ANTIGONE

R. X. Karvanis

FIRST PRINTING, March 2023.
Harry Markos, Director.

Paperback: ISBN 978-1-915860-03-3
eBook: ISBN 978-1-915860-04-0

Book design by: Ian Sharman

www.markosia.com

First Edition

Book I

Chapter One

In the darkest hour of night, when the first of the spring birds began the first of their pre-dawn harmonies, she was visited by Death. He came into her bedroom in a silence so thick that it woke her from her slumber. He came in, and He looked at her.

He stood before the window nearest to her bed. The streetlamp outside etched out the angles of His form, tall and twisted. Head cocked to the side, bird-like. He was a wraith in the shadows, and the silence stretched out, unbroken.

Until He spoke.

Antigone…

She gasped, her hand flying to her throat.

Antigone…

His voice was soft, smooth, a lover sighing in the dark.

Antigone. Look.

She stood in a clearing within a forest of tall, ancient trees. Dead leaves crunched below her feet, while live ones made a canopy above her through which the moonlight danced.

She heard a noise, a creak of wood. Spinning around, she beheld a single tree in the clearing, a young oak, lithe and supple. She reached to touch it.

Yet at that very moment, the tree began to change. Its leaves began to brown and curl, the branches withered, bark peeling and flaking away like dead skin. Within seconds, that beautiful, lonely tree in the clearing had shrivelled before her eyes, wasting away into a mere shadow of itself, twisted against the darkness of the forest.

Antigone…

Her head snapped round.

There, she saw. A dark shape, in the trees. On that branch. There.

She watched, squinting against the brightness of the moon.

A bird, she thought. Point of a beak, sharp as a knife. Yes, a bird.

Antigone…

A stab of pain – the voice not smooth now but rasping, a claw tearing into her. The bird's wings stretched out, feathers reaching down. She crashed to her knees, twigs and rocks digging into her skin, and her hand, still clasping her neck, tightened.

Antigone, Death beckoned her. *Wake up.*

And so she woke.

***

The man next to her shifted in his seat. Ann blinked the sweat from her eyes, and, on instinct, snatched the magazine out of the flap in front of her. Turquoise waters, rocky hills: an article on the Wonders of the Greek Isles. She felt the man's gaze on her face for a few seconds. Then he smoothed his button-down and edged himself into the aisle.

Ann let the magazine fall to her lap and peered out into the unfiltered dawn.

The light up here was so different. Brighter, harder. Burning in its intensity, even at sunrise. A different world altogether.

It made it impossible not to think of what had brought her here. Or how much everything had changed in a mere twenty-four hours.

She had never been on a road trip before, let alone on a plane, by herself, flying over thousands of kilometres of ocean. She couldn't shake the fear that she would be caught and sent back. That, at any moment now, one of the flight attendants would come trotting up the aisle and ask her to please accompany them to the front of the plane. Or something. In fact, Ann half wished they would.

But the attendants just kept serving out orange juice.

Ann put the magazine away and rubbed her eyes. She told herself she shouldn't be so paranoid. She'd done nothing wrong.

That's right. In fact, she had done everything right. Nice house, big car, handsome husband. And then she'd woken – was it really only one day ago? – with that echo in her ear. The mere hint of a whisper.

She'd tried to ignore it. She'd gone through the motions of her day. Gone for her run, showered, made the bed, vacuumed the already spotless carpet. In the end, it had been a note from her husband that had snapped everything into focus.

Have another meeting tonight.

Won't be home till late, won't need dinner.

Don't wait up.

That was it. A harmless little note scribbled on the edge of an old legal document. Addressed to no one.

Antigone. The voice in her dream had called her Antigone. No one had called her by that name since – since she was barely old enough to remember. Yet the voice had called to her, and everything had unravelled. Just like that. Just like that the bag had been packed, the ticket purchased, a note left. As if the whole tapestry, so hurriedly woven, was simply waiting for the right thread to catch before it could fall away completely.

"Off to meet a boyfriend, miss?"

Ann started. She hadn't noticed the man next to her return to his seat. She glanced at him quickly. His smile, through the grey beard, was kind. She shook her head.

"Your family, then?"

She hesitated, then nodded.

"I see, I see... Do they live in Athens?"

"...Yes."

"Forgive me for saying so, but you do not look Greek."

"My mother was Swedish."

"Ah, yes, I can see that."

He stared at her, waiting for more. Then he laughed.

"Am I disturbing you?"

"Sorry. No. I – I'm going to meet my brother."

"Ah, your brother. How nice for him to have such a lovely sister to make such a journey. What does he do, your brother?"

"He's a pilot."

The man's eyebrows shot up and he chuckled. "Oh, brave man. I never liked heights, myself. Heights make a man feel small, and no man likes to know his own insignificance."

Fiddling with a square of paper in her pocket, Ann didn't reply. The man watched her for a few more moments before sighing and picking up his own magazine.

Slowly, Ann pulled the paper out. She scanned the address scribbled there.

"Look, look at that!"

His voice was still clear in her memory. He had been pointing up at the swallows that swooped past their house at dusk.

"Look at the way they dip and soar together."

She had leaned her head against his back. They'd been fifteen years old at the time and these moments of peace had been few and far between.

"Think about it, my Anna," Nik had said. "With wings, we could go anywhere we like."

"I think we'd probably be too dense," she'd quipped.

"Huh?"

"Birds have hollow bones, don't they? So that they're light enough to stay in the air."

He'd twisted around to look at her then, instantly serious.

"One day I'll fly you away from here. I swear it. Even if I have to hollow us out first."

Ann shoved the square of paper back into her pocket.

She could remember it still, perfectly. The intensity of her brother's face. That inner burning which always seemed to transform his eyes from a yellow-brown into liquid gold.

Eyes so like her own, she'd been told.

It had been almost four years since Ann had last seen her twin. In fact, she'd had no news of Nik at all until about six months ago, when she'd received a call from an aviation school in Athens, Greece. The man on the phone had told her that as she was listed as "Niko's" next of kin, they'd be pleased to invite her to his graduation. She'd declined, but before the man had hung up, she'd obtained the address of the flight academy that Nik had been due to begin teaching at in a month's time.

It made sense that he'd become a pilot, of course.

Ann had always suspected that Nik's fascination with birds stemmed from the story that their mother told them about how she'd met their father.

It was early springtime, the story began. As a young Lotta Adamsson sat on the grass reading, she heard a shriek above her. Looking up, she beheld a mighty hawk shooting down towards the field. It collided with the ground in an explosion of feathers. When the feathers settled, she saw that the hawk was sitting atop a pigeon, its claws embedded in the smaller bird's sides.

So mesmerized was she that she failed to notice a young man approaching until a shadow fell over her, blocking out the sun. The man told her bluntly that he admired her strength. Taken aback, Lotta laughed and asked him what he meant. You never turned away, he told her. You do not hide from the brutalities of life.

For many years, it seemed as if Nik was continually begging his mother to repeat this story. Ann later realized that it had been, for him, like a light-house in the night, providing him with a fleeting connection to the figure whose absence had always seemed so significant to him.

"When did you marry him, Mommy?" a six year-old Nik had once asked.

Lotta had replied in her most forbidding tone. "I didn't."

Ann had tugged at her brother's arm, fearing one of their mother's explosions, but Nik had remained unfazed.

"But how were we born, then?"

"You were born when I was very young – too young," Lotta had snapped. She had then softened a little. "Look, I'm not saying it was a mistake and I'm not saying it wasn't, but I barely knew your father. All I really knew about him was that his family was from Greece."

Nik had taken a moment to process this. "But why didn't he stay with us?"

"I think he tried his best, for a while. But he was only a boy, really."

Nik hadn't understood. "But... didn't he like us?"

Lotta had looked away again and said quietly, "I don't know".

***

"Bread, miss?"

The bearded man next to her held out a bun. "I took it for you. I did not want them to disturb you, you looked so –" he gave a little laugh and shrugged – "far away."

Ann reached out to take it. "Thank you."

"We arrive in thirty minutes," he added.

Ann let the bread fall and roll beneath the seat.

"Miss?" The man frowned, leaning closer. "Miss, are you well?"

Ann nodded, one jerk of the chin.

"Really, are you certain?"

"Yes –" The word barely audible. She cleared her throat. "Yes."

The man placed his hand on her forearm.

"Forgive me if I pry... but am I right to think, perhaps, you do not want to get to Athens so soon?"

Ann said nothing. Her breath was beginning to come in shallow gasps.

"Would I also be right to think," he continued quietly, "that maybe you do not want to meet what – who – waits in Athens, so soon?"

Her silence confirmed. He nodded, squeezing her arm.

"You must *breathe*, miss. Breathing keeps us balanced. But I must ask. Why did you come so far if...?"

She swallowed. "He..."

"Yes?"

"He's the only one I have left," she managed. "I – I should never have – I should never have come. He doesn't want me. He doesn't want –"

The man took her by the shoulders and turned her to face him. "Look at me. Look at me, girl. Good. Yes. Breathe." He inhaled deeply. "And breathe." He exhaled.

Through the nostrils, out the mouth. Like running. She leaned back and closed her eyes.

The pilot came on the speaker, informing them that it was 7:00 a.m. in Athens. *Fifteen degrees Celsius and cloudy. No rain expected.*

Then she heard a voice, low and alarmingly close to her ear.

"Do not let him go, girl."

Her eyes flashed open. The man's face was only inches away.

"Family is the only thing we have in this life. Promise me you will not turn back. Promise me."

"Y–yes," she said. "I promise."

Chapter Two

Almost a week passed before Ann even tried to find her brother.

The noises and smells that had accosted her from the moment she'd disembarked had left her feeling anxious and raw – the hustle of the crowds, their shouts and gesticulations, the clouds of cigarette smoke, the honking of cars. By the time she'd climbed out of her taxi, the relative shelter of the hotel felt god-sent. She was worn out, bone-weary, with an exhaustion that threatened to smother. Ann tunnelled into the large, chlorine-scented bed with a sigh.

And slept through to the following day. She dreamt of nothing. It was early evening when she woke. Throwing on her running shoes, she ventured out into the maze of pedestrian streets that surrounded her hotel. She jogged slowly, drifting past stores with their imitation antiquities that spilled out onto the cobblestones, and the Parthenon on the hill above, lording it over the city with its columns fluorescent against the indigo sky. She ran for less than an hour and then returned to the hotel to sleep.

The next evening, she stumbled across an ancient ruin that was tucked away between the endless shops and restaurants. It was no more than a few broken walls and pillars – relics of a dead world, separated from the rest of the city by a simple iron fence. Just beyond reach. And yet – Ann thought – they were there. They endured, still.

***

Sleep evaded her that night. Once, twice, she almost drifted off, only to be pulled back by a breeze stirring the pad of paper on the desk. Or a rustle of feathers from beyond the open window. A whisper on the wind, echoing her name.

An imagination run rampant, she told herself as she fumbled for the remote.

The TV flicked on to some cheap thriller dubbed in Greek. She couldn't understand a word, but the shrill voices and flashing lights kept her calm, sedated, even if they kept her awake.

Yet when the first hint of dawn came, her thumb hit the power button and the room fell silent. She picked up the phone.

***

Two hours later, the taxi screeched to a halt.

"This is it?" she whispered, checking the crumpled square of paper again. "You're sure?"

"*Nai, nai, kyria*," the driver assured her. "Here, here."

Ann looked up at the nondescript building. She was breathing slowly, deliberately – preparing herself for the worst. That he would send her away. That he would not even acknowledge her.

What she was not prepared for was the woman at the front desk who checked a pile of papers then said, without looking up, that *kyrios* Adamsson had left his job a week ago.

For a few moments, Ann could only stare at the top of the woman's head. Then, clearing her throat, Ann asked if it was possible to have his home address.

Eyes still on her desk, the woman pursed her lips. No, that was not permitted.

"Please."

The woman finally glanced up then, and whatever she saw in Ann's face made her sigh, check another pile of papers, then scribble something down on a sticky note.

Another address. Not for a home, but another aviation school. Located on the island of Crete.

***

The island of Crete is situated southeast of the mainland and constitutes the southernmost point of Greece. It is the largest of the islands by far, possessing a rich geographical diversity, from fertile plains and pastures, to rivers and freshwater lakes, to the mountain range that Ann could see from the plane window, stretching from one side of the island to the other in jutting clusters. A little country in and of itself, the on-flight magazine said. Heraklion, one of Crete's major cities, sits along the northern coast, near the centre of the long island. The flight there took less than an hour.

The first thing that Ann noticed stepping down onto the tarmac was the salty tang of the wind sweeping in from across the water. She had never been so near the sea before and suddenly there it was, stretching out into the distance, shockingly blue and sparkling in the sunlight. The Mediterranean Sea. The breeze buffeted against her, teasing a smile onto her face.

ANTIGONE   15

Then she recalled why she was there. Clutching her knapsack to her chest, she followed the other passengers to the building.

The flight school operated out of the airport. The building was comparatively small; she found the right desk quickly. There was a middle-aged man sitting behind it, frowning at her as she approached.

"Um, excuse me." She gripped her knapsack tighter. "Does a Niklas Adamsson work here?"

The frown vanished. "Ah. You are his sister, yes?"

She stared.

"I see your face," the man explained quickly. "I think, of course, she must be Niko's sister."

"Yes, sorry, of course." Ann had forgotten the effect that she and Nik used to have on strangers. "Of course. Is he – is he here?"

"No, he come in around two. Soon."

He pointed to a clock on the wall just above the desk. Twenty minutes.

She settled in to wait. She perched on a chair opposite the flight school's desk. It was too still there, too restricting. She went outside to pace the parking lot. Too exposed. She took refuge in the women's washroom. Too stifling. She returned to her seat. Two o five. He was late.

Two ten. Ann's leg, jiggling against the chair, stilled.

Something had tugged in the back of her mind. No more than the smallest twitch, a sensory recognition, dim yet achingly familiar. A tiny voice whispering, *Here. Now.*

She glanced up just as a young man strolled through the sliding doors of the airport.

His hair was longer than she remembered, with sun-bleached waves pushed back from a square, tanned forehead. He'd put on weight, too: he was broader – no longer the scrawny teenage boy she'd known.

Everything about him, from his posture to his long, graceful strides, exuded confidence and good health.

Tears pricked the corners of her eyes. He was alive and well. And he was here. Her Nik.

A movement in her peripheral vision. The man behind the counter was standing, pointing toward her. Ann started to rise just as her brother began to turn. She froze, half out of her seat.

Nik's head jerked back – the impact from an invisible slap. Ann's knees went weak and she sat down again, hard. After a moment or two, her brother began to approach, very slowly, sunglasses hiding his eyes. He halted two meters away.

"What," he began quietly, "are you – *doing* – here?"

She could only stare.

"Ann?"

Nothing.

"Ann, what the hell is going on? Did something happen – are you okay?"

His voice was rising, sounding alarmed now. She managed a nod.

"Well then?"

After a few seconds, he sighed, running his hand through his hair. A nervous gesture he'd always had. It put her more at ease as he told her to wait and turned back to his colleague. They exchanged a few words in Greek, and then he beckoned in her direction.

"Come on."

They moved out into the sunlight. Ann jogged to keep up, her eyes on the back of her brother's head. About fifty meters out, in the shade of a stout palm tree, he whirled round to face her.

"Ann," he began, obviously trying to keep his cool. "Ann, what is going on?"

When again she didn't respond, he shrugged. "Okay. Fine."

He took a cigarette and a lighter from his pocket, lit the cigarette, and leaned back against the tree.

"You're smoking," Ann blurted out.

"Ah, it speaks."

"When – when did you start smoking?"

He blew a long line of smoke over his shoulder. "Oh, at least eight years ago."

Baiting her, she knew. She waited.

"Okay, two," he admitted, the corners of his mouth twitching. "Everyone here smokes." He took a deep drag. "Ann, for chrissake, tell me what you're doing here."

She dropped her gaze to her running shoes. "I thought you were in Athens."

"I'm not. I'm here and that's not an answer."

"Why did you come here so suddenly?"

"What does it matter, Ann? Why did *you*? Tell me."

"I..." She sighed. "I don't know."

He scoffed. "So you just woke up and found yourself sitting in the Heraklion International Airport? How extraordinary."

She knew he was going to lose his patience soon.

"I – I hadn't heard from you in so long. I was –" she paused, searching for a remotely adequate word – "concerned."

He raised an eyebrow at her and she crossed her arms over her chest. Smoke poured from his nostrils as he waited.

"I think I've just left my husband."

"Ah. This is the guy from –?"

"Yes."

He nodded and took another drag of his cigarette. "So what, then?" He looked away across the parking lot. "You'd had enough so you decided to... go on vacation?"

"I guess."

"I hear Barbados is nice this time of year."

She didn't respond. She wasn't really meant to. His profile was absolutely still, his cigarette now dangling between his fingers, forgotten.

"So," he began after a moment. "How d'you find me?"

"Your school called."

"Huh. And how long you planning on staying?"

She shrugged. Sighing, he dropped his cigarette into the grass and crushed it beneath the heel of his boot.

"Listen. I have to go back to work. Vasili's vouching for me, but if I'm late again in my first week…"

"Okay."

They walked back toward the airport, side by side this time, neither saying a word. Just outside the doors, Nik paused.

"So, my day off's tomorrow. But I can't take any other time, you know."

He said it defiantly, challenging her to object.

"Sure. Of course."

"If you like," he continued more softly, "you can meet me here tomorrow. We can do some touristy stuff or something."

"Alright."

"Eleven o'clock, then."

He moved to leave. Her hand shot out – a reflex.

"Nik."

He turned toward her, brows knitted. It was the first time, she realized, that she'd said his name.

"You really shouldn't smoke, you know," she mumbled after a moment. "It'll kill you."

Slowly, he removed his sunglasses. His eyes – a bright amber, so like her own – narrowed on her face. And then, without a word, he turned away again and disappeared into the building.

Chapter Three

At twenty past eleven the following morning, Ann sat on the curb outside the airport, knees drawn up to her chin. His whole life, Nik had never been on time for anything. In a way, it was reassuring that some things, at least, would never change.

All assurance vanished when her brother arrived ten minutes later. His face was a tight-lipped mask.

Again, he stopped a safe distance from her.

"You came." An accusation.

"Yup," she said, her voice sounding painfully false. "Of course I did."

"So… what d'you want to do then?"

"I'm easy."

He shifted his weight impatiently. "Well, I guess we could go see the old part of town, have lunch at a little *taverna* on the harbour that a friend of mine owns. There's also a big, ancient palace or temple or something about eight kilometres south of here. This guy outside the *kafeneio* was telling me about it this morning."

He passed her a wrinkled pamphlet from his pocket.

"Whatever you like," she said, glancing at the pamphlet and trying to smile. "Both sound good."

"I haven't seen this palace thing yet. It's pretty cheap, I think. Though, money's not an issue for you, is it?"

A genuine question. He dug his hands in his pockets and waited.

"Not really, no," she admitted.

He nodded slowly, as if to himself. "Well. We'll have to catch a bus."

He jerked his thumb toward a line of idling vehicles – buses much like any Ann had seen before, except that the side view mirrors curved down from the top corners. Like horns, she found herself thinking.

"Er – sure," she said. "That's fine."

And so it was settled. A bus brought them to the station near the port, where they boarded another bus with the sign "Κυωσός/Knossos" on its dashboard. Soon they were trundling through Heraklion, with its boxy buildings, backed-up cars, and signs for hotels and discount super markets. A city like any other. As the buildings began to thin out, Ann caught sight of the land rising before them in the distance. Every few seconds, the view would disappear behind the trees that bordered the road, but in those glimpses she beheld a single mountain emerging on the horizon. Its serrated outline made her think, unaccountably, of a human profile – open mouth, sharp nose, long hair spilling back from a broad forehead. The face of a man, sleeping beneath the hills.

"What mountain is that?" she asked her brother, breaking their long silence.

His eyes flicked toward her. "What?"

"That mountain in front of us. What's it called?"

"*Iouktas*, I think."

He'd already turned away. Ann looked back to the window. The mountain was hidden again behind the foliage.

"It's so green here."

"Huh?"

He hadn't even looked her way that time. She took a deep breath.

"I wasn't expecting it to be so green."

"Winter rains."

"Oh, right... Is it usually so warm here in winter?"

It was like she hadn't even spoken. Ann sighed and let her head fall back against the headrest.

"I think today's officially spring, actually."

She peered at her brother, and he offered a tiny, apologetic grin.

"The equinox," he went on, looking away again. "Rains are done and it's only gonna get warmer here on out. In a couple months, it'll get really hot – up to forty degrees, maybe."

She smiled. "I like the heat."

"That's true," he said quietly. "You always did."

The driver shouted out in Greek as the bus pulled into a large, empty parking lot. Ann and Nik alighted behind the few other passengers. All they could see of the site from this vantage point were hints of pale stone peaking through the trees. A dirt path stretched up in front of them, leading to a ticket booth with a small man slouched inside. Ann took the pamphlet out of her pocket and began to inspect it.

"I think we must be coming in from here," she said, pointing to the map.

"Mm. I think we're in for a treat."

She looked up and Nik jerked his chin toward the sky. The sun had disappeared above a ceiling of grey.

"Looks like the rain's not quite done with us after all."

***

He was certain it was going to rain at any moment.

Just my luck, Takus thought as he slouched further into his seat.

He had been sitting there for about four hours and only three people had come through. Leaning back against his chair in the ticket booth, he popped another pastry into his mouth from the open box on his desk.

This would be the one thing he would miss when he went home. You could find any kind of delicacy you wished in this place: cow cooked in dozens of ways, chicken wherever one looked, hundreds of kinds of cheese and sweets and breaded goods that he had never even dreamt of until he had come here half a year ago. Takus swallowed his mouthful and patted his belly. It was, he thought, like having a feast day on every day of the year.

Yet he was growing tired of it. All this sitting and waiting – always *waiting* – was making him restless. And fat. And, although he would not fully admit it to himself, he was nervous at the thought of leaving his wife unsupervised for so long.

"I am an *artist*," he grumbled. "This is a waste of my God-given talents!"

Takus was, in his crabbiness, perhaps a little more appreciative of his talents than they deserved. He was a mediocre painter at best, more an avid connoisseur of beauty than a skilled channel for it.

He caught sight of movement at the bottom of the path. He sat up eagerly.

People were walking up toward him. The first few were – he could see at a glance – the common variety of sightseers, with their camera bags and umbrellas, overeager to beat the tourist rush. But the two people who had fallen behind... Takus's mouth fell open slightly. They were something else entirely.

The man walked several feet in front of the woman. Takus regarded him with envy. This was the kind of man who would never find himself in need of a bed companion. He was tall and broad, with the kind of bright colouring a that made him seem to glow, despite the greyness of the day.

The first of the touristy-types reached the booth. Takus dispensed their tickets quickly, returning over-generous amounts of change. The young man approached the desk.

"Two tickets, please."

He dropped some money on the counter. A moment passed.

"Hello? Two tickets."

Takus was not attending. He was staring around the young man, and his thoughts were straying.

The young man snapped his fingers in front of Takus's face.

"Oh! My humblest apologies, young sir."

Takus made a long affair of the printing process to give himself extra time to consider the young woman. She was clearly the young man's sister. Twins, most certainly. He had never heard of twins of opposite sexes looking so alike, but here they were, like two versions of the same golden god. And those eyes – those eyes! Yellow, like those of a hawk.

The young man leaned over the desk. "Is there a problem?"

Takus looked up and gave the boy what he considered to be his most conciliatory smile. "No, no, of course not, young sir." He passed the tickets forward. "I hope you and your pretty sister enjoy your visit."

The young man led the girl away without a word and Takus sighed.

Why was it, he wondered, that loveliness touched him so? It was, in a way, like a pain to him: an ache in his chest that only paint and a fresh wall could release. If only he had his paints now, he would render an image of them both –

And then it hit him.

Barely able to contain his excitement, Takus reached down, slammed the "Κλειστός/Closed" sign onto the desk, and spun to watch the distant figures move into the maze of broken stones.

He had been promised very rich rewards. Enough luxury goods to set him and his family up in style for life. Maybe move into a harbour town. Make a priestess of his little girl, give her the status he never had.

He had been waiting for half a year. He was appalled that he had not recognized them immediately. They were exactly as they had been described. Takus supposed that he had become too indolent in this strange, foreign place to notice anything beyond his own stomach. No matter. He was going home and his wife would soon take him in hand.

The two golden heads vanished from sight.

It had been so disorienting when he had first arrived here, in this place he had known so well, unseen millennia having worn it away into a shadow of its former self. Yet still he knew these corridors like he knew the curves of his wife's hips – something that no time could take from him. Smiling broadly, Takus ran up the cobbled path and deep into the ancient palace.

***

Twenty minutes later, the skies were still threatening rain and Ann was still traipsing after her brother through the sprawling network of rubble walls. She had attempted many times to determine their location on the site map, but whenever she'd made any headway at all, Nik had charged off again, dragging them both further into the ruins. They had passed through tall rectangular doorframes, climbed worn stairways, wound their way around strange inverted pillars – thinner at the bottom that at the top – all without encountering another living soul. Every so often, a wall would rise up to block their path and Nik would simply take off in another direction like one possessed.

He'd been acting strangely ever since they'd arrived. Not that he'd seemed so relaxed before, but since they'd bought their tickets from that odd little man, he'd seemed even more impatient. More tense, somehow.

And the feeling was catching. Without understanding it at all, Ann could feel her heart thump with every turned corner, her palms now slick with sweat. She turned back to the pamphlet.

"According to this," Ann said, her voice carefully casual, "this place was the original Labyrinth, which actually meant 'House of the Double Axe'. It was allegedly home to the mythical King Minos and his Minotaur."

"The guy with the bull's head?" Nik asked vaguely as he strode toward a low wall.

"Yeah, I think so."

"Hm."

Nik was glancing both ways down the path. And before Ann had a chance to say another word, he'd planted his hands on the wall and vaulted over, disappearing from view.

Ann rushed to the wall and saw him squatting quite a bit further down in a narrow space. His face turned up to her.

"Coming?"

Ann wavered – but only for a moment. There was no way she was staying up there without him. Peering around and taking a deep breath, she scrambled over the wall and let herself drop.

Her feet hit the floor later than she expected – and for one dizzying, terrifying moment, she was certain that they were trapped. But before the panic took hold, she spotted a passageway to her left.

Not that it was much of an option. The corridor was draped in cobwebs, all light choked out only a few meters in. Swallowing hard, Ann uncrumpled the sweat-smeared pamphlet and continued reading.

"So it says, um, that not much is known about the people who – who lived here." She was whispering now. "They know that they thrived for over a thousand years, 'as a very prosperous and influential maritime power'... and that no one understands how their civilization – which was the very first in Europe, it says – came to its end in 1450 B.C.E."

Nik nodded absently. He was running his fingers over the stone of the wall.

"It also says here, that these people weren't actually Greek: 'They were replaced in their palaces by the Mycenaeans, the earliest Greeks, just after their downfall'."

Nik was no longer paying any attention at all. Neither was she, really. She was peering into the passageway nervously. The air seeping out of it smelled different – thick, stale. Like it hadn't been disturbed in a very long time.

A small rustling from above. Ann glanced up – and backed into her brother.

"Ann, what –?"

Nik followed her gaze and let out an impatient huff of air. A large tabby was sitting on the wall, tail swishing back and forth. Its eyes trailing the twins.

"For god's sake, Ann, it's just a stray cat. They're everywhere in this country."

"I hadn't noticed," she muttered, edging further away from it.

"Why am I not surprised?"

Ann tore her eyes away from the cat. Her brother shrugged.

"You tend not to notice much outside your own head, is all."

Maybe it was that sarcastic expression. Maybe it was the strain of being trapped in that eerie place, with that feline watching them, but before she fully registered what she was doing, Ann was ducking under the cobwebs and storming away into the passage.

Blood pounded in her ears, propelling her into the darkness, through the stale air, unthinking. Yet it was only a minute or so before her stride faltered. Before she came to a halt in the near blackness.

He was all she had. All she'd ever had, really.

She turned around.

And froze.

There, in the tunnel before her, a dark form. A deeper patch in the black, swelling and shifting as it approached.

Then something butted against her thigh, and coarse hairs pricked through her jeans as a deep rumbling filled the passage. Purring.

Ann released her breath as the feline began to wind itself through her legs. It was even larger than she'd thought, easily four times the size of the domestic cats she knew. More like a small mountain lion – which, conceivably, it was. A different kind of threat altogether: alarming, yes, but mercifully plausible.

And then she thought she heard it. Her name, carried in on a gust of rank air.

Antigone...

"Ann!"

Nik was running through the passage, his footsteps pounding on the stone floor. The dark shape of him halted meters away. Twisted, angular. Then she blinked and he was himself again.

"Ann, is that you?"

"*Yes – yes.*"

"And is that –" His laugh was low. "I didn't even see it leave the room."

The purring stopped. A moment later, Ann realized that the cat had moved away. She glanced over her shoulder and saw the shape of its head turn toward them, its eyes flashing faintly yellow. It yowled then began to trot down the passage, its claws pattering against the stone. A few metres further down, it paused, yowling again.

"I think it wants us to... follow it?" Nik whispered incredulously.

"Nik – it's a cat!"

But her brother simply grabbed her wrist and towed her after the creature.

The passage was brighter further along, striped with shafts of daylight from gaps in the ceiling above. The cat waited for them to catch up before continuing on, through another corridor, then another, then up a twisting stairway – steps slanting treacherously downward – and out into a large, open square.

"This place is enormous," Nik breathed as the cat continued across.

It was. Even fragmented as they were, the stones that bordered the space seemed countless, the building stretching on without end. To the south, the profile of the sleeping mountain rose up above the ruins, almost black now against the dark afternoon sky. To the west the structure was taller, with a long row of doorways set into its wall. And there the cat stood, the space behind it lost, once more, to darkness.

Nik set off at a jog.

"Nik!" Ann called.

He ignored her, hopping over the low chain that had been set up to keep tourists out of the main structure. She went after him. But by the time she'd reached the doorway, both her brother and the cat had moved on. She crept into the shadows of the sunken space and up into a small room, with a fountain set against one wall and a stone chair against the other. Nik was waiting for her there. He moved toward the next doorway, gesturing for her to follow.

They went steadily downward, following the breadcrumb hints left by the cat. A soft cry here, a tail whipping around a corner there. Ann kept meaning to protest but somehow never managed it. The passageways got darker, colder, damper – yet the urge to follow only grew, like a gravitational pull that became stronger the deeper they descended. When their path reached an abrupt end, however, her better instincts reasserted themselves.

"Nik, I think we'd better –"

"Hold on."

He knocked against the wall in front of them. It rang hollow. She was intrigued in spite of herself.

"Is that –"

"Wood."

"Bizarre."

"Yeah."

Nik fished around in his pocket and the space was lit up in a blaze of neon light. A cell phone,

Ann realized. It seemed jarringly out of place. The door before them was solid and heavy-looking, with a large, crude-looking handle and a bolt, both elaborately engraved with geometrical designs.

"Look at the detail on this... Is this bronze?" Nik tapped the hinges. "Amazing. The wood should have deteriorated years ago."

Something in her brother's tone made Ann peer into his face. There was the briefest of pauses, then –

"Nik, no. No! We shouldn't even be here!"

"Anna, come on. What's the worst that could happen?"

Anna.

One word. One childhood nickname, almost forgotten, and she knew she would follow him. She'd follow him to hell itself, if he chose to go.

"Famous last words," she grumbled to cover up her sudden joy.

"I always knew I was destined for fame."

Then he grinned at her – a lopsided grin that cut across the lonely years since she'd last seen it. Her own mouth tugged in response.

The passage went dark.

"Oh. Shit. Battery's dead."

She heard his hands sliding down along the wood. Then he leaned in and pushed. The door swung open easily.

"They must keep these hinges oiled or something," he muttered.

Ann grabbed the back of her brother's jacket as he slipped through the portal. The space on the other side was utterly dark, with a blackness so deep that the earlier passageways seemed bright by comparison. They heard the door thud behind them. Every hair on Ann's forearms pricked up.

"Nik, I don't like this."

He began to inch forward. "Just a little dark, that's all."

She knew he was scared too – she could feel it in the tension of his shoulders. Yet he continued to shuffle on over the uneven floor until something scraped behind them.

"Nik, please."

"Calm down, would you? It's probably just a mouse or something." She felt his shoulders droop. "Look, we can go back whenever you want."

Anna, he'd called her.

"Just a little further then," she whispered.

But they'd only taken a few more steps when a much louder noise sounded from behind – a bang against the door. Nik stiffened.

"Could it be that cat thing again, you think?" Ann breathed.

"Maybe. Wait here."

She clutched his jacket more firmly, following as he groped his way back. When he stopped, she felt his body tense again as he heaved backward. Nothing happened. He pulled again.

"The door's stuck!" he choked.

Her stomach dropped sickeningly.

"The damn thing won't *budge*!"

She moved around him and tugged against the handle. He pulled with her. It would not open.

Footsteps.

The twins froze. Someone was moving just on the other side of the door. Ann sagged in relief as Nik called, "Hey! We're stuck in here!"

The footsteps halted.

"Hello? We're stuck!"

The footsteps began again, more quickly. The sound fading, she realized. Moving away. Seconds later, they'd died out completely.

Nik's voice, carefully controlled, came out of the darkness. "Correct me if I'm wrong, but if we could hear them walking, they could definitely hear me yelling... Right?"

Ann nodded.

"*Right*?" he repeated.

"I nodded." After a couple more seconds had passed, she whispered, "I feel ridiculous just thinking this, but..."

"You think whoever that was just locked us in."

"...Yes."

"I think so too."

His confirmation cemented it. She leaned hard against the wall.

Another thudding noise echoed in the passage. Ann straightened, hopeful, only to realize that her brother was throwing himself against the door.

She inhaled, filling her lungs to the point of pain. "Nik. Nik, I don't think that's going to help."

"Really? You don't think?!" he shouted. "What the hell else are we gonna do?"

"Stay calm," she whispered. "Breathe. After that..."

He was quiet for a moment, then she heard his jacket scraping down the rough wall. She sat down beside him and wrapped her arms around her legs.

The twins remained silent for several minutes. The absolute darkness, at least, afforded them a kind of respite. A momentary stasis, where they could delude themselves into thinking that there were options other than the only one available to them. But, of course, it couldn't last.

"I think we have to go on," Nik said eventually.

When she didn't respond, he climbed to his feet. "Come on, Ann. Let's move."

Slowly, Ann rose up beside him. Then she let her brother take her by the hand and lead her back down, deeper into the blackness.

***

One summer, when the twins were five years old, Nik had been bed-ridden for two weeks with avian influenza. How he'd contracted the virus, the doctors could not say, but after a couple days in hospital, he'd been declared out of danger and was permitted to return home.

Ann remained just outside his door for days, listening as her brother tossed and turned and cried in his bed. Eventually, she decided that she would find him an animal to play with. Not a bird – his favourite, which she was convinced had made him ill in the first place – but something small and furry. Something harmless.

The woods that surrounded their family home were dense and dark. Ann had always been afraid of them. But, supposing the forest to be the best place to find animals, she marched off into it with her little chin held high. And after what had felt, to the five-year-old girl, like an eternity spent searching, she finally spotted a squirrel. The moment it spotted her, it scurried up a tree.

Ann only hesitated for a minute – she knew that her brother would not have been afraid. It was a few more minutes for her to reach the upper branches. And less than three seconds for her to plummet back down again.

An hour later, as the few patches of sky visible through the leaves were beginning to darken, Ann wiped away her tears to see her brother, in his pyjamas, hobbling through the trees toward her.

"Sorry it took me s'long," he sighed as he dropped to the ground next to her.

Ann threw her arms around him and covered his feverish face with kisses.

Much later that night, as the twins lay intertwined on a hospital bed – Nik sleeping soundly, Ann with both her legs in casts – Lotta asked Ann to repeat the story yet again.

"But were you yelling for Nik to come?" her mother asked dubiously.

Ann yawned and explained again. "No, I was too far. I just told him."

"But what does that mean, you *'told'* him?"

"Maybe," the attending nurse interjected, "it was one of those twin things, you know? When they know when the other's in trouble? You're always hearing 'bout stuff like that."

"No," little Ann insisted. "I just told him where I was."

"Annika," Lotta snapped. "That does not make any sense. What do you mean, you *'told him'*?"

Ann turned toward her mother then, amber eyes wide and solemn. "I was scared and I couldn't move. So I just told him where I was and he came and got me."

***

The twins' shoulders pressed together as the already narrow passage tapered further. They'd been walking for at least fifteen minutes, their shoes shuffling inch by inch, their free hands feeling along the wall ahead of them.

"What happens..." Ann trailed off, afraid to vocalize the thought. She cleared her throat and tried again. "What happens if we – if we meet a dead end?"

"Then we go back and wait," Nik replied. "Or I use you as a battering ram."

She wasn't in the mood to be humoured. "And if there's another door ahead?"

"We go through it."

"And if –"

"Anna. Enough already."

She sighed and they walked on in silence. A small, detached part of her mind was shocked at how quickly she'd accepted their implausible situation. Maybe, she thought, it was just implausible enough: it didn't really require believing. Or maybe she was simply very content to shamble along blindly, holding her brother's hand.

"Why does everyone here call you 'Niko'?" she asked after another minute.

"I don't see anyone here at all."

"Ha ha, very funny. Did you ask them to call you that?"

She felt him shrug. "It's a Greek thing, I guess."

"It sounds off for you."

"It's a nickname, Ann. What does it matter what people call you?"

"I don't know, it just matters."

"Besides, it never seemed to bother you."

"Me?"

"Everyone calling you Ann."

"That's my name."

"Not really. Hasn't always been, I mean."

Ann felt a chill like a cold finger running up her spine. "That's different."

"Is it?" He was silent for some time. When he spoke again, his voice had sunk to no more than a breath. "Or maybe it's actually kinda nice, isn't it? A different place, a different name..."

"What do you mean?"

He didn't respond. He had stopped walking – stopped breathing. She could feel his pulse beating within his palm. Matching her own.

Here. Now.

She could sense it clearly then, that gentle, tugging warmth deep within her mind. That space that had been closed up for so many years that she had long since thought it gone. The space through which she used to pass so often and so effortlessly. She exulted in it, carefully teasing it open. Then, as smoothly as she drew breath, she slipped through.

And they were there together. She felt their hearts miss a beat, then another. They were afraid, she felt. Very afraid. They knew He was near. They could taste His presence in the air and it was foul.

Who is it? she asked her brother silently. *Who is He?*

Her mind reeled away from his as Nik hurled himself backward, his body slamming into the rock. She could not see him, but she could feel the fury oozing out of him in waves.

"*You dare?*" he hissed.

"Nik, I – I didn't mean –"

"*You* –" His hands seized her, only to release her as quickly as if he had been burned. "*Stay OUT!*" he bellowed.

She could not utter a word. She stood suspended, mute and unseeing in the absolute darkness.

Then – a shift. A change both incomprehensible and lightning-quick. The air contracted and pulsed, pushing against her body, then in an instant it was gone, leaving her mind spinning and her body flushed with heat – only then to be swallowed in ice.

Antigone… the voice called to her.

The world was engulfed in brilliance. Bewildered, Ann found that she could see her brother standing before her, back pressed against the wall, staring up at a dazzling square of brightness as dark arms reached down through it to grab at them. She opened her mouth to scream, but no sound emerged.

Fingers fastened around her body, and she was hauled up into the light.

Book II

Chapter One

Ann was pulled to her feet and steadied by strong hands. Her eyes watered as they adjusted to the brightness. She could make out a face in front of her – blurry and dark, framed by darker hair. It was barking harsh, unintelligible noises at her. As another face appeared, and another, she was tugged forward. Stumbling, she let herself be led out of the room and through a maze of space, light and shadow.

It was only after an interval of quiet and stillness that she began to regain her bearings. She sat in a dim chamber, light sieving in from a space carved out of the top of one stone wall. It was a tiny room: against the opposite wall, just by her feet, were stacked bundles of what looked like bowls, or jugs, wrapped in coarse wool. Her brother sat silently just inches away, knees drawn up to his chin. Ann stared at the jugs, determined not to let her eyes wander in his direction.

The voice had spoken. It had been as clear as if the speaker had been right beside her. And Nik had felt something too. She wasn't imagining it, then. She wasn't imagining that disembodied sigh, that rasping breath that seemed to leak out of the air and seep out of the earth. That voice, that name, which left her heart cold and her hands shaking.

There was a noise beyond the door. The twins scrambled to their feet.

"Game time," Nik muttered.

The door swung open to reveal a small man with close-cropped hair. He was wearing an utterly strange, layered ensemble of leather, wool and fur. Like what Ann imagined a Viking chieftain might have worn. Only with a lot more embroidery.

She tore her eyes away from the outfit as the man uttered something. His voice was low, expressionless. Ann glanced at her brother, who shook his head at the man. After a pause, the man beckoned to someone outside and two much younger men appeared, dressed only in kilts. No shoes, Ann's brain noted pointlessly.

The cropped-haired man spoke again – a clear command – then turned and left the room. Taking the twins gently by their elbows, the two younger men guided them out. Following the older man, the group passed through several stone corridors that were very like the ones that the twins had travelled only a brief time before. They were brighter, cleaner, and infinitely busier, but they were the same. People stepped aside as they approached. Ann kept her eyes on the floor ahead of her, but out of her peripheral vision she caught glimpses of small figures, dark skin set against colourful clothing, each with a hand held up against their forehead, palm outward.

And as they walked on, the people began to multiply – exponentially, it seemed. Ann bounced against the swell of bodies as she was now all-but dragged forward. A drone of whispers followed close behind them. Soon, a broad doorway appeared ahead, an expanse of sky visible beyond: their literal light at the end of the tunnel. Yet as they stepped out beneath the clouds, Ann staggered to a halt.

A vast courtyard sprawled out before them. Ann gaped as her guide yanked her onward. Nothing, not even the building that surrounded the open space, seemed to stay in one place. The structure itself – towering three, maybe four storeys above in some places – was a teeming mass of lofty doorways, open balconies and inverted pillars. The walls were uneven, sometimes pushing in toward the courtyard, sometimes receding backward into the late afternoon shadows. And every surface was alive with colour – the reds, blues, yellows, and greens of flowers and frescoes, paint applied directly to the pale plaster in distinct patterns, or depictions of red-skinned men and white-skinned women, or drawings of sea life, of birds, of bulls – bulls, bulls everywhere, even in the stone horns that seemed to protrude from every balustrade and line the edges of every staircase.

And there were people, people packed into every opening that could fit them. They leaned over railings, crowded the many doorways. The courtyard overflowed with them. An ocean of dark hair and olive skin – with Ann sifting through, towering almost a head above the throng.

This was an alien race of men and women – with the kind of homogeneity that made them seem all the more *other*. The men, like her guide, were all half-naked, long-haired and clean-shaven, wearing embroidered knee-length kilts, which were longer in the front than at the back. The women were exotic, sultry, with kohl-lined, almond-shaped eyes, and tresses piled high to tumble down bejewelled necks. Their dresses seemed specifically designed to amplify feminine curve: full, flounced skirts and constricting belts; tight, short-sleeved jackets loosely tied at the front to expose as much cleavage as possible. Human bodies so in evidence, so in-your-face that after a few more seconds of open gawking, Ann tugged down the hem of her own baggy sweatshirt and dropped her gaze to the safety of the floor.

This was obviously a celebration of sorts – but something was noticeably off. The crowd became so dense that the twins' guides began bodily shifting people out of the way, yet the hum of chatter that pervaded the courtyard remained subdued. As if in anticipation. And it was growing quieter still.

Then the cropped-haired man stopped walking and the crowd fell completely silent. Ann risked raising her eyes again. Every person present seemed to be facing the tallest facade of the building. What little sunlight leaked through the clouds was hidden behind it. And embedded deep in the shadows at the base of the wall was a strange edifice – a shrine by the looks of it, with pillars and horn statues framing a high slab of a table, on which lay an enormous double-edged axe.

The cropped-haired man was speaking now, voice projected and sounding even more expressionless in the vastness of the courtyard. Ann tore her eyes away from the axe.

In a cleared space next to the altar sat a pair of thrones, and on them, two people. The woman appeared to be in her late sixties or early seventies, with iron-grey hair and a palpable tang of steel to her. The man next to her was some ten years younger maybe, with a quality about him that arrested the eye – something beyond the massively powerful body and the atypically short black curls and beard.

It took a second for the silence to penetrate Ann's brain. The cropped-haired man had stopped talking and was gesturing behind him – toward *them* – and stepping out of the way.

Her nerves, which till then had been simmering quietly beneath the shock, roared up to full alarm. The pair on the thrones – almost certainly royalty of some kind – was looking directly at her now. Her breath was lodged in a hard knot beneath her ribs.

Yet nothing was happening. The man – the king? – simply regarded the twins, frowning. The queen continued to sit, her thin, down-turned lips growing noticeably thinner as the silence stretched on. Ann remained completely still, not daring even to breathe.

Then the queen cleared her throat, the sound dry, scraping – snapping the king out of his trance. He blinked several times. He rose. Then he spoke a few words in the alien language. His voice was rich and impossibly deep. In the stillness of the courtyard, Ann imagined she could feel the vibrations of it in the flagstones beneath her feet.

Nik shifted his weight beside her.

"I'm sorry," he called out. "But we can't understand you."

Before the words were fully out, the queen was on her feet, sweeping through the crowd, which shifted like repelling magnets to let her pass. She halted in front of Nik, who had moved slightly, and was now half-blocking Ann.

The woman raised her arms slowly, her mouth pulled tight, a slash across her face.

"Welcome, Foreign Ones," she pronounced in thickly accented, yet oddly perfect English. "We have long been awaiting your arrival."

Chapter Two

A flurry of excitement broke out from a group of women standing behind the thrones as a murmur began to pass through the rest of the courtyard like a crowning wave.

"W-what's that?" Nik stuttered.

"It has been many generations since your arrival was foretold."

The woman was almost unintelligible at first, her emphasis oddly placed – as if she'd never actually heard the language spoken.

"We must thank the gods for sending you to us at last," she continued, "on this, the most sacred of days."

Nik's mouth clamped shut with an audible snap as the queen turned to communicate something to one of the women behind her. It was only then that Ann noticed that all the women in the cluster behind the thrones had tied the front of their jackets back to fully expose their breasts.

But the queen was addressing the twins again.

"I am Erea, *Kynra* of Kabyrnos and Sacred Mother to the holy Sisterhood. This –" she gestured behind her to where the king stood, still frowning – "is the *Kyn* of Kabyrnos, and indeed, of all of Kapreitu, our holy land in the sea."

The *Kyn* moved forward then to stand next to the *Kynra*. He took his time, walking slowly, deliberately. Reclaiming command of the space in a few measured steps. The courtyard settled back into silence. And then, in an equally deliberate gesture, the man brought the back of his hand to his forehead, and – astonishingly – bent forward in a low bow.

The courtyard filled with the rustling of thousands of shifting skirts as the entire crowd followed suit. Bowing down too, the *Kynra* explained,

"We honour you."

Nik caught Ann's eye. She could only stare back.

Then the *Kynra* straightened, hands now clasped before her. "We will have time to welcome you properly at a later point, Foreign Ones." She peered up at the still darkening sky. "At present we must commence the ceremony."

At the *Kynra*'s words, the atmosphere in the courtyard shifted perceptibly. The *Kyn* signalled a group of men left of the thrones – many of whom were dressed in the same leather-and-fur as the cropped-haired man. These men and the *Kynra*'s bare-breasted women began to move, arranging themselves in two lines that fanned out from their monarchs.

While people rushed to take their places, Ann felt someone take hold of her arm – tightly, almost pinching. She turned to find one of the bare-breasted females, a stocky woman, with skin pulled tight over horse-like features as she scowled up at Ann.

"Follow me!"

One barked command and the woman turned away from Ann toward Nik, to say (hands to herself this time), "You as well, please."

Then she marched off. After exchanging one wondering look, the twins hurried to catch up.

"Do you all know English?" Nik asked in a whisper as they were guided through the crowd toward the altar.

The woman glanced up at him briefly. "I do not understand."

"English. Does everyone here speak it?"

"English?"

"What you're speaking."

"The tongue of the Foreign *Kyn*."

"Er – sure. That."

She paused in the space next to the altar, turning to face him. Nik met her gaze evenly, trying very hard – Ann guessed – not to make eye contact with the woman's nipples.

"Only we of the Sisterhood learn to speak this tongue," the woman explained with evident self-satisfaction. "It is our sacred responsibility. We learn it in honour of our ancestral leader, and for those –" she bowed her head at Nik – "who are to succeed him."

Nik raised his brows.

The woman then shot Ann a brief glare – for good measure – barked at them to "Stay here!" and then strutted away to rejoin the line of bare-chested priestesses.

"Somebody doesn't like you much," Nik muttered in the growing silence. "You insult her dress or something?"

Ann glanced at him, taking in the full effect of that lopsided grin. Her arms still throbbed where his fingers had dug in to them, only a short while ago in the tunnel. Someone was speaking now by the thrones in loud, rhythmic tones. Ann turned away.

The *Kynra* was chanting, and the feeling of anticipation had intensified. It was so strong now it was almost a sound running beneath the woman's words like the humming reverberations that followed the striking of a bell.

And then, as if drawn by some thread, Ann felt her eyes pulled away from the *Kynra* toward the altar. The axe lay there, gleaming in the low light. It was intricately engraved, she saw, with animals – bulls and birds – twisting up the hilt and curving onto the silver blades like live creatures. Ann curled her hands into fists, fighting a strong, sudden urge to step forward and run a fingertip along a razor sharp edge.

Other women had joined in the *Kynra*'s hymn now. The priestesses wove their voices together, high and pure fluting around the low and guttural. Moments later, they were joined by the deeper tones of the robed men to the left of the thrones – priests? – and soon, the air was thick with their song. Ann felt as if she was drinking it in, pulling the river of voices into herself with every breath – and taking with it a flood of feeling. An indistinct welling of hope. A sharper pang of loss.

And then they were moving, they were all moving, following the *Kynra* across the courtyard. The crowd parted, opening up and joining the end of the procession one by one, the whole line of people swaying gently to the rhythm of the chant. And emerging up above them, above the wall they moved toward, was the profile of the sleeping mountain, nose pointing upward into the charcoal clouds. But the mountain soon disappeared behind the roof, and the voices lured them onward, into the building itself.

Darkness filled the corridors. Ann melted into it, a shadow lost among shadows. The movement of the dark forms in front of her, the brushing contact of the one behind. The second, ghostly procession moving counter to the flow, back toward the sanctum of the inner courtyard. Just more paintings, Ann's brain told her. Only paintings.

It was cold now, growing colder still as they re-emerged into open air. An outer courtyard, hedged in by pines, filling, slowly, with the whole swaying mass of people. The sky was lit with an unearthly, sallow light. And in the centre of the glowing space, a single, massive tree. Branches bare, twisted, and unnaturally dark. Scorched, she realized.

The singing had stopped. The crowd was still. The sky rumbled overhead.

This was not real, Ann told herself. This place was a dreamscape, these people just figments of a stagnating, solitary mind.

Not a single person in the thousands present uttered a word. The *Kynra*, standing close – surprisingly close – to Ann now, looked as pale and brittle as the stones of the massive building behind them. The *Kyn* too was there, bearded jaw tight, an expression in his brown eyes that made Ann look away again.

To find that Nik was no longer beside her.

Something tugged in her mind and she whirled round. He was not far: five, maybe six, feet away in the crowd. Just out of reach. His back was to her, his face hidden. Yet she knew, somehow she knew what she would see if he turned round.

She had seen those burning eyes before.

A muffled cry broke the stillness. In an opening around the tree knelt a woman, hair tumbling in front of her face. And she was sobbing, hands clasped before her – begging, desperately begging.

The crowd stirred to let a group of three pass. A young boy, maybe eight or nine, walked between two men bearing spears. The boy's cheeks were streaked with tears, but he was no longer crying. He allowed himself to be dragged to the oak, where the two men hoisted him up, and began to fasten his arms and legs to the limbs of the tree.

The sobbing woman sprang forward then, grabbing at the ankles of one of the men. Two more spear-bearers materialized to hold her back. Ann glanced around the courtyard to find that a small army of guards surrounded the space. Another strangled cry brought several of them forward. The woman clawed at the air as she was hauled backward, toward the outer trees, the sound of her screams piercing the air until, very abruptly, they were cut short.

Ann's hands were shaking now, her skin damp despite the cold.

This was not *real*, she told herself.

She turned back to the boy. His head had fallen back against the bark, his face blank and turned up toward the clouds.

The sky rumbled again. Louder, this time.

"What are they going to do to him?" Ann whispered aloud.

Someone next to her shifted. A priestess.

"What are they going to *do* to him?" Ann asked the woman.

The woman held her eyes but said nothing.

The *Kynra* moved forward. She began to speak again, although this time her words held no power. They were mechanical, meaningless. It took Ann a moment to realize that she was speaking in English.

The gifts of the gods, she said. The price of life. The sacred balance maintained.

"What is she talking about?" Ann asked the priestess desperately.

"Please be calm," the woman whispered. "It is what must be."

"What *what* must be?"

The *Kynra* was backing up now, the crowd moving with her, clearing a larger space around the tree. The priestess took Ann's arm and drew her back. Ann let herself be led.

Another rumble sounded above and the whole crowd glanced up. The black mass of clouds was roiling, with splinters of lightning dancing across its surface. Glancing back to the tall, lone tree, Ann finally understood.

This could *not* be real.

The sky flashed bright, once, twice, leaving the world dark in its wake.

The thunder grew louder.

The sky flashed again, illuminating the lines of the tree in an electric silver light. Ann could see the image imprinted before her even after the view had retreated again into blackness. The child had passed out.

Real or not, she had to do something – untie the ropes, haul him down, *anything*. But there was no time, no time to think, to –

Another flash of light. The heavens snarled in immediate response.

Ann's face turned to the sky.

Here. Now.

And with a mighty, cracking blast, an arm of lightning shot down and struck the very heart of the tree, blinding them all in a blaze of white.

Chapter Three

Ann and Nik had been sitting by themselves in the *Kyn*'s chambers for what felt like hours. Neither had said a word, nor had they touched the wine or fruit that had been left for them.

Immediately after the tree had been struck, the rainless storm had dispersed. Just as quietly and as quickly, the crowd had also disbanded, leaving what was left of the boy to the descending crows. The twins had been escorted back through the broad double portal and it was only once in the shelter of the corridors that Ann had lost control, retching down one wall. Their guide had helped her up and gently urged her onward. Nik had barely glanced her way.

By the time they were settled in the *Kyn*'s apartments, Ann had begun to recover. The chamber was dark and draughty, the seats they sat on backless and stiff, but they had been left with a pair of sheepskins and a few clay braziers for warmth. The braziers were odd-looking apparatuses, with three short legs supporting rounded heaps of embers. Like coal-bearing turtles, Ann found herself thinking. She was, she then realized, still in shock.

It was some time before Nik's face returned to its normal colour. It was longer still before his eyes could do more than stare blankly ahead. When he revived enough to notice Ann watching him, he rose to his feet and made his way over to a table. A pitcher of water sat there, swan-shaped and made of crystal – a thing of real beauty. Ignoring the silver tankards beside it, Nik brought the swan's mouth to his lips and drank deeply.

Just as he was replacing the pitcher, Ann heard the door creak open. The twins turned.

Three people settled in a phalanx before them.

The *Kyn* stood in the centre, feet apart, huge chest pressed out as he clasped his hands behind his back. He was not as tall as Ann had thought – shorter than her own five foot ten inches – yet for the moment he seemed to fill all the space in the room. He did not attempt to communicate. He merely observed the twins, his dark, intelligent eyes sparkling in the torchlight.

At his right shoulder was a woman, pale and well-muscled. She stood very still, with a charged kind of stillness that made Ann think of a loaded weapon. She wore a plain tunic and a dagger at her belt, her only adornment the silver diadem that she wore over her brow. She was some kind of guard, clearly.

The man to the *Kyn*'s left was lean and unusually tall. He was handsome, Ann supposed, but there was something almost too smooth about him. Something in the narrowed eyes, in curving edges of his smile. A smile that only broadened as the man caught her gaze.

The door opened again. The *Kynra* swept into the chamber, followed by one of her priestesses.

"Have you been offered something to eat?"

"Yes," Nik stated.

"Thank you," Ann added quietly.

The *Kynra* acknowledged the thanks with one sideways jerk of the head. For the first time, Ann noticed the quantities of onyx beads that were woven into the *Kynra*'s hair and wrapped around her throat and wrists. The torchlight seemed to catch every facet of every stone at once, making the *Kynra* seem more glittering goddess than human woman.

"As I said before the ceremony, we are very delighted that you have come to us at last. Very delighted, indeed."

Ann imagined that she did see something, some spark of intensity beneath the calm.

"And why exactly is that?" asked Nik, bluntly vocalizing the thought.

"Your arrival has been foretold for generations, Foreign One."

"So you said."

"So I did."

Shaking his head, Nik turned away, and as he moved back to the table with the water pitcher, Ann saw the *Kynra* stiffen. She was not – Ann guessed – used to such informal treatment. But the moment passed without comment.

"Explain this to me," Nik continued as the *Kynra*'s priestess began translating for the others. "How is it that you claim to know we were coming?"

"We need not go into these details tonight," the *Kynra* replied. "You must be very fatigued."

Her brother's chin shot up in a gesture that Ann recognized all too well from their teenage years.

"Or, for that matter," he went on, "how did you know that it was *us* you were waiting for? Did you have any specifications – or would any random stranger do?"

"How can it be doubted? One has only to behold you to know you have been sent to us by the gods."

Nik snorted and the *Kynra*'s face went totally still – an alarming contrast to the ceaseless shimmer of her beads. Ann shot her brother a warning look, and yet, when the *Kynra* did finally reply, she was very calm.

"Countless generations ago," she began, "in the late years of our Kypran forefathers, a foreign man like yourself came to our land in the sea, and through his virtues and talents, was appointed *Kyn* of Kabyrnos. A more noble, or judicious leader Kabyrnos has not since seen."

A pointed pause. As the priestess finished translating, Ann stole a glance back at the others. The guardswoman was tightening her grip on her dagger, nostrils flaring. The sly-looking one didn't appear to be listening at all: his eyes were still on Ann. Ann quickly looked to the *Kyn*.

The man had adopted a wry expression; Ann half-expected him to roll his eyes. Yet when he noticed her watching him, he smiled – only a hint of grin, but it was warm, conspiratorial. Ann felt the knot of tension in her chest relax infinitesimally.

The *Kynra* was talking again. "After the Foreign *Kyn*'s death, one of our priestesses who had the gift of Sight foretold the coming of others of his kind. She prophesied that their arrival would herald the advent of a new age for Kapreitans.

"We have been hoping that your arrival would be imminent. We have –" another pause, her eyes flicking toward the *Kyn* – "a very great need of change."

This time, the guardswoman growled a few words. The *Kynra*'s lips pursed, but she ignored the other woman. Yet when she opened her mouth to continue speaking, the guardswoman cut her off, anger plain in every snapped syllable. The *Kynra*'s eyes flashed darkly. She stepped forward in a surprisingly swift motion.

The *Kyn* said one word, his voice echoing in the cavernous room. No one moved.

Three heartbeats later, Ann threw her brother a desperate look. He caught his cue.

"So, anyway..." Nik mumbled. "I don't really think that we're, uh – what you're looking for."

"Nonsense," the *Kynra* snapped.

"Really, though – we're not, like, prophets or anything. You've obviously made a mistake."

The *Kynra* frowned at him. It was a minute change, the slightest pinching of her brows, but even Nik could tell he'd said enough.

"There is no mistake," the woman said quietly.

"Excuse me?" Ann felt the attention of the room shift to her. She moistened her lips. "I think that maybe we should... We're very tired."

The *Kynra* looked at her with approval. "Of course, Foreign One. My priestess will guide you to the apartments that have been prepared for you. Tomorrow, a servant will come and bring you to share your morning meal with me and I will answer all your questions in greater detail."

As the priestess translated this last sentence, the *Kyn* made a comment – a brief, almost lazy interjection. The *Kynra* turned, shot the priestess a scathing look, and then snapped at the *Kyn* in their native tongue. He simply bowed his head to her, still smiling pleasantly.

The *Kynra* looked back to Ann, mouth so pinched now it was barely visible.

"The *Kyn* and I will both see you in morning."

***

Unlike the journey from the outer courtyard, the walk from the *Kyn*'s apartments to their own rooms was very short. The High Steward had – the priestess explained – ordered a set of rooms for them in the upper eastern section of the palace. It was a great honour, she informed the twins. They were being afforded every possible luxury.

Yet, standing in the doorway of her chamber, Ann was sceptical. Taking up most of the room's length was a low bed – animal skin stretched over a wooden frame, topped with what smelled to be a hay-filled mattress. Beside the bed was another brazier – her very own turtle – and an engraved wooden trunk, on which sat a small assortment of things – clay lamp, stone jug, wash-basin. Not much else fit in the room beyond the little clay pot that sat in the only empty corner.

Carved into the upper portion of the inner wall was a narrow window, which opened into the common room that she shared with Nik. The common room was larger, containing several stools, a table, and two more glowing turtles. At one end of the room was a door that led out to the corridor, and at the other, a lightwell – a skylight of sorts that opened directly to the stars.

Nik sat beneath it, forehead resting on his knees.

"I'm too wired to sleep," he muttered as Ann re-entered the room.

"I'm too hungry."

He dug into his pocket and procured six shrivelled brown lumps. Dried figs, from the *Kyn*'s table. He tossed her three.

She slid down the wall. "Nik, what is this place?"

"Isn't it obvious?" he asked, popping a whole fruit into his mouth. "Still got that pamphlet on you?"

After a pause, Ann pulled the crumpled tourist guide out of her pocket.

"Nik… It can't be…"

"It can. It is." He sighed, passing a hand through his hair. "God, what I'd do for a smoke."

"We can't have – it's impossible." She shook her head, and scanned the pamphlet. "This is – at least – three and a half *thousand years*."

"Would it make more sense if it was only a couple of weeks?"

"Nik, it's impossible. It's crazy, it's – not…"

"I know. But what're the other options?"

She shook her head again slowly. "I know what you're saying. I know what I've *seen*. But, it just doesn't… compute."

"I don't think I really believe it yet either."

Ann looked down. Her fingers absently traced the wrinkled skin of the figs she'd dropped in her lap. Her mouth watered; she took a nibble. The fruit was grainy, with a concentrated sweetness that almost made her dizzy. It had been so long since she'd eaten.

And as she leaned against the wall, trying to calculate how many hours had passed since breakfast at her hotel, it finally settled on her that the hours had, in fact, passed. She could feel them in the rumbles of her stomach, in the exhaustion that pulled at the back of her eyes. Despite every protest her mind still wanted to make, she began to accept that this – that all of this – was really happening.

She balled up the pamphlet and tossed it to Nik. "Take this. I don't want it anymore."

And then Nik was on his feet, chucking the pamphlet onto the nearest smouldering turtle.

"This is ridiculous!" he yelled. "I mean – we just – I was only supposed to take *one day*. Everything was *fine* and then –" He glared at Ann. "This is just *unbelievable*!"

And it ended as abruptly as it had started, with his sudden deflation against the wall.

Ann smiled as she watched the pamphlet shrivel, flames consuming it from the edges inward. She was used to this, Nik's outbursts of impotent rage. They calmed her, made her feel, oddly, more at home than she'd felt all day. Than she'd felt in years, really.

"And what are *you* grinning at?" he demanded.

She lost the smile. "Nothing."

Another minute passed.

"So," she ventured, "if we really have gone… 'back in time'–" she felt ridiculous just saying it – "what are we going to do about it?"

"Try to get back, I guess… Right?"

After a pause, Ann nodded and Nik straightened, tossing the last of his figs onto the glowing embers.

"Right. Tomorrow night, then."

"Tomorrow night," she repeated, watching him disappear behind the curtain into his own tiny bedroom.

Chapter Four

Despite her exhaustion, it took Ann most of the night to fall asleep. She tossed on her scratchy mattress, startled by every hoot of an owl, every whistle of the wind over the lightwell. Her mind preyed on her. She heard voices on the other side of the thick walls, whispering to each other. Whispering to her. In every shadowed corner she saw some lurking thing, watching her, waiting...

Ann buried her head under the wool covers. Her imagination was bad enough; reality was – in this rare instance – worse. That mother's screams. That young boy's face as he'd stared up at the gathering storm. If a horror like that could happen, what else was possible in this barbaric, elegant world?

And then there was Nik. Nik, who had, only that afternoon, taken her hand. Who had smiled at her and called her Anna. But – his face in that outer courtyard. His voice as he'd screamed at her in the tunnel. That *voice*...

No. She forbade the thought.

As the night crept on, Ann found herself wondering – wondering about this place, these people. About the currents that seemed to run underneath them all, unseen yet already profoundly felt, like a spark of electricity from a frayed wire.

Best steered clear of.

And then, just before dawn, Ann was hit by a thought so momentous that it left her breathless. If Nik was right, if her senses told true, then they'd somehow been brought to a world that lived and died before the time of Olympic myth. A world that existed well before the philosophers had spun their golden tales, before Christ had been born to captivate and compel. A time before legend. They were, at that very moment, at the beginning of it all.

***

Someone coughed.

Ann scrambled into a sitting position, pulling her blanket to her shoulders. The curtain of her doorway was pulled back and dim light leaked through, highlighting the small, plump form of a young woman. The woman's hands were resting on rounded hips and she was frowning at Ann as if locked in internal debate.

Ann cleared her throat. "Can I help you?"

For a moment, the girl continued to stare. And then, with a sideways flick of the head, she seemed to make her decision.

"Good morning."

Her accent was thick – thicker than the *Kynra*'s – and she spoke slowly, articulating each syllable.

"Are you a priestess too?" Ann asked dubiously, eyeing the girl's plain, calf-length dress.

The young woman's frown deepened. She was uncommonly pretty, Ann noticed.

"No. I am not priestess," she said. "Do not tell others, please, that I talk to you. Yes?"

"Sure. Yes."

The young woman smiled then, a sweet, dimpled smile that seemed to relax her whole body. Her hands dropped to her sides. "That is good."

She marched over to the stone jug and poured some water into the bowl. "You will clean, now. And after, you will dress, and after, you will eat."

Pushing the bowl towards Ann, she promptly left the room.

An efficient little person, Ann thought as she splashed water over her face. She then eased out of bed and was about to go in search of a bathroom when her eyes fell on the little covered pot in the corner.

She groaned.

One awkward minute later, just as Ann was buttoning her pants, the curtain flew aside and the young woman marched back into the room with a pile of clothing. Little sprigs of dried herbs scattered the floor as she shook out a dress and held it up for Ann's approval. It was similar to the one the girl was wearing, but in a much finer cloth, with geometric patterns embroidered along the hems. Ann eyed the deep V of the neckline apprehensively.

"Er – I'm fine as I am. Really."

The young woman regarded Ann's dirt-smudged jeans and wrinkled sweatshirt. "I think not."

Ann tried a few more feeble protests, but it was not long before she was pulling the dress on over her jeans as the girl stood by, hands on her hips.

"So, what's your name?" Ann asked as she turned away to remove her bra.

"I am called Hersephona. Hersa. And you?"

"Ann."

The young woman's laughter was light and tinkling. "That is not a name. It is a *sound*."

Ann couldn't help but smile. In their rich, rolling tones, the name did seem a little incomplete. Hersa moved forward to help her wind the cloth belt.

"How did you learn –" she gasped as the girl tightened the belt around her ribcage – "to, to speak this language so well?"

"My friend who is priestess, she teach me. In secret."

The girl handed her the final article, a rectangular pad of wool, with strings attached at each corner.

"Why in secret?"

"Only those of Sisterhood have the... privilege, I think you say. Yet it is worst, I think, for servants to know. So, you must not tell."

"Oh. Yeah, I see. No problem."

Ann angled away again to fasten the strings over her hips. She thought of this girl, surreptitiously practicing a foreign language in what was likely very minimal spare time. And as she turned around to inspect herself in the polished bronze mirror that Hersa held up, Ann found herself imagining what it would be like to stay. In high school, she had excelled in languages, picking up French easily, even learning a bit of Spanish before circumstances had made it impossible for her to focus on her studies. Immersed as she would be here, it wouldn't take her long to become fluent.

An image of the boy on the tree flashed through her mind.

No. They would return tonight.

"You like?" Hersa asked.

"Uh..." Ann wriggled her shoulders in the short, tight sleeves as she tugged the front flaps of the dress over her chest. "Is there anything to, you know, pin this?"

Hersa looked confused.

"It's just a little... revealing."

The girl gestured to her own ample cleavage. "It is nice, yes? Though you do not have much – you need to *eat* –" she laughed, pinching Ann's collarbone gently. "Yet you are so beautiful, it matters not."

Ann wrapped her arms across her chest as Hersa squeezed around and began to tug at her ponytail.

Ann yelped, hands flying to her head. "What now?"

"I fix your hair."

"What's wrong with it?"

Hersa laughed her tinkling laugh. "You look like… it is 'horse'?"

Ann sighed, but found – oddly – that she was smiling again. "Do you have an opinion on everything, Hersa?"

The girl considered this for a moment. "Yes, I think this is true. It is maybe not wise, in my position, though I – how do you say it? I cannot help myself."

***

The two women emerged from the bedroom still laughing, with Ann's hair still up in its ponytail. Nik, who had been sitting on a stool outside, rose, eyeing Hersa with interest.

"You girls sounded like you were having a lot of fun in there."

The women exchanged smiles.

"Nice threads, Ann." He turned to Hersa as Ann tugged at her neckline again. "Don't I get some too?" He flashed her a smile. "Clothes, I mean. Not fun."

"In your trunk," the girl stated shortly.

When Nik returned minutes later, he was wearing an embroidered kilt that only just brushed his mid-thigh.

"Are there any shoes to this delightful ensemble?" Nik inquired with another flash of his teeth.

"You are *indoors*," was all the little servant said before moving to the door and announcing, "I will take you to the *Kynra* now."

And she marched out. Ann peered at her brother.

"You insult her dress or something?"

Nik just grunted and strode after the girl.

The twins followed the little servant back through the corridors they'd travelled the night before. Ann walked mutely, watching the sunlight slant through the lightwells to touch the stone of the walls. The morning had brought a sharpness with it, dispelling the dream-like quality of the previous evening.

"What are they doing down there?"

Nik had paused and was peering down over a balustrade.

"Training," Hersa replied without slowing her pace.

Ann glanced over the railing. There were clusters of people tumbling and grappling on the flagstones of the vast inner courtyard one storey below. Men occupying the one half, women, the other.

"What for?" Ann asked.

"Many things." Hersa thought for a moment. "It is how to show thanks, to the Earth Mother, for her gift of life. You understand?"

Ann looked back down at the bare, glistening limbs that heaved and twined together. No, she did not understand.

"And the men must keep their bodies strong too. It is their duty. In case of –" Hersa paused, searching for the right word – "battle. War. We have no war in many generations, yet..."

Hersa beckoned them onward, leading them into another enclosed corridor. "Also, some of the men may train for the Great Tournament," she said over her shoulder.

Nik perked up. "The Great Tournament?"

"Yes. It happens again one year from now."

"Who competes?"

The girl shushed him as another servant appeared at the end of the corridor bearing several empty breakfast trays. She led them silently to the double doors of the *Kyn*'s apartments. After knocking once, she bowed to the twins – hand to forehead, eyes to ground – and then retreated as another servant came to usher them inside.

Nik watched her leave. "Funny little woman, huh?"

***

The twins were escorted out onto a veranda, which overlooked the people training in the courtyard. The inner wall was painted with dolphins swimming through seaweed. A tranquil scene set against the grunts from below.

"Morning's greetings, Foreign Ones."

The *Kynra* sat, back straight, in the shade of an awning. She was surveying their attire. "You are both looking very well."

She herself had abandoned the formal flounced skirts of the day before and was dressed very similarly to Ann, only with the same abundance of onyx she'd worn the previous night. In the daylight, however, the black beads seemed dull, heavy – almost cumbersome as the woman swept her hand toward a table against the wall.

"Please," she said. "Eat."

Nik folded his arms across his chest and remained where he was. Ann politely helped herself to a few pistachios.

"You must have many questions."

Nik let out a low laugh. The woman regarded him for a moment, then said, slowly,

"Your mistrust is understandable, Foreign One. I sympathize. It will take time."

He laughed again. "And here I was thinking you expected us to start performing miracles straight away."

"I *expect*," the woman said, her voice low, "that you adhere to our laws during your stay here. You will be counted among our elite, however you will be required – as are we all – to conduct yourselves with decorum, and to fulfil your responsibilities – yes, Foreign One," she added in response to Nik's look. "Every person in our city has a duty, an occupation. Honouring these roles is what maintains the balance in our hearts and in our society. All of our people respect this – or there are consequences."

Recalling the previous night, Ann gave a tiny shudder. It did not escape unnoticed.

"What is it, Foreign One? Do not be timid."

The woman had leaned forward and was staring at Ann with an uncomfortable degree of interest.

"I was just… Last night, with the tree."

The *Kynra* sat back. "Ah yes. The sacrifice. An unpleasant yet necessary business –"

The door flew open, crashing against the dolphins. The *Kyn* stood there, a dark cloud on his face as he glared around the room. Seconds later, he whirled back around and was gone.

The *Kynra* continued as if there had been no interruption.

"The Day of Life marks the beginning of the Season of Life. On this day, we give thanks to Mavros, the bull god, for His protection, and to His Mother, the Earth Mother Pritymnia, for Her bounty. They give and so must we. To maintain the sacred balance."

"Balance, again," Nik said.

"Balance *always*. It is the shield against chaos."

The *Kynra* was silent for a moment then, her mouth pulling down into its lipless curve. "Yet I fear that the people have been led astray…"

The door opened again and the *Kyn* re-entered the room, this time followed by a scowling woman. The horse-faced priestess from the day before.

The *Kynra* flew to her feet, black stones flashing, and snapped a few words in the native tongue. The priestess merely pointed at the *Kyn*, who had already settled himself on a bench in front of the dolphins and was munching on raisins. The two priestesses exchanged a look, then the younger woman, reluctantly, began to speak.

"I am commanded to speak for the *Kyn*."

The *Kyn* said a few words.

"He asks your names."

Nik leaned against the wall, arms still folded. "I'm Niklas – Nik – and this is –"

"Ann," Ann stated.

The *Kyn* turned to peer at her curiously. The horse-faced priestess sneered.

"'*Ann*'? What kind of –"

The *Kyn* growled a word and her face sunk back into its customary sullen expression. Then, looking straight at Ann, the *Kyn* placed a broad hand on his chest and said,

"Zelkanus."

Ann smiled shyly. The *Kyn* continued speaking.

"He says that he hopes that both of you, Niklas and *Ann*, will stay here for as long as you wish. He says that he, and his people, would be honoured."

Nik's eyes narrowed. "Thanks."

"Yes," Ann added. "Thank you."

The *Kyn* bowed his head and spoke again to the younger priestess.

"He says that appropriate occupations will be found for both of you. I am now instructed to go fetch a steward, like a common servant, so if you will excuse me."

As the woman stalked out of the room, Nik turned to the *Kynra*. "And who's she?"

"She is Aralys, a Sister in the Sisterhood," the *Kynra* responded stiffly. The *Kyn*'s re-appearance seemed to have smothered her zeal for the moment. "She is most proficient in your tongue and will escort you through the palace later this morning."

Moments later, Sister Aralys returned. And slithering through the door behind her was a large tabby cat.

The twins exchanged glances as the woman announced that the High Steward was expected shortly. Ann watched the creature patter over to the *Kynra*, laying down at her feet.

As Aralys and the *Kynra* began to speak together quietly, Nik leaned over the stone balustrade to continue watching the people below. Ann, not wanting to attract attention to herself, remained where she was, peering over at the dolphin fresco from across the veranda.

The painted creatures that spanned along the length of the wall were flat, heavily-outlined and done up in bright, solid blues. Not lifelike at all, they were more like icons on the wall of a church: symbols of beauty, of peace, painted to ward off all that was ugly in the world.

The shield against chaos.

There was a movement at the edge of her vision. Ann turned to find the *Kyn* next to her, offering her a bowl of olives.

Tentatively, Ann took the bowl. The *Kyn* selected an olive, and placing it in his vast palm, he said a word. On his prompting, Ann repeated the word. The *Kyn*'s brown eyes crinkled warmly. Then, uttering another word, he mimicked the act of eating. Ann repeated that word, fixing it in her memory, and followed it with the word for 'olive'.

The *Kyn*'s laugh was deep and rumbling. He offered her the fruit to eat. Ann popped it into her mouth, smiling.

"What's going on?" Nik asked, drawing up beside them. His eyes were on the *Kyn*.

"He's teaching me some... Kapreitan?" Ann looked inquiringly at the *Kyn*, who smiled back.

The door opened again, drawing everyone's attention for the fourth time, and in sailed the sly-looking man from the previous night. He was decked in an arsenal of armlets and rings that gleamed as he swept into a bow. Ann tugged again at the front of her dress.

"Watch out for him," Nik whispered to Ann as the *Kyn* took his High Steward aside.

"No kidding."

"No – not *him*."

Ann frowned. "... Zelkanus then? Why on earth?"

Nik's brows shot up. "'*Zelkanus*'?"

Sister Aralys interrupted them then to announce that the High Steward had promised to present them with a selection of occupations the following morning. It was now time, she said, for her to show them the palace. She informed them that it would take some time, as the place was *very* large and *very* confusing – "for some".

Farewells were made. The High Steward bowed again. The *Kynra* bade them a cold goodbye. The *Kyn* only smiled. And as Ann followed the short, strutting priestess out of the room, she thought to herself that, however misguided, her brother's warning had also been pointless. If all went as planned that night, she would never see any of these people again.

Chapter Five

The twins sat in their dark apartments waiting for the palace to fall silent. They were both drained, tapped dry, wanting nothing more than sleep – yet still they waited. It could not be much longer now.

Hersa had come and gone hours ago, bringing with her a dinner of spiced lentils, unleavened flatbread and boiled greens with lemon. She had then taken Ann into her chamber to present her with some feminine supplies: an ivory toothcomb, pots of kohl and rouge, woollen pads, a pair of wide-edged bronze tweezers – and, finally, a necklace.

"From the *Kyn*," the young woman had informed her as she'd fastened it around Ann's neck. "It looks well with your hair."

Ann had protested, fingering the heavy golden collar. She couldn't possibly accept.

"You must," Hersa had replied. "Proper women wear such things. And – how can you refuse?"

When the girl had left, Ann had removed the necklace immediately. Strange creatures intertwined along its length. Griffins, she'd recalled: crossbreed monstrosities with leonine bodies and eagle's wings unfurled.

She'd dropped it on her pillow and returned to Nik in the common room.

He was in one of his moods. They had spent the entire day trudging after Sister Aralys. The palace *was* enormous – its inhabitants numbering in the thousands – and their guide was irritable. To put it mildly. She'd buried them in an avalanche of information: which rooms were allocated for magistrates and which for the distributors of goods, the names and locations of the many entrances, the numerous halls, the countless shrines. Ann had begun by not paying any attention – there was no real point – but it had not been long before she'd been captivated in spite of herself.

The extent and sophistication of the building was astounding. It boasted laundry pools and baths and even – to Ann's exasperation – real lavatories. These were all connected by a sewer system, the water for which was brought in on raised canals from a spring on holy Mount Crytus – the mountain to the south. The Mountain of the Sleeping God, the locals called it. There were dozens of underground cisterns that collected rainwater for the dry seasons, and scores of small workshops, teeming with the bustle of industry: weavers at their looms, potters shaping their clay, masons with their chisels and drills, paint- and glaze-makers grinding stones and shells – all pausing to gawk as the twins were ushered by. Aralys had bragged that the fine goods produced in those workshops were the most sought-after in the known world. They were what made Kabyrnos – the palace and the surrounding city – so famous amongst the peoples of the Akrean Sea.

That and its beauty. The structure of the place was stunning, with its soaring ceilings, clean rectangular lines, and its open, airy halls. Natural light channelled into every room through lightwells and balconies and rows of open doorframes. There were also smaller instances of grace that had fairly taken Ann's breath away. Nestled within winding staircases were colourful little gardens, inhabited by butterflies and birds. Water splashed out of mosaic fountains, it trickled into sparkling pools that were sunken into the stones of the floor. The palace was truly alive with hidden pockets of loveliness.

But by the afternoon, Ann had become numb to the beauty of the place. She was a system in shock. Gone were the stillness and solitude she was so used to. People were everywhere – running past you, bumping baskets into you, ogling you, babbling at you, bowing to you in every corridor. *Animals* were everywhere – packs of dogs swarming, lines of sheep and cows hauled in for clerical tallying. The building was a thriving metropolis, a city unto itself. And it seemed never, ever, to stand still.

It also seemed entirely without plan. No sense of logic or symmetry to the place – just a dizzying jumble of rooms and halls, all connected by a warren of corridors. Aralys had explained that the palace had been evolving and growing since the days of their first *Kyn*, Kabyrn, son of Kapreita (for whom the island was named). From the blessing of the Earth Mother – she'd said – the building had ripened into being. Like a living creature in its own right.

Yet the only way that Ann could make sense of it at all was to think of the central inner courtyard – the Blessed Courtyard, the priestess had called it – as dividing the palace into four loose quadrants: north, facing the ocean; east, greeting the rising sun; south, toward the mountain; and west, the setting sun. And the burnt tree.

It was in that direction that they would have to head that night.

Yet their guide had refused to let them set foot there. There were very few reasons to enter the ground storey of the western quadrant, she'd warned: if you were a servant, loading or emptying the main storerooms there; if you were a supervising guard or tallying clerk; or if you had holy business in the Sisterhood rooms. No one else was permitted.

Her caution had been discouraging enough on its own. But late that night, after the twins had changed back into their ordinary clothes, Ann considered how unlikely it was that they would be able to find their way back even to the central Blessed Courtyard. And yet, they had to try.

So they waited.

The glow from their turtles had long since faded. The only light in the room now was a pale radiance that poured in from their lightwell, along with a draught of night air. Arms wrapped around herself, Ann moved to the lightwell and glanced up. The full moon was directly above them now. She shivered. She was no expert in the lunar clock – something you'd have to be, in this place – but she was fairly sure that this meant that half of the night had expired.

She turned back to the shadowed room, to her brother sitting hunched over at the opposite end. The pale square of his face turned up toward her.

"Time, you think?" he asked.

"Probably best."

He nodded and began untying his laces. Ann followed suit, cringing as the chill of the stones seeped in through her socks. Nik rose without a sound, moved to the door and opened it. Ann peered over his shoulder. Bright shafts of moonlight pierced the darkness of the corridor, lending a thickness to the shadows that made her move, instinctively, closer to her brother's back.

Nik started forward at her touch. Taking a deep breath, Ann slung her running shoes over her shoulder and tiptoed after him.

Passage followed passage as the twins slipped through the darkness. All was silent – no wind now, no stirring from the chambers they passed. Nik showed no sign of uncertainty as he wended through the corridors, quickly and without pause. Ann followed, growing increasingly more uneasy. Falling steadily more behind.

Something was pricking at the back of her mind. Something indefinable – a kind of resonance, an energy, almost like static – that grew clearer and more undeniable with each minute. Almost like the presence of the voice, but different somehow: cleaner, stronger, with a bolder flavour to it. It seemed – impossibly – to hum in the floor beneath her feet. It was a rising and ebbing breath. A soft pulse within the stones.

A living creature in its own right.

A hiss from the end of the passage. "Ann!"

She had stopped walking.

"*Jesus,* Ann, keep up!"

"Sorry," she whispered as she hurried to catch up with her brother. "Sorry."

But he had already moved on. She continued through the dark, Nik leading her faster, the pulse rising in her ears, resonating in her brain. She kept her eyes dead ahead, fixed on the form of her brother's back as it flitted in and out of the moonlight. She watched for him, focusing all her attention on the movement in front of her, until suddenly, in the middle of a chamber that was open on one side to the night sky, he went still.

"I know this place," he breathed.

She looked around. A square room with the faint outlines of benches and tables. A room like thirty others.

"That painting." He pointed to the wall ahead. "The one of the crane hunting in the grass."

She squinted at the wall. Black shapes sprawled across it, vague, indeterminable.

"I think if we go down those stairs there, we come out into one of those greeting halls just off the courtyard."

A gust of air blew in from outside, ruffling her hair along her neck.

"You sure?" she whispered.

"Yes."

The twins stole across the hall and down the stairs. The stairwell was narrow and steep and seemed to plunge downward interminably. As she groped along the walls, easing herself from step to step, Ann felt sure that her brother was leading her into the lowest levels of the eastern quadrant – the part of the building that was cut deep into the slopes of the valley. The tightest, darkest place they'd visited earlier that day, with its innumerable storage rooms and workshops. They'd never make it out before dawn. But when the steps abruptly ended and she emerged into an enormous chamber – almost dazzled by its comparative brightness – she realized that, miraculously, Nik had been right. She took a step out into the hall.

A hand clamped over her mouth.

She struggled, her scream muffled. The hand tightened, another one snaking around to secure her arms against her sides.

"Shut up, Ann, *shut up!*"

She froze, locked in her brother's arms. Everything around them was absolutely still. No hint of movement in the hall, no stirrings in the dark. Just the pulsing hum. After a long moment, Ann wiggled her chin, and Nik's hand slipped down, freeing her mouth.

"What?" she asked. "What did you see?"

He remained totally motionless. Not breathing, not loosening his hold. Her arms were starting to grow numb.

"Nik?"

He said nothing.

"Nik, you're hurting me."

He let her go, stepping away quickly.

"Sorry," he mumbled.

"What *was* that?"

"Nothing. It was nothing. Doesn't matter."

He continued toward the bright square of light at the opposite end of the hall. Still shaking from the shock, Ann hurried to keep up. She needed to stay close. She needed to concentrate on his nearness, on the warmth of another human body – on the fact that just beyond the wide expanse of courtyard, her normal, boring, *safe* life was waiting.

The Blessed Courtyard was vast, stretching out like a moonlit desert between them and the western quadrant that rose up in the distance. The balconies and rows of doorways carved out of its face were dark, the space beyond blotted out. It made her think of blank, staring eyes.

"So many goddamn doors," Nik muttered.

Ann took a shaking breath and dredged up the images of the previous afternoon. The maze of broken walls. The stale air below, the caution tape foolishly ignored. The cat, standing in one of the doorways to the right of a wide, truncated staircase. The very staircase that rose up before them now, its upper steps lost to blackness.

"There," she whispered. "Just north of those stairs."

Nik nodded and moved out into the moonlight, his shadow running swiftly behind him. Ann's eyes scanned the perimeter of the courtyard as she ran.

There was no one – that she could see. But directly ahead, getting closer with each second, was the axe on its altar, glimmering faintly in the glow of the moon.

A dizzying jolt, like a strike to the back of the head.

Ann stumbled to a halt three quarters of the way through the courtyard.

The ground was rumbling, it was *shaking*, no build-up, no warning. An earthquake – but the air was vibrating with it too. Nik had stopped just feet away. Ann struggled to close the distance, but her whole body was trembling now, her knees impossibly weak.

A roll of thunder boomed through the air.

Greetings, golden children.

Ann's hands flew up to cover her ears. This voice – so unlike that rasping sigh that whispered her name – was a vice against her skull.

That will not aid you, human.

Wincing, she brought her hands down.

To wander Kabyrnos at night is to invite peril.

Nik stepped forward. "We – we're trying to find our way back home."

I know this.

"Can you – can you help –"

Nik stopped mid-sentence. He was staring northward. Slowly, Ann followed his gaze.

The form of a powerfully-built creature stood in the shadows of the open pathway which led down through the northern palace.

I will return you to your home, the figure said at length.

The pressure in the air was building. A wave of nausea rolled over Ann.

Yet the passage between the worlds opens only on the first day of every year. On the Day of Life.

"Wait," Nik began, his voice now shaking. "You can't mean –"

Yes.

"One year..."

A short time.

Ann's breath was coming in gasps.

I will warn you, however, the figure continued. *These people are my most cherished.*

His words were pushing down at her now, like the weight of an ocean, the exertion of his will, crushing her.

You will not *disrupt the balance of their world. It is, at this moment, poised on a thread. The interference of outsiders could result in disaster.*

Just at that moment, the moon broke out from behind the clouds. Ann gasped. Protruding from the sides of the figure's heads were two great bull's horns.

"You –" Nik breathed, "You're –"

The god raised His chin proudly.

Nik was on his knees now. Black spots sparked at the edges of Ann's vision. Another moment, she knew, and she would pass out.

You are warned, the bull god boomed.

Another cloud passed overhead and He was gone.

***

Nik had moved away from her. She had no idea when. The wind whistled past, pushing damp tendrils of hair off her face. She was sitting on the hard stone of the courtyard, and she was shivering now.

A faint sound. Footfall against stone.

"Oh," her brother's voice came from somewhere behind her. "It's you."

She should be alarmed, she knew. But she couldn't muster the energy. Slowly, she turned.

A woman stood on the bottom steps of the broad staircase, the moonlight glancing off the wide silver band on her forehead. She stood completely still, her hand resting – as it had the previous night – on the dagger at her belt.

Ann reached for her shoes from where they had fallen, several feet away. She could feel the woman's gaze shifting, locking on her. Ann tied her laces unhurriedly, and then rose to her feet.

The woman descended the last two steps. She moved so gracefully that Ann could not help but feel a grudging admiration. Everything about her seemed to give the impression of a tiger, pent-up and lethal.

"Easy there," Nik said, getting up. "We're going back."

The woman's eyes narrowed slightly, but the resignation in Nik's voice was enough to make his meaning clear.

"Come on, Ann."

He walked past the guardswoman, past his sister, back toward the eastern side of the courtyard. Ann followed. She did not look back at the woman, nor did she peer at the northern passage. She simply walked, one foot in front of the other, again watching her brother's back as it moved away from her.

A year.

A year under that watchful gaze. Under the thumb of the *Kynra*. A year in a place where children were sacrificed like animals, and powerful men gave you extravagant gifts. A year in a world where gods lurked in dark corners.

A whole year trapped in the prison of these beautiful walls.

Nik had vanished into the gloom ahead. Ann walked on without direction. She'd either find her way back or she wouldn't.

Book III

Chapter One

Antigone, the voice called to her. *Antigone. Get up.*

Ann swung her legs out of bed. Her bare feet met the cool stone of the floor and she stood, shivering slightly. It had been months since she'd slept with a blanket; so close to midsummer, the nights were already too warm. But not tonight.

Antigone. Come.

The room was very dark. Ann felt her way along the wall toward the curtained doorway. Her fingers met cloth and she pulled it aside.

She found herself looking into a clearing within a forest of tall, ancient trees. The light was dim and the branches were half bare. The moon hovered over the western horizon, orange and nearly full.

An Expectant Moon, they called it. Almost half-way through yet another month.

Antigone...

The voice was as she remembered it: rasping, seeping through the air like a fog, a damp breath. Yet the horror it had once held for her was absent. It was simply one of the many voices in her life – calling to her, directing her, demanding of her. And she'd learned months ago that if she simply did what was asked, she would soon be left in peace.

"I'm here," she called.

The voice answered her, its cold breath pricking her skin, urging her forward. It spoke no words, but she could feel it telling her that soon, it would be time to wake up again. To get up. To *move*.

Just off to the side of the clearing, very near to her path, was a lovely young tree – an oak, with a crown of golden leaves on its thin branches. Ann slid her palm against its bark as she passed. It was warm and seemed to stir at her touch.

No! the voice snarled.

Ann snatched her hand away.

Enough.

And she was alone. Ann swayed on the spot, a hand shooting out to steady herself. Stone. She was within Kabyrnos. She could feel the soft, beating hum of it enfolding her. As her eyes began to adjust, she realized she was standing in the doorway of Nik's bedroom. She stared into the darkness, not moving. He wouldn't be there, she knew. He hadn't slept there in months.

Ann made her way back to her own bed. It would be time to wake up soon. But not yet.

***

The first shafts of light hit the wall of her bedroom. Any moment now, the servant would come with a meal and a fresh chamber pot, and it would all begin again. Another day.

Sighing, Ann dragged herself to her feet and reached for her clothes.

She'd gone through this routine every day for months now. Shake out dress, pull over head, wrap belt around waist. And yet it was only today that she noticed how the material hung off her frame like a curtain from a rod. Tucking the ends of the belt in against her ribs she found herself wondering when she'd last eaten dinner.

A question that was all too easy to answer. Palace folk were served their midday meal at their place of work and the evening meal they took in the dining halls, in the upper northern quadrant. After that first day, Ann had never stepped foot outside the eastern quadrant where she slept and worked.

So nearly three months then.

But could it really have been that long? The only marker of time that every really caught her notice were the days of rest, which occurred on every ninth day. Those were the worst days, when the workshops remained empty, the looms still, and Ann was left with nothing to do but sit in her chamber and wait for their afternoon lessons. At first she had tried to work regardless, but when Dramelka – the stern Mistress of the Loom – had found out, she had forbidden it, insisting that all her workers needed a day to rest or their work would suffer. Which, in Ann's case – the woman had then added – was hard to imagine.

Yet her spinning had improved and Dramelka had since offered to teach her to make dyes, or even to weave. Ann had refused. She was fine where she was.

But not this morning. As usual, she arrived at the weaving rooms while the rest of the palace was still at their exercises. Yet as she sat amongst the mountains of unspun wool, dangling her clay spindle whorl and methodically massaging and twisting the attached wool into thread, her mind simply would not smooth out. Today, the repetitive rhythms held no hypnotic power for her. Today, she was bored.

So when the first three women arrived, prattling away as they did every morning, Ann was so relieved for the distraction that she actually greeted them – almost eagerly – in Kapreitan.

The women halted. Stared. Eventually, one of them returned the salutation stiffly. The two others just continued staring.

Like the people she'd passed in the corridors that morning, Ann recalled. Staring and saying nothing until she had moved on.

The three women continued to their seats further along Ann's wall, where they gathered their clouds of wool and their picks, and began their usual routine. Comb out the fibres. Complain about their husbands. Boast about their children. Gossip about their betters.

Ann listened to their chatter every morning – for the words, not the content. She never tried to partake. She couldn't remember the last time she'd spoken with anyone except the priestesses who gave her and Nik lessons every afternoon.

Nik never spoke to her directly, of course. He always arrived slightly after the priestess, dutifully engaged with the woman for the time they were there, and then disappeared in search of dinner. Ann wouldn't see him again until the following afternoon.

He was working in the stables, she thought. Or the aviaries. The threading women mentioned him from time to time. They'd talk about how their sons had told them that Niklas had been so witty in the gathering hall last night, amusing them all with tales of his homeland. They talked about how he'd been seen kissing a prominent painter's daughter. Or how he'd been drinking all the night before with two of the *Kyn*'s dancers. The usual drama.

Which – inevitably – there was more of this morning. Two people, caught in a storage closet. A real scandal, because one of the two was married.

The wife of the Master Bronzesmith. The other was the High Steward.

Not surprising, Ann thought. And the threading women seemed to agree. Never – they whispered – had Kabyrnos housed a more brazen womanizer. The few times Ann herself had encountered the man, he'd gone out of his way to show her the kind of exaggerated deference that seemed more mockery than respect. He'd stop, step out of the way, bow – then stare, smiling at her until she had rushed past.

The threading women had moved on. Ann listened, surprised to find herself interested in the city's news – for once. Well, no, it wasn't the first time. There had been one detail, a couple months back: a body that had been found deep within the western quadrant, in the cellars below the Sisterhood rooms. The decaying corpse of a painter, who had been reported missing by his wife half a year earlier. His head had been nearly severed at the neck – Ann remembered that.

But today's news was more mundane. There was to be a midsummer festival in two days' time. The Day of Light. Feasting, music, dancing, and bonfires after nightfall. And a hunt had been organized for tomorrow morning. A boar had been terrorizing Kartissus, the village on the lower slopes of Mount Crytus.

Then the women fell silent. It was a pause so abrupt, so pointed, that Ann immediately understood that they were looking her way. She kept her face blank and her eyes on her work. When they spoke again, she could barely make out their words.

"– certain that he has joined the huntsmen?"

"Larodys told me, and he had it from the Master of the Hunt himself."

"Yet he has no experience –"

"The creature is said to be rabid!"

They were silent for another moment.

"He is a young man, for all he is god-sent," one woman whispered. "Young men see no danger until it has gored them with its horns."

A shattering sound halted their whispers. Ann peered down to find her spindle lying in pieces at her feet. Slowly, aware of the dozens of eyes on her, she dusted off her lap, stood and left the room.

Out in the privacy of the corridor, Ann rested her forehead against the wall. Fear had overtaken her so suddenly and so completely it was as if it had been simmering beneath the surface all morning, just waiting for its chance to boil over.

She couldn't stay here. She had to get out – to *move*. Straightening up, she marched off down the corridor, picking the first destination that came to mind.

***

It took Ann most of the morning to track down Hersa. She had not seen the little servant for some time. In the early days, the girl had come to visit her regularly. Then she had come occasionally. Then she had stopped coming altogether. Ann couldn't blame her.

Finding her now was a lot more complicated than she'd anticipated. Hersa would, Ann guessed, be attending to the women's residences at this point in the morning. A simple enough destination: the residences took up the larger part of the western third storey. Yet on her way there, Ann somehow managed to interrupt two official meetings in the southern commerce region, an illicit game of gambling in the men's gathering hall, and a

Sisterhood ritual that involved a life-size statue of a nude woman, two vats of oil and a dozen or so very irritated priestesses. Ann only began to make some real progress when she was stopped by two guards, standing to attention on either side of a low door.

She stuttered a request for directions. After a brief, hushed discussion, the door was unlatched and Ann was instructed to follow.

The corridor was very long, very low and very dark. As Ann hurried behind the guard, trying to keep within the flickering sphere of his torchlight, she noticed doors – a long row of them, square and heavy-looking – running along one side of the passage.

She cleared her throat. "Where – what place…?"

"These are the western storerooms, *Prona*."

Ann was silent. The honorific was still jarring; more shocking still was the fact that she'd been permitted access – even chaperoned as it was – to this out-of-bounds area.

During one of their afternoon lessons, a priestess had informed the twins that the supplies that were kept in the western cellars were the life raft of Kabyrnos: there were enough dry goods, oil and wine stored there to sustain the entire city for up to a full year. She'd then mentioned that the stores had been depleted of late, as the rains had not been as plentiful in the past Seasons of Darkness – the winter rainy season.

"How many moons could the supplies now last for?" Nik had asked (infinitely more at ease in the native tongue than his sister).

"Enough."

Peering now at the long row of storage closets, it struck Ann how very tenuous life on this island really was. Beneath the veneer of grandeur and longevity – the halls, the art, the rituals, the traditions – lay the very real possibility of extinction.

The balance of a world, poised on a thread.

A thought better left alone.

The corridor ended abruptly in another door. This second and only other threshold to the storeroom passage was guarded by paunch-bellied men (an unusual sight at Kabyrnos) who stooped over their oil lamps to scratch symbols on tablets of clay. Clerks, Ann realized. The guard handed her off to one of these men, who, in turn, passed her on to a servant with the instruction that she be escorted to the women's residences.

The residences (which reminded Ann more of a dormitory than a place of permanent habitation) were found to be empty. Where, she then asked in her slow, clumsy Kapreitan, would the servants who worked there be now?

"Perhaps resting before the midday meals are to be served, *Prona*," her guide told her. "In the servants' dwelling."

"Can you take me to there?"

A sideways flick of the head: the Kapreitan nod.

Ann followed her guide up a narrow stairway. One short flight and she found herself emerging onto the open rooftops.

The overwhelming exposure of it. The searing pressure of the sun, unfiltered and relentless. The crushing weight of the sky after living so long in small, dark places. Ann's instinct was to retreat. To shield her stinging eyes and fly back down into the cage.

But then she beheld the city – the city that she'd lived at the heart of for months without fully realizing it – sprawling outward from the palace walls like an immense spider's web. Pale buildings, cobbled thoroughfares, all aflame in the late-morning sunlight. For a moment, it was just as it was on her first day: the alarming number of people, the sheer presence of their collective, with lives lived in the public spaces of street-front gardens or workshops, open second-floor rooms and rooftops. Then she blinked and her eyes were up, past the city to the country beyond.

This was a world transformed. The sun had dried out the greens of winter, leaving a land of brown, rocky hills and olive-coloured scrub. A land of jagged horizons, hedged in by blue expanse. An already ancient land, with weathered bones exposed. The air tasted of sun-warmed herbs. It sounded of distant voices: people calling to one another, the brays of livestock, the cry of a hawk overhead. The purr of the breeze. It felt of pure heat, warming to the core. It was a vivid world that sprawled out before her now, bright, brittle, and unyielding. A world poised on a thread.

As if being closer to death had somehow made it more alive.

The servant coughed behind her. "The servants' dwellings are just here, *Prona*."

"Yes – yes."

Peeling herself away from the view, Ann followed the servant through the rows of hanging laundry and into a burrow of rooms at the opposite end of the rooftop. Low mudbrick ceilings, six dirty mattresses and a chamber pot to one room. The habitation of the lowest caste.

And there, in a tiny chamber overlooking the city and the sea beyond, sat Hersa. Ann hesitated in the doorway. There was something very private about the way the young woman sat, staring out into the distance.

The guide coughed again. Hersa started, spinning toward them, her big eyes glossy with unshed tears. She turned away again, wiping her face, and the guide bowed out. Ann didn't know whether to follow him or not.

"You took your time."

The little servant was standing now, waiting, hands on her hips. Demanding an explanation. Ann dropped her gaze to the ground, to the mattresses stacked there and the linens folded next to them, darned in so many places that Ann wondered that they were still serviceable.

"I'm sorry, I shouldn't have intrud –"

"In Kapreitan, Ann."

Ann looked up, surprised.

"You want to become proficient, do you not?"

Ann nodded – sideways. The Kapreitan nod.

"So we must practice."

The girl sat back down and patted the sill next to her.

***

"I heard you're going on a hunt tomorrow."

Nik halted, hand on the door. They had just finished their lesson and the priestess's skirts were disappearing into the corridor. He was clearly twitching to follow.

"And?"

"Are you... are you sure that you should?"

His eyes flashed darkly in the low light. He was different, Ann noticed; she was surprised at herself for not noticing earlier. His longer, lighter hair, his darker skin. His ease in nothing but a kilt.

"You don't think I can handle it?" he asked.

"That's not what I'm saying."

"Then what *are* you saying?"

Ann didn't know how to reply. Hersa had told her that although hunts were never safe ("especially with a rabid boar"), the Master of the Hunt would not have agreed to take Nik if he did not think he could take care of himself. Then the little servant had reconsidered. It was possible, she'd said, that the Master had not had much choice.

"What do you mean?"

"A decree of both *Kyn* and *Kynra*," the girl had explained. "The Foreign Ones are to be afforded *sythamus* in every possible way."

Sythamus, Ann now reflected: an honour, a general privilege, that might very well amount to a death warrant.

"Just – be careful, Nik. Please."

His eyes were fixed somewhere over her head.

"Yeah. Sure. No problem."

And the door slammed behind him.

In the silence that followed, Ann sat back and waited for the approaching dusk. The glow from the lightwell was fading, the room growing colder. More than that, she could *feel* the night advancing, the beating hum of the palace rising up to fill the absence of daylight. Ann had been aware of this pulse – in that vague, half-awareness of a dreamer – since the night they'd met the bull god. But tonight, tonight it throbbed in her ears, angry and unquenchable. As if – she thought – in finally opening her eyes to the brightness of the world around her, she'd opened herself up to something more. A darker tide, flowing beneath.

Chapter Two

The next morning began much like the previous day. Ann dragged herself out of bed at dawn, dressed, picked at her breakfast, and went to the threading room early. She greeted the others as they arrived. Today, they all greeted her back. Everything appeared as it should. Familiar. Innocuous.

Yet beneath the calm, Ann's nerves were sizzling. She flinched at every bang from the carpenters down the hall. Her fingers shook; her thread was lumpy, unworkable. She tried to take refuge in blankness, to smother and anesthetise, but the inactivity was straining her to the point of rupture.

She reached her limit just before midday. Winding her thread around the new spindle, she placed it on its shelf and headed for the door. She walked slowly, waiting for someone to object. And although voices quieted and eyes snapped up as she passed, no one said a word to her. Hersa had been right, it seemed: *sythamus*, in every possible way.

Ann strode through the passages, her limbs buzzing with a restless energy. A good, long run – that was what she needed. She'd been sedentary for months now, and her body was wasting away. And clearly taking her mind with it.

She picked up the pace and soon found herself on a broad terrace overlooking the Crytus Valley to the south. The city continued some hundred feet below the palace at this point, and there, rising up beyond, was the sleeping profile of Mount Crytus.

Ann stopped a passing servant.

"When did the men – the hunters – leave?"

"For the boar at Kartissus?"

She nodded.

"Before mid-morning, *Prona*."

Ann peered toward the mountain then squinted up at the sun. She was still a novice in gauging distance by eye, and time by the passage of sun and moon. The mountain was maybe an hour's brisk walk away, mid-morning about three hours past. The hunters would likely be well into their pursuit by now. They might even have already killed the thing.

But they had not. She knew it with an absolute certainty.

She paced back and forth along the terrace and tried to focus.

It was there. Beneath the bustle of the city, she could sense it still, the pulsing energy, that humming force – dulled, though, seared out by the sunlight. Yet present nonetheless, with a tang of urgency to it, like a dampened electric shock.

Something was about to happen. Something had gone wrong.

Antigone…

She whirled toward the mountain, heart thudding. The whispered voice not a threat now, but a confirmation. A call to action.

She ran to the nearest person.

"How do I get –" she began, in English.

The man stared at her, eyes wide.

Ann took a breath and focused. "I have need to go to Kartissus. How best is this to be done?"

He pointed to the long road that rose up into the south. "The South *Kyn*'s Road will take you through the Kypran hills, Foreign One. After the graves of the outer city, just beyond the quarries, the road will fork. Take the western path."

Ann thanked him and hurried off toward the grand, zigzagging steps that led down the face of the valley. As she flew down, the sane part of her brain warned that she was behaving like a lunatic – that even on the slim chance that there was something wrong, there was no one less equipped to deal with it than her.

A pointless caution. By the time she reached the bottom of the steps, her calves were aching, her chest was hammering, but her mind was reined by the simple urge to go. To *move*.

And move she could. After the initial discomfort, it was almost easier to keep going than it would have been to stop. She'd spent years training for this. Breath after breath, step after pounding step, heart racing, sweat trickling down her spine, blood, bone and muscle pumping together. As disused as it was, her body would not let her down here. Here – if only here – she was in control.

If it wasn't for all these goddamn *people*. Ann pushed her way around mule-pulled carts and burdened travellers, trying not to inhale the clouds of dust they kicked up. She fought every instinct to sprint; she couldn't afford to burn out or injure herself. It had taken nearly two months for her heels to stop aching from the unforgiving stone floors, and another month altogether to build calluses thick enough to protect her from the occasional pebble or shard of clay. Running barefoot along cobbled streets was a whole other matter. People stared as she hurried by, wincing.

Yet the buildings eventually thinned and travellers became scarce. It was not long before Ann found herself alone, running up a dirt path. She had passed the quarries, with their cliffs of exposed limestone bitten out of the hills; she had passed the temporary mass graves, trapdoors sealed in the dirt until the bodies within were no longer bodies but bones, ready for re-internment. The land had begun to rise more steeply after that – and so too had her panic.

She was too slow, already too tired. She met the fork in the road and paused to catch her breath. Wild olive trees, with their pale, gnarled trunks, rose up around the path. Ann doubled over, sweat dripping off her skin into the parched dirt. Her mouth was caked with dust. She spat and straightened.

Time to move.

She shot off to the right, dodging the stones and roots that protruded from the path. The slope grew steeper, the mountain rising directly above her now, and she found herself hardly running at all, only rocking forward on the balls of her feet. Ann kept her eyes on the ground, willing herself upward with each step. As she did so, she slid into the warm space within her mind and tried to feel for her brother's presence – even a hint of it. But there was nothing. Nothing but that pounding energy, that friction in the air, hounding her like the endless drone of insects.

Yet there was a new noise too – an actual, physical sound, audible over the hiss of cicadas and the wheeze of her own breath. An uneven, pounding rhythm, coming from above. Ann glanced up.

A wall of glittering light was descending on her. She blinked, clearing the dust and sweat from her eyes, and the image focused: a squad of men, armed from head to foot in shining bronze. They carried spears and had rectangular, cow-hide shields slung over their backs like knapsacks.

Two rushed forward to pull her up straight.

"Are you well, *Prona*?"

"Terkys, your water –"

"You are –" Ann wheezed – "hunters of Kabyrnos?"

"Yes, *Prona*."

"May we assist you in some way?"

One of the hunters offered her his waterskin. She drained it, eyes busy scanning the group.

"Where –" she croaked – "where is he?"

The men exchanged glances. There could be no doubt as to who she was or to whom she was referring, yet no one said a word.

"*Where is he?*"

The two men closest to her stepped back.

"We do not know, Foreign One," one man said. "We have not seen him since after our arrival in Kartissus."

"The villagers told us where the boar was said to den. We sat down to eat before venturing out, and…"

"He was gone."

"Gone," Ann repeated.

"Yes."

"All morning he appeared… strange."

He was gone.

"Very strange," agreed another.

Always, just – gone.

"Like one asleep," added another.

"Like one touched by the gods."

"Where?" she demanded. "Which way?"

"*Prona*?"

"The – den. Which way?"

"Please – we are not – we will escort you to the village –"

"Forget it."

Ann peered up the mountain and, taking a deep breath, she rushed off the path and began to scramble up the rocks before her. She heard the men behind her calling out, telling her to come back; she heard the scrape and slide of metal as someone clambered up after her. She knew they'd stop her if they could.

No, she thought. Not a chance.

She threw herself up the slope, ignoring the ache of her muscles and the sting of shrubs scratching against her skin. Little lizards scrabbled out of the way as she ploughed through the undergrowth, and the calls of the hunters below soon faded to nothing.

She grabbed hold of a branch to steady herself, and reached out with her mind.

There. She could feel him now. A spot still in the distance – but he was there.

She readjusted her course and sprinted off, concentrating only on her precarious footing and that vague point ahead of her. Her breath burned in her chest, blood pounded in her ears. She pushed harder.

She could sense him clearly now. And he knew she was coming too – she could feel it. He was trying to tell her something, but she was too exhausted, too absorbed in her task. The land was levelling out in a small plateau. Low branches whipped at her face, and as she struggled to fend them off, her foot caught on a large rock and she went slamming down, her breath knocked clean out of her.

For a split second, there was absolute silence as she fought to pull air into her lungs.

Then came the heavy breathing. A very nasal, grunting breath.

Her body stilled. Her eyes lifted.

Standing thirty feet away was a black mountain of a beast.

Her heart bucked in her chest. She didn't move – she couldn't. The boar was staring at her, its long tusks protruded from the edges of its mouth, curling its lips up into a mocking grin.

And then, like a surge of adrenaline, her brother was in her mind.

Ann. You need to get up. Slowly.

He was frightened too – she could feel the fear roiling in his stomach, compressing his lungs – but his mind was razor sharp, pinpointed on the giant.

His clarity centred her. With infinite care, Ann pushed herself to her feet. The beast did not move. Resisting every urge to flee, she risked a glance to her right – to where Nik was, perched on a boulder. Her eyes shot back to the boar. She now saw a wooden spear sticking out of bulky hind quarter. It didn't seem bothered.

I only have two left, Nik told her. *You need to move this way. You're too exposed there.*

She scanned the area quickly before returning her gaze to the boar, who still seemed – incredibly – content to simply watch her. The rock Nik was on was the largest in the area, but she wasn't sure it would protect them if the animal decided to charge. Without a better option, she began to edge toward him.

The creature roared. The sound was deafening – a grating scream that froze her to the spot. But Nik's hold on her was firm; it steadied them both. And the boar still hadn't moved.

The thing was most definitely not rabid, Ann realized. Everything about its appearance suggested a beast of clear-cut savagery, but its eyes – so tiny and black in that hulking skull – seemed almost to be *considering* her. And for a second, she imagined she could feel the boar's contempt for her – its amusement. But that was impossible.

No, I'm not sure it is, Nik told her.

In the space of a second, Ann understood. Nik had been stuck here for some time, the animal stringing him along, growling and half-charging whenever Nik made to escape. Like it was toying with him. Like it was waiting for something.

The boar cocked its head at her, bird-like. Then the ground shook as the creature took its first steps towards her. Ann's body convulsed, every muscle shrieking at her to move – to run – *now*.

Yet, somehow, those tiny eyes held her in place.

Ann felt her brother snap her out of her daze like a physical blow to the face. She gasped. The boar snarled, swinging its hideous head from her to Nik, as if it had somehow sensed his interference. Then the creature quickened its pace, aiming itself at the boulder now. Within a second, its huge body was thundering through trees at an astonishing speed.

Ann heard Nik's '*Shit.*', she felt his last, hasty thought. And just as her fingers curled around the shaft of the spear he'd tossed her, the creature slammed into the boulder and Nik's body sailed through the air and crumpled against a tree.

Ann winced, feeling the hammer of impact on her brother's back. She felt his mind flickering out.

She called out to him, screaming at him with her mind. He blinked and groaned.

Up! she cried, putting some of her own strength behind it. *NOW!*

His eyes flew open and the boar circled to face her. She brought her spear up to shoulder height, and backed up slowly, feet fighting for balance on the rock-strewn ground. The beast's breathing was rough, shaken from the impact. Its powerful shoulders heaved from side to side as it lumbered, slowly, toward her.

Nik was back on his feet.

We have to run, he thought to her. *Uphill.*

Ann hesitated, glancing across the boar to the steep slope beyond. *Takes us too near.*

But they were given no other option. The boar screeched and vaulted forward then, and the twins darted off, diagonally, up and away.

Ann scrambled like a frenzied animal, nails tearing into bark, scraping on stone as she hurtled up the slope. The ground vibrated beneath her: the beast was behind her, she knew it, those pounding hooves shooting closer to her with every second, its tusks at her back, just moments from skewering. She could almost feel it, the tearing of flesh, the shooting pain through her heart. Any moment – any moment now.

But then came the surge of pure terror from her twin as a tree he'd just passed was splintered to pieces.

There was no time. Ann threw her arms out and, bracing herself against a trunk, launched herself back down the slope. For a few perilous moments, she plummeted, letting gravity take her. Then the ground levelled out and she flew, flinging herself around trees, leaping over rocks, and finally, skidding out into a wide, dust-filled clearing.

A split second's mirage: a dark, moonlit space, within a forest of ancient trees.

Then back, with Nik hunched over in a cloud of dust, and the boar slowing in its charge near the edge of the clearing. The dust was clearing and Ann could see her brother desperately yanking at his foot – which had jammed between two rocks as he'd thrown himself clear.

And the boar was circling back.

"Oh god."

Without thinking, Ann shifted the spear that she still – miraculously – held to her left hand and stooped, grabbing a rock the size of her fist. She hurled it at the side of the boar's head. Shockingly, the rock struck true. Blood welled – but the boar only unleashed another bellow.

To your left! Nik called out to her.

She understood immediately. Not far from her was a sheer cliff that bordered the clearing, and in it, a cave – a crevice – just large enough for her to slip through.

The boar was bucking its head madly as it galloped toward Nik – now a wild, frenzied thing that was somehow less terrifying than the cold, calculating creature of earlier. Shifting toward the mouth of the cave, Ann found another rock and let loose.

A strike to the shoulder – enough to divert the creature's attention. It swerved sharply – too sharply for its ungainly bulk – and stumbled, its hooves skidding beneath it. The beast's tiny eyes were furious now, one swamped with blood from the wound on its head.

Ann felt Nik roll the rock off his foot.

Go for the other one! he called.

The boar was crashing toward her now, a mere twenty, fifteen meters away. Ann bent, took hold of a pebble, exhaled and found – strangely – that she knew exactly where to aim. Putting her whole torso into it, she shot the pebble directly into the beast's clear eye.

The responding shriek almost sent her reeling. The creature slid to a stop, kicking its hind legs and squealing, so close now that Ann was sprayed with sand and blood. But then Nik was there, pulling her back into the cave, and shouting for the beast's attention.

The squeals subsided; the boar's muscles tensed.

Using all of their combined strength, Ann and Nik jammed the butt of the spear into the earth at their feet, and kneeled down, bracing. The sharp bronze point extended out, past the face of the cliff, pointing directly at the boar's underbelly as the creature hurtled toward them.

The impact was like nothing Ann had ever felt. A detonating bomb, smashing them both into the rock – followed by total disorientation, head spinning, ears ringing. She felt a warmth pouring down her chest. Blood – her own this time – from a gash across her collarbone, a long shard of splintered spear protruding from her skin. She grimaced and dragged it out.

Nik had scrambled to his knees beside her and was crawling towards the opening.

The boar was lying on its side in front of the cliff. Twitching – the broken spear embedded in its neck. Its blood had already soaked the dirt a dark brown. Nik rose, edged out of the crevice and hoisted up the final spear. There was a low thud and a squeal as he buried it deep into the boar's chest.

He turned back toward her and sighed. It was over. "Let's go."

Arms around each other's shoulders, the twins limped past the convulsing animal, and began to head across the clearing, downhill. The going was slow. Skin throbbed, pain blazed in every bone; hearts pounded in tune, still labouring away beneath cracked ribs. The mountain was quiet. The calm was absolute.

Nik paused.

"Did you feel that?"

"Feel what?" Ann mumbled, leaning against him.

He was silent for a long moment. Then –

"That."

"No." She sighed. "There's nothing, Nik. Let's go."

But when they'd shuffled down only a few more steps, she felt it too. A quiver, the slightest tremble in the mountainside. She faltered, peering up at her brother. He was craned around, looking back the way they'd come. And what she saw in his amber eyes made her knees go weak.

"*Impossible*," he breathed.

Standing silently in the shade of the trees above them was the boar.

It was a ghoul of nightmare. Its eyes red, bloody saliva streaming out of its mouth. Three spears jutting out of its body like skeletal limbs.

"The devil Himself."

Something in her brother's tone made Ann look at him sharply. He was staring up at the creature, mouth open, eyes unfocused. And written on every slack line of his face, a resignation. A submission so absolute it chilled her to the core.

Like one touched by the gods.

The monster took a lumbering step toward them, sliding several feet down the slope.

She took hold of Nik's wrist in both hands.

"Nik, come on – we can still outrun it."

He shook his head slowly. The ground trembled.

"Come *on*!"

She heaved at his arm but barely moved him half a foot. Gently, very gently, he pulled out of her grasp – and began to climb.

Ann stood, looking on in horror as her brother moved up toward the beast that was balanced on the slope above them. Again, the thing seemed to be grinning down at her, its breath quiet, rasping. It took another skidding step down toward them –

– and lurched sideways as a streak of grey shot out of the trees to pummel it in the ribs.

Nik halted. Ann gaped, utterly uncomprehending as the boar tottered, then began to slide down the hill, scrambling, squealing, sand and dirt flying up. And then the thing was on its knees, on its side, rolling, crashing down the hill, foliage flattened beneath it. With Nik still standing in its course.

Ann ran – she *ran*, as fast as her battered body would let her, closing the gap between her and her brother, slamming into him, smashing him into the ground just as the giant body plunged past.

She pushed up on her elbows, her brother unconscious beneath her, and her head whipped round. Snarls – low and ripping – filled the air as the grey animal tore down the slope. She half-rose to her knees to get a better look. The grey thing – a dog, Ann could now see, large and lean – met the boar in an explosion of motion. The larger beast was prostrate, but its hooves were kicking madly as the dog wove in and around, taking nips and snaps where it could. It was only a matter of time, however, until one kick landed – and the dog was thrown, bouncing against a tree to land in the dirt with a thud.

For one terrifying moment, Ann thought the dog was dead – with the boar rolling itself to its feet, and Nik still unconscious. But soon the dog was back, flying at the boar, twisting underneath its bucking head, snapping and tearing at tender flesh.

The boar's breaths were coming in huffs now, its movements slow, laboured. When, minutes later, it crashed to the ground, it was with earth-shaking finality. The dog swept down for the last time, buried its teeth into the large black neck and ripped the great beast's throat out.

With one jerking shudder, the thing went still.

Letting the gory tatters drop from his mouth, the dog scrambled back up to where Ann still crouched, frozen over her brother. His tail was wagging, his tongue lolling out of his wide, bloodstained maw – every inch the proud, prancing puppy. He prodded Ann's face with his nose, sniffing.

The sun flared through the leaves overhead. Ann blinked at the scruffy grey creature.

"Well," she muttered, sinking back down onto the ground. "Aren't you handy."

And then, leaning into its warm fur, her eyes fluttered closed, and she let herself fall away.

Chapter Three

Ann woke to the sound of an angry voice.

"If you are well enough to strut around and flaunt your battle wounds, then you are well enough to dress *yourself*."

The only response was a bark of laughter.

"Hush! Do you want to wake your sister? What kind of –"

Something wet and cold inserted itself into Ann's neck. She flinched away – and immediately regretted it. Her whole body ached like one big, raw bruise. There was a clamber of readjustment, the bed shifting beneath her, and Ann found herself blinking up at two round eyes which stared soulfully back at her through a scruffy grey fringe. Then the dog licked her, chin to forehead.

The little room flooded with light, and there was a squawk of outrage.

"Get out of here, beast!"

The dog was dragged backward, tongue still lolling, tail still wagging. It scampered out of the room as Hersa came forward.

"Ann! Oh, Ann, thank *Mavros*."

"H-how –?"

"The hunters brought you in. You have been unconscious for almost a day. The healers thought…

Cracked ribs, a shoulder out of socket, strained ankle, wrists… Oh Ann, you could have died."

Hersa helped her to sit up, packing sponge-filled cushions in behind her. Ann sagged against them, her vision spinning.

"You will not be able to work for some time, I am afraid."

Ann peered down at her hands, lying limp in her lap and bandaged from forearm to knuckles. What skin was visible was covered in a crosshatch of cuts and bruises.

"I'll live."

Hersa kneeled down beside her, lovely eyes wide. "You killed that boar, Ann. A beast larger than a bull, they say. And you two killed it alone. It was…" She blinked, recalling herself with a disapproving click of her tongue. "It was a very stupid thing to do."

"We didn't do it alone."

As if on cue, a long furry snout poked around the doorframe. One tentative sniff and the dog was bounding back in, filling up almost the entire chamber. The creature had obviously been cleaned, but even without the blood and dirt, it was a feral-looking thing, with half an ear missing and a patchwork of old scars visible through long fur.

Which Hersa had, again, grabbed by the fistful.

"It's okay, Hersa," Ann said weakly.

"It certainly is *not*!"

"He saved our lives."

"It is a *wild animal*, Ann!"

"He's very gentle…"

"He is very *dirty*."

Ann stared at the other woman.

Hersa sighed and released the dog. And as the little woman squeezed out of the room – "… as stubborn as that brother of hers…" – the dog placed its forepaws on the bed, burrowing its head in Ann's lap. Ann gave a weak laugh.

"I like you," she whispered to him.

He licked her fingertips.

"Good. Glad it's mutual."

Hersa marched back in, dumping an armload of clothing on the bed.

"For now, the dog must leave – no arguments. We must prepare you and there is not much time."

"Prepare –?"

"Today is the Day of Light. And your banquet."

"My *what*?"

The next hour proceeded in one skirmish after another: getting fed, getting sponge-bathed, having honey-salve reapplied to her wounds without the dog licking it off, manoeuvring into a twenty-pound fortress of a dress. Discussing the finer points of public presentation.

"You simply cannot go before the whole city like *that*," Hersa declared, waving her hand at Ann's ponytailed hair. "You must look your finest. It is expected."

Ann eventually gave in, and humming away, Hersa tugged and scraped at Ann's poor scalp. When she was done, she held up the mirror to display her work. Ann gaped.

The image was transfixing – a bizarre collision of the elegant and the grotesque: tawny dress with golden embroidery over sunburnt, blistering skin; tumbling, oil-shined curls framing a bruised, puffy face; golden griffin necklace sitting above an angry-looking gash.

"It could be worse, my friend," Hersa laughed. "You are fortunate that you are so lovely, or you would be intolerable to look at right now. Now –" the girl reached for a tray – "the final touch. Picked out by the High Steward himself."

Ann peered down at the small fortune in jewellery spread out for her selection: gemmed hairpins, sun-ray coronet, silver armlets, heavy golden earrings. "The High Steward picked these out?"

"Yes… On behalf of Kabyrnos, of course."

The girl's eyes were dancing.

"He is known for his taste," Hersa went on mercilessly. "In jewellery, in music. In women."

Ann felt herself flush as the other girl laughed.

"I am teasing you, my friend. It is said that he has been much engaged with the palace beauty of late."

"The who?"

"Afratea, wife of Hefanos, Master Bronzesmith." Hersa's eyes rolled skyward in the universal gesture. "That woman has an endless need for attention, and it is said that her husband gives her none of it. A very unsociable man."

The curtains swished aside.

"Who's an unsociable man?"

The dog squeezed into the room again, but Hersa ignored him, glaring instead at Nik. She puffed out to her full five foot two inches.

"You enter other people's bedchambers without announcement? Have you no manners at all?"

"Nope."

"Leave!"

"In a minute." Nik held out his fingers to the dog. "Here, boy – you ran right past me."

The dog regarded him coolly, then turned his adoring gaze back to Ann.

"You see," Hersa scoffed. "Not everyone rushes to do your bidding."

Nik didn't respond. He was looking at Ann.

Their eyes met, only for a moment – two seconds, at most. Yet it was enough.

Sighing, Nik eased himself onto the foot of her bed, hand to his bandaged ribs. "What'll you call him, Ann?"

Ann thought for a moment, scratching the scraggly cheek. "Kaenus," she announced at last.

Nik let out a bark of laughter. Hersa's hands shot to her hips.

"You cannot think of something more *unique*?"

Kaenus was the Kapreitan word for a male dog.

"It suits him." Ann cupped her hand under the dog's chin. "Does it work for you?"

He barked.

"Kaenus it is."

Hersa leaned back against the wall. "Actually, it reminds me of an old story of a dog named Kinelaepus. He was said to be very loyal too. Also very ugly."

Kaenus looked up at her with a whine.

"Yes," Hersa said, rapping him on the nose. "Ugly."

"I don't think so," Ann said.

"*You* are in love," Hersa laughed.

"Kinelaepus," Nik repeated. "I've heard that name before. He was the dog of –"

"Kapreita, yes."

"She was important, right?"

"What are you – stupid?" the girl snapped at him. "You think islands are named for people who are *not* important?"

"I can see this is going to be a very accepting learning environment."

Hersa glared at him, but her twitching lips gave her away. "If you want to *learn*, do not speak – *listen*."

Nik clasped his lips shut tight, and leaned forward in mock attention – then stiffened with a hiss of breath, hand back at his rib. Hersa was grinning openly now.

"Do you want to hear about Kapreita, or do you not?"

"Yes, please," Ann said.

After another chuckle, the girl began.

Kapreita was a young Northern girl back in the days of the Kypran tribes, when the island was without name or palace, and those in the northern mainland of Gyklanea still lived in caves. The Great Mavros, son of Pritymnia, coveted Kapreita, for she was very beautiful.

"Tall, with golden hair – like you, Ann."

Mavros tried for many days to separate the girl from her people – first swooping down on them in the guise of a hawk, then, approaching them one night in the shape of a white bull so magnificent that they ran away in terror.

"For it is said that to meet a god in his truest form gives great fear – and great pain too."

The twins' eyes met for the briefest moment.

Yet the god was gentle with Kapreita. He lay down at her feet, inviting her to climb onto His back. And when she did so, He immediately leapt up, and, ignoring her cries of protest, flew away to the south – across the sea, away from her home and her people, toward the holy mountain where He was born. There she conceived a child. And there she was abandoned.

"Pritymnia, feeling great shame for what Her Son had done, sent forth Kinelaepus – a noble hunter dog, born of the finest line of the earth."

Kaenus barked and wagged his tail, knocking the stone jug off the trunk.

"Do not flatter yourself," Hersa grumbled as she retrieved the pitcher.

Kinelaepus led Kapreita to the homestead of the Kypran tribe, where she was married to their chief, and soon after, bore a son, whom she named 'Kabyrn', meaning 'of the Sacral Axe' – the holy symbol of the Mother.

Kapreita ordered a palace built in the sight of the holy mountain: a temple in honour of Pritymnia, and a place for Kabyrn to govern after his adoptive father had passed. In the meantime, the chief oversaw the running of the land – holding it in trust for the Earth Mother – while Kapreita gave spiritual guidance to the people.

"And such has been the role of every *Kyn* and *Kynra* since," Hersa explained. "Although I believe Zelkanus has taken a much more active role in both. Out of necessity, some might say."

Kapreita had three other sons by her husband, who were sent throughout the island to build palaces in the image of Kabyrnos. Melkus to the northeast, Zaffronos to the east, and Phernos to the south. Xanu to the west was built later. These four ruled the holy island, and the three born to the chief were sworn to send tribute to Kabyrn every year, to honour their exalted brother and his divine ancestors.

"And so it remains still," Hersa concluded.

"Still?" Nik asked. "You're seriously telling me that every year these people fork up a portion of their own stuff just because the ruler of this place, so many generations ago, was alleged to be the son of a god?"

Ann expected another outburst from Hersa, but to her surprise, the girl looked thoughtful. "I think that you do not understand something. I will not blame your lack of intelligence, because it was difficult for me to grasp too, at first."

Nik snorted.

"The Kapreitans may *say* that an action is holy and right, yet they *do* it because it is necessary.

Kabyrnos maintains all Kapreitan trade routes and colonies. It holds the most important events, like the Great Tournament in the coming Season of Life, where it must host people from all over the island and Gyklanea too. It has need of extra resources.

"To you, you might think, why would these other cities not want their independence? And to be truthful – *in confidence* –" she fixed them both with a stern stare – "I understand that. I was born in one of the Ceklydonic island colonies. Yet this is not how Kapreitans think. They believe that every person, every peoples, have their place, and that order must be maintained at all cost."

After a long moment of silence, Ann asked quietly, "So what happened to Kapreita?"

Hersa sighed. "What happens to so many women. Her husband died, and she married another. It is said that, eventually, she chose her own death by walking into the sea, northward, toward her lost homeland."

"But this island was named for her?"

"Her sons did that. They also commissioned several images of her – statues – to sit in the central shrines of all four palaces. Most were lost in earth tremors – except the last one, I believe, which rested in the Blessed Courtyard here until the rule of Cryklonus. Zelkanus's father. Then it too was lost, along with many other relics. The Sacral Axe rests there now."

Ann was scratching Kaenus's head absently. The tragedy of the story was, somehow, painfully familiar. A story she'd once read, or a picture she'd once seen, maybe. A young girl standing alone on a moonlit beach as she was approached by a great beast. Her thrill of exhilaration – of fear – as the bull took off. The terror when He revealed

Himself. The pain – then the hope that grew with the first stirrings of a child within her. And the emptiness that followed. All children eventually gone – their mother left with nothing, and nothing left of her but a heart-breaking tale.

A loud knock on the door. All four of them started. Hersa jumped up, snapping at Nik to ready himself. As Nik limped out, the little woman hoisted Ann to her feet, muttering about men who were never ready when they were told to be.

As they inched out of the bedroom, the little servant's words echoed in Ann's mind.

What happens to so many women.

***

"You're really a very beautiful girl, you know, Annika," Lotta observed one day when the twins were thirteen years old. "I think it's time to start making the most of it."

In the months that followed, Ann learned that "making the most of it" meant no more tussling with Nik and his friends, or letting her legs loll apart at the dinner table. It meant no more comfortable jeans or hand-me-down sweatshirts. It meant a new wardrobe of mini skirts, kitten heels and crop sweaters. It meant everything in miniature. After a year had gone by, Ann had been told so many times to fix her hair, to put her lip gloss on, and to smile smile smile, that she no longer felt comfortable without her perfectly manicured mask.

And then Lotta informed them that she was going to be married.

The man was a partner at an advertising agency. He lived in the city and seemed to like toting their mother around to charity fundraisers and client dinners. Within the month, they'd moved into his downtown mansion and the twins were enrolled in private schools.

"But why do we have to go to different schools?" Ann had asked her mother as they were unpacking their boxes.

"Oh Annika, don't give me a hard time, okay? I've got too many things on my plate right now. You're going to a girl's school, Nik to a boy's. You'll like it, you'll see."

But Ann never did like it. The other girls only ever received her shy, glossy smiles with poorly concealed sneers. Nik fared better than she did: he could fit in anywhere. And when the two schools met up for their first formal occasion of the year, things became much worse for Ann. The other girls could not fail to notice that it was always Ann to whom the boys' eyes strayed, Ann who they asked to dance, Ann who they talked about.

Eventually, Ann stopped styling her hair. She stopped putting on makeup and she stopped smiling. But Lotta never said a word about it. Lotta rarely said anything those days.

And so their lives continued, hushed and unrelenting, until the twins' fifteenth birthday.

***

A litter. An honest-to-god litter, altogether with gilded poles, an awning, and four shirtless men to bear it around on their shoulders.

Nik was having the time of his life, lounging heads above everyone else, grinning and waving down at the crowds of palace folk. Of course, his wounds made him look more dashing than ever. The Foreign *Kyn* come again, the people whispered.

Kaenus – whom Hersa had, again, failed to detain – also seemed to be loving every moment of this fame by association. He strutted ahead of both litters, tail high, nose held proudly aloft. Nobility personified.

Ann, on the other hand, only sunk further into her seat as people in the corridors craned to look. As they cheered. As they reached out to touch. And when a group of ogling teenagers started tossing wreaths of flowers, Ann found herself thinking that she'd almost rather try her luck on the mountain again. This could not possibly get any worse, she told herself.

Which, of course, it did. As they approached the doorway that led into the Blessed Courtyard, the servants stopped to set down the litters. The crowds had vanished; all but one waited beyond. Standing there, bedecked in the mantle of his office and waiting to escort, was the High Steward.

In an instant he was beside Ann, so close that she could smell the sickly sweet of his perfumed body oil. Flowers and resin – and something headier. Something distinctly male.

"It saddens me, *Prona*, to see you so injured," the man said. "If you have need of any small service throughout the day, do not hesitate to ask. I will personally see to it that your comfort is restored at once."

The man's voice dripped honey, his eyes locked to her face in a flawless expression of sympathy. Yet, at the corners of his mouth – almost imperceptible – the perennial smirk. Beneath the façade of concern, the man was almost leering at her.

Ann swallowed. "Thanks."

"No. It is I who must thank you. You have given much for our people." A pause, the man holding her gaze for one, two, three seconds. "Now. The people await your arrival. Shall we?"

And with that, he strode off into the courtyard. One of the litter-bearers turned to Nik.

"*Psydu*, may we proceed?"

Nik, who had been watching the interaction closely, leaned back and gave a lazy wave of the hand. "Yeah. Sure. Proceed."

So, with a heave and a lurch, the litters moved out into the blaze of the Blessed Courtyard.

Chapter Four

"You are blessed of Pritymnia, Huntress."

The flat of the Sacral Axe had settled on Ann's skull, compressing her spine.

"Continue in your unparalleled service to her people."

How the *Kynra*'s eyes had glittered. Like the silver of the weapon's blade.

Huntress.

Ann had since been deposited onto a wooden throne in a hall that overlooked the Courtyard of the Dying Sun, with its blackened tree. Beside her sat Nik, finally looking a little worse for the wear. It had been a long ceremony.

Other people were beginning to trickle in. The elite of Kabyrnos, embroidered, scented and plumed within an inch of their lives; a line of painted peacocks, coming to pay their respects. They were introduced, they bowed, hands to foreheads, but they did not linger. Ann's head rang with names – Lynnos, Gerytus, Trynu, Zyklos: all important clan surnames that she knew she should remember but could hardly differentiate.

The commoners feasted in the courtyard below. Ann, sitting with her back to the outer courtyard, could hear their songs and laughter as they gathered round the fires where their meals were still roasting on spits.

Fifty cows in total. Legs tied, blood drained. Jugulars severed by the *Kynra* herself, with the same blade used to anoint the twins only moments before.

"Great Deathless Mother," she'd called in the silence before the act. "We, Your most blessed people, who dwell in the shadow of Your holy mountain, honour You. Please accept our humble sacrifice."

Honour and blood. Servants were circulating now, passing out refreshments. One approached Ann, offering a glass of wine. Red. She refused.

Introductions complete, pipe music began to float in from a corner of the hall, calling all to fodder. People milled about, devouring the grilled octopus, honeyed prunes and seedcakes that the servants bore in on trays. Kaenus was nowhere to be seen – he'd be camping out by the spits, no doubt. A few guards had taken up stations throughout the hall. Ann spotted the Guard Commander – as she'd since learned to call the guardswoman – standing alone against the inner wall, looking starkly out-of-place with her plain tunic and stony expression. There was no doubt in Ann's mind that the woman was very, very bored.

Not surprising, really. Yawning herself, Ann's gaze drifted away and up.

Her mouth snapped shut. A bull, heavy-shouldered and enraged, was painted onto the plaster of the inner wall. Slender figures closed in around the beast, flipping over its back, grappling with its bloodstained horns.

Ann shivered. Those horns.

"Excuse me, Huntress."

A small man bowed before her. Short grey hair, priest's robes. Ann felt a stirring of recognition.

"The *Kynra* has requested a private audience with you."

A gut-clenching request, uttered in so unsettling a voice. Empty, like the hollows of his face.

"Now?" she asked, bewildered.

The gaunt priest watched her for a moment. "Will tomorrow evening suit?"

She nodded mutely.

"I will come to fetch you then."

Then he was gone, lost in the sea of colour and noise. Like a mere figment. Ann glanced around. No one seemed to have noticed – not even Nik beside her, who was preoccupied with something on his other side.

An outbreak of cheers drew Ann's attention to the main doorway. The *Kyn* had appeared and was being greeted as if he – and not the twins – was champion of the day. Which, in a way, he had been.

Ann had never heard anyone speak the way he'd spoken that afternoon. His voice so deep, so sonorous, his words seeming to quiver from his entire body. Casting a net over them all.

The Hunter and Huntress, he'd knighted the twins. Their new beacons of hope. Of strength. Of selfless sacrifice for the welfare of all.

"Today is the day that we take these two heroes as our own," he'd declared amidst the shouts and cheers. "Today is a new beginning, where we turn away from the years of hardship. For I need not tell you what you yourselves have suffered. What person present has not hungered in the cold? Or lost home or friend to the ever-increasing tremors? Or seen loved ones devastated by plague? These dark times have been a true trial."

His voice had entreated them; it had consoled them. And the crowd had seemed to reach toward him, hunger plain on their faces.

"And then came this beast, like a monster from the darkness below," the *Kyn* had continued. "Let no one here doubt that it was sent for one purpose and one purpose alone. To test – our – strength! We are not being *punished*, fellow Kapreitans. We are not *cursed. We are blessed.* The most god-favoured of all peoples in the Akrean Sea! And this, this is the price we must pay. For it is only through hardship that we can show our true mettle. And today, as we embrace the heroism of these two golden people, we take our first steps back into our rightful place of honour!"

His people had screamed their approval. They'd stomped their feet and pumped their fists into the air. The Guard Commander, standing at her *Kyn*'s shoulder, had slammed the butt of her spear onto the stone floor, nodding fervently. And the High Steward, who, until that moment, had been lingering behind Ann, had moved to begin preparing for the feast – but not before sweeping up Ann's hand and promising,

"Later."

A smiling threat, which had hung over her head all afternoon as she'd watched the man darting in and out of the hall, issuing orders and surveying trays. And now, with the roasted meat being hauled in on platters, she knew her time was up. The man was weaving through the crowd toward her.

"How much longer do you think we have to stay?" she whispered at her brother's back.

He shot an impatient glance over his shoulder. "What?" he asked in Kapreitan.

"I am –" her exhausted mind struggled for the right word – "tired."

A woman's voice cut in from around Nik.

"I am sure we can arrange to have your litter fetched if you are too fatigued, Huntress."

As the speaker rose to her feet, Ann found herself sinking further into her chair. Never had she seen such a woman. Those long, fluid curves, the sensually arched back. The siren glided around Nik, wielding her body like a weapon.

"Such attention must be very tiresome for you," the woman went on. "You are above such things. Ah. I see a servant attending to the elder Gerytus – shall I fetch him for you?"

Ann dropped her gaze to her lap. Her fingers – swollen, scratched – were fiddling with the cloth of her skirt.

"I didn't mean –"

"I see you have met our guests of honour, Afratea."

Ann was shocked at the force of her relief. The High Steward had arrived and was regarding the woman with the same smirking expression that had paralyzed Ann only hours before. But the woman – "the palace beauty", no kidding – seemed unfazed.

"I have, and they are charming. And so attentive."

The High Steward took a sip of his wine. "Who would not be attentive to you?"

Afratea's lashes fluttered down modestly.

"And where is your illustrious husband today?"

The woman gave a toss of her curls, but not before shooting a glance at Nik. "Oh, at his forges, no doubt."

"Afratea is married to our Master Bronzesmith," the High Steward informed the twins. "A most revered figure in our city."

Nik stared back. "Great."

"I did not know he was so popular with *you*, Heremus," Afratea said.

"Why would he not be?" the High Steward asked. "He is a skilled man, who fulfils all of his duties with care and attention. Well. Almost all of them. It is *such* a shame not to see him here with you today."

All coyness vanished; Afratea glared.

"We've met before, haven't we?" Nik asked the High Steward as he leaned back in his chair. "You're the *Kyn*'s servant, right?"

"Not quite, Hunter. Although, in a way, we all serve our great leader."

"Sure. And weren't you our escort this afternoon? Or was that some other servant?"

"It was an honour to attend you," the man replied smoothly. "An honour that I would like to repeat, if you will permit me – Huntress?"

Ann blinked. She'd been so absorbed in their sparring match that she'd forgotten that they could see her too. Not waiting for a reply, the High Steward snapped his fingers at a servant, who procured a stool. The man folded himself onto it as if the others no longer existed.

The High Steward took another sip of his wine and smiled, flashing red-stained teeth. "Tell me, Huntress, is our city very different from your homeland?"

Ann nodded tightly. The smell of him was overwhelming. Nik and Afratea, meanwhile, had risen and were moving away. No doubt in search of their own private corner.

"The Foreign *Kyn*," the man continued conversationally, "was famously known to have said that the land he had come from was 'much more advanced, yet far less wise'.

"My own clan, the clan Trynu –" he indicated a seal ring on his index finger – "traces its lineage to the time of the Foreign *Kyn*. The Zyklos clan, the clan of the *Kyn*, are said to be his direct descendants... It is a great shame that that noble line must finally come to its end."

The High Steward paused, bait dangling. Ann was intrigued in spite of herself.

"Oh?" she asked.

Another flash of teeth. "Zelkanus has no heir, you see. No son, no brother or sister sons. For the first time since Kabyrn, rule will not pass to a direct blood relative. A great shame indeed."

The man plucked a piece of meat off a passing tray and bit in with relish.

"But why is that line so… important?" Ann asked.

The High Steward's jaw worked slowly, his eyes never leaving her face.

"An interesting question," he said at length. "The Foreign *Kyn* took the place of Kabyrn's dead son, introducing customs that we maintain to this day: water transportation, local crop distribution, foreign trade. He painted our future as the gods intended, bringing our people into a new age."

The advent of a new age for Kapreitans.

"Yet the time has come to move on, I think." The man's eyes narrowed slightly, his voice dropping. "The next *Kyn* must be selected – and soon. For the stability of the island."

He continued chewing, continued watching. Yet all Ann could think of was a darkened courtyard. And a warning.

The High Steward leaned back, carefully wiping his fingers on an embroidered handkerchief.

"One can never quite tell what you are thinking, Huntress."

Ann came back to herself with a sharp intake of breath.

Huntress.

It was sudden, so sudden, as if the weight of the past two days had settled on her all at once, crushing her with a single word.

"Are you well, Huntress?"

"Please don't call me that," she whispered.

The man's bare knee shifted slightly, pressing against her thigh. "What may I call you, then?"

Ann stiffened. "The – the *Kyn*."

The High Steward jumped to his feet and sank into a bow as the *Kyn* stopped before them.

"Huntress," he boomed in his impossibly deep voice, "you are not well. Heremus, fetch the litter. It was foolish to keep her here so long."

The High Steward muttered his apologies and departed. The *Kyn* continued to stare down at Ann, thick brows pinched together.

She struggled to sit up straighter. "I'm – fine."

He nodded and strode away. For a split second, Ann was filled with a curious sense of loss. But a moment later, he was back, with a tankard of barley beer. He held it to her mouth.

"Drink."

She drank. The beer was light and fresh. Exactly what she needed.

"There." The *Kyn* stood back, regarding her. "That is better. May I?"

He gestured to the High Steward's abandoned seat. And as the wood creaked under his bulk, Ann was struck by the contrast to the stool's former occupant. This man commanded attention, drawing her eyes as unconsciously as the other had repelled them.

"You look like you have been through a war, Huntress."

"I'm fine," she repeated.

"Of course you are. You are strong, I can see that. There are many men I know who could not last as long as you have today with such injuries."

Ann did not reply. The *Kyn* chuckled.

"You do not care for praise."

"I... I guess not."

The man pierced her with a stern look. "You 'guess', or you know?"

"I –"

"Never apologize for who you are, Huntress. Nor what has made you so. I cannot understand how you did what you did, yet I can honestly say that there must be no woman equal to you."

The Kyn's attention was, in its way, much harder to bear than the High Steward's. Ann looked away for a moment's relief.

But directly across the hall, still standing to attention beneath the bull fresco, was the Guard Commander – the stone of her face having acquired an edge that Ann could not understand. They held eye contact for only a second, but it was enough to leave Ann a little dizzy.

"She is a good woman, Palthenra," the Kyn said, having followed Ann's gaze. "With a very strong sense of justice. Fiercely loyal too. A great asset to me and to this city. As for the rest…"

The man heaved a sigh and then burst into chair-rumbling laughter.

"You have bewitched my tongue, Huntress," he laughed. "You simply sit, watching me with those unnatural eyes of yours, and I spill out the workings of my mind." He shook his head, still smiling at her. "May I call you by your name, Huntress?"

Ann was unexpectedly pleased by the idea. "Oh – of course."

"Then I must be Zelkanus."

She hesitated.

"Say it."

"… Zelkanus."

"Good. Now we are friends."

Zelkanus held out his hand. It was warm and it enveloped hers completely.

"I was thinking, Ann, about what miracle brought you here to Kabyrnos."

"I try not to," she admitted quietly.

He chuckled. "Yes, I can imagine the shock it must have been for you." He sighed again, his massive chest deflating. "There are simply too many things in this life that one cannot understand."

Ann thought back to his speech, to the unequivocal certainty with which he spoke to his people. Then, as if reading her thoughts, he added,

"Yet as a leader, you bear the doubts of your people upon yourself. A *Kyn* must provide answers."

"And if..."

"Yes?"

"If you don't have them?"

"The answers?" Zelkanus smiled sadly, patting her hand and finally letting it go. "You do your best. To give the people what they need."

"So you don't really believe what you said?"

The question had slipped out before she could stop herself. But Zelkanus just looked at her thoughtfully.

"You have lived for how many years, Ann? Twenty? Twenty-one?"

"Twenty-one."

"Twenty-one years," he repeated slowly, as if to himself. "Yes. I thought as much. I have lived almost forty."

Ann stared, mouth falling open slightly. She'd been under the impression that he was much older. Yet, now, a single glance told her how absurd that would have been – especially in a world where seventy was considered ancient. His face was lined, but not heavily, and his hair was barely dusted with grey. He was, to all appearances, a vigorous man only entering middle age.

Strange that she hadn't seen it before. Stranger still that the discovery made her so uneasy.

"And I have led this city for eighteen of those years," the *Kyn* continued. "Of course, any thinking man will have his doubts. That we Kapreitans are the favourites of the gods is not a proven fact, particularly in light of recent years."

These people are my most cherished.

"Yet I will hope, and I will give strength where I can. For the welfare of my people. As any *Kyn* would."

Zelkanus turned then, glancing over at the litter that was making its way through the hall. He rose.

"You will learn the truth of what I say in time, Ann. I am sure of it."

She frowned. "What do you mean?"

The man peered down at her, his eyes unreadable. Then, slowly, he picked up her hand again and brought it to his lips.

"We are honoured to have you among us, Huntress."

***

It was only later, when she'd been stripped of her finery and was lying prostrate on her mattress, that something occurred to her.

The sun was fading and the Day of Light ceremony had officially begun, marking the beginning of the summer season with a city-wide party. Music, dancing and bonfires. Ann could hear the laughter and voices carried in on the breeze through the lightwell. Having gorged himself thoroughly, Kaenus was snoring on the floor next to her. Nik, however, had still not returned. If he would return at all.

The griffin necklace that the *Kyn* had given her lay in a heap on the trunk beside her, where she had discarded it the moment she'd been left alone.

Ann lay watching it, the gold glinting, winking at her through the increasing gloom.

A kiss on her hand. The gesture had seemed, at the time, so natural. So safe. But hadn't she learned well enough by now that nothing like that was ever safe? Every touch, every smile came with expectation.

And every expectation caged her. These people, these walls, these fractured bones – all bars on that cage. And she'd been warned, she'd been warned not to interfere.

So she would just have to stay out of the way – stay out of any more trouble. She would just have wait. Only nine months more.

Chapter Five

The following evening found Ann balanced on a seat in the common room, shrouded from foot to crown in a new set of bandages. She'd barely been conscious an hour. She'd slept long but fitfully, the ache of her body throbbing into her dreams. And the moment she'd woken, the servants had descended, embalming her in salve, mummifying her, leaving her hardly capable of movement. A sitting target, awaiting her escort in a nervous silence.

Yet, when the knock came, the face that appeared around the door was not the gaunt one she'd been dreading, but that of a teenage girl. Black, lively eyes, mouth turned up in a shy smile. The crimson belt of a Sisterhood acolyte tied around her waist. The acolyte bowed and asked if the Huntress was ready. The Huntress was not, but she nodded anyway.

After the previous night's revelries, the palace was quiet, subdued. Ann was grateful for it, just as she was grateful for the girl who led the litter – and Kaenus, following close behind – through the winding corridors with barely a word. Yet as they crossed through the rows of post-and-lintel doorways that led from the Blessed Courtyard into Sisterhood territory, the atmosphere altered perceptibly.

There was a buzz of activity here, yet it was hushed – and all the more nerve-wracking for its restraint. Solemn-faced priestesses glided through the antechamber in silence, watching the litter as it was set down before a broad door.

The acolyte knocked, barely tapping knuckle to wood.

"Enter!" was the imperious reply.

They entered. The chamber beyond was small and painted in earthy reds and browns. The sound of trickling water greeted the newcomers from a mosaicked pool sunken into the floor. Branches from an overhanging tree trailed into the water like fingers over the side of a boat, while a pair of doves nested in the leaves above. This was a place of deep serenity.

If not for the three people by the opposite wall.

"Set her down by the waters," the *Kynra* commanded the litter-bearers, never turning away from the two women who stood before her throne.

One of the women Ann recognized immediately by her scowl. The other was unknown. She had masses of springy curls, and similar prominent features to Sister Aralys beside her – yet she lacked that tight, pinched look that seemed suggestive of chronic stomach pain.

While the litter was deposited by the pool and the black-eyed acolyte silently departed, Ann heard the *Kynra* utter,

"This is the end of the matter. Any more of this infantile behaviour will not be tolerated."

Aralys sniffed audibly. "Sacred Mother, I –"

"*Enough*. You are a priestess of the Sisterhood of Pritymnia. I suggest you leave now before you disgrace yourself further."

After a few more seconds, Aralys stormed out of the room – the litter-bearers exiting a safe distance behind. The *Kynra* arched her brows at the remaining reprobate.

"You too are excused, Sister."

Ann noticed that her voice had softened somewhat.

"And please," she added wearily. "Please *try* to control yourself."

"Of course, Sacred Mother," the curly-haired woman responded lightly. "I will try to, I will. And I *do*! It is only so difficult –"

The *Kynra* pointed at the door.

"Yes, Sacred Mother. Apologies, Sacred Mother."

The curly-haired woman made her way quickly across the chamber, yet just as she reached the door, she paused. There was only the slightest turn of the head, but Ann could have sworn that one bright, hazel eye had winked at her.

"Forgive my lack of welcome, Huntress," the *Kynra* said as the door shut. "Siblings rarely see eye-to-eye and sometimes persist on acting like children regardless of age or rank."

She rose to approach Ann's litter. "You must also forgive me for sending an acolyte to fetch you. It was meant with no disrespect. My personal attendant was assisting me with an urgent matter, and no one else was on hand."

Ann muttered a polite "Of course," and the *Kynra* halted in her tracks.

"And perhaps you will ask your friend to stop drinking from the basin."

Kaenus looked up guiltily, spraying water across the floor.

"He may not mind," the *Kynra* continued drily, "yet it is usually reserved for ceremonial purposes."

The woman settled herself on a stone bench near Ann, and beckoned the dog with one snap of her onyx-laden fingers. She leaned down as he approached, reaching out to clasp his chin.

"And who are you, my noble creature, that you feel entitled to drink from the sacred waters of the Chamber of the Earth Mother?"

Kaenus chirped and wagged his tail, all contrition forgotten.

"Interesting." The *Kynra* sat back, then after a moment, turned her gaze back to Ann. "Did you enjoy the ceremony yesterday, Huntress?"

"Oh, uh, yes. It was… interesting."

"What struck you most?"

An image of a horned head, limp, lifeless and streaked in crimson.

"You, uh, mentioned something about the, the Mother," Ann stammered. "You called Her… Deathless, I think you said?"

"Ah. Yes. The Earth Mother alone is immune to death."

"But – she has a Son, right?"

"She has countless. All those who live are children to the universal Mother."

"I meant a more –"

"You meant the god Mavros."

Ann narrowly suppressed a shiver. She'd cringed away from any mention of the name since the moonlit encounter several months back. And the *Kynra* was looking at her oddly now, her slate-coloured eyes boring into hers. As if she could sense Ann's secret and was trying to pry it from her.

But the moment soon passed.

"Even a god eventually dwindles," the *Kynra* continued. "They fade, as we all do, into the earth. You must understand, Huntress, that all gods derive their power from the *krythea* of humanity." She tapped her chest over her heart. "*Krythea*, you know? Yes. Yet it is the Earth Mother who sustains *us*, for it is Her love, Her belief and devotion that *we* depend on."

The woman rose from the bench and moved toward the low hanging branches of the tree. Reaching up, she eased one of the doves from its nest. The bird did not resist, only sunk down into the cup of her hands.

"It is the inescapable course of fate, Huntress," the woman went on. "It is told that Pritymnia deeply regretted bringing Mavros into the world. He was a glorious being, supplanting His Father in the *krythea* of humankind almost immediately –"

"His Father?"

The woman waved an impatient hand. "A god of the heavens – it is of no import. His name has long since been forgotten. I mean to say that although Mavros was adored, the Earth Mother regretted bringing Him into a world so hard and unforgiving. It was a condemnation, you see: even if His existence spanned a thousand, *ten* thousand lives of men, it would – and it will – eventually end. Like His Father's before Him."

The *Kynra* stroked the bird's back, her eyes drifting up to fix on some unseen distance.

"It is said," she continued, "that Pritymnia considered freeing Her Child from this bondage."

She paused and was silent so long that Ann finally whispered, "But She didn't."

"No, Huntress, She did not. For, in the end, He was Her Son."

A knock sounded from the other side of the door.

The *Kynra* exhaled. "Enter."

The door opened, a small form etched against the brightness from outside. As Ann's eyes adjusted she recognized the gaunt priest.

"You have fed her well?" the *Kynra* asked him, moving to return the dove to its nest.

"Yes, Sacred Mother."

That voice, so completely devoid of life.

No, Ann thought as the other two continued their conversation: it wasn't a lack of life that sent a shiver racing over her skin. That would be clear, clean, like a body missing a limb. It was the depth that she could sense beyond the vacuum. The arm that was there after all, concealed behind his back.

The *Kynra* had turned back to Ann. "Huntress, you will allow me to introduce Darkylus, a priest of the Brotherhood."

As the man bowed to her, Ann caught a glimpse of a lithe figure snaking around his legs.

"And this is my dear one," the woman said, stooping to stroke the cat's mottled fur. "She has no name for herself. She is kept, like the doves, to remind us of the two halves of the Earth Mother's nature."

Ann eyed the feline nervously. Then, recalling Kaenus for the first time since the *Kynra* had begun speaking, she attempted to crane round in her litter to look for him. Yet her view was limited to one half of the room.

"Darkylus," the *Kynra* went on, "I believe you have met our Huntress before?"

"Yes," the man replied. "Twice."

Ann looked at him in surprise.

"I conducted you to the Blessed Courtyard upon your arrival at Kabyrnos, Huntress."

Of course. Ann recalled that first surreal moment when she'd beheld his strange, formal garb, and she found herself wondering what he must have thought of *them*, two dishevelled strangers crouched on the floor of a storage room.

Whatever he thought, then or now, those blank eyes gave nothing away.

"Darkylus, keep watch over my dear one for the rest of the day," the *Kynra* ordered as she lowered herself into her throne again. "See that she does not misbehave again."

"Certainly, Sacred Mother."

The woman sighed, patted the cat's head, and then straightened in her throne.

"Huntress," she began.

They had arrived at the point. Ann felt her back prick with sweat. She swallowed, unable to shake the childish fear that she was about to be punished.

"I told you once that maintaining the sacred balance was of paramount importance."

"Yes," Ann said slowly, thinking not of their conversation on that first evening but, again, of the horned figure in the darkened courtyard.

"I am afraid," the woman went on, "that that balance has been upset."

Ann's heart stilled.

"As the Mother gives, so must we. I told you this. If we are not deserving of Her love, we shall diminish. It is what we of the Sisterhood guard – with the aid of our Brothers. It is the most sacred of our responsibilities."

Ann remained motionless, eyes glued to the woman's lipless mouth.

"Yet, as much as it pains me to say it, we are failing. Worship of the Earth Mother has become merely token amongst the people. Perfunctory, *meaningless* gestures! They sacrifice a cock for their evening meals, they leave clay models at sanctuaries and they believe this is an adequate substitute for true presence! True prayer!"

Ann's heart had restarted in irregular little thuds. The *Kynra*'s eyes were still fixed on her, but they had lost their focus.

"And now our city suffers. The Earth Mother allows us less and less of Her life-giving waters with every passing year, while Her Son tears our land apart with His tremors and storms."

Kaenus had reappeared now, materializing by Ann's elbow. Ann reached out a hand and rested it on his head.

"And no matter what is told to the people, this is no *test* –" the woman spat the word – "it is a *punishment*, and if we do not mend our ways, we will be visited by a devastation equal to the Great Atonement of our ancestors!"

The *Kynra* sat back, hands clutched together, thin chest rising and falling. And the cat had moved, Ann noticed, closer to the open door. It was standing between the priest's legs, its queer yellow eyes trailed on Kaenus. Ann curled her fingers into the dog's fur.

"Yet, although we may err, our Mother loves us always."

The *Kynra* had risen again and was approaching Ann.

"It is told that when a time of very great need arises, our Mother will not neglect us as we have Her."

She reached the litter and leaned down bring her face level with Ann's. Ann tightened her grip on Kaenus's fur.

"Kapreita was sent to us as a saviour, you see."

The woman was so close that Ann could see the beads of sweat on her upper lip.

"She was selected, the Chosen of Pritymnia, to set us straight upon our true path."

Kaenus was growling now, so low that Ann could only feel the vibrations of it through her fingers.

"And now, Huntress," the *Kynra* said, eyes gleaming as flat and hard as two of her onyx beads, "in this time of need, the Earth Mother has Chosen another to save us."

Oh no, Ann thought. Oh god no.

"Pritymnia has Chosen you."

***

Later, Ann wondered at how quickly it had all unravelled. Those horrible words, uttered like a starter's pistol to send the cat flying across the room. The brief, bloody battle that had ensued, Kaenus emerging the undeniable victor. Her own fervent apologies – her stuttered denials – as the servants had been called in and the dog dragged from the chamber.

"You don't understand," she'd finally managed to say. "There's got to be some mistake. I'm not – I *can't* be…"

Then the awareness setting in. The recognition that she *had* been lured, she'd been reeled to this very point. And that she was helpless to say why any of this – coming to this place, hunting the boar – had happened. Or whose voice it was that was bringing it all about.

Yet, perhaps worst of all, had been the *Kynra* sensing her hesitation. Sniffing out the weakness like a bloodhound and bending it to her will.

"The gods work in unknowable ways, Chosen," she'd said, holding her pet as it licked its wounds. "Who are we to explain or deny their will? Would *you* bear that weight? Or would you do what little you could to help a people who are desperately in need of aid?"

Ann's silence had, apparently, been enough. There were to be more lessons, the *Kynra* had said – once Ann was well, of course. Possibly even involvement in the most sacred Day of Death ceremony at the end of the season. And after that, who was to say?

The woman had paused then, stroking her cat slowly, careful not to touch the marks that Kaenus's teeth had left. The cat had sat still through this, Ann recalled, those yellow eyes fixed on her.

"You see, we must take care to embrace every prospect of salvation that is presented to us, Huntress," the *Kynra* had said, still stroking the animal. "For mercy is granted only once."

Chapter Six

The following days were spent recuperating in bed from an exhaustion oddly more mental than physical. Ann's brain smarted from an overstimulation so extreme that she lay in a healing stupor for three days. Three days, then Hersa came for her.

"Great Mavros on Crytus!" the girl exclaimed, hand flying to her nose as she pulled aside the curtain.

She spun on her heels and marched out, returning some time later with fresh linens, handfuls of dried sage and lavender, and a vial of perfume, all of which she applied liberally to Ann's chamber and person. Once the room had been thus exorcized, the tiny servant turned on Ann.

"It is time," she told her, hands on her hips.

"But –"

"No arguments, Ann."

"I just –"

"It is time. You must *bathe*."

Ann had stumbled across the communal baths only once before, and what she had seen had been enough to convince her that a year's worth of sponge-bathing wasn't so bad a fate after all. And as she stood at the threshold now, clinging to the single layer of linen that protected her, she was convinced that she'd been absolutely, one-hundred-percent right.

Even to a modern eye, these baths were the very picture of luxury. They had sunken, steaming pools, mirrored walls of polished bronze, baskets of sea sponges, vials of scented oils. But, in Ann's opinion, they lacked the one feature essential to any bathing experience: privacy. Bathing was – apparently – a social sport in Kabyrnos. Everywhere Ann looked she saw women: women laughing, women lounging, women plucking and massaging. Women with downy legs and darkened armpits, who stared at Ann as she stood clutching her towel tighter around her.

"Unless you are growing feathers under there, there is nothing to be ashamed of," Hersa snapped, reaching for Ann's towel.

Ann was still weak; the merciless girl won easily, and then ushered her, stumbling and exposed, toward the salt bath.

The water stung at first, especially around the scab under her collarbone, but it was only a matter of minutes before the salt began to work its way into her muscles, loosening and smoothing. Ann grew so languid that when two bath attendants came to gather her up, she was helpless to fend them off. She was carried to the massage table, where she was scrubbed down with sand, her face and scalp massaged with clay, her body rubbed with olive oil and scraped clean with a dull bronze blade. She was kneaded, rolled out, as insensate as a lump of dough. She could only moan as she was dragged back, deposited into a more tepid pool, and left to float in bliss.

Later, after she'd been tucked back into her clean, fragrant bed, Hersa insisted on capping off the day with an enormous meal: grilled fish, boiled legumes with sesame, bread and goat's cheese, and a dense, honey-soaked wheat cake.

"To put some meat back on those bones."

Ann was surprised to find herself ravenous, devouring the whole platter in minutes. When she was done, she licked her fingers, leaned back into her pillows and yawned. She then asked her friend how the Day of Light celebrations had been.

To her surprise, Hersa's rosy cheeks grew rosier. "They were fine," she said quickly.

Ann frowned at her.

"They were fine!" the girl repeated, her blush deepening.

"Hersa! What happened?"

"Nothing."

The two women stared at each other for several seconds.

"It is a very busy day for servants, Ann," Hersa insisted. "We have to serve the food, attend on the celebrations…"

"What happened, Hersa?"

The girl exhaled and sat down on the edge of the bed.

"There is a man. I… had not been with him for several moons, yet…"

"You still like him."

"He is not for me."

Ann made a noise of protest, but the girl held up a hand.

"He is not for me, Ann."

After a few more moments, Hersa leaned back against the wall and sighed. "And how did you enjoy your banquet?"

Ann groaned and told her everything. Hersa listened attentively, saying nothing. However, when Ann mentioned her brief sighting of the Guard Commander, the girl interjected.

"Take care, Ann. She is not a woman to cross. It is said that she once cut off the hand of an urchin simply because he spoke rudely to the *Kyn*."

"*What?*"

"The boy was sentenced to a year of servitude for the theft of a magistrate's sword. He was incensed, claiming injustice – I do not know the details – yet he did say that if he – if the *Kyn* – were not so blinded by pride, the city would not be suffering as it was."

"And the Guard Commander…?"

"She simply removed the boy's hand – and his livelihood with it. He was a potter's apprentice."

Ann was silent for a moment, digesting this. "He did say she was loyal."

Hersa smiled wryly. "Zelkanus rescued her – as he has rescued many. She was a refugee from the north, and the *Kyn* took her in, sending her to the guards when she was of age. Most foreigners to the island do not succeed as she has done."

The girl went strangely quiet then. After a minute, Ann cleared her throat and began to tell her about her meeting with the *Kynra*. For whatever reason, she chose not to say anything about the Chosen. But when she mentioned the gaunt priest, Hersa shuddered.

"Unnatural man. Erysia told me –"

"This is your priestess friend?"

"Yes. She told me that the man is the *Kynra*'s cousin, who came with her from the city of Xanu when she was married, at the age of twelve."

"*Twelve?* Wait. But the *Kyn* –"

"This was Cryklonus, Zelkanus's father."

"Wait, *wait*. The *Kynra* was married to the current *Kyn*'s father?"

"Is that so unusual?"

"Yeah. Where I come from, it's unusual."

"Well, it is common enough here, if the bride is of child-bearing years. Yet she would not have born the *Kyn* an heir, regardless. Erysia told me that the oldest priestesses say that when she first came here, the *Kynra* locked herself in her rooms, refusing to see her husband – or anyone except her clansman. Even when she emerged many moons later, she would not allow her husband to enter her bedchamber."

"Who was the current *Kyn*'s mother, then?"

"A chambermaid, I believe."

Hersa shrugged – a casual gesture, but again, the girl seemed unusually subdued.

"Hersa –"

The girl hopped to her feet. "It is late and you should rest. You still have much healing to do. And I –" the little servant turned away – "I have much work to attend to."

***

In the following weeks, Ann's strength grew quickly – as did her curiosity. Once she was well enough to move around on her own, she began to venture out into the city.

She had procured a pair of sandals and a hat from Hersa. The sandals – essentially two leather straps with soles attached – felt awkward after so many months without. She abandoned them quickly, opting to remain barefoot as so many others did in the warm seasons. The hat, however, proved very useful. Ann knew it looked ridiculous – a broad, flat, starched thing, perched on her unfashionably ponytailed head like a plate on a spoon – but it kept the sun off her face, so she wore it gratefully.

The first place she visited was the Courtyard of the Dying Sun. She had avoided it too long. And, in fact, filled as it always was with groups of talking, busy people, the place had lost some of its horror for Ann. Some of it. Day after day, while she was still too weak to go further, Ann would sit in the courtyard, eyes on the blackened tree. Watching it carefully, though she could not say what for. The tree remained lifeless, an unchanging mast lost in the swell of the city – practically invisible to the townsfolk who flowed around it.

But they were preoccupied with their lives, Ann supposed. What fish was to be had for dinner. How the goat kid had stopped nursing, or how an unseasonal storm had threatened the wheat crop. A common topic, Ann found, was Kabyrnos's dealings with the Gyklanean mainlanders to the north. Makrona, one of the more powerful Gyklanean cities and a longstanding trading ally of Kapreitu, had recently terminated their contract to supply Kabyrnos with timber and silver. They simply did not have enough to spare, they'd claimed. Horse's shit, the cityfolk grumbled.

As Ann became stronger, she would often walk out along the West *Kyn*'s Road with Kaenus. Girl and dog would meander past the armoury that sat in the shadow of the palace, past the forges, the tanneries, the olive oil and wine facilities. They would wander out into the countryside, and it was there, far from the activity of the city, that Ann first became aware of the earth's frequent tremors. Like a giant, shivering in its sleep. At first, these quakes unnerved her and she would turn back, but she soon became used to them, and her walks grew longer and more frequent.

The Kapreitan countryside mesmerized her. The softness of the morning, the layered silhouettes of distant peaks fading as they blended into the sky.

The flat, golden glare of midday on the fields of wheat, as the labourers stashed their sickles and sledges, and led their oxen back to shade. Then the magic of twilight, the low sun sharpening every curve of the distant hills, the divide between light and shadow deepening then vanishing altogether.

Often, when Ann returned to the apartments at dusk, she would find gifts left at the door to her room: embroidered bands of cloth for her hair, bouquets of late poppies, sweets and other local delicacies (which Kaenus happily dispatched on her behalf). She had an uneasy feeling about these tokens, but as the giver never declared themselves, it wasn't too difficult to just tuck the gifts out of sight and out of mind.

Occasionally, the *Kynra* would send priestesses to check in on her. In the early days, Ann would play up her injuries until these women went away again. As she became more mobile, she found it more effective to simply spend her days outside the palace.

The Season of Light was, to Ann, loveliness incarnate. Bright, hot day followed bright, hot day like the golden beads of a necklace. Long naps became welcome midday necessities and at night, cityfolk would stay up late, playing music in the streets, then sleeping on rooftops to stay cool. Fresh fruit abounded: early grapes, sour yet flavourful; sun-ripened plums, juicier and sweeter than any fruit Ann had ever tasted. Farmers brought stalks of wheat to local shrines for harvest blessings. Small children ran naked through the streets with white-and-purple caper flowers clasped in their hands and streaming through their hair. The city was in celebration and Ann ached to join.

When Ann finally returned to her work, she began to learn to weave. The looms were intimidating

– upright, wooden monsters – and the noise they made was appalling, clacking and banging as the shuttles of thread were shunted back and forth between hanging layers of wool. Ann found the work surprisingly soothing. Yet still, when the workday was finished, she was always the first through the door. The season was at its height in the world above.

***

Ann wandered in the pastures just east of the palace. It was hot still, the sun glaring down to bake the earth and everything on it. Yet there was shade where she walked; the pines grew close together here, the ground carpeted in their needles, the air thick with their perfume. Dry, but sweet. Almost floral.

Ann moved silently in the fragrant air, thinking of how long it had been since she'd left home. She wondered if time was advancing as quickly there, and, if so, what her husband had made of her disappearance.

How could she even begin to explain herself, once the year was up?

Where would she go?

A hot breeze came in from over the valley, blowing north. Ann followed it. Till the sun set, she was free and time ceased to exist.

She soon drifted into a grove of fig trees. Most city fruit was cultivated on the fertile slopes of the valley, but these wild orchards could crop up in the smallest given space. As if in reminder to the city: We were here, they said. We were here and we will be here, long after you are gone.

The hot wind blew again. Ann slipped through the grove, and past the clan villas that perched on the crest of the valley, with their white walls covered with the violent pink of bougainvillea. She floated through the livestock paddocks, past the bull's pens that made her quicken her pace, and along the curve of trees that almost completely blocked from view the workshops of the Craftsmen's District to the west. Beyond that, Ann knew, was the Northern District. Serf grounds. The final barrier of city before the open stretch of hinterland that lay between Kabyrnos and the harbour town of Kylondo.

Yet for now, rising just before her, was a wall of cypresses.

Ann approached slowly. There was something forbidding about these trees that grew so close together, like a ring of tall, slender sentinels. Gently pushing into the foliage, Ann peered into the heart of their circle.

A huge expanse of sand. The sun seemed to burn brighter here, scalding the ground, with heat rising up in waves to distort her view of the heavy stone benches beyond.

This, she realized, was the arena.

Everyone seemed to be talking about the Great Tournament these days. Next spring, people would be descending on Kabyrnos from all over Kapreitu and Gyklanea. The event was long awaited: it took place only every fifth year. And the hopes of being chosen as one of "the Five" to represent Kabyrnos was running rampant. Almost every young man under the age of thirty (and their mothers) could be heard bragging about his athletic prowess. Dawn exercises seemed to stretch well into mid-morning for this demographic, and no one seemed to object. Often, on her way in from the western fields, Ann would pass groups of old men leaning on their staffs, or labourers standing in their sweat-stained loincloths, hotly debating past victory records and placing bets on which city would come out the highest this coming Season of Life. These discussions were usually punctuated by a strong undercurrent of hostility against the Gyklaneans. The Makronans in particular – Ann gathered – usually sent the very best.

Ann continued on her way. To the southeast, past a small copse, was a long building of timber and mudbrick. She headed toward it. Horses grazed in the surrounding paddocks, tails swatting flies, muzzles hovering over the parched grass and the lavender bushes that grew in abundance there. Ann bent to pick a purple-tipped stalk as she neared the open door of the building. She brought it to her face and inhaled.

Something stirred in her memory.

"Let me think about it," her brother's voice drifted out from the barn.

Ann froze.

"Of course, Hunter." A woman's voice, deep and humourless. "Inform me when you have made your decision."

"You know –" Ann could *hear* the grin – "you can call me Nik."

There was a pause, then a laugh – Nik's. Then silence. Ann waited, still not moving.

A figure appeared in the doorway and Ann took an involuntary step backward.

But the Guard Commander had already seen her. Ann remained fixed to the spot, praying that the guardswoman would continue on her way.

No such luck.

"I have a message for you," the woman said as she halted a few feet in front of Ann. "The *Kyn* has asked to see you. Whenever it suits."

"Okay."

Another moment passed in silence, the woman's eyes trained on Ann's face, unblinking. Hand resting, as always, on the dagger at her belt. Ann swallowed, trying to steady her voice.

"Is there anything else?" she asked.

Another few moments passed. Then the woman spoke.

"If I were you, girl, I would tread carefully."

She said it plainly, not a threat, but a fact.

"I do not know your business with the *Kyn* –" her lip curled ever so slightly – "although it is not difficult to guess. Yet if I even suspect that you are doing anything underhanded, I will not hesitate to act."

Ann remained silent.

"Am I understood?"

Ann looked down at the lavender flower still pinched between her forefinger and her thumb. She nodded.

The guardswoman stepped back. "I will tell the *Kyn* that his message has been passed on."

***

In the very early morning of the twins' fifteenth birthday, Ann was woken by the gentle creak of her bedroom door.

The twins had been kept up till past midnight by the screaming in the living room. Their stepfather's heavy tread on the stairs had sent Nik flying back to his own bedroom, but their mother had remained downstairs. Until now.

"Annika?" she whispered. "Annika – oh. You're awake."

The light from the streetlamp outside shafted through the window, falling on half of Lotta's face – warping it, aging it prematurely, so that the person who bent down over Ann's bed was not the young, beautiful mother she knew, but a ravaged old woman.

"Annika, listen to me carefully. Are you listening?" Her mother placed an envelope on the mattress by her elbow. "It's a bank draft. For fifteen thousand dollars."

Ann said nothing.

"It's in your name."

Still, she said nothing.

"Keep it. You'll need it someday." Her mother sighed, the crags of her face deepening. "Did you hear me, Annika? Fifteen thousand." She paused, then added, "Don't tell him, okay?"

After a moment, Ann nodded.

"I mean your brother. Don't tell your brother."

Silence.

"Am I understood?"

Again, Ann nodded. Lotta leaned further down, dropping out of the light's path.

"Listen to me," the voice from the shadows whispered to her. "Promise me you won't tell him. I know you, but you don't need to worry about him. He's a *man* – he'll be fine. But you, you'll need to tread very carefully from now on."

Another few seconds of silence, and the voice grew stern.

"Keep the money and don't tell a soul. Promise me. Now. I want to hear the words."

"I – I promise."

A moment passed, then Lotta rose, a lock of her hair brushing Ann's face as she stood. Her shampoo smelled of lavender, Ann recalled.

"Take care of yourself, Ann. No one else will do it for you."

***

Ann watched the Guard Commander walk away until she had disappeared from view.

That look the woman had given her.

"Ann?"

Her brother stood in the barn door, pitchfork in hand. His bronze skin glistened with sweat, his waves of hair shining a bleached gold in the sunlight. A glowing, irascible god.

"What are you doing here?" he demanded.

"I was just..." She looked around helplessly. "Wandering."

He cocked an eyebrow at her. "Oh, yeah?"

"Yeah."

He readjusted his grip on the fork. "Alright then."

He turned back into the barn. After a moment, Ann followed.

"What was *she* doing here?"

He thrust the fork into a pile of hay, pitching some into one of the empty stalls. "She wants me to join the palace guard."

Ann absorbed this.

"Well," she said at length, "at least she likes *you*."

Nik chuckled. "True."

Ann stood for a minute, watching her brother work. His body was whole, his skin smooth, unmarred by bandage or scar. It was as if the hunt on the mountain had never happened. Like so many of the things they'd been through together.

"Nik?"

He shot a glance over his shoulder but continued working. Ann noticed now that the lavender sprig was gone. She must have dropped it outside.

"Have you ever wondered –" She paused, taking a breath. "Have you ever wondered where..."

"Where what?"

He had straightened and was staring at her now.

He's a man, their mother had said. Ann remembered that especially – the way she had uttered the word like a profanity.

Ann exhaled. "Nothing."

Nik gazed at her for a few more moments. "Okay, well… I should really finish up here."

"Right. Of course. See you later then."

She turned back only once before losing herself in the trees. Nik was a distant figure, almost obscured in the shade of the building, but she could see that he was not working now. He was standing still, leaning over his pitchfork. Shoulders hunched, forehead resting on his knuckles.

He's a man, she told herself as she turned away. He'll be fine.

Chapter Seven

Time passed, taking the prime of the season with it. The days grew shorter; the heat's intensity waned. Yet left behind were the marks, the testimonies of change that the summer had wrought on Ann. Work-hardened hands, road-toughened feet. Weight gained and skin browned. A strengthened body, a roused mind – both impatient for more. At long last, Ann was ready.

But she was finding it difficult to convince Hersa that she hadn't taken leave of her senses.

"Let me ensure that I understand you," the girl said. "You wish to venture out alone, into the unprotected countryside, under the *sun*, to… run?"

"Yes."

"*Why?*"

Ann shrugged. "Exercise?"

"You want exercise? Join the others in the courtyard at dawn. *Horses* run wild in the fields, not humans."

"This human does."

Eventually, the girl gave in, bestowing Ann with a woman's training outfit: a plain tunic with looser sleeves, slits up the skirt to hip level, and a tight breastband. As Ann dressed, Hersa observed her, hands on her hips, eyes narrowed.

"I understand now."

Ann peered at the girl, wary.

"They have been saying that you are not fully human, you know. No human woman could make it up the mountain, slaughter a boar and live to tell the tale. And I understand now. Your hair in its horse's tail, your long, bony legs – this need to *run*…"

Ann sighed.

"Though I do not care to think what this says about your mother's preferences."

"Ugh. Very nice, Hersa."

Hersa tossed her a waterskin. "Such things are not unheard of. And, truly, there can be no other explanation for this behaviour."

Ann tucked the waterskin into her belt. "Well, I'll leave you to puzzle that one out on your own." She went to the door and whistled for Kaenus. "But if we're not back by nightfall, send out the scouts."

***

Ann paused on the broad southern veranda. The city was quiet under the early morning sun. It was a day of rest. Kaenus drew up beside her, inserting his snout under her dangling hand. She patted his cheek as she looked out at the outline of Mount Crytus.

"Didn't turn out too well last time, did it, buddy?" she asked the dog.

"Does he understand you?"

Ann whirled round. The *Kyn* was walking through the broad doorway that led out from Commerce Hall.

"I – I don't know," she replied.

The man squatted down as Kaenus padded over to him. "What do you call him?" he asked, scratching behind the dog's mangled ear.

"Kaenus."

The man looked up at her, brows raised. "No embellishments for you, I see." Sighing, he heaved himself to his feet. "In which case, I shall ask you directly."

He moved closer to her.

"Join me for an evening meal."

Not a question.

"Ann?"

"Okay. I mean, yes. Of course."

He clapped his hands, brown eyes crinkling. "Excellent! Next day of rest, then. Meet me at my apartments for sundown."

He looked as if he were going to leave her then – but he lingered, eyes flitting down over her attire.

"Where are you headed dressed like that, Ann?"

Something in his tone rankled. Instead of replying, she shot a glance back at the mountain.

"Ah, I see," the *Kyn* said. "Confronting one's fears. You have courage. Yet you must take care, Ann. One never knows, what one may find on the mountain of the sleeping god." He was silent for a moment, gaze fixed on the profile in the distance. "It is a cursed place, I think."

Then, after another deep sigh and a nod, he departed – leaving Ann alone on the veranda to fully catch her breath.

***

Ann's muscles eased back into a familiar loping rhythm as she moved along the empty road. The air was still only warm, the sun still low. The few workshops found in this Southern District were quiet. Outside the traveller's inn, a line of mules stood feeding drowsily. This was the time of year for the distribution of harvested grain, and deliveries were being made to the palace daily. But, for now, the city slept on.

Buildings soon melted into countryside. Girl and dog rose and fell with the hills, passing through orchards where Ann stopped to pluck figs so ripe that purple flesh had burst, exposing the jam of their interior. Soon, they reached the fork in the road; this time, Ann chose the eastern path.

Unlike the route to Kartissus, this road was paved with well-worn stones, which ran diagonally up the slope at a gentle incline. And yet, after the first fifty metres or so, the path became almost undetectable, with roots and bushes creeping further in over the cobblestone the higher it climbed. Ann was forced to proceed more slowly, picking her way through the scrub, while Kaenus wandered freely in the surrounding area, nose to ground.

The air grew hot, and the incline steepened. Ann drove herself up the slope towards the serrated peaks above, fighting to follow the almost non-existent path and sometimes losing it completely. She clambered up rock face, dragged herself upwards by the spiny arms of trees. She exulted in the strain, completely absorbed by the thrill of the challenge.

Until her ascent ended abruptly in a stone wall.

The wall was long and tall, completely blocking her view. Ann worked her way around the perimeter, hoping to orient herself with a sight of the city, surely hundreds of feet below by now. She came upon a ramp, rising further still. Again, she climbed. Her legs were shaking, her tunic soaked through, but she was consumed by the urge to rise, to soar up as high as her body would take her.

She stepped out of the shelter of the ramp and into a mistral gale. Her hair whipped around her face, her sweat cooling instantly as she took in the broad stone terrace and the vast expanse of sky beyond, the earth falling sharply away. Bracing herself against the wall, she inched toward the edge of the terrace. The wind tore at her, pushing her back; she leaned into it, gazing down at the land that stretched out far below.

It was so remote from her – a painting of contrasts, with the brown contours of the land, and the azure breadth of sky and sea. An image made of dream. And standing there, perched on the precipice of the world, Ann forgot her fear and was gripped by a surge of pure wildness. She was both dreamer and dreamed, a bird taking wing – soaring into an existence so simple yet so extreme that she felt that to fly further was to descend into madness. This was no place for mortals; it was the throne of gods. Yet, for one ecstatic moment, Ann was one of them, elevated and untouchable.

Kaenus barked once, twice, calling her back. Resigned, she turned to retreat.

And stopped short. Only inches from her feet, cracked into the stone of the terrace, was a long, jagged fissure. Ann reeled away, knocking against an old stone altar. She gripped the stone hard, her heart thudding against her ribcage as she peered down. The fissure was three, maybe four feet at its widest, and its depths were black. A chasm, utterly lost to shadow.

She heard Kaenus bark again, closer this time – then he was there, a warm presence at her side, guiding her away from the altar, away from the fissure, toward the opposite end of the terrace. And the shelter of the building there.

It was a lonely, forgotten place, nestled on three sides by the craggy rock of the mountain. An abandoned shrine, Ann guessed as she took in the collapsing timber roof and the crumbling plaster of the doorway.

From which emerged a tiny bundle of a person.

At first sight, the figure seemed more apparition than human, with thick swathes of colourless robe writhing in the wind behind its stooped body. But the weather-beaten face that soon came into view was undeniably real: it was an ageless, genderless visage, humour tugging and twitching at the folds around the eyes.

Ann climbed the last few steps up to the building's porch, and the apparition bent forward in a swirl of robes to pat Kaenus on the head.

"Good dog," the apparition said, voice crackling like a dry leaf.

As Kaenus disappeared around the building, snout once again to ground, the person turned back to Ann. She – he? – grinned so broadly that Ann could see the holes where four teeth should have been.

"You must be cold, Huntress."

Ann stared into that beaming face. "I… am."

"You must come in, then, come in!"

Ann followed the stooped figure out of the wind. A few short corridors later, she found herself standing in a dark, cramped room. There was a fire-pit in the centre, heaped high with ash and rubble, a stool beside it, and three stained mattresses piled against the far wall.

The apparition ushered Ann to the stool. "Sit, sit, sit!"

Ann sat.

"Now you must have some tea."

The apparition looked about the room, limp hair swinging from side to side, as if he – she? – expected to find a steaming mug amongst the crumbled brick and dust. Then the weathered face fell, folds sagging comically. One second passed, then two, then –

"Andrylea!"

Ann jumped, almost knocking over her stool.

"*Andrylea!*"

A woman appeared at the apparition's elbow.

"*Andry* – oh!" The apparition clutched her – yes, definitely *her* – thin chest, gripping the swathes of material there. "There you are, Andrylea! Do we have any tea?"

Andrylea's chin flicked upward: no.

"Can you fetch some?"

Andrylea's chin flicked to the side.

"Good, good, good. Go then – and go quickly!"

Andrylea disappeared and the old woman made to turn back to Ann – but paused, then rushed back out into the corridor.

"Take care what herbs you pick this time, girl!" she shouted.

She came back into the room, a bit out of breath but smiling once more.

"Forgive me, Huntress," she sighed. "Andrylea is young, and therefore given to bouts of daydreaming."

Andrylea was, to Ann's best guess, at least forty.

The old woman settled herself on the ground in front of Ann's stool. Sitting there, with her limbs tucked beneath her robes and most of her face hidden by hair, the woman looked rather like a small pile of dirty laundry.

"Can I ask," Ann began, "how did you know that I –"

A bony hand flashed out of the robes, silencing her. "Do not waste your breath on *that*."

Ann sat back, rebuked. But the woman continued to watch her with owl-like intensity, so a few moments later, she tried again.

"What – what's your name?"

The woman released a heavy sigh. "Klochistropa."

"What a –" Ann swallowed, eyeing the inexplicably crestfallen face – "what an unusual name."

"Is it not?" the old woman cried, animated once more. "My father told my mother that no man would marry a girl with a name like this, yet my mother insisted. It was an important family name, you see – her mother's name, her mother's mother's before her. Yet it turned out that my father was right!" She tossed her hair back with a cackle. "No man ever *did* want to marry me."

A long period of silence followed this statement. Ann fidgeted under the woman's gaze, unable to ignore the feeling that she was meant to say something. Yet when she began to ask another question, the old woman's hands flew out of her robes again.

"You must be famished, my dear! Would you like some lentils?"

"Well, I –"

"Andrylea! *Andrylea!*"

Another, entirely different woman appeared at the door.

"Do we have any lentils for our guest?"

Andrylea the Second's chin went up.

"Oh no. Anything else to eat?"

Andrylea the Second's chin went to the side.

"Good, good, good. Bring it."

Andrylea the Second disappeared and Klochistropa turned back to Ann. "I cannot *tell* you what a pleasure it is to have you here, my dear. My girls are very loyal, it is true, and very kind to an old wretch, yet they are not what one would call talkative."

"I had noticed that, yeah."

"Very perceptive of you, my dear."

As Ann smothered a smile, Andrylea the Second reappeared, setting a chipped stone bowl on the ground.

"They are both mute," Klochistropa stated.

"Oh!" Ann eyed Andrylea the Second's calm face apprehensively. "I'm – so sorry."

"Very kind, very kind," the old woman chanted, waving the other woman out of the room. "Yet it can be very dull up here, with only those two sulky girls for company."

"But they can't *both* be named Andrylea," Ann commented as she picked an almond out of the bowl at her feet.

Klochistropa's beady eyes narrowed. "*Very* clever of you, my dear, very clever."

As Ann tried to decide whether or not she was joking, the woman refolded herself into her robes and went on.

"Call it an old woman's weakness. I never *could* remember their names, and they never *could* straighten me out, so you see…"

Ann laughed; she couldn't help herself.

"You have a very pretty laugh, my dear. You should laugh more often."

Ann's smile fell away. After a moment, she picked out another couple almonds and asked,

"So, what is this place?"

Klochistropa did not respond straight away. "Careful, my dear," she said quietly. "You only have one left."

"One –?"

"This place," the old woman cut in, "was once a site of great importance. The people cannot be bothered to make the pilgrimage now. They worship in their palaces, like the arrogant Pyitans in their sands to the south, who believe not in gods of sky and earth, but in deities of stone and mortar." The woman paused then, observing Ann with one long, canny look. "You see, this temple safeguards the birthplace of Mavros."

Ann froze, half bent down toward the bowl.

"Yes," the woman said slowly. "The womb of the Mother."

Ann thought of the fissure – of the darkness within it. She shivered.

A heavy shawl was wrapped around her shoulders. Ann looked up to find Andrylea the First, smiling quite kindly and holding out a cup of steaming liquid. Ann reached for the cup, but Klochistropa got there first, sniffing its contents suspiciously. Slowly, the old woman relinquished the tea, returning to her spot on the floor.

"Very nicely done, Andrylea," she said reluctantly.

Andrylea passed Ann the cup. Ann smiled her thanks. The tea was warm and soothing. Sage, she thought.

But the old woman was talking again. "It is a very lonely place now. It saddens one to see it."

"But you're here," Ann observed.

"You *are* quite clever, are you not?"

Ann blinked at her.

"Yes, I am here," the woman repeated. "For many long years now. And before that, I made the journey often. Ah yes, I loved it here... Then." Her voice had grown quiet, her eyes intent on Ann's face. "Perhaps he thought he did me a favour, banishing me here."

"Who –"

Another flash of a hand, the old woman's index finger held out.

One. *One left*.

At last Ann understood. She was quiet for some time, then, very carefully, asked,

"*Why* were you banished?"

She was rewarded with another broad, hole-punched smile.

"Good, yes, good, very good, my dear. I was banished for my gift, you see. The gift of Sight –

the gift of my mothers. You must understand, I was very gifted. Not with one of those common gifts of charisma or intuition..." Klochistropa trailed off, watching Ann intently again. "Your – shall we call them gifts? – are not so common either."

Ann stared at the old woman.

"You think every person can sense the things you sense?" the woman whispered, leaning in toward her. "You think every person wakes in the night hearing what you hear?" Her voice was no more than a breath now. "You think many others can speak into the thoughts of another?"

"H-how –?"

"No, no, no, my dear," the woman said, wagging her finger in Ann's face. "I have said too much already... Yet I *will* warn you – and it *will not count* –" she shouted defiantly – "for I am just restating what I have already said! As I have more than enough cause to know, not all gifts are blessings. And the stronger the gift, the more dangerous. You must beware, my dear."

Abruptly, Klochistropa scrambled to her feet.

"I know, I know, I *know!*" she yelled, flapping her hands in the air as if to swat at invisible flies. She whirled toward Ann. "It is time for you to leave."

Ann's could barely open her mouth to protest before she was hauled up and ushered out of the room.

"Andrylea!" the old woman cried. "*Andrylea!*"

The two women appeared as if from nowhere, one reclaiming the mug and shawl, and the other depositing a sling – full of nuts and a fresh waterskin – into Ann's hands.

"Girls, girls, have you seen that dog?" Klochistropa asked. "He was sniffing around here, up to his usual mischief, no doubt –"

Andrylea the First pointed into the room where Klochistropa and Ann had been sitting.

"*Oh!*" the old woman shrieked. "Oh! Oh!"

She disappeared in a storm of flailing material, the Andryleas just behind her. When Ann arrived back in the tiny room, she found Kaenus with his front half submerged under the pile of mattresses, the Andryleas approaching him cautiously, and the old woman flapping in the background.

"Oh! Oh! Oh!" she yelled. "Stop him! Get him *out*!"

The Andryleas descended, grabbing hold of his tail and heaving backward. But Kaenus was too strong. With a low growl, he lurched forward, and one of the Andryleas lost her grip, staggering back into Ann. Ann steadied her and the woman dove back into the fray, taking hold of the dog's shoulders this time. Kaenus growled, digging in with his forepaws.

Then Klochistropa let out a barking cackle.

"Oh," she cried, "let him *have* it!"

Everyone turned to her, including the dog.

"Let him have it, I say! We have held it long enough."

Both Andryleas sighed in unison – looking, for the first time, a bit put out by the old woman – and began to shift the dirty mattresses aside. Kaenus had been digging at a low mound of dirt, a spot in the floor where the tiles had broken away. Presently, his head emerged with an oblong object, wrapped in filthy rags. He pranced over to where Ann stood and deposited it at her feet.

One of the Andryleas stooped and placed the object into Ann's sling.

"You have water?" Klochistropa asked, hands pushing at her back again.

"Y–yes."

"You have food?"

"Yes."

"Good, good, good."

The wind met them as they stepped back out onto the terrace.

"Well then, my dear... Be gone with you."

One final shove sent Ann stumbling down the steps, back toward the ramp. Yet when she had just about reached the opening in the wall and was preparing to begin her descent, she heard a cry from behind her, calling her back.

The old woman was flying down the steps, hair and robes tearing around her.

"One final thing," she whispered as she caught up to Ann. "If you find yourself wandering this way again, *please* –" the smile stretched across her face, showing not four, but at least six missing teeth – "would you bring some lentils?"

Chapter Eight

Once Ann's legs had recuperated from their second foray up the mountain, running became a regular part of her daily routine. Every morning she would jog through the city and out into the countryside beyond, passing many cityfolk along her way. After a few days, she tried smiling at some of the people she passed. She was surprised to find that they were always more than ready to smile back.

To her relief, the mysterious gifts stopped coming. The *Kynra*'s priestesses had not, but they didn't take much skill to evade: a sharply turned corner, a back-room exit into the steam clouds of the dyeing workshops – problem temporarily solved.

Yet it soon became impossible for Ann to ignore the sense that was growing in her mind, like the building of an aura along the fringes of her vision. A sense of waiting – though what for she couldn't say. There was just something – something that, no matter how fast or how far she went each morning, would always be there to meet her when she returned. Something that whispered her name from the stones of the great building. At one time, she would have dismissed this as pure nerves. After her meeting with the old woman on the mountain, she had to wonder.

But before she knew it, it was the late afternoon of the day of rest – only four days out from the autumnal equinox – and Ann had more pressing things on her mind.

That evening, she was to meet the *Kyn*.

She had the apartments to herself. Nik would be drinking in one of the gathering halls no doubt, and Kaenus would be roaming as usual. Probably near the kitchens (she'd already received two complaints about him). For now, however, there were no complaints, no dog, no brother. She was alone and there wasn't much time left to prepare.

She'd have to dress well, of course – in deference to his position. But not too well. Her blue dress with the yellow embroidery was a little looser, a little longer. A little more concealing in the front. She'd wear that. The griffin necklace she left in its corner at the bottom of her trunk.

By the time she was dressed, it was almost dusk. As she turned to leave, something caught her eye. Something dirt-smeared, poking out from beneath her bed.

The sling – and in it, the oblong object. Exhausted on her return from the mountain, she had dropped it on the floor and promptly forgotten all about it. Ann kneeled and eased it out of its filthy rags.

It was a figurine of a woman, mud-caked and about a foot tall, wearing the formal, flounced gown of a priestess. Breasts bare, arms held out to the side – a bird in one hand, and, in the other, a snake. Ann submerged the statue in her basin of water, smoothing away the dirt. The crystal faience of the surface had chipped away in many places, but the colours were still clear. Skin fair, eyes dark. Hair yellow.

There was a knock on the door. Ann placed the dripping statue on her trunk and hurried into the common room. It was past time to leave anyway.

But waiting in the corridor, with cupped hands held together in front of him, was the High Steward. He stepped in, uninvited.

"Huntress," he said, bowing slightly. "Much time has passed since I have seen you last. You are well? You certainly look it."

Ann felt the usual flood of heat in her cheeks. "Yes – thank you."

"I wondered…" The man hesitated, shifting slightly from one foot to the other. A practiced motion, Ann thought. Very smoothly executed too. "I wondered if you have been receiving my… well, my tokens?"

"I have," she said with an inward sigh. "Thank you."

He watched her for a moment, the edges of his wide mouth snaking up.

"You are most welcome." He shook his cupped hands gently. "May I?"

Ann nodded warily and the long fingers opened. Out flew a small, yellow butterfly.

"I saw it in the gardens and I thought of you."

Ann bit her lip. "Oh."

He took another step toward her. "May I come in?"

"Actually," Ann said. "I'm late to meet somebody."

"I am sure your friend would be happy to wait a little longer."

"No –"

"I am sure it would be a pleasure to wait however long for *you*."

"I don't think the *Kyn* will see it that way."

She'd said it quietly, almost a whisper – a shameful admission – but its effect was immediate. The High Steward's smile froze in place.

"You are to meet the *Kyn*?"

"What's going on in here?" came a voice from the corridor. "Cattle blocked the road again?"

The High Steward backed out swiftly as Nik strode into the room, eyes on Ann.

"I was just leaving," the High Steward announced. "Huntress."

With a curt bow, he marched out, back straight, shoulders stiff. Half-crushed butterfly flapping near the floor.

"You going too?" Nik asked as he poured himself some water. "You got yourself a date, I heard."

"It's not like that," Ann replied. "But I am late."

She turned to leave.

"I don't like it, Ann."

She halted in the doorway.

"It's not my business, I know, but I don't have a good feeling about him."

Ann kept her back turned, her eyes on the ground.

"I just don't think you can trust him, okay?" her brother went on. "And sometimes, it's like, I dunno… It's like I can feel him watching me or something."

Ann turned to raise an eyebrow at him.

"Look," he snapped, getting defensive. "Everyone knows the man's had dozens of mistresses, okay? They all talk about it!"

Ann fought to keep her voice calm. "Nothing's going to happen, Nik. He just asked me to eat with him."

"Right."

"*Really*." The word sounded so flimsy. "How could I say no?"

"Easy. Just say it."

A moment passed in silence.

"Nik," she said. "I appreciate where this is coming from, I really do, but you don't need to worry."

"You're right. It's none of my business. What do I care if my own sister starts up with some creepy older guy?"

"You didn't care the last time."

The words flew out before she'd had a chance to think and the moment she'd said them she knew she'd gone too far. She watched Nik's face go still, his hand tensing around his cup. And when he placed it back on the table – so quietly that it barely made a sound – she watched him slip past her and leave the room without a word.

***

True to her mother's wishes, Ann did not tell her brother about the money. She didn't tell him that first day, while their stepfather raged through the house, breaking lamps and screaming at them. She didn't tell him when she found him crying later that week, nor when she found him tearing up all the photos they had of her. Perhaps she had felt that her promise had bound her. Or perhaps she'd felt that the money was a burden that she should bear alone, like a black mark on their foreheads that only she could see. A penance she would make on behalf of them both.

She was always a quiet girl, but over the course of the following year, Ann stopped talking almost entirely. She cooked and cleaned for her brother and stepfather, accepting as much responsibility as quietly as she could. Her only outlet was running. She joined the track team, and every morning, for an hour before school, she would run and run and run, growing faster, going further each day.

For those first six months, she and Nik clung to each other, instinctively knowing that it was their best chance of survival. The path between their minds was always open but silent, like a tight hand hold that linked them firmly but did not threaten to shatter the brittle restraint that kept them going.

They rarely spoke – and never inside the house. Their stepfather, when he was home, provided enough of that for the three of them.

"Don't you brats realize how lucky you are?" he would yell. "I pay for your food, your clothes, your schools, and you aren't even my own children!"

He told them he'd get the law down on their mother if he could ever find her. He said a lot of things to them, but they never spoke back.

As the months went by, their isolation thickened. Ann and Nik stopped clinging to each other, and their mental bond slowly wasted away. Nik began to spend most of his time with his friends, leaving his sister to fend for herself at home. Their stepfather was quieter when Nik was absent. He would come home from work, sit in his armchair with a glass of scotch and watch Ann prepare his dinner. When Nik did come home in the evenings, though, there would be more yelling. At sixteen years old, Nik had finally learnt to fight back.

Life continued this way for well over a year, Ann trying to become as small as possible amidst the storm of their existence. She knew they couldn't live like this forever, but like a ship lost at sea, any port was preferable to none. So she clung to this life, terrified of the day that one of the men would go too far.

***

Ann stood on a balcony overlooking the darkening hills to the southeast of Kabyrnos. There was a table in the centre of the space, laden with a feast's worth of food – fish, honeyed squash, cumin mashed lentils, fresh greens, flat bread, wine, fruit – and behind it, a bench scattered with an assortment of cushions and animal skins. On the opposite side of the balcony was a curtained doorway.

The *Kyn* was not yet there. His servant had told her to wait, gesturing to the bench. The evening was growing cool, he'd said; better to keep warm. No thanks, Ann had replied. She'd prefer to stand.

There was a rustling of fabric. Ann turned away from the view, catching a glimpse of the torchlit room beyond the curtain. A few richly decorated trunks, a table, and one very large bed.

"Ann, are you unwell?" The *Kyn* came forward, his face softened with concern. "You are very pale. You do not look well, truly."

Ann tried to smile, tried to tell him she was fine. All she managed was a weak nod.

"Please," he urged. "Sit."

He guided her to the bench, then draped a skin over her lap. A lion's skin, Ann noticed as he settled himself next to her. Headless.

"Eat," the *Kyn* commanded, passing her some bread. She ate. "Now tell me. What troubles you?"

She continued to chew, the bread as dry as ash in her mouth. Was it just the evening light or did the *Kyn* seem larger somehow – his bare chest, with its dusting of black curls, improbably broader, his arms impossibly thicker?

"Tell me," he repeated, "or I will start to guess, and that, no doubt, will embarrass us both."

As he spoke, the *Kyn* reached across the space between them, laying a heavy hand on her arm. Ann flinched, noticeably. The man frowned, drawing his hand away.

"Are you unhappy here, Ann?"

His voice was sad, his eyes now turned toward the dusky hills. Swallows dipped and soared in the sky ahead, the air full of their calls.

"No," Ann whispered. "I just..." She sighed. "I was just thinking about my brother."

"Ah." The *Kyn* leaned back against the wall. "You are very different from your brother, I think."

"Yes."

"He has a talent, I have noted, for being liked."

"When he wants to be."

"Yet he is not – how should I say it? I would guess that he does not have much in the way of backbone."

She peered at him.

"No grit," he explained. "No fight to him."

She let out a mirthless laugh. "And you think *I* have fight?"

The *Kyn* laughed too, a deep, rumbling sound that Ann could feel in the stone of the wall behind her.

"That you do, my girl, that you do."

Ann was quiet for a moment. "I think you've got it wrong."

"Then you have underestimated yourself most gravely."

She could think of nothing to say to this.

"Not everyone is blessed with family, Ann. It is not a thing to be lightly tossed away... Yet nor –" he added, as if to himself – "is duty."

Ann watched him, waiting for the explanation. The man dipped his bread into the lentils and chewed meditatively. After a few more bites, he went on.

"Never doubt, my dear Ann, the value of respecting and adhering to the set order in life."

His eyes were fixed on the distance, his mind clearly miles away from the balcony.

"Does the field-worker, or the tanner – or even the *Kyn* – rail against his fate because he must fulfil a task that was passed to him at birth? No. Does he seek to rob another man of his place because he is dissatisfied with his own lot? No. He knows the value of a life ruled by duty. This is order. It is balanced and it is right. It is what provides purpose in an otherwise senseless world."

"The shield against chaos?" Ann offered.

"Indeed. And *that* is a thing to be most jealousy guarded." The *Kyn*'s hands clenched to fists in his lap. "For there are always those who seek to rob us of it."

The light was fading quickly now, the man's face blurring in the thickening shadows of the balcony. And from deep within the palace, Ann could hear it building. That low, pulsing herald of night. "Who is it?" she whispered.

"The Makronans."

The *Kyn* spoke quietly, as if he too could sense the need for restraint.

"They call off time-honoured agreements with no warning, and *now* –" his bearded jaw tensed, his fist grinding into the muscle of his thigh – "*now*, they open their own trade routes with *our* trade partners, mimicking our art, trading it for *half* the value... They make no outright, honourable challenge, yet they have made it clear that they seek to take what is rightfully ours!"

The fist came down against his leg with a dull smack. But, after a few silent seconds, the fingers began to relax. Hand flattened against skin, massaging the muscle slowly.

"Yet – there is always a 'yet', is there not, Ann? *Yet* these cowards lack our advantage." He turned to face her head on. "To speak frankly, they lack you."

Ann sat very still for a moment. Then she leaned back, and pulled the beheaded lion skin up to her chin. She reached for the glass of wine in front of her. Took a long, deep drink. The *Kyn* remained silent, watching her.

"What," she began after another minute had passed, "do you expect me to do?"

"Your mere presence here is a great advantage to us. And there will be times when I will call on you. And your brother, if he will come. To show your support for Kabyrnos."

Ann said nothing.

"I *am* sorry, Ann." He shifted closer to her – still not quite touching. "I understand the pressure you feel, I do. Yet I must be very honest with you. As it stands, my people may not survive another decade. It strikes me to the core to say it, yet it is the truth. Our way of life has continued uninterrupted for a hundred generations, yet it is now failing. In my reign. For ten years we have suffered – longer than that, truly. It began with my cursed father's rule."

The man was quiet for a moment, the bitterness of his last words echoing in Ann's mind.

"Perhaps it is the gods' choice that we should perish now," he whispered. "Yet I am not so resigned. They would not abandon us without a last chance for redemption. No, I am not resigned. What I *am* is desperate."

She could hear it, the desperation – the pain – in his voice. And she was struck by the strength of her own response to it.

"Is this –" she hesitated, swallowing hard. "Is this because you think we're the successors of the Foreign *Kyn*? Like the *Kynra* said?"

The *Kyn* smiled wryly and shook his head. "The people crave a saviour who will spring from the earth, bringing rain and plenty with him. They are angry, and they are tired and worn. What they have need of is fresh hope. It is hope that you must give to them."

"But – *how*?" she asked, her voice now pitched to the note of panic.

"It is simple, my girl."

The *Kyn* reached out again to place his hand on her arm. This time, she did not cringe away.

"You must stop holding yourself back."

***

The rest of the evening passed in a daze. They ate – a lot. They drank even more, Ann in a panicked sort of despair, the *Kyn* in patient good humour. Once the wind picked up, they even moved into his bedroom – but it was nothing like what Ann had feared. The man sat her down at a low wooden table and introduced her to the game of *mestra*.

Mestra was rather like chess, but inverted, where it was the square one's pawn landed on that dictated the possible movements. Ann quickly found herself out of her depth, her ivory lion's head figurines smoothly dispatched one by one by the *Kyn*'s bull's hooves.

It was very late when Ann stumbled back out into the corridors. She made it only a few steps before she had to stop and lay her face against the cool stone of the wall. The pulse was there still – "*Always*," Ann grumbled – but it was quieter than the hammering in her head.

"Don't *interfere*, Ann," she muttered to herself, rolling off the wall. "You're the *Chosen*, Ann. *Beware*, Ann." She took a few more lurching steps. "Stop holding yourself *back*, Ann."

She groaned, clutching her head.

"Did you enjoy yourself tonight, Huntress?"

Ann reeled back into the wall. A glowing figure stood in the corridor ahead, backlit by a lightwell. Ann blinked rapidly, waiting for the vision to disappear.

"I must say, I thought that you were too proud to be any man's mistress. Yet perhaps I was mistaken. He is a *Kyn,* after all."

"How – *no* –"

Her vision's laugh was high and cruel.

"Excuse me, Huntress. It is late."

And the vision was gone, melted into the dark.

Chapter Nine

"Tell me about the *Kyn*'s father."

Hersa paused, readjusting her grip on the basket of soiled sheets. It was the day after Ann had dined with the *Kyn*, and they had just left the residences, where many of the palace women were taking their midday rest. Despite her persistent headache – and the little servant's objections – Ann had insisted on accompanying Hersa on her laundry-run. She needed information.

"Zelkanus's father?" Hersa repeated.

"If you don't mind."

The girl peered nervously over her shoulder, but all the other servants were well ahead.

"You wish me to tell you about Cryklonus –" she whispered the name – "*now*? *Here*?"

"Please."

The little woman turned without a word and continued walking. Ann hustled to keep up, knowing to stay silent.

"Cryklonus ruled in Kabyrnos for over twenty years," Hersa began at last. "Over twice the usual period of reign, I am told. Though his son's has been nearly as long."

For the first years of his rule the city continued to thrive, but it was only a few years more before the *Kyn*'s greed ran the city into disrepair and dishonour.

Then, in the tenth year of his reign, the earthquakes and drought came. The people began to truly hate their *Kyn*.

"A prophecy was made in the year of his marriage to Erea," the girl continued. "If the *Kyn* were to father a son, that son would be his demise."

Cryklonus laughed this off, punishing the seer who made the prophecy. He had no son, he said. Yet only a few moons later, a young servant girl who he had attacked one night in a drunken fit gave birth to a boy in secret. She named him Zelkanus, which meant "storm's child".

As he grew, Zelkanus became widely beloved. A clever and courageous child, he often protected the other children from the caprice of Cryklonus's Followers. By the age of eight, the people of the palace began to call him *Kounros*: boy hero.

Hersa paused. They were nearing the women's gathering halls, and they could hear shrieks of laughter coming from ahead.

"And then one day," the girl went on, more quietly now, "when Zelkanus was nine years of age, he disappeared. Many feared that Cryklonus had had him killed: the *Kyn* feared the boy's popularity, you see. Yet word soon spread that Zelkanus was alive, hidden away – in the mountains, they say. Though no one knows for certain."

Another explosion of shrieks interrupted their story. Ann winced, and, holding her aching head, peered around the pillars into the gathering hall. A large group of women sat clustered together, leaning on silken cushions. There was something mesmerizing about them – something darkly fascinating in their whispers, in their rapt expressions and hungry eyes. Like a brood of harpies, contemplating their next meal.

Ann hadn't realized she was staring until one pair of those kohl-lined eyes flashed up to meet hers.

"Ann, are you coming?" Hersa asked impatiently from up ahead.

"Yes – yes. Sorry."

The girl continued. The years that followed Zelkanus's disappearance were the darkest that Kabyrnos had even known. Years without order or law. Serfs were used as cattle or worse. Clansfolk were stripped of their titles and properties at whim. Mass executions took place for any who were suspected of speaking against the *Kyn*. The palace became a prison of fear.

The only stronghold in this time of madness was the young Sacred Mother, Erea. She offered what solace and protection she could to the people of the city, and, for the most part, her husband let her alone.

"For it is said that godless Cryklonus feared his wife. She was, to him, one touched by the divine, and the man feared what he could not understand."

And then came the twelfth Day of Life after Zelkanus had disappeared. Cryklonus and his Followers were in the Blessed Courtyard – drinking and gorging themselves on what livestock was left – when a tramp appeared, as if whisked there by the gods. The tramp lost no time in challenging Cryklonus to a duel. The *Kyn* saw that the tramp limped and had no weapon with him. He accepted the challenge readily.

"They say that the fight was very short," Hersa said, pausing at the end of the corridor and setting down her basket. "The tramp ran away towards the altar – without even the trace of a limp – which the drunken *Kyn* took as an act of cowardice. Cryklonus charged, yelling like a madman – until the tramp whirled round and cut short his cries with the blade of the Sacral Axe."

Ann let out a long breath. "So Zelkanus killed his own father."

"Some say yes, some say no. It is rumoured that Cryklonus was not quite dead when he was brought to the oak later that day."

"The oak?"

"Yes. In the Courtyard of the Dying Sun. As you saw on your arrival."

The boy on the tree.

"There is a sacrifice every year. Yet they say that when a *Kyn* hears his call, he must offer himself to the Earth Mother. It has been this way since Kabyrn."

Ann thought of Zelkanus, his powerful body bound to the trunk of that twisted, blackened tree.

"A *Kyn* of Kabyrnos is asked to give all for his people. And there are not many among us who do not owe Zelkanus some great debt. Our *Kounros*."

The girl's eyes were shining, the laundry forgotten on the floor. On impulse, Ann reached to take her hand.

"That was a *wonderful* story."

Ann spun round to see Afratea, posed against a doorframe of the women's hall, harpies pouring out around her. Hersa snatched up her basket and bowed her head.

Afratea let loose a high, cruel laugh.

That laugh.

"Huntress, you never cease to surprise me! One evening, cavorting with the highest in the land, and the next day, hauling wash with the lowest."

The harpies tittered as the woman beckoned Hersa with a lazy wave of her hand.

"Girl, we are thirsty. Fetch us some wine."

"*Prona*," Hersa replied, head still bent over her load. "There is wine in the women's hall, if you would care for it."

"I do *not* care for it. It has grown sour... Perhaps the *Kyn* has finer wine?" Those kohl-lined eyes flicked to Ann. "Huntress?"

Hersa's face snapped up; she stared at Ann.

"Did he serve you only the best of his cellars last night?" Afratea let the question hang in the air for just a moment. "How tactless of me. I did not mean to embarrass you before your little friend."

Ann stood mute as Afratea and her coterie turned their backs on her and returned to their silk-lined halls, still laughing. When they were gone, Ann turned to her friend.

But the little servant was gone too.

**

The next morning, as Ann and Kaenus made their way out through the corridors, it was impossible not to be aware of the hush that travelled with them like a fog. The conversations that paused until she had moved past. The hiss of whispered voices once she was thought to be out of earshot. Ann knew that palace folk would soon find something else to entertain – yet still, she could feel their eyes on her, burning, a brand against her skin.

Not nearly soon enough, they moved out into the narrow, cobbled streets of the Craftsmen's District. This district was dominated by workshops, and the days here began early. Even now, the sun barely above the Thyrtu mountain range to the east, forges were roaring to life, sharpening wheels were sending sparks out onto the street. Men and women ran between the buildings, exchanging morning's greetings and yesterday's borrowed tools. These people had more important things to occupy them than palace gossip.

As they pushed further north, paved road yielded to dirt laneway, workshop to residence. It was an area not dissimilar – at first glance – from the Western or Southern Districts, home to artisan and working-class labourer. Communal water wells, street-front vegetable gardens and fruit trees, pomegranates just reddening. The houses here were smaller, it was true – with many cracks in the mudbrick that had yet to be mended. But it was not these disparities that made Ann pick up the pace as she moved deeper into the northern serf's district.

It was here, in these modest, well-swept laneways, that the hush returned. Women shaking mattresses over roofs pulled their burdens out of sight as Ann moved into view. Running children were snatched out of her way with muttered apologies. Men setting out to field, roadside or workshop moved aside and waited until she had passed, eyes down.

Ann was almost used to the quiet manners of the women who brought her breakfast every morning. She had almost come to terms with the deference and caution she was treated with whenever she'd visited Hersa in her rooftop residence. But these wary, sidelong glances, this utter refusal to meet her eyes, or even to carry on with their lives in her presence, was something else altogether.

Ann hurried on her way, Kaenus at her heels, and it was not long before they made it out onto the open road. Besides a few men leading fish carts, the road was empty. Kaenus loped in the long brown grass that bordered the footpath as Ann pushed into a sprint. The strong breeze rippled through the pines, teasing the cicadas into a reluctant, closing summer hymn. The sky was cloudless, the road dusty, rising and dipping as it made its way down to the water. Ann pushed harder, letting the world melt away in the pumping of her arms and legs, the rush of air through her lungs. And, much sooner than expected, she found herself at the top of a hill, looking down over the port town of Kylondo – and beyond it, the sapphire of the Akrean sea.

Kylondo was set in the curve of the Delun Bay, nestled between the wetlands and the cliffs that made up the better part of the bay's coastal region. The perfect point of access for any coming in from the north. Approaching from the south, Ann slipped into the narrow alley streets that were already swarming with people: old women carrying baskets of shells and sponges, men with faces crisped to the texture of old leather, fish mongers flaunting their gaping prizes. Ann pushed her way through the market square, weaving around fish stalls, ducking beneath lines of hanging octopi, and finally, breaking out into the open space of the wharf.

The wind was stronger here. Ann walked towards the water's edge, her face misted with spray. The waves were tall, sometimes spilling over the gunnels of the high-prowed ships that were anchored just beyond the pier. Sailors were busy loading hulls with clay *pethys* of wine and oil taken from the portside warehouses. Ann closed her eyes, filling her lungs with algae-scented air, tasting the salt on her lips.

"*Prona*?"

Ann turned to find a boy – a strange-looking kid, with the full cheeks of a child, but the lined, weathered skin of someone four times his age.

"You are the Huntress, are you not?" He jerked one callused thumb over his shoulder. "My mates, they made me ask."

Ann glanced behind him to see a group of boys sitting along a low wall. They had paused in their work of untangling a fishing net to stare.

"My mates, you see, they want to meet you."

When she didn't answer right away, the boy's gaze narrowed, accentuating the absurdly premature crow's feet that fanned from eye to temple.

"You do not have to if you do not want to."

"Of course I'd like to," she said.

The boy shrugged. "If you say so."

Ann followed him back to his friends, who immediately dropped their net and slid off the wall. One boy, the shortest and thickest of his companions, stepped to the head of the pack, arms crossed, chin levelled up at her.

"Is it true, Huntress, that you and the Hunter took out that boar with only your bare hands?"

Ann was surprised into a yelp of laughter. The boy's friend – her escort – leaned forward, and whispered, "I *told* you, Prytos."

The sturdy boy stabbed his chin out further. "Is it true that the beast was as large as five bulls?"

Ann bit her lip. "Well –"

"It cannot be *five,* Prytos," said another boy from the rear of the pack. "My father says even the Hithutan beasts of the east are no larger than *three*."

Another boy – a tall, lanky one – chimed in.

"Not true! *My* father says there is a great white beast that sometimes wanders these shores at night –"

"Shut it, Laerkys."

"He has *seen* it –"

"Your father is a drunk!"

"*Your* father cannot tell the right end of an oar!"

Laerkys's knobby fist shot out to add force to his point. As if on cue, his friend – and three others of the pack – launched themselves at him and Ann suddenly found herself in midst of a brawl. For a few seconds, she could only blink down at the swarm of limbs, but just as she was beginning to consider intervening, a voice piped up.

"Did you get to keep the boar's tusks, Huntress?"

The attention of the pack snapped back to her at once.

"Uh – I didn't ask."

"Did you stab it with your spear?" cried another, unhooking his arm from around his fellow's neck.

"Well, *yes*, but –"

"Did it kick you?"

"Did it gore you?"

"Do you have any scars?"

"Yeah," Ann said, choking down another laugh. "I have a scar."

The boys exchanged sideways glances; the sturdy one stepped forward again.

"Can we see it?"

Ann pulled down the neck of her tunic to expose her collarbone, and the boys let out one long, collective whistle, all leaning back. Then the lanky one – Laerkys – lifted his long arm to point back in the direction of the market.

"Is that your dog?"

Ann swore under her breath. Kaenus was galloping out of the market toward her, tentacles streaming from his mouth, as a man ran behind him, waving a copper knife.

Ann grabbed Kaenus by the scruff, and began to wrestle the remains of the octopus from his jaws. The man caught up and was pointing the knife in accusation.

"Is this your dog?"

"Yes, it is hers!" one of the boys behind Ann exclaimed.

"I am –" Ann gave the octopus another tug – "*so* sorry."

Two of the tentacles ripped free. The man's eyes slid from the mess in Ann's hands to her face.

"That was my last one – *Prona*. My wife said I was to barter it for milk."

He glared at her expectantly.

"Tell him who you are!" one of the boys hissed.

"Show him your scar!" cried another.

Ann's teeth bit down on the inside of her cheek to stop herself from laughing. "I'm really very sorry. I can –"

Her arms flew out to steady herself.

A jolt, a sharp one, like a colossal shift in the earth beneath her feet. She glanced back at the boys. Their faces were instantly drawn, eyes wide in alert.

And, only seconds later, another spasm.

"Down!" someone cried.

The boys dropped to the ground – hands over their heads – just as the earth began to shake in rolling shudders that seemed to be rising, swelling up toward the surface from deep below. Ann fell to her knees, throwing one arm over Kaenus. The tremors mounted swiftly, clattering her teeth, grating her bones, and unravelling her thoughts with a din so immense – the land roaring, pottery and glass smashing against cobbles. A rumble sounded from somewhere inland as a cloud of dust shot up into the air. Ann buried her face in Kaenus's fur and held him close as the shaking went on and on, tearing the earth – tearing *her* – apart.

Then, with one last, violent jerk, it was over.

Ann remained motionless, crouched over her dog. The sudden stillness was almost as bewildering as the very first jolt had been.

"Great Mavros have mercy on us," she heard the man next to her whisper.

Raising her head, she saw the copper knife on the ground inches from her face. Slowly, she picked it up and held it out to the man. He stared down at it as if he had never seen it before.

And then there were hands on her arm. Lanky Laerkys, tugging at her.

"Huntress, we must go!"

The urgency in his voice snapped her into focus. She rose to her feet, joints loose, legs quivering. He tugged her arm again then they were running, all running – the boys, Kaenus, the man, the others who had peeled themselves up off the pier – rushing away from the shore and into the town.

"Where are we going?" Ann shouted as they passed through the abandoned market.

"Out," Laerkys called over his shoulder. "Higher."

He darted a glance back toward the harbour. Ann peered back through the gap in the buildings. The water had receded, she saw, the slickly pebbled underbelly of the shoreline exposed. And beyond it, a white-crested wave, rolling in toward the pier.

She flew after the boys.

It was only when they reached the outer edges of the town that Ann dared to look back. The shore was hidden behind the buildings, but the masts of the ships were visible above the rooftops, seesawing wildly. Mercifully still afloat.

A commotion up ahead drew her attention.

"Find your parents," Ann ordered the boys as she began to move toward the crowd that had formed around a half-collapsed building.

The throng was densely packed. Dust-covered people passed back chunks of brick from a large mound of rubble.

"I can hear you, Lyndu," Ann heard a woman cry out. "They are coming!"

Ann worked her way around to the edge of one of the remaining walls, where fewer people stood watching as the pile slowly – too slowly – dwindled. She could see the woman now, a shrunken figure huddled within the broken structure. Ignored in the rush to free whoever was trapped beneath the rubble.

And above her was what little was left of the ceiling. Wooden beams jutted out like exposed ribs, creaking under the weight of the collapsed roof.

An instant's indecision – that one moment to look around, certain that someone else must be handling the situation – then in Ann went, pushing through the line of people, clambering over the debris and into the shadow of the crumbling house.

She took the older woman by the shoulders.

"Please, *Prona*, you must come –"

"Leave me!" the woman shouted, shoving Ann's hands away. "Lyndu, Lyndu – I am here!"

"*Please –*"

The dust filled Ann's lungs, pitching her forward in hacking convulsions. But then – a sound, muted and minute, which nevertheless pierced through the scrape of her breath and the clamour of voices around her. Breath lodged in her throat, Ann craned upward to see a crack racing across the surface of the ceiling.

Her heart stalled in one painful squeeze as the people outside started shouting, the danger now obvious to everyone but the old woman.

Ann hooked her arms under the woman's armpits and heaved backward. The woman shrieked and began struggling like a wild animal, kicking out with her feet – sending Ann stumbling back, fighting for purchase on the uneven ground.

Two large chunks of brick fell and smashed only feet away, showering them both with shrapnel. Then, a loud snap from above, followed instantly by a warning scream. No time to look, Ann clenched her teeth, and launched them both backward.

Into a wall of hands. The old woman was hauled away and Ann was dragged back onto the grass as the bricks began to rain down, shrouding the rubbled remains in a veil of dust.

"Lyndu!" the old woman sobbed, crumpling to her knees.

But Ann was still being led back – doubled-over, almost choking now – through the crowd and out. She was urged down onto a rock, and a waterskin appeared in her blurred vision.

Ann took a long draught. Her throat cleared. She inhaled deeply. Coughed. Inhaled again. Then squinted up at her rescuer.

"What are –" another cough – "*you* doing here?"

The High Steward's smile was uncharacteristically solemn. "I could ask the same of you."

Before she could retort, the man took hold of her shoulders and gently pushed her against the rock.

"Rest, Huntress. You are overtaxed. I will return to escort you to the palace soon."

She tried to raise her head in protest, but his hands remained firm.

"Rest."

***

"Do you think she is dead?"

"No, look – she breathes."

"Well, she was *almost* dead."

A mixture of awe and disappointment in the pre-pubescent voice.

"Do you think she will cry?"

"Girls always do."

A sharp smack and a low grunt.

"The Huntress does not cry!"

Something wet slid against her cheek and her nose filled with the unique bouquet of dog breath. Ann held her hand out to pat Kaenus's neck and the boys fell quiet. She sat up, looking around at their expectant faces.

"Did they –" she swallowed, the glue of her saliva smacking audibly – "did they get the man out?"

"He was crushed," was the matter-of-fact reply.

"It is no wonder," added another.

"A very old house," said a third. "Only the oldest cannot withstand these smaller tremors, my father says."

Ann gaped. "Small?"

The boy shrugged bony shoulders. "Last year, one of the tremors washed out half the town. Over fifty people were drowned."

"And there was the Great Atonement."

The sturdy boy, the *de facto* pack leader, moved to stand next to the rock. When he was certain that he had Ann's full attention, he went on in a low, sombre voice.

"They say that many generations ago, on a day very like this one, Mavros brought down his wrath upon the people for their impious ways. The skies darkened to the colour of dried blood. The ocean wailed like a thousand widows as the waves came down, destroying everything in their path. Every city from the island of Fernu to the villages south of Kabyrnos was smashed to dust."

The boy paused, frowning at someone over Ann's shoulder. Instantly, the pack shifted, moving closer to the rock.

"Huntress," the High Steward beckoned. "It is time."

Ann sighed. "I've got to go now."

As the pack reluctantly moved aside, the man gripped Ann's elbow, pulling her upright. She nodded back at the boys and let herself be half-dragged toward the road.

"I see that, despite your love of mortal peril, you have found yourself some able bodyguards," the man remarked as they waded through the dry grass.

A gurgle of laughter escaped before she could stop it. The man peered back at her, a strange expression on his face, but he said nothing until she turned to start walking southward along the road.

"Where do you think you are going?"

She frowned. "Back to the palace?"

"Not that way, Huntress."

He gestured to a tree on the other side of the road. There was a single horse tethered to its branches.

"But, but," she stammered, "there's only one…"

The edges of his mouth curled up then, his long eyes glinting.

"Is that a problem?"

***

"You must *relax*," the High Steward told her.

Ann was leaning against the front of the saddle, holding herself as still as each jarring step would allow. She tried to readjust, to loosen up – she was so damn sleepy for some reason – but the warmth of the man's arms around her was like an actual, physical strain on her muscles.

"If you do not relax, you will fall off the horse."

They were moving at a brisk walk, Kaenus trotting easily beside them, totally oblivious to Ann's distress.

"Traitor," she mouthed at him when he glanced up, tongue bouncing.

"May I ask what you were doing in Kylondo?" the High Steward inquired after a few more minutes had passed.

Ann's head had been lolling forward, but she snapped it back up.

"Oh, I was just on my morning run…"

"Ah, yes," he said. "Your 'runs' are widely spoken of."

The silence that followed this somewhat scoffing statement was so pronounced that Ann could easily guess where the man's thoughts had strayed. Her runs were not the only thing being spoken of at the palace that day. This thought stayed with her, needling her more with each jolt of the saddle.

"And why were *you* in Kylondo?" she demanded irritably.

The High Steward sighed, his breath warm against the back of her neck. "I personally inspect all of the estates in the Kabyrnos region once a moon cycle."

"Oh." Ann squirmed in her seat again. "Bad timing today, I guess."

"You must not fidget so," the man scolded. "You are making the horse nervous. As for my timing, I believe it was divine will, Huntress. If I may say so, you should not simply charge off alone. You could have been seriously injured today. Or worse."

The reproach was irksome; the fact that he was right was nothing short of maddening.

"*You* went off on your own."

"*I* had five attendants with me," he replied. "I sent two of them off to the palace to seek further aid and had the remaining stay behind to ensure that no one else was hurt." He paused for a moment. "I do not know what kind of place you come from, Huntress, yet I feel I must tell you that Kapreitu is not a tame land where young women may safely roam wherever and whenever they choose."

Ann chose not to respond to this. Another long minute passed before the High Steward asked,

"What are you thinking of now?"

"Nothing," she sighed.

"Please. I am interested."

She leaned back ever so slightly. "I was just thinking. Not being free to roam, or see new things, or meet new people... It's not really living, is it?"

It was the High Steward's turn for silence. The horse slowed to a rhythmic amble as the man's arms sank to his sides. Ann began to yawn.

"You are not very like the women I know, Huntress," the man said slowly. "To your advantage, I think... You are as wise as you are fair."

Ann's yawn cut off with a groan. "Oh, please."

"Please?"

"Please no flattery. I'm too tired for it."

The man surprised her with a laugh, loud and brash. "You forbid me my greatest ally!"

Eyelids drooping, Ann chuckled. "You'll get over it..."

"Perhaps."

***

An anxious voice pierced her sleep.

"What happened? Is she okay?"

"She is well, Hunter, only worn out," said another voice, much nearer – so near, in fact, that Ann could feel the vibrations of it in her body.

Her eyes fluttered open. The stables stood before her, and she was now fully nestled in the curve of the High Steward's torso. She could smell the tang of his sweat, feel the pressure of his jaw resting against her ear.

She lurched upright, smacking his chin with her temple. The man grunted as Ann's vision spun. She began to fall forward.

Arms wrapped around her, easing her off the horse. She blinked up into round, tawny eyes. *His* eyes, so like hers. Smiling faintly, she let her own drift shut again as she leaned into her brother.

"I do not think she has had much to eat or drink today," she heard the High Steward say.

"I'll get her back to our rooms," her brother replied. "What happened?"

"There was another earth tremor."

"Yeah, I felt it. Was it that strong, though?"

"It was in Kylondo."

There was a pause.

"What was she doing in Kylondo?"

"She was… running."

Ann heard the restraint in the last word. Then she heard both men chuckle.

"Sounds about right," her brother said. "Well, thank you, High Steward. I should get her back."

"I will send a servant to you with water and food. Please let me know if you think she needs the attention of a healer."

"Yeah, of course. Thanks."

Nik set off, Ann bouncing gently in the cradle of his arms. She lay limp against his chest, letting his familiar scent wash over her.

He must have mistaken her for sleeping, because as they passed into the sweetly-scented shade of the pine grove, Ann felt the arms around her tighten. Then she felt the stubble of his cheek press against her forehead.

"Thank God," her brother whispered. "Thank *God*."

Chapter Ten

The shuffle of her feet over the dewed, crisp grass. The chirping of crickets, the call of an owl. The air outside was moist and cool as the world slept on under the mantle of darkness.

Only now could Ann begin to calm herself. Only now did her heart beat slow enough to let her notice the trees gliding past as she padded back out through the eastern pastures. She paused under the low branches of a wild olive tree, recalling the previous day – being fed, watered and washed, then put to bed in sight of the yellow-haired statue that stood on her trunk. That sisterly presence, watching over her as she slept.

Yet she'd woken later swamped in fear. Night had long since staked its claim and the pulse had returned, the walls seeming to pound with it – shaking, the stones shaking, narrowing in around her like a constricting throat. Before she'd properly understood what she was doing, she'd found herself running out into the open air. Pulse still perceptible, but left behind. For the time being.

Ann hoisted herself up into the branches of the olive tree. She leaned her head against its bark and watched the moon as it arced above her, back toward the palace. Eventually moving out of sight.

The darkness grew thicker. Ann remained as she was, motionless, perched in the tree. Watching. Waiting. But there was nothing.

Then came the whispers of a new day. The first of the autumn birds beginning their pre-dawn harmony. The shapes of the mountains in the distance sharpening in the evanescent light. This was a spectral world of monochrome, of dusky silhouettes. A world of illusion, fleeting and untouchable. A world out of time.

Time, now, to return.

As she passed through the eastern portal and back into the dark passageways, Ann felt the hum of the palace envelop her, the soft, pulsing pressure against her skin. She moved quickly, these corridors now well-known. Ten minutes and she'd be back in her own bed, ready to greet the sun as if she'd never been without it.

She paused. Footsteps, from the adjoining corridor.

Knowing it would still be some time before the palace folk woke, Ann moved to the edge of the wall as silently as possible and peered around.

A dark figure at the end of the next passage. Shifting, swelling, moving toward her.

Ann's head whipped back around the corner, hand over her mouth.

She listened as hard as she could, every nerve in her body trilling high alert. The footsteps drew nearer, shuffling and brisk. Ann risked another glance.

"Halt!"

The two women faced each other through the shadows. The other's features still unrecognizable – except for the silver halo that flashed as she took a step forward.

The Guard Commander.

Ann ran.

"*Halt*, I said!"

Ann hurtled down the corridor and wheeled around the corner. She heard the pounding of footsteps behind her as she flew down the next passage, then veered to fling herself down a flight of stairs.

She knew this was idiotic: she hadn't done anything wrong. But when she heard the dull smack of the other woman's feet at the base of the stairs behind her, her legs propelled her faster, and she raced onward, no thought to direction.

She was approaching a series of sunken halls, separated from the passage by a low wall. Without thinking, Ann planted her hands on the wall and vaulted over, landing a few metres down with a grunt. She pushed herself hard against the wall. Several breathless seconds later, she heard the Guard Commander run past.

But before she could exhale, the footsteps stopped.

Moments passed in total silence. Except for the stairs at the other end of the hall, the room was closed off.

The Guard Commander was moving again. Fifteen, maybe twenty feet to Ann's right. Just by the staircase.

"Huntress –" an urgent whisper, just by her shoulder – "in here. Quickly!"

Ann bit her tongue to stop herself from screaming. The voice had come from a dark recess, a small opening in the wall at her back.

She heard the Guard Commander's footfall on the steps.

Ann whipped around and squeezed herself through the gap. She landed about three feet down, her breath flattened out of her. And as she lay gasping noiselessly, she heard the soft scraping of stone, and a gentle thud.

Utter blackness. She could tell that the space was narrow – she heard it in the muted movements around her. The dulled clicks and scratches; the muffled swishing of material.

And then, light.

A woman stooped over Ann, her thatch of curls brushing against the ceiling of the tunnel as the lamplight flickered across her face.

The winking priestess from the *Kynra*'s Chamber.

"You look done in," the priestess observed, smiling.

"How did you – how could you know I was there?"

The priestess shook her head, curls bouncing. "Intuition."

"Intuition."

"Yes. Intuition."

The priestess's grin widened, the shadows deepening in the creases of her face. Making her look distinctly impish. And just a little bit crazy.

"So who was it?" the priestess asked.

"Who was –?"

"Chasing you."

"Oh. The Guard Commander, I think."

Ann felt a twinge of misgiving as soon as the words were out; this was not a face to trust too quickly.

But that curly mop was shaking again. "Unpredictable as the sea, that woman. So calm and still, nary a cloud in sight, then – without a splash of warning – a storm is upon you."

"Personal experience?"

"My father was a fisherman."

Ann blinked. "No, I meant –"

The priestess leaned in abruptly, so close now that Ann could see the earthy green tints of her eyes twinkling in the lamplight.

"I feel I should tell you," the priestess said, "I believe we shall be great friends."

Ann blinked again, several times. "And you are…?"

"Erysia, at your service. Sister of the Sisterhood."

"Oh. You're Hersa's friend."

The priestess leaned back, clapping her hands together like a small, delighted child. "She has mentioned me then!"

"Many times."

"Good. It is always nice to know you have made an impression." Then the priestess turned away and bent to retrieve what appeared to be a small mountain of robes. "Now we best be on our way. Come."

She dumped the entire armful into Ann's lap and turned away into the passage.

***

Ann let out a groan of relief as she tipped her load into the only empty nook left. They'd been walking in the tunnels for at least ten minutes, Ann often forced to stoop so low that her knuckles had grazed the earthen floor.

"There," the priestess said, surveying her hoard with satisfaction. "The last of the lot. You bed in the eastern quarter, correct? This way then."

Erysia swung back in the direction they'd come from. They walked for less than a minute before she swerved left at a fork in the passage, then almost immediately left at another. Ann wiped the sweat off her brow, trying to ignore the feeling that this warren of tunnels went on without end, in ever-tightening circles.

"How do you know your way so well?"

"I have been wandering these passageways since I was a girl," Erysia replied over her shoulder. "They were dug out of the earth in the early days of Kabyrnos. I doubt if any others know of them now. Very handy in a tight spot, they are."

The priestess turned left again then paused at what appeared to be a solid wall. Passing the lamp back to Ann, she placed both of her palms against the upper wall and shifted the stones sideways into a hollow space.

"Come, Ann, and quickly. I must be back before they wake."

Ann clambered out and followed the woman through the still-shadowed corridors to the door of her own apartments. But the priestess did not stop there. Without breaking stride, Erysia opened the door and walked through into the twins' common room.

The light from the lightwell was growing brighter, illuminating Kaenus's snoring form below. As usual, there was no sound from Nik's room.

"Is this your bedchamber?" Erysia asked, pointing to Ann's curtained doorway and stepping in without waiting for a reply.

Ann peered over the woman's head at the narrow room that had become so familiar to her – the low, rumpled bed, the trunk, the watchful little statue. A private sanctuary, now disturbed by this unlikely intruder.

"Hm," the woman murmured. "Very nice."

And then she was hastening back to the door, where she paused, flashed back another grin and winked.

"I expect we will see each other very soon, Ann."

And the door shut silently behind her.

***

The sun was higher now, the morning light glistening off the near-nude bodies that filled the Blessed Courtyard.

Ann took another step back into the shade of the column.

After the previous day's adventures in Kylondo, she'd thought that maybe she could use a change of pace, a day or two's break from running. But as she stared out at the masses of people grappling and grunting their way through morning exercises, she realized she might have been too hasty.

The courtyard was a battlefield. The men were sparring and wrestling with open hostility, brotherly even in competition. The women were leaping, tumbling, their graceful movements barely concealing the covert looks and whispered remarks. Ann could see her brother, his golden head dipping in and out of the fracas. She caught a glimpse of Afratea, tossing her tresses as if the world was watching.

Ann turned away.

She skirted along the perimeter of the courtyard, keeping within the shadows of the building. If she rushed, she could squeeze in a run through the city. But she had only just passed the grand staircase before she was forced to stop, caught up in a flurry of activity.

Women – obviously angry women – were crowding together in the pillared space just off the courtyard. It took Ann a few seconds to realize that, although they were garbed in plain dresses, these were priestesses. This was Sisterhood ground.

"Quite the sight, do you not think?"

Erysia was leaning against the pillar to Ann's left.

"Rather like hens, running about without their heads."

"Sisters!" cried a voice from within the swarm.

The women fell silent. Ann peered back at Erysia, who was smiling vaguely at nothing in particular. She turned back to the crowd: the priestesses were stepping aside as someone made their way through.

"Brace yourself, girl," Erysia whispered.

The throng parted, and out strode the Guard Commander, flanked by two of her guards. The guardswoman looked around, her eyes falling on Ann, then – incredibly – skimming past to land on Erysia. She approached.

"Sister. I am charged to discover the whereabouts of certain ceremonial garments. As I am sure you are aware, they went missing some time in the night."

A small noise escaped Ann's throat; the guardswoman's gaze snapped toward her.

"And only a day before the ceremony too," Erysia sighed. "A true tragedy."

The Guard Commander's attention snapped away again. "It was suggested to me that you might have something to say about this."

"Oh, I have far too much to say in general, Guard Commander. The Sacred Mother often tells me so. Yet I do not think any of it would interest you. The affairs of the Sisterhood, you know."

The guardswoman merely waited, unblinking.

"It must all seem so dull to you," Erysia went on. "You, who lead such an exciting life, upholding order. Thrill of the *chase* and all that."

The guardswoman's eyes narrowed to slits. Ann felt sweat prick at her upper lip.

"Erysia!"

All three women turned to find Sister Aralys pushing her way through her fellow priestesses – who were all now watching the corner in silence.

"The Sacred Mother wishes to see you," Aralys barked. "In the Chamber."

Erysia only smiled serenely at her sibling.

"Now!"

"Of course, Sister. No need to raise your voice." Erysia turned back to the guardswoman. "My apologies, Guard Commander. We will have to save our chat for another time."

Then, with another angelic smile, she flitted away through the angry swarm of priestesses.

Ann turned to make her escape.

"I will offer you a piece of advice, Huntress."

Sighing, she turned back. Aralys was glowering up at her, teeth bared in a sad pretence of a smile.

"If I were you, I would not keep company with my younger sister. She brings only shame to all those who know her."

"Perhaps the Huntress wishes to follow the Sister around, rescuing her victims one by one," the Guard Commander interjected, waving her guards off to return to the throng. "It would certainly be a swifter path to glory than lurking in mountains or waiting for earth tremors."

The woman turned to follow her guards then paused, as if struck by a thought.

"Though perhaps not easier than the occasional visit to an illustrious bed."

Aralys brayed. The guardswoman shot her an irritated glance before taking her leave.

Ann lost no time in following her example, storming back in the direction she'd come from – intent now only on putting as much distance as possible between herself and the snare of Sisterhood chambers.

"Huntress!"

Ann groaned. "What now?"

An acolyte, red-sashed and wide-eyed. Her black-eyed escort from the day after the banquet.

"Apologies, Huntress. The – the Sacred Mother has summoned you."

Ann pressed the heels of her hands against her eyes, hard.

"H-Huntress?"

She dropped her hands, unlocked her jaw. "Yes. I just… I had a feeling it would be something like that."

***

Erysia was gone by the time Ann entered the Chamber of the Earth Mother. Only the *Kynra* was there, straight-backed on her throne, waiting as Ann took her place before her.

"It is not often that we see you in these parts, Huntress."

Ann replied with a bow. As she straightened, she forced herself to meet the woman's gaze, holding it. Briefly noting the firm – but not pinched – curve of her mouth, and the cool – not glacial – glint of her eyes. It appeared that the *Kynra* was in a good mood.

"I had hoped to see more of you during this past season," the woman said. "Alas, I understand what it is to be young in the days of Light. The world awaits, does it not?"

Ann nodded cautiously.

"And I understand that you have been seeing much of my charming husband."

Ann shifted her weight, careful to keep her face neutral. "Not much, no."

"You have joined him. In his private chambers."

"He asked me there, and I went. You asked me here, and I've come."

"How obliging of you."

A slice of the usual steel; Ann finally let her gaze drop.

"I would warn you against him," the woman went on after a moment, "yet I know youth loves nothing so much as a challenge. So I will tell you only to take care."

Ann peered back up at the *Kynra*. The downward parabola of the woman's mouth was stretched flat in what Ann could only assume was meant as a show of sympathy.

"For we women have so little margin for error in this life, Chosen."

A few seconds passed, the chamber silent except for the trickle of water in the fountain. The rustle of the doves in their nest.

"Tomorrow is the celebration of the birth of Mavros," the Kynra said. "The Day of Death, we call it. I wish you to participate."

Not a request.

"What does that – involve?" Ann asked slowly.

"A sombre procession. You will walk with us through the streets of the city. March at my side for all the people to see. After nightfall, there will be private celebrations."

"Private?"

"The citizens feast in their homes."

"And the priestesses?"

A flicker of something passed over the Kynra's face, quickly suppressed.

"We celebrate Pritymnia's aspect of the Mother. We shall await the Epiphany."

Those slate-coloured eyes locked on hers. Cool, unyielding. Offering nothing more.

Then the woman's head turned toward the door. "Ah, Darkylus."

Ann had not noticed him enter. The gaunt priest moved forward without a sound and deposited a parcel in the Kynra's outstretched hands. For a few seconds, the woman simply held the parcel, thin fingers stiffening around it protectively, like a cage. Then, slowly, she peeled back a layer of the wrappings.

The Kynra's head fell forward into her hands and she exhaled. A small, shaking sound, an indistinct sigh of pain or pleasure and then nothing. Time seemed to pause with her as she remained half-collapsed around the parcel.

"This confirms all."

Her voice not even a whisper, the words carried out on the draught of her breath. Then, slowly, she straightened. Thin cheeks quivering, hands working quickly yet delicately, stripping away the remaining wrappings.

To reveal a statue.

"I – I found it on Mount Crytus," Ann stammered, offering an explanation though none was requested.

"This confirms all," the *Kynra* repeated, her finger tracing the curves of the statue's breasts, the flow of its yellow hair. "Be here tomorrow, Chosen. After the midday rest. Now you may go. Both of you."

***

At first, it had been uncomfortable. Embarrassing, even. Yet the monotony had quickly driven Ann to the tranquilized state of the long-sufferer. She'd watched the hem of the *Kynra*'s skirt swing over the petal-strewn street in its ceaseless sweep; she'd eyed the faces of the Southern District, the Western District, the Sanctuary District, all melting into one another as they passed. Always silent, the city struck dumb by the relentless passage of the Sisterhood procession. Only the smallest sounds of life had escaped: the rebellious shuffling of young feet; the occasional grunts of the priests behind, bearing the weight of the litters on their shoulders as they'd marched on and on. Ann wondered that they were still standing. She wondered that their passengers had not passed out from heat. The still-stifling heat of the first day of autumn.

She'd been shocked when she'd first laid eyes on these women – at least twenty priestesses, all within days of childbirth, born up to parade swollen breasts and bellies for all to see. She and Nik had been told in no equivocal terms that the Sacred Mother was extremely strict about the Sisterhood vows of celibacy. Clearly, there was an exception. Ann had been curious enough to ask, but the opportunity had not presented itself. From the moment she'd arrived back in the Sisterhood antechamber, the *Kynra* had kept her close.

The old woman had been unusually quiet throughout the afternoon, maintaining a silence that seemed to sizzle in the air around her – an impression aided by the onyx beads that seemed to have multiplied, covering her body in a darkly flashing second skin. Ann had kept her mouth shut, but her eyes open. Searching, if truth be told, for her new, delightful "friend".

It had to have been Erysia who'd told the *Kynra* about the statue. Ann still couldn't guess why; she was more preoccupied with the thought of that creepy man slinking into her bedroom. As the afternoon wore on, and Erysia still had not shown her face, Ann began to accept that she was not going to get an explanation any time soon.

The procession had finally returned to the palace, making its way up the open northern passage – the Bull's Corridor, the palace folk called it – and up into one of the western halls that overlooked the courtyard. It was dusk now, the last of the sun pouring in from the windows of the adjoining hall. The servants began to filter in, handing out bowls of food. The *Kynra* had disappeared. Ann slumped back against the wall, tugging at her tight, heavy gown. At least she'd been permitted to keep it tied in front.

After most of the bowls had been emptied, the priestesses began to rise. The *Kynra* still absent, a quiet hum of chatter grew, dispelling the sense of frozen twilight that had kept Ann fixed in her seat. She wandered alone amongst the other women in their groups of two or three. She saw many of her old tutors, solemn-faced Mothers who nodded to her as she passed. She made brief eye contact with Sister Aralys, who was glaring at her from across the hall as if trying to impress on her the depth of her unwelcome. The skies had deepened to purple. The last slivers of orange light vanished from the floors. Soon, the priestesses fell back into silence, and Ann knew without looking that the *Kynra* had returned.

Just at that moment, the pulse slipped back in, almost unnoticed between her own quickening heart beats. Gently, like an old friend greeting her, wrapping its soft, throbbing arms around her.

The *Kynra* was standing in one of the doorways of the hall, glittering arms held out to the side and bent at the elbow. Like Ann's statue. She began to speak. She spoke simply, quietly, her voice carrying throughout the hall. She spoke of the day of Mavros's birth. A day of life and a Day of Death. For it is the moment we are born, she said, that we begin to die. And so we give ourselves a day to mourn – and a night to celebrate the new life of the Mother in every child. And the sacred balance is maintained.

"Balance, again."

Nik's voice rang clear in Ann's memory.

"Always," the *Kynra* had rejoined. "It is the shield against chaos."

Chaos. A man crushed beneath his own house. Half a town, washed out to sea – an entire island, shaken to pieces. Young flesh melted to the bark of a tree. A yellow-haired woman swimming out into oblivion. A boy forced to take the life of his own father for the freedom of his people.

Where was the balance in all this?

Antigone...

The voice swelled around her with the beat of the pulse, soft and rasping. The light was gone now.

Antigone...

"Huntress."

The sea of priestesses parted, their faces turned back toward her. Blank, featureless.

"Huntress, come."

Hands pressed at her back, gently urging her forward as the floor pulsed beneath her feet. Then one hand gripped hers, nails digging in. The *Kynra's* voice blared in the foreground while Ann's mind floundered in a pool of dark.

The lost Idol of Kapreita, the woman was saying. Found – at last. Reclaimed from the rock of the Sleeping God.

The collective gasp of the priestesses like a sigh of wind rippling over water as Ann struggled to keep afloat.

"And she who found our relic for us," the *Kynra* cried, "she who is Chosen to bring our people back to their proper place at the feet of Pritymnia, shall, for this night of Darkness, be reborn in the body of the Mother. Fellow Daughters, let us honour our Epiphany!"

***

The moon had not yet risen. The priestesses were visible only as shadows, flitting back and forth quietly, quickly. No one spoke. The only sounds were the rustle of dresses, the snapping of wood, the trickle of water somewhere nearby.

They'd walked for a long time, another procession out through the emptied streets of the city, stopping on the parched banks of Ados – the river that ran from the northern shores of the island to the south. The river of passing souls, they called it.

The air was growing colder. There was no pulse now – not so far from the palace – but still Ann remained unmoving in the night. Watching, waiting.

A light flared ahead. The faces of crouching acolytes blazed into view then faded back into the dark. Slowly, the light grew again, illuminating a pyramid of branches from within as the fire licked upward.

Ann watched the fire grow, barely perceiving the movements around her – the Mothers stepping out of the circle to take glowing objects from the kneeling acolytes. The one woman who approached her, holding a clay vessel to her mouth.

A trickle of sweat ran down Ann's forehead, cool against her burning skin, as the slender nozzle slipped between her lips. Smoke filled her mouth, thick and sweet as incense. It burned as it travelled down her throat. Her head spun. She took another breath, then another, then the nozzle was removed.

Ann ran her tongue over her lips and felt the night air flush against them before they warmed again in the heat of the fire. That one sensation occupying the whole of her attention until she noticed the clouds of smoke billowing upward. She could almost hear the smoke dissipate, like the gentle hiss of water on a hot element. Her mind shifted inward. To the sluggish beat of her heart, the throbbing just beneath her skin, blood drawn to the surface by the fire's heat. The heat that burned, yet did not hurt her.

The pyramid of fire shifted and crumbled, sending sparks flying upward like a rush of fireflies. Beyond the dancing flames, the *Kynra* waited.

"Daughters of Pritymnia!" The woman's face was a fire-lit mask, eyes lost to shadow. "Tonight, we honour Mavros, the bearer of Light and the bringer of pain. He who protects, and He who calls at the end of our days, drawing us back into the Dark."

Ann's heart gave a reluctant thud; she felt the blood course through her body in a rolling wave as she watched that mask, its slash of a mouth moving – speaking only to her.

"Tonight we call on Him in His own element of darkness. Oh Great One who dwells beneath the land, hear our plea!"

Then the mask fell back, exposing the shimmering length of throat, and the woman let loose an ear-splitting cry. The other priestesses joined in her call, a pack of wolves howling at a moonless sky. Ann swayed on her feet, staring into the crater of fire. Lips shaping the name without speaking it.

Mavros.

The cry stopped, but the name rang on in Ann's ears like the sounding of a knell.

A flash of light drew her eyes. A glowing knife, plucked out of the fire.

Then the *Kynra* was beside her again, her hand gripping Ann's once more. The pressure sent delicious currents up Ann's arm as she stared down at the glowing blade, orange heat rippling over its surface. The blade that was meant for her.

Because she was Chosen. But not by the Mother, no, not by anything so whole and good. She was Chosen by the Son, in His darkest, foulest form. The voice, the bull god – one and the same. It was *His* voice that called to her in the darkness, *His* heartbeat that hammered in the walls, *His* horned form in the courtyard that night, promising to return them, warning them against interfering – though it had been He who had dragged them to this place to begin with.

In a way, she'd always known it. And she could face it now, numbed as she was by the drug. She had felt Him watching her, waiting for her, ever since she'd arrived here. Perhaps even long before.

"Oh Great Mavros, hear our plea for mercy!" the *Kynra* cried. "She who is, this night, the vessel of Your Mother, will offer You Her life's blood. Take this sacrifice, this blood of the Mother, and have pity on us!"

The *Kynra* dragged the knife across Ann's palm. It seared, white hot, the pain radiating out in exquisite release.

Then her arm was wrenched up and the priestesses unleashed another roar. She felt the hot liquid trickle down to her elbow; she felt the adrenaline surge, building at the base of her spine.

The roar abated, rolling into a chant as the women moved back, clearing the space around the bonfire. Fingers threaded into the base of Ann's hair and her head was jerked back.

"*Move*," the *Kynra* hissed.

Then those hot, thin hands travelled down her neck, down her back to settle on her hips, guiding them from side to side. The chanting rose, swelling up into the night like the fire that roared on, flames licking at the borders of her vision. The heat, the voices, the ache in her hand, in her heart – everything rolling together in one pounding rhythm. She danced, her whole body quivering with the sound of the singing, growing louder and wilder as the singers broke apart. A cacophony of screams, calling her back into the black pit of her soul.

And then Mavros was there with her, as suddenly and absolutely as if He had never left her side.

Antigone…

She danced on. She could feel His pulse inside her chest, His breath frozen in her lungs. She brought her hands in front of her face to find that they were not hands at all but claws, smeared with her own blood. Claws curling around her throat.

Antigone...

She danced faster, her body thrashing, the pressure around her neck tightening. As the darkness edged in around her vision, she let out one cry. And, as if from a very long distance away, she heard the *Kynra* cry out too and then a wave of echoing voices, letting loose in their ecstasy.

Her knees folded and she crumpled to the ground.

Antigone.

Book IV

Chapter One

The days following the night of Death were the some of the darkest Ann had ever known. That first evening, Hersa coming to find her soaked in her own sweat, hand still caked with dirt and blood, and swollen with infection. Then, the fever dreams taking hold. The dreams that sent her down into the labyrinth of her mind – only to be pulled out after an age by the deep rumblings of a man's voice.

Nine days, he told her from her bedside. Nine whole days not knowing whether she would live or die. Then her damp hair was smoothed off of her face as she lay with eyes closed, thinking that the alternative might have been preferable. She was tired, so very tired.

That dreadful night of the bonfire stayed with her even as the infection waned. The beautiful haze of the drug, mutating as the night wore on. Then, the moon rising, a dull red against the ebony of the sky, her body shaking on the ground beneath it. And those faces. Those featureless faces, those monsters of smoke and ember – twisted abominations, half-man, half-beast, crawling out of the river toward her. The nightmare demons sent to recover her, to drag her back down into the blackness beneath the earth.

It was a night of horror, leaving her with so many questions and only one certainty, one fact as clear and immutable as the angry gash across her palm: He had claimed her. Mavros had claimed her, and His mark on her was now impossible to hide.

Especially from Nik, who could – she was sure – smell His presence on her like a foul odour. He would always come after nightfall, when she was likely to be asleep. The curtains would rustle aside and he would step into the room, his face half-hidden in the shadows. He would stand there only for a minute or so before he would disappear again, and the curtains would fall closed. And she would be left alone again with her dreams.

***

One afternoon, the brightness that poured in through Ann's window darkened to grey, bringing with it a cool, moist breeze that had her shivering in her bed. That night, Hersa brought her another blanket and a couple warmer dresses. The little servant came every evening, and although Ann rarely spoke, the girl would sit on the edge of the bed and tell her of the world outside. There was very little rain, she said – much less than there should have been at this time of year – yet it would be enough, she thought, to bring some of the flowers. She sketched out an image for Ann of the pink, gold and white blossoms that would soon dust the hills. She explained how, on Kapreitu, the Season of Death was, in fact, a season of new life. A season of healing.

Then one evening, Hersa did not appear. Ann waited until the daylight had faded completely before she returned to a restless sleep. The next evening, the girl still did not come. So, on the following day, Ann went in search.

And found her friend, sitting on her window sill in the servants' residence, mending a dress.

"Ah, good," the girl said when she spotted Ann ducking through the doorway. "Tomorrow you will go running, yes?"

***

Ann moved out into the eastern pastures with Kaenus at her side, too weak to run but feeling her strength grow with each step out into the warm air. Hersa had been right: this was autumn reimagined. The few bouts of rain had washed away the dust and haze of summer. The grass was soft beneath her feet. The cypresses that ringed the stadium seemed taller, greener. The Thyrtu mountains seemed so close that Ann felt that to stretch out her hand to them would be to prick her finger on one of their razor sharp peaks.

And without the oppression of the heat, the valley had burst into life. Labourers lay nets beneath the olive trees, shaking out the green fruit with long rakes. Women carried woven baskets that brimmed with quinces and grapes up the valley slopes as children snuck down to pick at the fruit that was left behind to dry in the sunshine.

It was truly a season of healing. Even the slash on her palm was now no more than a red, raised ridge. It was hard to recall, with the sun on her face and Kaenus bouncing at her side, the thoughts that had preyed on her for so many days. As if that sense of taint was a mere symptom of the infection, now expunged from her system.

An encouraging thought. And one that Ann was, for the moment, more than willing to believe.

***

Again, Ann found herself staring out at the early morning tumult of the Blessed Courtyard. It had been several days since she'd returned to the weaving rooms, and this morning she had woken knowing it was time to join the others for exercises. Why, she couldn't say exactly. Something new, perhaps. Something to keep her facing forward.

This time, she only let herself hesitate for a few seconds before stepping out under the open sky. A group of five women not too far from her laughed as they attempted double handsprings and front flips. They made it look easy. Fun, even.

Ann gazed into the south, searching – she only realized once she'd finished – for her brother, who was very obviously absent. But toward the centre of the courtyard, a crowd had formed, with men and women alike massing in a large circle. Flashing movements shot up above their heads. Curious, Ann moved forward.

She heard them before she could see them, the pair in the cleared space, breathing hard as they brought their staffs in at full force. She was mesmerized by the rhythmic dip and swing of the weapons, and barely noticed the two that held them – or the people that moved out of her way as she approached, eyes following her instead of the match. The moment she registered who the two men were, however, she took a step back in retreat. But the circle had closed again behind her.

The *Kyn* and the High Steward, both slick with sweat, moved with incredible speed as they laced in and around each other. The *Kyn* had just knocked the other man's staff to the ground and was lunging forward in attack; the High Steward dodged the expected blow, snaking in to grab the larger man's weapon. The *Kyn* braced himself and heaved his staff up and around. Ann had never seen strength like that; she had never seen anyone move the way the High Steward moved when he broke his fall in a somersault and bounded back to his feet in an instant. But the *Kyn* was on him again, storming down in a shower of strikes that the younger man would have managed to evade had he not become distracted. His eyes met Ann's over the *Kyn*'s shoulder – and then he was on the ground, his ankles swiped out from below.

Polite applause followed, quickly petering out. The *Kyn*, still turned away from Ann, was booming with laughter as he helped the High Steward to his feet.

"Not so superior are you now, my friend?"

The High Steward did not respond, and after a moment, the *Kyn* turned to find out why.

Ann could feel the stillness that spread out into the courtyard then, gripping them all for no more than one, two seconds at the most. The two men looking at her, her looking back – the rest of the courtyard looking back and forth between the three of them. Then the High Steward stepped forward.

It was in that moment that Ann understood that something had shifted. The *Kyn* hung back, merely nodding at Ann, as the High Steward closed the distance between them. Whatever barrier there had been for him before was now gone.

And if she had noticed, the palace folk certainly had. It wouldn't be long before her name was pried from the *Kyn*'s and joined with the High Steward's. They wouldn't care which man she was attached to, she knew. So long as someone had claim.

"Huntress," the man greeted her, slightly out of breath. "I cannot tell you what joy it gives me to see you so well. Do you wish to join our exercises? Perhaps I can make some introductions? Find you –"

"No – no, I'll be fine."

It was a moment before he replied. "Of course you will be. Everyone knows that the Huntress is more than capable of taking care of herself."

Before she could think of a reply, the man bowed. "I shall bid you good day, Huntress."

And he returned to the *Kyn*, who slapped him on the back and declared a rematch.

Ann stood for a second, stunned. Then she turned and walked, eyes fixed straight ahead, back toward the southern quadrant, when she paused just behind a laughing young woman.

"Excuse me?"

***

Ann lay on the flagstones. The girls had shown her a standing somersault – a manoeuvre that they'd clearly considered very basic. One hour later, the best Ann had managed was a glorified face plant.

The girls all smothered their smiles. The quiet-looking one, Tefkelerea of the Zyklos clan, helped her to her feet. The courtyard was beginning to empty. Ann dusted off her tunic, rubbed her elbows, and let her eyes roam over the courtyard – for the first time, really taking the time to look.

"Athyla?"

The musician's daughter unfolded her long limbs from a stretch and looked up.

"Where do the servants exercise?"

"Servants do not partake," Helkys, the youngest of the group, declared.

Ann turned to peer at the girl. She was thirteen, maybe fourteen. She had uttered the statement with the kind of innocence that only a child could get away with.

"Why not?"

"Dawn exercises are a privilege, Huntress," Athyla explained. "A form of worship of the Mother. And of course, servants are not permitted to take part in rituals of any kind."

Ann didn't respond. The courtyard was now nearly empty, and she could hear the sounds of the palace kicking into gear. The muted bangs from the lower eastern workshops, the clang of metal from the guards' barracks, just off the Bull's Corridor to the north.

Then Alrydia – beauty of the Gerytus clan – giggled. "Look, girls."

All five followed her gaze to the north: a few men were emerging from the Corridor – one man much taller than his companions, with a towel draped around his neck, blond hair dark with sweat.

"I hear that he exercises in the official training grounds now," Alrydia whispered breathlessly. "Is it true, Huntress?"

The girls all swivelled toward Ann. Backs straightened, eyes brightened. This was a transformation Ann had seen countless times.

"I don't know," she replied. "Where is that?"

"Out in the city," Lyndea whispered.

"It is where all the most promising trainees train," Alrydia sighed.

Ann frowned, not understanding.

"For the Tournament," Tefkelerea explained quietly.

Ann looked back at Nik sharply. He had spotted her now; his eyes lingered on hers for a moment before he slowed, said something to his companions then broke away to head in her direction. Two of the girls let out strangled little squeaks as he drew near. He paused, bowing.

"*Pronae*."

Ann felt the fluster of activity around her – the adjusted tunics, the hair brushed off faces.

"May I borrow my sister?"

"Of course, Hunter," Alrydia and Lyndea chimed in unison.

He unleashed the full force of his smile on them. Somewhere behind her, Ann heard Helkys sigh.

"Ann?"

She turned to the girls. "I'll see you tomorrow?"

Tefkelerea was the only one to reply. "Yes, Huntress. Tomorrow."

Neither Ann nor Nik said a word as they moved past the still-gaping girls and down the steps of the winding staircase toward the baths. Nik, Ann could tell, had something on his mind.

"I hear you're training for the Tournament," Ann ventured as they turned down an empty corridor.

"Mm."

"And when's that taking place again?"

He shot her a look. "*Very* subtle, Ann."

They walked another minute or so before he spoke again. They'd just entered the corridor of the baths, steam pouring out of the two doorways ahead, when Nik's fingers grazed her elbow to hold her back.

"I was wondering," he began, eyes fixed somewhere over her shoulder. "Do you think that we... I mean, it's just that, the longer we're here, the harder it is to believe sometimes that we're ever..."

He trailed off and Ann swallowed a surge of panic – the inevitable response to anything that reminded her of that night, not yet far enough behind her. Or what she had learned then.

"That we're ever going back," she finished for him.

"Yeah." Nik took a breath, a slow in and out. "Sometimes I think that I dreamt it. That – man. In the courtyard. You know?"

She couldn't respond.

"Ann?"

"No," she managed after another moment. "You didn't dream it."

Nik nodded slowly. Then he inhaled, pushing his shoulders back.

"Alright then."

He began walking again. But just before they reached the point where they had to break off from each other, he turned back to her.

"Can I ask you a question?"

She nodded.

"Do you really *want* to go back?"

Ann was silent for another moment. "I... don't think it's up to us."

***

The days settled into a steady rhythm, all irregularities smoothed out or tucked safely beneath the surface. Ann completed her first workable web of fabric – a plain, patternless thing that even the Mistress of the Loom described as "good enough". She began to alternate her morning routine between running and joining the practices in the courtyard, where she worked on loosening her body, stiff from years of hard runs and soft chairs. She soon came to understand that the gymnastic manoeuvres she was being taught were not only feats of skill but leaps of faith: they required a deeper level of trust in her body, in the muscular memory that made flipping her legs over her head as habitual as putting one foot in front of the other.

More than that, it took a belief in the fact that if legs fell short, or hands faltered, the consequences would be bearable.

The days grew shorter, cooler. Midday rests were now a thing of the past, and people worked through to the late afternoon – a time when palace servants were still kept busy. Ann spent more time than usual on her own, rambling out in the eastern pastures or in the valley orchards. She always returned early, though. She wanted to be well toward unconscious by the time the sun set.

One evening, she was returning to the common room when she heard a giggle come from Nik's room. She froze, hand still on the door. By the time Nik's lower tones had joined the giggler's, she was backing out as quietly as possible. When she returned later, the room was silent.

The next morning, Nik's curtain was still closed. She tiptoed to the common room door – and found, waiting on the other side, the *Kyn*'s servant.

She was expected the following evening, he informed her. At sundown.

The fever dreams returned that night. The black outline of horns rippling against the brightness of fire, and the voice, rasping, whispering to her that she ought to take more care. That she ought not to interfere. Then the laughter, cawing, shrieking like a crow's – jolting her from her sleep. Leaving her shivering, blankets drenched in sweat, walls still pulsing to the beat of His mirth.

The moment that the first hint of sunlight hit the floor of the common room she was up and out. She ran hard, long, going north, towards the sea, stopping at a fork just before the descent into Kylondo, then continuing east. It was just after midday when she and Kaenus returned to the palace.

To find the door to her apartments open.

Kaenus slipped through as she reached for the handle. She heard him bark even before she'd stepped in to see him at the door to her bedchamber. Curtain ripped down. Mattress half-blocking the doorway, straw spilling out.

Ann stood blinking down at the wreckage of her room. After almost a full minute, she stooped, brushed aside her dented mirror and picked up her gown, the one she'd worn to her banquet and the Day of Death ceremony. It had been left lying in the centre of the room, spread-eagled, its skirts stripped to ribbons. Ann's hands tightened to fists around the shredded material. The dress was not well-loved, it was true, but she was only too familiar with the kind of labour that went in to making a garment like this.

This was a ruthless act of vandalism. Pure intimidation.

Tugging a strip of the yellow cloth from the bodice, she strode out of her room, out of her apartments, leaving the door swinging behind her and Kaenus scampering to catch up. The whole way down to the Blessed Courtyard she could think only of one person. One person who might have heard of her meeting that evening. One person who *liked* to intimidate.

Ann hammered her fist on the door that led into the guards' barracks. She could hear laughter and shouts coming from within.

The door opened and a teenage boy gaped up at her. Beyond were a handful of men, sitting around a lamp-lit table, in the middle of a game of gambling. One of these men paused in shaking a handful of flat clay tiles, and asked,

"Can we help you, *Prona*?"

"I need to speak with your Guard Commander."

"Her patrol ended at midday. She should be back presently."

"Good," Ann said, striding in past the boy. "I'll wait."

As the men tentatively returned to their game, Ann paced along the length of the long, windowless room, which smelled strongly of fresh beer and old sweat. Affixed to the inner wall were weapons and armour of all kinds – spears, short-swords, helmets, breastplates, and a few mottled cow-hide shields that Kaenus found particularly intriguing. Ann was reaching up to touch the smooth, wooden curve of a bow when she heard the door open behind her.

"– and I shall need to you to double your rounds of the north-eastern main." The guardswoman strode into view, looking over her shoulder at the four guards who followed her. "Head Cook has made some complaints, though the gods know the man sees mischief in every passer-by. Tell Niklas too, whenever he deigns to arrive –"

She halted, finally noticing Ann by the weapons wall. "Are you planning to wage war, Huntress?"

Ann tried to force a smile. "You could say that."

The Guard Commander regarded her for a moment then moved over to the table and poured herself a glass of beer. She gestured to the men – one flick of her finger – and they stood and exited the room. As Ann approached, the woman settled herself onto one of the emptied stools and took a deep drink from her tankard.

"Can I offer you anything?" she asked, stretching out her legs and sighing.

"No."

The woman shrugged, drained her tankard and began pouring herself another. "How can I help you, then?"

Ann dropped the strip of material onto the table; it fluttered down, settling over the gambling tiles.

The Guard Commander glanced down at it, then back up at Ann.

"You shall have to elaborate."

"Someone has been in my rooms." She said it slowly, holding the woman's gaze. There was scarcely a flicker of reaction. "They've destroyed everything."

The guardswoman placed her tankard back on the table.

"I see. And nothing is missing? No. Well, I can tell you that this sort of thing does happen from time to time. I will have two of my men search your rooms to see if there is any sign of the intruder's identity. Beyond that, I would advise you to use the bolt when you are in, and keep anything of value safely hidden."

Ann watched the other woman carefully. Her thick, blunt fingers curved around the handle of her tankard, the weary lines around her mouth deepening as she looked up at Ann.

"Huntress," the guardswoman sighed after another couple seconds had passed, "the upper eastern residences are already patrolled ten times per day. That is over three times as often as the other residences, with the exception of the servants', which are only patrolled once, if that. I do not have the manpower – nor the inclination, if I am to be quite frank – to increase the number of patrols."

Ann was taken aback. "That's not what I –"

"Then is there anything else I can do for you?"

Ann stood for a moment staring down at the strip of material on the table.

"Was it you?" she asked.

The Guard Commander's gaze was cool and appraising. After long moment, she nodded down at Kaenus, who had been drawn to the table by the tone of Ann's voice.

"That is a fine dog you have, Huntress. A true, loyal warrior, I can see." She held out a hand, and Kaenus's nose jutted forward to sniff it. "No, it was not I who snuck into your bedchamber. Subterfuge is not, as you might say, my weapon of choice."

"No. You prefer blunt threats and violence."

The woman brows shot up, and then – to Ann's amazement – she laughed. One bark then she crossed muscular arms over her chest and leaned back against the wall.

"You have been listening to gossip."

"Excuse me?"

The Guard Commander heaved her feet up onto another stool with a small grunt. "People are always willing to believe the worst – especially of outsiders. A truth best remembered, Huntress."

Ann regarded the woman as she stretched out, sipping her beer. Here, in her natural habitat, she was almost a different person from the sentinel who patrolled the palace corridors.

"I see," Ann said, at length.

"At last. Now, is there anything else I can do for you?"

Ann shook her head and made her exit.

***

Ann had only just left the barracks when Kaenus darted away from her, zipping north along the Corridor. Within seconds, he had disappeared into the north-eastern passages – heading, Ann suspected, for the kitchens. She rushed after him.

Yet just as she'd reached the turn-off, a curly-haired figure darted out in front of her, cutting her off, and a voice from further down the corridor screeched, "Come back with that food, wench, or I will have your flesh for stew!"

Erysia paused only long enough to make a face at Ann. Then she was gone, disappearing into a narrow passage on the western side of the Corridor.

"*Guard! Guard!*"

Ann heard the man thumping in from the east; she heard the jostle of metal coming from the south.

She'd had her fill of guards for the day. She veered west.

The passage she followed was narrow and dark. Ann walked on for some time before she spotted a doorframe ahead, a light flickering from within. She felt a twinge of misgiving, but continued on. As she passed the doorway, a voice called out,

"Chosen."

Ann froze. The chamber was cavernous, lit only by a single beeswax candle that was wedged onto the ground by the door. Ann could only just make out a long pool sunken into the stone of the floor.

"Chosen," the *Kynra*'s voice repeated from the darkness beyond. "Come."

Ann moved forward slowly, her eyes adjusting as she went. The *Kynra* was standing up to her hips in the water, totally nude except for a few strings of her onyx. She was painfully thin, Ann saw, her breasts flat against her ribs, as if in evidence of an exhausted motherhood, suckled dry. And cradled in her bony arms, a child of clay.

"We bathe our idols in sacred waters once a day, Chosen," the *Kynra* said as Ann stopped by the edge of the pool. "To refresh the spirit within them. How is your hand?"

Ann's fingers balled around the still-tender ridge. "Healing."

"You are honoured, Chosen. It is the divine mark of the Earth Mother."

Ann said nothing.

"I knew that you would find your way to me eventually," the woman went on. "I have something I wish to say to you."

The *Kynra* stooped over to submerge the statue of Kapreita in the pool.

"I wish you to join our Sisterhood."

The words reverberated against the walls of the chamber. Ann remained silent, her eyes on the spot where the woman's wrists disappeared beneath the black, rippling water.

"You will swear in as a Sister – and move up quickly, I suspect. Yet it is not a step to be taken lightly. Once you bind yourself to Pritymnia, you are bound to her rules of devotion – and, above all else, of chastity. There can be no turning back."

"Sacred Mother?"

The *Kynra* looked up toward the doorway where Sister Aralys was entering. The statue's yellow head bobbed to the surface.

"It is time for the Blessing. I have brought your robes, as requested."

The priestess helped the *Kynra* into an undyed robe. As she stepped back, her eyes flicked up to Ann. And her lips curled into a tiny, gloating smile.

Not an unusual look for her – but still, it made Ann think.

Yet the *Kynra* was on the move and Aralys was scuttling ahead to retrieve the candle. And as the older woman swept through the chamber, robes flapping behind her, her voice echoed back to Ann.

"I await your decision, Chosen."

***

That evening, Ann was ushered into the *Kyn*'s brightly lit antechamber. The *Kyn*, who seemed to have been waiting on the edge of his seat for her, welcomed her warmly, drawing her over to the turtle braziers, draping a shawl over her shoulders, offering her some wine. Once he was assured that she had everything she could possibly want, he settled back onto his bench and started asking her questions – about her health, about how she was spending her time. He did not directly mention the brief encounter in the courtyard; he only asked how she was enjoying the exercises.

She replied that she was enjoying them very much. Then she mentioned that she had noticed that there were no servants partaking.

The *Kyn* looked thoughtful at this. He began talking about how having the various exercise grounds throughout the city was a relatively recent development. Before that, he told her, people were forced to take exercise in whatever space they could find – or to forgo it altogether. Now, it was a proper community endeavour. It brought the city together. And a cohesive city is a strong city, he said.

After a slight pause, he mentioned that he had relied heavily on his High Steward to bring it all about.

"A fine man, Heremus," the *Kyn* said slowly. "Well-respected, too. From one of the oldest families on Kapreitu."

Ann fiddled with the beaded fringe of the shawl.

"And he has a very high regard for you, Ann."

When several more seconds had passed in silence, the man leaned back and sighed, combing his large fingers through his curls.

"I have a favour to ask of you, Ann."

Ann waited, apprehensive.

"In a short time from now, we will be visited by an envoy of Pyitan and Hithutan ambassadors, our most important trading allies. This will be the last visit before the rains set in, and it is essential that we make a good impression.

"Meet them at my side. Let me show the world the mark of the gods' favour on our people."

Ann's hand balled around her scar again as the man continued speaking.

"Let me show them our Huntress – and, I hope, our Hunter. Talk to you brother for me, Ann. Convince him to attend. I believe he will listen to you."

"I doubt it…"

"He will."

Ann pulled the shawl more tightly around her shoulders. "I don't… do very well," she said. "In big, public affairs, I mean."

The *Kyn* regarded her for a moment.

"A bargain, then," he said. "What if I were to say that if you do this thing for me, I will return the favour? Anything that is within my power."

"… Anything?"

"Within my power."

Ann sat for few moments, watching the torchlight play over his features. It was hard to tell what the limits of his power might be. It was easy to imagine them boundless, here, in this vast room, within this immense palace, which seemed to her almost a universe of its own. And he, its only true god. She looked into those eyes, glowing in the low light. Watching her, waiting for her response.

"I'll do it," she whispered. "And I can't promise anything, but I'll manage Nik too."

He smiled. "Thank you, Ann. And your request?"

She inhaled. "Permit the servants to join the morning exercises. In the Blessed Courtyard – or wherever they want. The city serfs too."

The *Kyn* was quiet for so long that Ann was certain he was going to refuse her.

"This is what you truly wish?"

"It is."

He took a long, deep draw of air – the taking on of the weight of the world, it seemed.

"Then consider it done."

***

The rest of the evening passed pleasantly, any lingering tension dispelled by the arrival of dinner. Sesame scallops and herbed legumes, Ann's favourite Kapreitan meal. It was followed by a game of *mestra*. As with their previous games, Ann was defeated quickly. They began again, the *Kyn* trying to explain to her the tactical advantages of each move – trying to drill the principles of the game into her head. Yet after she proved her ineptitude twice more, he decided that she'd suffered enough.

"For tonight," he added. "As with every skill, Ann, one must practice to attain excellence." His eyes twinkled at her. "Or mere competence, for some."

Ann left promising to return in nine days. She then slipped through the corridors, trying not to think of the hum of the walls around her. Or the mess that still waited for her in her chamber.

Or what would come of her request the following morning.

Yet it was a couple of mornings after the *Kyn*'s proclamation was made that the changes began to take effect.

Hersa was among the first of the servants to come to the Blessed Courtyard – to be met with total silence. Ann joined her in the north-western corner, where they spent a long, tense session going through the motions, never permitting their eyes to wander away from their own little group.

They were joined half-way through by Tefkelerea. At the end of the session, the servants filed away to the sound of muttered comments, and a familiar, scornful voice remarking loudly that "some people will do *anything* for attention."

"Well, that was bleak, was it not?"

Erysia was leaning against the courtyard wall, just out of sight of the Sisterhood rooms. Peering into the priestess's lively face, Ann recalled that there was something that she'd been wanting to ask her. Something she was upset about, from before that dark, dark night. Yet it was hard to bring to mind. All the smaller things of before seemed so distant. Sighing, she settled herself beside the priestess and peered down again at her palm.

"I heard them, you know."

Ann glanced up. The sound of Sisterhood chanting was now floating out from the rooms beyond, and the woman's hazel eyes were unusually serious.

"In the Chamber," the priestess went on quietly. "He was very angry."

Ann was about to ask who, but then realized she already knew.

"He said that she could tyrannize her priestesses all she liked, yet she was not permitted to hook you into your schemes and risk your life again."

It was a moment before Ann could reply. "And the *Kynra*?"

"She said it was not his decision to make. No danger would befall you from within the Sisterhood, she said."

Something in the priestess's words resonated. Ann mulled it over for a moment and realized that the Sisterhood did offer a kind of sanctuary. A layer of insulation between her and the world at large. And it was just possible that, in devoting herself to the Mother, she might also be protected from the Son.

The chanting had grown louder. Erysia sighed, pushing off the wall. Before she rejoined her Sisters, she gave Ann another sombre look and said,

"Take care, Ann."

The sky was growing brighter but Ann remained where she was, standing alone in the courtyard.

Something was mounting within her. A thought, a picture that had been forming in her mind for some time now, though she'd refused to look at it head-on.

She was a pawn here. That fact seemed unavoidable now. But appeasing powerful players – both seen and unseen, with motives clear and unclear – was not a game for which she had any skill. Nik, with his talent for pleasing, would have been a much more suitable contender. Despite this, Ann had been telling herself she'd been scraping by. That she'd been steadily and unobtrusively chipping away at her remaining time here. However much time that was.

Yet if that horrible night – or even the past few days – had shown her anything, it was that her grace period was coming to an end. The time was fast approaching where she'd be forced to make a choice. And standing there, utterly exposed in the glare of the courtyard, Ann simply prayed that it would be the right one.

Chapter Two

Over the next few days, Ann abandoned her runs in favour of courtyard exercises. It took some time for all of the other girls in her group to join her and the servants in their corner, and by the time they had, more servants had joined and were already making groups of their own. Ann was surprised that so many servants wanted to add to their already very full days, but remembering Hersa's secret lessons with Erysia, she thought she understood.

When she joined the *Kyn* in his rooms for their next appointment, he congratulated her on her "triumph" in the courtyard and she was forced to admit that she had not yet approached Nik about the ambassador's welcome. The man fixed her with a stern gaze and informed her that the envoys were due before the next day of rest. She assured him that she would take care of it, and then spent the remainder of the evening being methodically out-manoeuvred in game after game of *mestra*.

The following morning, Ann went out on her first run in many days. It was promising to be a perfect autumn day: warm without being hot, sunny without glaring. The flowers that Hersa had promised had appeared, along with fresh winds blowing in from the south, bringing with them dustings of red sand from the Charnerat Sands across the sea. The mountain peaks from east to west had acquired caps of snow and rings of cloud; the lowlands, a deeper hue of green. The island was abloom.

Ann returned to her rooms with hands full of blossoms. She stepped into the apartments just as a girl stumbled out of Nik's bedchamber.

"– it's not that late," came Nik's voice from behind the curtain.

"H-Huntress," the girl stuttered. She stood, frozen in the act of tying a red sash around her waist.

Nik emerged. "You can prob–"

He spotted Ann. Swore. Rushed to the door and slammed it shut. He thought for a moment, then tore the flowers out of Ann's hand and thrust them toward the black-eyed acolyte.

"Take these. You can tell the Sister you went for an early walk. Go."

The girl nodded, her face white as Nik opened the door again and peered both ways down the corridor.

"Go," he urged her. "Now."

The girl obeyed. Nik closed the door softly behind her, and then stood for several moments before turning back to his sister.

"Ann –"

"I forgot to mention," Ann said loudly. "There's an envoy of ambassadors coming in the next couple days, and we were asked if we would greet them. In an official capacity."

"Ann, I know –"

"Will you do it?"

Nik let out a heavy breath, his whole body deflating with it. "Sure. Yeah. Just tell me when."

He took one final look at her and then slunk out of the room. Ann waited for the thud of the door behind him, then she sunk onto a stool and buried her head in her hands.

"Oh shit," she whispered. "Shit, shit, *shit*."

***

A few days later, the Pyitan ambassadors arrived. The official welcome was set to take place on the following afternoon, but the *Kyn* had requested that Ann and Nik be present to greet them. Ann arrived at the large southern terrace just as the Pyitans were being escorted up the steps of the Mountain View Entrance by the High Steward. She was shepherded to her position behind the *Kyn*'s right shoulder – next to her brother, who did not acknowledge her arrival.

There were about fifteen Pyitans in total, all male, followed by a line of slaves who were bent-backed with gear and ushered out of sight immediately. Having lived so long in Kabyrnos, these men looked almost more foreign to Ann now than the Kapreitans had at first: the darker skin, the shorter, bluntly-cut hair, the beaded collars – the feminine, kohl-lined eyes. A few of them wore tall, golden headdresses too – none taller than the one worn by the youngest man, to whom the *Kyn* addressed himself.

Ann had come to understand that the Pyitan visit was a great honour bestowed upon the Kapreitans. The land-loving race rarely ventured from their sandy kingdom, yet when the *Kyn* had sent a small fleet of his own vessels to Pyit, the *Pyirat* had, in turn, sent back a younger son and several of his most trusted advisors.

The Hithutans from Higard – the largest settlement along the eastern mainland coast and Kapreitu's point of access to all the tribes further inland – arrived the following morning. Nik was summoned to greet them; Ann was not. She began to understand why when she joined the welcoming delegation that afternoon in the Hall of the Charging Bull.

The Hithutans were – to all appearances – a rugged band of warlords, complete with greasy beards, shaggy hair and weapons dangling openly from their belts. They stared at Ann and the other women present in a way that made her flesh crawl. Their eyes stayed on her during the *Kyn*'s speech and the presentation of the gifts; they only looked away while the dancers were brought in to perform the Flight of the Cranes. Pressed up against the wall with the painting of the bull, there was nowhere to retreat. Ann almost cried in relief when the *Kyn* invited them all to follow him to the hall that overlooked the Blessed Courtyard.

The courtyard had been transformed. Stone blocks with jutting horns formed a vast ring in the middle of the space. Within the ring, the flagstones had been covered with sand; outside it, along the border of the courtyard and craning over the roofs and balconies, crowded the people of Kabyrnos. When the *Kyn* moved into view, the crowd began to cheer and stomp their feet. The moment he raised his arms, the noise stopped.

"Every person here knows what balance is required in this life," the *Kyn* announced, his voice booming out into the space. "It is a never-ending dance between mankind and the divine forces that rule it. For the will of Mavros is as unknowable as it is steadfast."

As the crowd murmured its assent, Ann felt herself go cold – as if a wind had passed right through her, chilling her to her marrow. She squinted down at the bright patch of sand nervously.

"The painting," her brother whispered beside her.

The painting. The charging bull that she'd felt at her back throughout the entire welcoming ceremony.

The *Kyn* was still talking. Age-old alliances. Survival in an unpredictable world. Only together – he was saying – could they be strong.

Then a braying roar ripped through the courtyard and the crowd erupted once more. Four people dressed in coloured tunics appeared at the mouth of the Bull's Corridor. Like acrobats they flipped, leaped and tumbled their way into the horn-enclosed space as the people of Kabyrnos screamed and threw flowers into the sand.

The roar sounded again and the crowd simmered. The four acrobats backed up to form a straight line along the middle of the arena. One of them – a man dressed in blue – called out.

She saw the heads of the crowd turn, gazing north again. She heard the Pyitans and Hithutans murmuring their appreciation as she too looked toward the Corridor.

An enormous bull was tethered in the opening, heaving against his ropes.

She felt her brother stiffen beside her. She felt it in her own muscles, his adrenaline coursing through her veins. Their eyes met for a single instant before returning to the bull. To those horns, thrashing in front of those very same walls.

The beast's ropes were cut just as a spear was thrust into its hindquarter. The bull's shriek was lost in the cry of the crowd as the creature vaulted forward, thundering through the gap in the barrier – which was immediately closed as another stone was dragged in place behind it, sealing the beast in with the four acrobats.

Three of whom were sprinting forward now, the red acrobat to the east, two green acrobats to the west. The red acrobat drew out a long siren from the back of her belt. The blare of the horn sounded over the cries of the mob and the bull veered, swinging toward her. The two greens were now sprinting up and around, behind the bull, as the blue acrobat blew twice on his own siren from the south.

The two green acrobats were within feet of the beast as it slowed, turning to face the blue acrobat. They lunged forward, springing off their hands, off their feet and into the back of the bull's protruding horns.

Ann gasped along with the crowd as the green acrobats curled their bodies up around the horns – dragging the bull's head down with their weight. The creature screamed again and kicked its hind legs out, sending a storm of sand into the air.

The acrobat in blue was moving forward, slowly, holding his hands in the air, displaying himself for the crowd, who cheered and clapped to the beat of his steps. Ann heard a few of the Hithutan lords shout from the other side of the balcony, slamming their goblets into the balustrade as the man in blue continued to stroll toward the wild, bucking creature.

Then the man stopped. He crouched. Placing his siren in the sand, he launched forward into a full sprint, toward the bull's head. The crowd fell silent as he plunged into a series of rolls and flips, then sprung forward to take hold of the bull's horns – just as his two green companions dropped and rolled away. The bull's head bucked upward; the blue acrobat was tossed into the air. Ann followed his soaring form as it curved up, then back down, hands touching briefly on the bull's back then springing forward again – directly into the waiting arms of his red partner.

The crowd roared, the acrobats bowed as the bull's handlers climbed into the ring, tossing spear after spear. Bringing the beast to its knees within seconds.

Ann felt a hand on hers, prying her fingers apart. She tore her eyes away from the scene below to find that she'd been gripping her brother's arm so hard that she'd left white marks on his skin.

Nik took her hand, drawing her back from the screams, from the clanspeople and their applauding guests. Back from the sight of the sand, now soaked to a deep, dark brown.

**

A few days before the twins' seventeenth birthday, Nik arrived home with a stack of failed tests that needed to be signed. Their stepfather signed them, but not before letting Nik know that stupid punks were often kicked out of school if they weren't careful. Which would not be permitted. Not in *his* house.

The following week, the principal called during dinner to inform their stepfather that Nik was being expelled.

The argument that followed was their most vicious yet. Ann remained plastered to the kitchen wall, unable to look away from the two men who stood on opposite sides of the room, hurling everything they had at each other. Their stepfather screaming that Nik was a loser who would never amount to anything. Nik shouting back that their stepfather was an impotent drunk who couldn't keep a woman happy even if he paid her. Then the plate of pasta being smashed against the wall as their stepfather warned Nik to watch his filthy mouth – or he'd get what he had coming to him.

Nik left then. Left the kitchen and then the house. Ann cleaned up the mess as quietly as possible, then slipped upstairs.

It was two weeks before her brother returned. Ann lived every moment of those weeks in the terror that the phone would ring, bringing news of some horrible accident. Of a body found in a ditch somewhere. When he did return, slinking up the stairs late one night, he didn't say a single word to her before disappearing into his bedroom. And their stepfather said nothing about his closed door the next morning. He merely took his coffee, picked up his briefcase and went to work.

Only two weeks before, Ann would have sworn that there was nothing worse than the screaming that reverberated in their day-to-day lives. Over the course of the next month, however, she discovered that what was worse – far worse – was the silence.

It was during this time that Ann met a handsome young man, a lawyer who'd come to her school to talk about the courtroom. He'd been waiting for her in the parking lot afterward. How old was she? he asked. Seventeen, she replied. Oops, he said, grinning. No harm in a friendly coffee though, was there? No, she said. No harm.

In fact, it turned out that it was those friendly coffees that made her life bearable in the following month. Without them, she thought, she would have had nothing at all to hold on to.

When the month was up, however, and her brother had left for good, she finally understood what it really meant to have nothing.

***

"Are you okay?" Nik asked as he closed the door to their apartments.

Ann collapsed onto a stool, then nodded. Nik began pacing the room.

"You?" she asked.

"Yeah."

After a few more seconds, he stopped pacing. Turned toward her.

"You're not going to tell anyone, are you Ann?"

She sighed, passing a hand over her face. "Of course not."

"I didn't mean to get you involved."

"I know."

"We only came here because there was nowhere else to go. I figured it was the safest option."

A long pause.

"What is it, Ann? Spit it out."

"The safest option would have been not to do it at all."

Nik blinked, then began pacing again.

"I don't see why. She's of age. She wanted it too."

"It's against their laws, Nik."

"It's only a stupid rule made up by the *Kynra*."

"And who do you think has the right to make rules?"

Nik's chin shot up but he said nothing.

"You heard her on that first day," Ann went on quietly. "People are *punished* when they break the rules."

He rolled his eyes. "Preach me another one, Sister Ann."

A strike that was too close to home. She rose from her seat.

"You still think you can run away from anything, don't you?"

He stopped pacing again, back now against the wall. He opened his mouth to say something but then snapped it shut and looked away.

"Don't you realize the position this puts that girl in?" she demanded.

"Don't patronize, Ann. Of course I do."

"You *think* you do, but you couldn't have possibly thought it out. Because if you had, there's no way you would have put her at such risk."

"Jesus, Ann, you're such a goddamn *mouse*!" His handsome mouth twisted as he stepped away from the wall toward her. "You hide away, terrified of speaking out of turn or stepping on anyone's toes. At least I'm *living* my life. Grow a pair, would you?"

"Why?" she said coldly. "So I can use people to make me feel like a man?"

His whole body went still.

"You *bitch*," he uttered. "No wonder you're always alone. No one can stand to be near you for long."

Ann's mouth fell open.

"You spoil *everything* around you," he hissed.

She took a step back, staring at the man that was her brother.

"Who *are* you?" she whispered.

* * *

Ann ran through the empty corridors, tripping over her heavy skirts, unaware of where she had gone or where she was going. Tears blurred her vision, her brother's twisted face in her mind. Eventually, she stumbled to a stop, pressed her forehead against the wall and burst into tears.

He found her there minutes later.

"Huntress?"

She jolted away from the wall, wiping her eyes with the heels of her hands. The High Steward stepped forward.

"Huntress, what is wrong – who has harmed you?"

"N-nothing," she stammered. "No one."

He gently took hold of her shoulders. "What is it, then?"

She looked away and sniffed. "What are you doing here?"

"I came looking for you when you left so suddenly. The banquet is beginning shortly, and I thought –"

"Go back," Ann urged, trying to pull away. "I'm fine."

"You are not."

She felt his fingers on her chin, pulling her gaze up to his. His face was surprisingly sympathetic. Ann felt the tears pricking at the corners of her eyes again.

"Was it the bull ceremony?" he asked softly. "I can understand that for someone who is unused to such things –"

She shook her head, not trusting herself to speak.

"Please, Ann."

If he hadn't used her name, she might have been able to pull it together.

"It's *nothing*," she sobbed. "Nik's just so – he – he just says whatever – *hurts* whoever –" She buried her face in her hands and tried to steady her breath. "It's nothing. Really."

The High Steward was silent for a long moment. "Do not concern yourself with this now," he said slowly. "If you cannot return to your rooms, go to the women's baths, or somewhere quiet. I will tell the *Kyn* that you were taken ill."

Ann dropped her hands. She hesitated, then gave him a small, watery smile.

"These troubles have a way of sorting themselves out, Ann. You will see."

She let out a shaky breath. "If you say so."

"I do."

***

The foreign envoys remained at Kabyrnos for another thirteen days. Ann attended a few more events where she was required to stand by the *Kyn*, smile, and occasionally nod as the Pyitan dignitaries spoke at her. They seemed fascinated with her – her mysterious appearance so many moons back, her hair, her height, her eyes. By the end of their visit, she was half-convinced that they thought of her as some kind of visiting deity. The Hithutans, however, never spoke to her. They only leered from across the hall as they downed their host's wine and devoured his food.

Nik did not attend any further gatherings. Ann did not see him again in their apartments, nor out in the eastern pastures where she escaped at every possible opportunity.

On the morning following the ambassadors' departure, Ann was intercepted by the *Kyn*'s manservant, who told her to meet the *Kyn* in his apartments after the midday meal.

"We are going for a walk," the *Kyn* informed her when she arrived. "Fetch your shawl, fetch your dog and let us go!"

The *Kyn* led Ann and Kaenus out into the city. He took them to the wine and olive oil facilities, hectic in post-harvest production. He showed Ann the water-filled *pethys* where the crushed green olives were stored until the oil had seeped out and risen to the surface. He then brought her to the enormous Royal Armoury, where he led her through rows of hanging weapons to a door at the back of the building, sealed in wax and stamped with an impression of his own ring. This chamber – he told her – was only opened rarely, and by him. It housed ancient relics, such as the sword that had belonged to Kabyrn, the furs of their Kypran forefathers. It even used to hold a necklace that had once belonged to Kapreita. A golden collar shaped with beasts, half-lion, half-eagle.

The *Kyn* then led her back out into the city, where he began to explain the economic system that sustained Kabyrnos. The estates in the region were mostly run by the clans, he told her – although, technically, they were all owned by the Sisterhood.

"This is because all earth belongs to Pritymnia, you understand? Although," he added, his lips twisting slightly beneath his beard, "it is I who decide who oversees each estate."

He then went on to explain to her how the large part of whatever was produced on an estate – be it wheat, barley, olives, wool – would be sent to the palace, where it would be redistributed throughout the region.

"This way," he told her, "every person is given what they need. We Kapreitans support each other."

"But wouldn't it be easy for people to keep back more than their share?"

The *Kyn*'s eyes hardened. "The most severe punishments are saved for those who put their own needs above the needs of all."

They began to wander back toward the palace.

"You were very quiet today," the *Kyn* observed at length.

Ann shrugged, but he continued to watch her for a minute before speaking again.

"I hope you will join me one morning in Commerce Hall, Ann. Watching me fulfil my duties as High Magistrate may seem dull to you after listening to me blather on all day, yet I can assure you – it is an incomparable distraction if one is feeling a little… overcome by things."

***

The next morning, Hersa caught Ann by the arm the moment she'd stepped into the courtyard.

"Have you heard?" she asked breathlessly, towing Ann toward their usual corner.

"Heard what?"

"The horses – two of the *Kyn*'s prized horses – they have been stolen from the stables."

"That's too bad, I guess," Ann remarked slowly. "Do they know who did it?"

The rest of the group had joined them. They were all watching Ann and no one was speaking.

"Well?" she asked, looking around at them. "What is it?"

"Have you seen your brother recently?" Athyla asked, long arms folded over her chest.

"What? No. Why?"

Helkys was shaking her head. "This does not bear well on him."

"Nonsense," Hersa snapped at her. "You do not know of what you are speaking."

The younger girl dropped her gaze, duly chastened. It had not been long after the servant had joined their group before the others had begun to yield to her natural authority. Out of the five original girls, only Athyla refused to submit.

"Why does it not bear well on him?" Ann asked.

"*Because*," Athyla said, staring down at Hersa, "he was the only one working when the horses were taken."

"And that proves he stole them?" Hersa challenged, hands on her hips.

"It as much as does."

The two women glared at each other.

"He wouldn't be that stupid," Ann said. "What would he do with them anyway?"

"The details do not matter, apparently," Hersa scoffed. "Some people need very little cause to start casting blame."

Tefkelerea moved to rest a hand on Ann's shoulder. "It will not come to anything, Ann," she said. "I am sure of it."

Yet Hersa's words were soon proved to be true. For the next few days, every person Ann encountered spoke of nothing but Nik: his possible means and motivations for stealing the horses, his inevitable punishment. Most people quieted when they saw Ann approach, but there were always those who demanded her input. On every such occasion, Ann would declare her brother's innocence and be met with pitying looks. On more than one instance, she found herself arguing with Athyla, who insisted that Ann couldn't possibly be as certain as she was pretending to be. Sometimes, Ann found herself wondering if the girl was right.

Eventually, when no official action was taken, the general conversation moved away from Nik's involvement in the horse theft and took a sharp turn into what Ann considered far more dangerous waters. Suddenly, the whole palace seemed fascinated by his personal life. Where there'd always been an interest before, the current obsession seemed fired by a kind of mob momentum that only increased as the list of known conquests grew. On this subject, Ann refused to say anything. She only hoped, worried, *prayed* that one particular affair would remain an absolute secret.

Then, one morning almost half a moon cycle after the theft, Ann hit her breaking point. The women in the weaving rooms had been whispering all morning, repeating some sordid tale of seduction that was getting so far-fetched that even Helkys would have wondered at it, when Ann slammed down her shuttle, snapped at them to mind their own damn business for once and stormed out of the rooms.

She moved south, mounting stairs and winding through corridors until she found herself standing in the massive pillared doorways of the *Kyn*'s domain.

Commerce Hall was an enormous chamber, totally devoid of ornament and almost impossibly full of people. Guards lined the walls, servants zipped back and forth bearing messages, lesser stewards moved about trying to maintain some semblance of order to the throng that waited for an audience with the *Kyn*. After making a few inquiries, Ann pushed her way through the wall of bodies, ignoring the muttered complaints and dirty looks, and eventually broke out into a small space at the far end of the hall.

The *Kyn* was perched on a stool there, with a look of complete serenity on his face as he listened to the bickering of two clansmen. When he caught sight of Ann, he beckoned her over. A servant brought her a stool, placing it next to his.

"Yes, *Psydu*," the *Kyn* interjected, addressing himself to the elder clansmen – a sallow-faced man with an unpleasant scowl. "I understand your feelings, yet your father's petition was clear. Under the circumstances, I was given no choice other than to cede to his will. Your brother shall inherit the oversight of the estate."

The younger clansman grinned as the elder all-but-screamed, "No choice?! The *Kyn* always has a choice!"

"No, *Pysdu*, he does not. Even a *Kyn* is bound by duty. Especially a *Kyn*. I cannot look to the interests of one man above the interests of Kabyrnos. It is vital to us all that the land be overseen only by one who is competent to do so."

"*Competent – ?!*"

"Now I suggest you calm yourself, *Psydu*. I am certain we can find you some alternative occupation."

The elder clansman seemed on the cusp of saying several very rude things, which he wisely omitted. Eventually, angry and helpless, he turned his scowl on Ann.

"And what business does *she* have here?"

A note of thunder crept into the *Kyn*'s voice for the first time. "The Huntress is observing and assisting me. *Your* business here is complete."

The *Kyn* gestured and the clansman was escorted out. As the next supplicant stepped forward, the *Kyn* turned to Ann.

"Gripping, is it not?"

It was. Over the course of the morning, Ann witnessed another heated dispute of inheritance, a vicious he-said-she-said match over a delivery of rotten fish with which the lower magistrates had clearly been unable to cope, a complaint about the vandalism of a sacred space, and, finally, a sentencing for rape.

Ann sat as still as possible throughout the resolution of the final matter. Three children had seen a carpenter lure a young woman into his workshop. They had heard her screams, seen her struggle on the earthen floor. Ann could almost see it too as the girl was brought forward, her face blank as she repeated the facts of what had been done to her.

The *Kyn* gave the carpenter his choices.

"Exile – or castration."

The carpenter pleaded with the *Kyn*, complaining that the girl had been toying with him, then swearing that it wouldn't happen again. But the *Kyn* remained unmoved.

"Make your choice," he replied coldly.

The man chose exile and the *Kyn* called an end to the day's hearings.

"It is difficult sometimes," he said to Ann as the hall emptied, "to see my people harm themselves and others in such ways. Yet, what can be done?"

He then heaved himself to his feet, told her he was glad she'd come, and left the hall.

As she made her own way out, Ann thought of all the people she'd seen that day, so caught up in the troubles of their own lives. She too had been caught up lately, but not in her own life.

At least I'm living my life, he'd said.

She hadn't seen her brother since that argument. Yet here she was, fighting his battles as if they were her own. Had he not made it abundantly clear that he didn't want her involvement? That he wanted nothing to do with her?

And, as the *Kyn* had said, what could be done?

Really, what could she possibly do anymore?

***

That night, Ann was in the dining hall with Tefkelerea, Athyla and a young bronzesmith named Trydus, who was telling them about the arrowheads ordered for the Tournament, when a distant shout rang in through the windows. When the second shout came, Ann was on her feet – her bench upturned, Athyla squawking – and moving toward the door as swiftly as her feet would carry her.

She could never mistake those yelling voices. One had been the *Kynra*'s. The other, Nik's.

Ann was down the steps and out into the Blessed Courtyard within a minute. She slowed to a quick walk.

A small group of people stood by the altar. The *Kynra* was facing Nik, blocking the form of someone on their knees behind her. Darkylus lurked only feet away, as did Sister Aralys, who was looking so pleased with herself that Ann could have slapped her. Other priestesses huddled further back in the row of doorways.

Ann looked around quickly, her eyes falling on a guard near the door to the barracks. She raised a hand to beckon him – but then hesitated.

This was not her business.

Another shout sounded. Nik had stepped toward the *Kynra*, gesturing violently; the woman had shifted and Ann could now see the black-eyed acolyte cowering against the altar, arm held in the older woman's grip.

She hailed the guard.

"Fetch the *Kyn*," she said as he neared. "And your Guard Commander. *Quickly*."

The guard moved away at a run, and Ann picked up her pace. She was close enough now to hear their voices.

"Do not *lie* to me, you impudent whelp," the *Kynra* hissed. "It is a *known fact*. You *forced* her –"

"I did not!" Nik growled.

"That is not what my priestesses say," the *Kynra* persisted, gesturing back at Aralys. "You have soiled a sanctified daughter of Pritymnia!"

"Your priestesses are out of their fucking minds, then!" Nik shouted.

"You will not speak to me in that way!"

The *Kynra* tightened her grip on the acolyte's arm and the girl whimpered. Nik began to step forward again, but Ann closed in on him, grabbing hold of his arm. He shook her off easily.

"If you're going to accuse me of raping someone," he snarled, "I will speak to you in whatever way I fucking choose. You are a lunatic old woman –" he stepped forward again – "who imposes insane rules on those beneath you just so you can pretend you're not as obsolete as everyone here knows you are!"

The look on the *Kynra*'s face made Ann's heart go cold.

"You have soiled a daughter of Pritymnia," she repeated slowly. "You will be punished accordingly."

"P-please," the acolyte whimpered as the *Kynra* reached over her head to the axe that lay on the altar.

"Hold your tongue, girl," Aralys snapped.

"Please, Sacred Mother," the girl insisted, her voice breaking. "He – he did not force me."

The *Kynra* froze. Ann glanced down at the hand that held the acolyte and saw the knuckles turn white. The girl let out a sob.

"What?" the *Kynra* whispered. "What did you say?"

"I s-said – *I went to him freely!*"

Afterward, in the solitude of her bedroom, Ann would relive the moment a hundred times, wondering how she could not have seen it coming. How she could not have somehow intervened. But it happened so quickly – so impossibly *fast*. It could not have been more than three seconds, she knew. Three seconds from the moment of the poor girl's cry to the point when her body had collapsed on the flagstones, the Sacral Axe buried in her neck.

The *Kynra* stood over the twitching body, blood gushing and spraying over her bare feet. Her mouth was open, her breathing ragged. She twisted the axe free, and held it in her hands as if it weighed no more than a knife. Ann stared at her, so stunned that all she could wonder was how in the name of all that was holy that wasted old woman had the strength to wield such a weapon.

Then the *Kynra* took a step toward Nik.

Ann lunged forward, taking hold of her brother's kilt. She *heaved*. He staggered back, making no attempt to resist.

"Huntress, control yourself," the *Kynra* uttered, face horribly, terribly calm. "This is not your concern."

The woman took another step forward.

And then it came to her, so softly this time it was almost a caress. It seeped out from the walls, from the stones at her feet, calling to her from the very beating heart of Kabyrnos.

Antigone…

Ann stepped forward into Nik's place.

A flicker of irritation passed over the *Kynra*'s face. Ann heard several barks in the distance as Darkylus slunk forward.

"Huntress," the man uttered. "It is the law. The offending member is now forfeit."

Ann heard a strangled groan behind her.

"Enough blood has been spilled," Ann said.

Kaenus was there now, growling at her elbow, hackles raised.

"Step aside," the *Kynra* demanded, raising the axe again.

When Ann neither moved nor replied, the woman's eyes grew wide in outrage.

"*Step aside, you foolish girl!*"

"No."

"You *dare* –"

"I do. I am the Chosen of Pritymnia and I will take responsibility for this man on her behalf."

The *Kynra* inhaled sharply. Ann stared straight into the woman's face and felt the weight of her own words press down on her.

"Will you deny me this right?" she asked quietly.

The *Kynra* was never given a chance to respond. A shout like an enormous roll of thunder boomed through the courtyard. Ann spun round and was shocked to find that a crowd had formed: Athyla, Tefkelerea and Trydus were there, and the Guard Commander too; she was supporting Nik, who sagged against her, eyes wide and sightless.

Then the crowd split open to reveal the *Kyn*, storming through with the High Steward in his wake.

Ann had never imagined that the man could look so terrifying. Within one lightning gesture, he stayed the High Steward – who had lurched forward when he'd spotted Ann – and stilled the entire crowd.

"*Have you lost what was left of your mind, woman?*"

"It was within my rights," the *Kynra* spat back. But the axe had been lowered.

"Within you rights to take a *life – here? In the middle of my palace?!*"

"*Your* palace?" she cried, sensing she'd caught an edge. "This is not *your* palace, you fool. You are a mere steward here – a temporary blight on the life of the Earth Mother's temple. No matter how hard you may try to forget that fact!" She readjusted her grip on the axe. "It is time for a new leader!"

The *Kyn* took three thundering steps forward and took hold of the axe's handle.

"I would agree with that," he uttered. "You have terrorized those poor women long enough."

He wrenched the axe from the *Kynra*'s hands so violently that she staggered forward, crashing to her knees on the flagstones. Darkylus rushed to help her up. And when the woman had straightened, her hands and dress now slick with the acolyte's blood, she spat, directly into the *Kyn*'s face.

"Just like your brute of a father!" she screamed.

The *Kyn* wiped the saliva from his cheek with the back of his hand.

"Count your time by the path of the moon, old woman," he uttered – so quietly that Ann, standing only steps away, could barely hear. "For it is soon done. Now get out of my sight."

"Gladly."

The *Kynra* gathered herself up and swept out of the courtyard.

***

Night had fallen when Ann re-entered the empty courtyard. She still couldn't quite believe it had happened. Blood covered her dress in spattered constellations, yet it all somehow seemed like a dream. Just vivid images and feelings, stitched together into a twisted, implausible scene.

When the *Kynra* had made her exit, the Guard Commander and Ann had dragged Nik into the barracks, where he'd stared down at his blood-spattered legs and shook. The guardswoman had sent for a servant, and once Hersa had arrived, she'd managed to make him drink some wine and then put him to sleep on one of the cots that were kept stowed in the back. Unable to remain still, Ann had left Kaenus to stand watch over her brother and ventured back into the courtyard.

As she neared the altar now, she saw a large, dark shape looming before her. She hesitated. Then the figure's massive chest heaved a sigh, and Ann continued onward.

The blood-stained axe lay on the ground near the *Kyn*'s feet. The body had been removed. As Ann approached, the man lifted his head and his shadowed eyes met hers for an instant before falling away. In this darkness, he seemed twenty years older.

The two stood there for some time in silence. Slowly, the *Kyn* released another long breath and stooped to pick up the axe. He stared at it for a moment before placing it back on the altar.

"This is what comes of a person putting themselves above others, Ann. Never forget it."

Chapter Three

A pall descended over Kabyrnos as the palace held its breath, bracing itself for what would come in the aftermath of the incident by the altar. Yet, for two days, nothing happened. Ann went about her duties quietly, carefully, willing herself through every step of each day. Nik lay in his bed, eating nothing and speaking to no one.

On the third day, however, hushed word began to spread that the horses had been returned. People began to say that it could not have been the Hunter after all, as it was known that he was bedridden at the time of their return. Ann overheard these whispers out in the city, in the baths, as she stood at her loom – yet when the whisperers noticed her attention, they all fell silent.

There had been a marked change in the palace folk's behaviour toward her. The reserved respect they'd always held for her seemed to have magnified into a kind of awe. Ann soon came to understand that in challenging the *Kynra*, they believed she'd somehow managed to conquer the unconquerable.

She, of course, knew better.

So when she found Darkylus waiting for her in the corridor outside the weaving rooms, she knew that the time of her reckoning had finally come.

***

"Huntress, welcome," the Kynra greeted Ann as she was guided into the small, plain bedchamber.

The woman sat on the edge of the bed, hair falling loosely around her shoulders. Today she was without the usual rows of onyx that Ann had come to think of as an inseparable part of her. She looked strange, shrunken. A bird without its feathers.

"Thank you, Darkylus. You may leave us."

The door shut quietly and Ann was left alone with the Kynra. She stared resolutely over the woman's head at the blank wall behind her.

"You cannot imagine the joy it gives me to know that you have finally accepted your true roll and responsibilities, Chosen."

The woman's tone was flat, as if she was merely stating a fact – and not a particularly interesting one at that.

"There is no reason now to prolong your oath-taking. You shall be sworn is as priestess by the end of the moon cycle, on the day that we celebrate Pritymnia's aspect of the New Bride."

Ann said nothing. There was nothing to say.

"Unless."

Ann finally met the woman's gaze. Those slate-coloured eyes were weary, sad – like the eyes of the old woman it was easy to forget she was.

"Unless?" Ann asked.

"I have given it much thought," the Kynra said, voice still curiously flat, "and it has occurred to me that your appointed task here can be accomplished in more than one way."

Ann waited for her to go on, but the woman seemed to be waiting for something from her.

"What do you mean?"

"Your destiny is to revive the glory of Pritymnia."

Again, the woman waited.

"Yes," Ann agreed reluctantly.

"Yet, it is possible that this might be achieved from outside the Sisterhood – and in a way that forces all of the Akrean world to acknowledge the superiority of a daughter of the Earth Mother."

"I still don't know what you mean," Ann said slowly.

"The Tournament."

Ann frowned, not understanding.

"Yes, Chosen. The Tournament."

"You…want *me* –?"

"Yes."

The woman was sitting up straighter now.

"But –"

"Who better? Sisterhood laws forbid a priestess to engage in secular rites, yet *you*… You are taller than most all men, you are faster, I suspect – no, I have seen you. And you are marked by the Mother. As for the rest –" she waved a hand almost lazily – "you will have a full season to prepare."

"I don't think –"

"No woman has ever competed, Chosen. Do you not see?"

"Sure, but I still don't think that *I* –"

"Chosen," the *Kynra* uttered. "I once told you that mercy was granted only once. You should consider yourself fortunate that you now have a choice before you."

Not a sound could be heard in that tiny, cell-like chamber. Not the flicker of the only lamp that lit it, nor the breath of the woman that sat on the edge of the narrow bed, watching. Waiting.

"Do I have some time to think about it?" Ann asked.

The *Kynra* refolded her hands in her lap.

"You have until the end of the moon cycle. By the morning following the Day of Darkness, I expect you to have agreed to my terms."

***

Ann floated through the corridors back to her own rooms.

"The Tournament," she whispered to the walls.

Kapreitan men, Gyklanean men – the best of the best – competing in fierce rivalry against each other. In front of thousands of people.

Would she even be on Kapreitu by then?

She would never be picked. Not in million years. Not over men who were undeniably more skilled than she and unfathomably stronger.

But if she was?

She stopped short, seeing a small, plump figure loitering outside her door.

"Hersa?"

The girl spun round guiltily.

"I –" Hersa glanced back at the door – "I was helping your brother out of bed –"

"Nik's out of bed?"

"Yes, yes – I had to practically drag him out, yet – the High Steward, he came …"

Ann stared back at her friend, mystified. "What? The High Steward? In there? With Nik?"

Hersa nodded, eyes wide.

"Huh."

The two women stood silently for several seconds.

"Well," Ann said casually, "It's my room too, so…"

She moved to the door to find it already slightly open. She shot a glare back at Hersa, who merely shrugged. Then both girls inched forward, pressing their ears as close to the crack as they dared.

"– hope you will forgive me, Hunter. It was childish and petty."

"Don't worry about it, man," came Nik's weary voice.

"I do worry about it," the High Steward continued. "I have humiliated myself and injured you. It was unforgivable of me."

"But here you are. Asking for forgiveness."

A lash of the usual sarcasm. Ann smiled: Nik must be feeling better.

"*The horses*," Hersa whispered.

Ann turned to peer at the girl. Of course she was right. She knew she was right. She just couldn't fathom *why*.

But the girl was staring at her pointedly – as if to answer the unspoken question.

Ann shook her head. "No way. That doesn't –"

The door swung open. Both women gaped up at the High Steward.

"I just got here," Ann blurted out.

Hersa had stepped back and was looking more like a submissive servant than Ann could have thought possible. No help there.

"I was on my way to the baths," Ann added needlessly.

"Oh," the man asked, finally speaking. "Indeed?"

"Hersa?" came Nik's voice from inside the room.

Without a word, the girl slipped past Ann and the High Steward, and closed the door firmly behind her. Ann cursed her silently.

"Perhaps I can escort you?" the man asked after a moment.

And so Ann found herself walking back through the corridors, the High Steward at her side. His hands were clasped behind his back, his head hanging slightly, the curtain of his hair hiding his face. Neither spoke. They descended two flights of steps silently, and passed by the priests' halls, where they heard soft chanting floating out from behind a row of screened doorways.

"How much did you overhear?"

Ann glanced over at the High Steward. "Uh, oh – not much."

"You are kind, yet I do not deserve your kindness." The man stopped walking and turned to face her. "Perhaps it is worth some small mercy that I did it out of indignation on your behalf?"

"*My* behalf?"

The man looked abashed, confused. Humble, even. Yet there was still a hint of something in his expression that made her uneasy.

"Why else?" he asked. "When you told me that he had hurt you..."

"When did I – oh. No, that's not..." Ann's head was beginning to spin. This was too much, too much for one day. "I need to sit down."

The High Steward led her to a nearby lightwell. A cool breeze was blowing down to rustle the plants in the garden beneath it. Ann sat on the low wall, leaned her head back against the stone and closed her eyes.

She heard the man settle himself next to her. "I know it is not honourable to offer justifications. Yet it is important to me that you know that, misguided though I was, I only ever wanted to make everything in your life as beautiful and as perfect as you are."

Ann's eyes flew open. The man was gazing at her now with such frank admiration that she realized that the time had finally come to set things straight.

"High Steward – Heremus. I am not perfect. Not even close. As for beauty..."

She glanced down at the garden beside her, filled with dancing butterflies. She thought back to the yellow butterfly he'd once brought her.

"I'm convinced it's more of a hindrance than anything else."

He opened his mouth to protest but she cut him off.

"No – it's true. It doesn't make you happy. It wouldn't make *you* happy. It just…" She shook her head, sighing. "It just blocks out what's *real*."

The man was staring down at the butterflies now too. He did not look up as Ann rose to her feet.

"Thank you for your concern," she said, touching him softly on the shoulder. "Really. But I don't think my problems will ever be fixed that easily, or by anyone but me."

***

Nik was still in the common room when Ann returned to the apartments. She smiled, seeing that Kaenus had wandered over to place his head in her brother's lap. Nik appeared to be napping. And from the sounds of it – violent crashes, disgusted scoffs – Hersa had taken the opportunity to clean his bedroom.

"Do you *never* tidy in here?" the girl demanded from the other room. "There are at least a hundred spiders living beneath your bed. Along with the rest of your belongings…"

Nik's eyes did not open, but his mouth curled into a small smile. "Don't touch them," he mumbled. "They're not bothering anyone."

"They are bothering *me*."

Ann plopped herself onto the floor with a sigh. Kaenus came to her and she leaned her face into his warm fur, breathing deeply. Inhaling the earthy, musky scent that she loved so much.

She heard another exclamation from the other room. She glanced up, ready to be amused, and found her brother watching her.

"Ann."

She looked at him for a long moment. Then she nodded. "Don't worry about it."

Hersa stormed into the room holding a pair of filthy, muck-covered sandals out as far away from her as her arms could reach. "What in the name of Mavros on Crytus did you *do* to these, Niklas?"

"I work in the stables, Hersa. And please stop calling me Niklas. You sound like my mother."

Ann peered at him curiously. She'd not once, not since their mother had disappeared almost seven years ago, heard Nik mention her.

"From the way you carry on, *Niklas*," Hersa said, "I would say that you certainly could have used a good mother."

Nik snorted, but his eyes, which darted over to Ann, were serious. "There's a mouthful."

Ann buried her face back into Kaenus's fur. Her mind was deliciously blank. When she re-emerged minutes later, Hersa had returned to her crusade and Nik had fallen into a doze. Climbing to her feet, Ann wandered into Nik's room, where she found Hersa on her knees, half-submerged under the bed. She felt a rush of pity for Nik's spiders.

"You know, I've never been in here before," Ann commented, looking around the room that was the mirror image of her own.

"Consider yourself blessed," came Hersa's muffled voice from under the bed.

"Hersa? Can you call a truce and come out here for a second?"

The girl pulled out and sat up, her dress covered in dust and cobwebs.

"What would you say if I told you that I was thinking of entering the Tournament?"

Hersa's brows snapped together. She was silent for a long time.

"I would say," she began eventually, "that you were very brave. And very stupid." Her face changed then, the frown relaxing. "And I would say that there is no better woman for the task."

***

The palace was still unnaturally hushed a few days later. Every evening, the dining hall filled with people who retrieved their dinners, ate and left without having spoken above a whisper. The courtyard was avoided like the Darkness's Plague. Morning exercises had simply stopped. At any given time of the day, the vast space remained utterly empty. Until suddenly, one morning, it was not.

It was full of trunks.

It seemed that someone had rearranged all of the belongings in the elite residences. The Head Clerk's trunk was found in the Second General's chamber, the Second General's in a Kaftanu elder's, the clan elder's in the Master Bronzesmith's wife's, and so on. For half a day, the courtyard teemed with indignant people – no one more indignant than Afratea, who seemed incapable of getting over the shock of finding an old man's loincloths where her own gowns should have been. The trunks had been hauled down to be reclaimed, and for the first time in almost six days, the courtyard was full of life again.

Ann ran into Erysia the next day and asked if it had been worth the trouble.

"Everything that is worth anything requires some trouble, Ann," the curly-haired woman responded haughtily.

Morning exercises resumed. Nik returned to his training and to work. Ann, who had quickly grown used to having him around their apartments, expected him to start making himself scarce again, but to her delight, he did not. That evening he returned to the common room after dinner and asked if she wanted to go for a walk.

He took her to the roofs. Cold wind whipped across the flat expanse, pushing at them as they made their way toward the mudbrick structure that was perched along the southern edge, overlooking the Crytus Valley. Muttering about shawls that were too thin, Ann pulled her wrapping tighter and followed her brother as he ran ahead to unlatch the door.

The aviary was lit by a single, barred window and smelled strongly of musk. Pigeons swarmed the floor and the window ledge, their droppings crusting almost every surface. Nik went to the clay jug in the corner and scooped out two handfuls of seed. The birds swarmed him, flapping eagerly. Ann stood with her back pressed against the door as he scattered most of the seed out into wide arcs, keeping a small amount in the palm of his hand to lure one of the birds close. The bird hopped onto his hand.

"You know," he said, "these birds are actually really intelligent. And look at the colours on this one's neck. Beautiful, huh?"

Ann watched her twin closely – the soft expression on his face, the callused fingers stroking the bird's head with perfect gentleness. She'd almost forgotten this side of him.

Nik settled the bird back on the ground, dusted off his hands and beckoned Ann to a door at the opposite side of the room. The chamber beyond was larger, brighter and colder; almost the whole southern wall was open to the sky beyond. The inmates of this room were chained by their ankles to long wooden posts, every one of them sharp-beaked predators. Their yellow eyes followed the twins as they moved toward the window.

"Isn't this view amazing?" Nik asked her.

Ann looked down into the Crytus River, almost a hundred and fifty feet below them.

"It's... really high up," she said weakly.

"Right," Nik replied. "I forgot you don't like heights. I come up here pretty often."

Ann closed her eyes, leaned her head against the window frame and tried to focus on how solid it was against her skull. Solid, but pulsing ever so softly. When she opened her eyes minutes later, she saw her brother still staring off into the distance, his face unreadable in the dusk.

"What is it?" she whispered.

"I... I didn't even know her name, Anna." A chain rattled behind them as one of the birds shifted its weight. "I didn't even know her name and I got her killed."

Ann placed her hand on his shoulder and the twins stood for several more seconds like that, not speaking.

Then Nik moved away and her hand fell back to her side.

"Anyway," he muttered. "I think it's time we get back."

***

When they returned to their apartments, they found Hersa standing in the common room with an armload of animal skins.

"Here," she said, pushing her cargo into Ann's arms. "Now you can stop complaining about how cold it is."

"I haven't complained –"

Hersa rolled her eyes. "Please. The only times you have opened your mouth in the past few days was to comment on how cold it was."

Nik was biting back a smile. "It's all you ever talk about, Ann."

"See?" Hersa demanded. "Thank you, Niklas."

Ann glared at them both and stalked off into her bedroom to examine her new gear: a short, warm-looking fur cape, and two sheets of leather with leather thongs which she assumed were to wrap around her feet and calves. Fastening the cape around her neck, she re-entered the common room to ask Hersa how to wrap the boots.

She stopped in her doorway. Hersa and Nik had settled themselves on the floor, Kaenus between them, and Hersa was telling Nik about the rocky cliffs of her childhood home. Nik was watching her, silent and smiling. Neither had looked up when Ann had entered.

Ann backed up into her room. The boots could wait for tomorrow.

**

The next evening, on the day of rest, there was a knock on the door soon after Ann returned from the dining hall. She opened it – thinking it was a little early for Hersa – and was surprised to find the *Kyn*'s manservant, who politely informed her that she had been expected for the evening meal. Flustered, Ann told the servant she'd be there presently and practically slammed the door in his face. But for several minutes afterward, she merely leaned against the door and smiled.

After what had happened at the altar – after what she'd declared – Ann had assumed that the *Kyn* would not want to bother with her anymore. It had hurt, more deeply than she wanted to admit, but she had accepted it as an inevitable consequence of protecting her brother. Shaking her head, she berated herself for being so stupid.

But as she walked the short distance to the *Kyn*'s quarters, she wondered if it had actually been foolish to stay away. She was now firmly tied to the *Kynra*; did she really want to entangle herself further with the *Kyn*? Every time she saw him, their bond grew stronger – she could feel it, a connection that was becoming as unyielding as it was involuntary. When she was around him, her mind was full of his expressions, his gestures, his words. She was captive to the sheer force of his personality. It was so easy to forget, in the ordinary course of things, that he was not just the charismatic man he appeared to be. She'd seen him in Commerce Hall.

"He is a *Kyn*, first and foremost," she whispered as she stood outside his door.

Then the door opened.

"I thought I heard something," the *Kyn* said, smiling. "Come in, come in!"

He drew her into the glow of his chamber. Ann glanced at his face, so warm in the firelight, and let out a deep breath.

"I thought you had forsaken me, Ann," the *Kyn* teased, eyes dancing.

Ann smiled back and told him she had just lost track of the day.

***

Later, lying in her bed, Ann asked herself why she had not mentioned her meeting with the *Kynra* over the course of the evening. Zelkanus could have helped her. At the very least, he could have given her guidance, helped to set things straight in her muddled mind. But as she tossed and turned, it occurred to her that it was for exactly that reason that she'd remained silent.

She needed to make this decision on her own – to be free of influence, to the extent that it was still possible. And as long as no one else knew about it, it seemed to her that she had all the time in the world to mull over her options in peace.

Chapter Four

Ann could not remember a happier time. With mornings spent with friends in the courtyard or out in the countryside with Kaenus, and evenings with the *Kyn*, or Nik and Hersa, Ann's life was full. It was complete. A vivid painting whose colours and patterns she could admire with satisfaction.

Yet she was careful never to look too closely. At the brush strokes, sloppily applied. At the shapes that distorted the nearer one drew. She never let her mind wander to the *Kynra*. She never allowed herself to think about the voice that seemed to call to her every night, her name carried in on the ever-cooling wind. And she never, not once, tried to enter the common space in the minds of her and her twin.

The pull was very real. Spending as much time with Nik as she was now, reaching out to him in that way felt as natural and as compelling as breathing. But the fear was stronger. She tried to ignore it, but there were moments when the dread would crop up again, unexpected and irrepressible. Moments when Ann would catch Nik looking at her with hard, wary eyes, or when he'd pull away mid-conversation, or refuse to look at her at all. She was careful to keep their interactions light. For as long as he was willing to give it, she was more than contented with his ordinary friendship. Just as she was more than happy to continue on in the ordinary life that she'd built up around herself like a barricade.

Ann had not given the Tournament more than the occasional, fleeting thought. She told herself she had time. She always had time. And then, one afternoon, time caught up with her.

Ann was luxuriating in the baths before going to meet the *Kyn* again, when she heard a woman tell her friend that she'd have to keep working through the evening if she wanted her dress to be finished in time for the celebration.

"What celebration?" Ann asked, sitting up so suddenly that she almost swamped her neighbour in a wave. "When?"

"The Day of Darkness, of course," the woman replied. "The day after tomorrow."

Ann was stunned. As she dried off, she asked herself how she could possibly have ignored all the signs that were so obvious to her now: the hum of activity in the priests' halls, the young men bragging about their masks, the women making arrangements to send children to city relatives for the night.

She was still in a state of shock when she entered the *Kyn*'s rooms later. She clung to the feeling, knowing full well what would have to come once it faded: the choice would have to be made. She knew she was being a coward, but as long as there was some time left to her, she would hide behind it.

The *Kyn*, when he arrived, was in a foul mood. Over dinner, he did nothing but complain about the food. Over their game of *mestra*, he snapped at Ann for her inability to learn even the most basic strategies. With some effort, Ann bit back to the retort that she was only learning the game to please him. Instead, she released a slow breath and asked what was bothering him.

"Nothing," he muttered.

Ann suppressed a smile. Sitting there, hunched over and glowering at the game board, he looked rather like an oversized, pouting child.

"Are you sure?" she asked him, more gently this time.

He glanced up at her and his scowl melted away. He ran a hand over his face, kneading his features out of shape.

"I apologize, Ann. What a day I have had."

He told her. Word had come that afternoon that Makrona had turned a few minor Kapreitan trading posts to their own service. These posts were stationed on some of the smaller Ceklydonic isles and were entirely local-run, so there was not much that Kabyrnos could do about it. But it was almost an outright act of hostility.

"And we cannot challenge them now," the *Kyn* said wearily. "Not with the Season of Darkness upon us."

"Is it really that bad?"

"No," he sighed. "Not yet... Though in a few short moons, they will be here for the Tournament. And then we shall see what we shall see."

The man smiled then, a slow, almost cruel smile.

"For now, however, the rains and winds keep us at home, and I only have to concern myself with domestic matters." He shook his head, making a sound of disgust. "That wife of mine."

Ann shifted in her seat uncomfortably. "What about her?"

"She accosted me on the southern terrace on my way here."

He took a deep drink of his wine, and moved his pawn two spaces across the board.

Ann was careful to keep her voice steady. "And what did she say?"

"Two days ago I reallocated the remaining priestess-run estates to some of my more prosperous merchant families. Today, my wife found out. She was... not pleased."

The *Kyn* seemed more amused by this than anything else. Ann cautiously nudged her pawn one space forward.

"Well," she asked, "did you really expect any different?"

He swept his own pawn in, knocking hers to the marble with a clatter.

"As a matter of fact, I did," he replied. "I sometimes have very high expectations of people."

Slowly, very slowly, he picked up the fallen pawn and placed it on the table in front of her.

"I... I hadn't decided yet," Ann muttered.

"Well, if you were intending to keep it a secret, I am afraid that you will be disappointed. Your patroness was overheard by half the palace."

So much for her choice.

"What did she say?"

"The usual drivel. That it was time for a new champion of Kabyrnos, that the Tournament would show the whole world a thing or two. Then she spoke of me, trying to stem your potential. It was not difficult to deduce her meaning."

If Ann hadn't felt so decidedly queasy, she would have been tempted to laugh. The *Kynra* had not been trying to force her hand, then. She'd simply let her temper get the better of her again.

Then the *Kyn* leaned across the table and covered her hand with his.

"Ann," he said quietly. "What is going on here truly? Tell me."

It was all the prompting she needed. The words poured out like water overflowing a dam as she told him about the *Kynra*'s belief in the Chosen of Pritymnia, and how Ann had been forced to accept the role on the night of the acolyte's death.

"To shield your brother?"

Ann nodded and went on to explain how she was now cornered into an impossible choice. She tried to remain calm, but after the words stopped coming, Ann laid her head on her arms and wept – and wept and wept, new waves of release breaking over her. The *Kyn* crouched beside her, hand on her shoulder, and waited for her to spend herself through. And when she finally looked up, swollen-eyed and runny-nosed, he smiled at her.

"You need not worry any longer, Ann."

Ann made a sound of disbelief.

"The woman is not as powerful as she pretends to be. Not even close." He said it was such calm assurance that Ann was tempted to believe him. "She may enforce her rules on those under her direct authority, yet that is all. If she so much as touches a golden hair on your head – or your brother's – I will break her neck myself. I would be glad for the excuse."

Ann stared at him, unable to speak.

"I will come with you, the morning after the Day of Darkness. We will refuse her together."

For several more seconds, all Ann could do was blink at him and sniffle. And then her chest expanded, clean air rushing into her body, buoying her up.

She was free. Free of the *Kynra*. She could do as she pleased.

"There now," the *Kyn* said, cupping her cheek and rising. "That is better." He settled himself back into his seat with a sigh. "I was worried, I must admit."

Ann held a hand to her forehead. Her head was still spinning. "About what?"

"About *you*, Ann," he said with a laugh. "This Tournament is no game to played at. It pushes a man to his limits and beyond. Men are often maimed, even killed." He took a long drink from his wine glass. "It is certainly no place for a woman."

And suddenly, her mind was razor sharp again.

"I would not have forbidden you from trying, of course, if you were set on it," he went on. "Although I doubt very much that you would have been selected. You are a very capable young woman, of course, yet you would have been vying for a spot among the strongest, most able men of Kabyrnos!" He laughed as if to emphasize the absurdity of the thought. "You must have been very strained indeed to even have considered the possibility. Now," he said, tapping his finger against the board, "I believe it is your turn."

Ann stared down at the board, unmoving.

"What is it, Ann?" Again, the *Kyn* laughed. "Are you afraid of losing? You should be used to it by now."

Ann looked up at him slowly. And then, with deliberate care, she reached out and pushed her pawn three spaces forward.

***

The next morning during exercises Ann was having a hard time concentrating. She'd mastered the front and back handsprings, and was now working on the front flip. And although she'd managed it a couple days before, today it was beyond her. Athyla, Hersa and the others had laughed the first few times she'd landed on her back, but she'd glared at them so ferociously that, eventually, they pretended not to notice at all. By the time people were beginning to disperse, Ann's back was aching, her face was beet red, and she was peeling herself up off the floor for what felt like the hundredth time. It was at this opportune moment that Afratea chose to make her entrance.

"Huntress, *really*," she laughed. "You will have to do better than that if you plan to qualify for the Tournament."

Ann dusted off her tunic and began to walk away. She did not have the patience for this today.

But the woman was following her.

"I am surprised to see that you still practice with us. I thought you would have joined the men in the training grounds by now. I know how much you love their company."

Ann spun to face her.

"What do you want, Afratea?"

"Me?" the woman asked, eyebrows arching. "I would think that it was *you* whose behaviour was wanting. It is not seemly for a woman to display herself so publicly."

Ann let out a bark of laughter. "That's rich."

"I shall let you in on a little secret, girl," Afratea hissed, all pretence vanishing. "You can kill as many beasts, enter as many Tournaments and bed as many men as you like. *It will not work.*"

"What is going on here?"

The women turned to find the High Steward approaching. Afratea perked up instantly.

"Your darling and I were just having a little chat," Afratea chimed.

"Indeed?"

"She is such a sweet, timid thing, is she not?"

The man sighed. "Afratea, run along now." He waved a hand in her face, shooing her, like a dog. "You tire me."

Ann had to hand it to the woman: she was persistent. She took a few undulating steps toward the High Steward, and said, under her breath,

"I used to tire you quite thoroughly, did I not?"

But the man only sneered. "Go back to your husband. See if *he* can still stand you."

This finally seemed to make some impression. And as the woman stalked away with what shreds of dignity she could muster, Ann couldn't help feeling a little bit sorry for her. A very little bit.

"I am sorry, Huntress," the High Steward said once they were alone. "That woman is a serpent."

"It's fine," Ann muttered. "I'm fine."

"Postpone your bath." He smiled at her, not unkindly. "There is an initiation rite taking place outside. You look as though you could use the diversion."

After a moment, Ann agreed. She wasn't sure why she did, but she soon found herself – again – walking silently with the High Steward as he led her out of the palace to the stepped stage arena just beyond. A crowd had gathered around the steps to watch several pairs of boys – no older than nine years old, heads freshly shaven – who stood facing each other.

"What are they doing?" Ann asked, leaning in so the High Steward could hear her over the crowd.

The man leaned closer still. "This is final stage of their rites, which began at dawn. They will compete to prove their strength. Once they have finished, their shorn hair will be burnt and offered to Mavros, and they will be made men."

A horn was blown and the boys lunged forward, wrapping their arms around each other's necks. Ann grimaced. They looked more like scrabbling animals than men.

Something tugged in her mind.

Her brother. He was there, standing on the opposite side of the crowd. His face grim as he watched the boys grunting in the ring.

"Where are the girls?" Ann asked after another minute.

"They will be in the palace now," the High Steward explained. He drew a line across his stomach with his finger. "Offering their first blood."

Ann stared down at the red ridge that ran across her palm. She imagined a line of little girls, baring their bellies to the *Kynra*'s knife. She clenched her hand into a fist. The second round of boys had taken their places.

"I don't understand these rituals," she blurted out. "I saw a betrothal rite a few days ago, and this man and this woman were weaving their hair together, and the whole time the girl was crying her heart out. But everyone went on acting like everything was just fine."

The horn was blown again and the second set of boys flew at each other.

"It is because her family knows what is best," the High Steward replied.

Ann spun on him. "*Why*? Why is it 'best' for her?"

The man blinked down at her in genuine surprise. "All women who are not priestesses must marry, Huntress. It is the way of things."

"And let me guess," she snapped, not bothering to keep her voice down, "this is because there was some ancient, divine proclamation stating that any woman who refuses to marry is perverting the sacred balance."

People were beginning to stare. The High Steward drew her away from the crowd and into the shade of a nearby tree.

"No," the man said cautiously. "It is because we must sustain our people. If our women do not marry and bear children, then we will die out."

Ann was somewhat chastened. For all its obvious differences, it was easy to forget that this was not the world she was born to.

"Sorry," she muttered, looking back to the ring.

"It is no matter," the High Steward replied. "I like your temper. It adds spice."

Ann ignored him. One of the boys in the arena had knocked his opponent to the ground, and was now straddling him, raining punches down in a wild frenzy. There was another, stronger tug in Ann's mind as she felt her brother's muscles tense. She felt him step back, away from the ring, as the boys were pulled apart. His heart was pounding; she touched her own chest.

"Do you truly find the idea of marriage so repellent, Ann?"

The High Steward had moved to stand directly behind her now.

"I will not flatter you, as I know you do not care for it," he whispered. "I will not tell you that you are the loveliest woman I have ever beheld, as I know that you would not care for that either. I also know that you believe my feelings are not sincere. Yet I can assure you, Ann, they are."

He took her by the shoulders and turned her around to face him.

"Bind yourself to me, Ann."

She was silent for a few seconds and then she whispered, "I can't."

"Nonsense," he laughed. "I am asking you to be my wife – to stand by me always."

"I know. And I can't."

There was a flash of confusion in his eyes. He had not – Ann saw – even considered that she might refuse.

"Why ever not?" he demanded, releasing her.

"I don't love you."

Again, the confusion – with a dash of something else. "You will learn to."

"I'm sorry, Heremus, I really am, but I won't."

The man spun away from her, pacing away and then back again. The crowd applauded as the next round of boys took their positions.

"Do you not understand, Ann?" he demanded. "Must I speak it? I will be *Kyn* after Zelkanus. He has all but told me. Which means that *you* would be –"

"*Kynra*," Ann whispered, eyes wide.

For the second time in less than a day, Ann found herself wondering at her own blindness. It was there, this whole time, right in front of her – she'd simply refused to see it. The tours of the city, the invitation to Commerce Hall, even her lessons in *mestra*. The *Kyn* had been training her, driving her towards this from the very first, with the ease in which he pushed a pawn across the board. And with just as little resistance.

"I don't want to be *Kynra*."

The High Steward scoffed. "What woman would not be thrilled to hold such a position of honour?"

Ann thought back to the old woman, standing naked and alone in the dark waters of her sacred pool.

"It wouldn't make me happy, I know it."

"I cannot understand you, Ann," the man snapped. "You have gifts that others would die for – beauty, status – and you repudiate them!"

"Don't you see, then?" she pleaded. "We value different things. We couldn't make each other happy, not really."

"Happiness again! Let me tell you something, Huntress –" he took a few steps toward her, leaning in close – "you must take what you can get in this life, mark my words. You think it is your beauty that blocks out what is real? You will wake up one day as a wasted old woman and realize that the one true hindrance in your life was *you*."

His words staggered her. She stared up at him as he breathed heavily down into her face.

"Maybe so," she whispered. "But this is not the way to find out."

"You stubborn girl!"

And with that, the man strode away from her. Ann sagged against the tree and covered her face. She realized suddenly that Nik was closer — she hadn't felt him approach. She dropped her hands to look for him, and found the High Steward was standing before her again.

"Enough with this, Ann," the man uttered. "I will only ask you once more. Bind yourself to me."

"No."

Something twitched in his jaw. "I do not accept that. Give me one reason — one *true* reason. No more of this idiocy."

Ann wrapped her arms around herself. Her sweat was drying and it was much colder here, out of the sun. She decided to give the High Steward an excuse that he could understand.

"I'm already married."

The man looked dumbfounded. "...You are lying."

"I swear it. I was married when I was still a girl, to a man who wanted me for exactly those 'gifts' you mentioned. He was kind to me, at first, and then — not so kind. I won't repeat the same mistake."

The High Steward was silent. Ann made to walk away.

She was pulled back. The man gripped her arms, his fingers digging into her flesh.

"You led me on," he hissed.

"Let me go. I *never* –"

"You – led – me – on." He shook her with every word, then held her pressed up against the tree. Her spine ground against the bark as she tried to twist out of his grasp. Her hands were growing numb, her heart was hammering in her chest. And all she could think was: Not this. Not this. Oh please, not this again.

"*That's enough!*"

The High Steward sprang away from her as if he had been struck by lightning, and Ann crumpled to the foot of the tree. Nik stepped forward, golden eyes livid.

"You've forgotten yourself, High Steward. Leave. *Now*."

His shout had drawn the attention of the people along the outer edge of the crowd. The High Steward flashed them a glance, then looked back at Nik. Then, without a glance at Ann, he strode away.

Nik kneeled down beside his sister.

"Anna, Anna, look at me," he said, gently shaking her shoulders. "Look at me."

She looked up into his eyes. *Her* eyes. He took her hands in his and then he was open, totally open, his concern, his love pouring into her like rain into a parched riverbed. Their hearts beat, once, twice. Three times.

And then she was alone again. He dropped her hands.

"She's okay," he whispered. "She's okay."

"I'm okay. I just need a minute…"

Ann laid her head against the bark and closed her eyes, knowing that, by the time she opened them again, her brother would be gone.

***

On a cold winter day almost five years earlier, the twins' stepfather lost his job. He came home that night and locked himself in his bedroom without a word. In the morning, as Ann headed off to school and Nik went wherever it was he went during the days, their stepfather was still hidden away. When Ann returned that evening, however, he had emerged.

"Where were *you*," he asked her, slumped in his chair with an empty bottle of scotch beside him. "School ends at four."

"I was at track practice."

He staggered to his feet, lurching out into the hallway. Ann could smell the sourness of his breath as he reached forward to finger the collar of her running jersey.

"Yes, I can see that. Or maybe that's just want you want me to see."

Ann backed up against the railing of the staircase. She had never seen her stepfather this far gone.

"So much like her mother," he muttered. "Where were you really, you little slut? With some football player behind the bleachers, eh?"

He laughed, spraying Ann with spittle.

"I was at track practice," she whispered. "You can ask my coach."

He tottered a few steps forward, almost pinning Ann against the banister. "Where were you *really*?"

"I swear –"

"*Don't lie to me!*"

He whipped his hand back and brought it down across Ann's face.

Nik found her huddled against the bottom step ten minutes later, still holding her throbbing cheek. He rushed over, leaving the front door wide open behind him.

"Anna, Anna, what is it?"

He gently peeled her hand back. His nostrils flared. Ann could feel the fury bubbling up within him, almost choking them both.

"Nik, no –"

He shot up and flew into the living room, where their stepfather was now passed out on the couch. Ann scrambled across the floor just in time to see her brother haul the man up and shove him against a picture on the wall. Their stepfather's eyes were barely open, his mouth sagging – Ann remembered that face, that red, gaping mask, harmless and grotesque. Without hesitating, Nik leaned back and drove his fist straight into it.

There was a shattering of glass as their stepfather's head smashed back into the picture frame. He dropped to the floor. Nik stood over him, chest heaving. His back was to Ann.

"*Don't you touch her ever again!*"

Cold air blew in from the open door. The stepfather blinked up at Nik, blood pouring out of his nose and down the wall behind him. Then, quite unexpectedly, he began to laugh. Loud, braying shouts of hysteria.

"I know –" he laughed – "I know, I know your *secret*, little boy –"

Nik didn't move.

"I know –" their stepfather went on. "I *see* –"

He was silenced with a swift kick.

"*Shut up!*" Nik shrieked.

He spun around, and for one brief second, the twins' eyes met. It was just for an instant before he turned away, but in that instant Ann felt the grief and the fear and the isolation of the last two years finally well up, threatening to pull her under. He felt it too, and for that instant, his heart reached out to her, like an outstretched hand. But it was quickly snapped away again, with a force more jarring, more painful than her stepfather's slap.

"Nik –" she gasped.

But he was gone. Ann watched the front door slam behind him, shutting out the cold night beyond.

Chapter Five

That night, Ann dreamt of many things. She dreamt of cold winter winds and empty houses. She dreamt of Hersa's voice, lovely and sad as she sang a song of lost loves and forgotten lands. She dreamt of mountains, of moonlit beaches, of dark caves and darker waters. Then she dreamt of nothing.

And when she woke, it was with the certainty that she was not alone.

There was something in the room with her. Not a person, no, but a presence as lively and as warm. It reminded her, unaccountably, of Erysia. It tickled and tugged at her as she dressed in her warmest woollen tunic, careful to avoid the new, livid bruises that ringed her upper arms. It was a smell, almost, or a taste – something light and fresh, like the first hint of spring.

Which was odd, Ann thought as she found Kaenus already pawing at the common room door. Because today was the shortest and darkest day of the year.

After nine months, Ann was used to the strange sensations that emanated from the walls of the palace. Yet this was unlike anything she'd felt before. And other people could feel it too – she saw it in the ready smiles and laughter that greeted her around every corner. Moreover, the feeling was much more potent out in the sunshine than it had been in the shadows of the palace. And it got tangibly stronger as the morning advanced. Kaenus became harder to control, galloping off after every butterfly, rodent and snake within a ten metre radius. The worst moments were when they passed another dog – especially a female – and Ann's shoulders were almost wrenched from their sockets as she tried to haul him away. By the time they returned to the palace, she'd given up with a laugh and let him bound off. She didn't think anyone would mind. No one – she could tell – was impervious to the day.

It was well past midmorning when Ann headed to the baths. She was moving slowly, finding it harder to ignore the warmth growing in the pit of her stomach. She passed a few men who eyed her in a way that would normally have made her cringe, but she – to her horror – could feel her body responding to their stares in flutters and waves of heat. Head down, she picked up her pace, certain that the steaming, salted pools would relax her. But the hot currents just made matters worse. She left within minutes of her arrival.

There was, in her opinion, no worse moment for her to cross paths with the High Steward. When she spotted him walking in her direction along the passage, she stopped to flee, but he'd already seen her. His step faltered. His face hardened. And then he continued onward, brushing past her without the slightest acknowledgement. Ann waited for him to disappear around the corner before fairly sprinting back to her quarters.

As the afternoon wore on, Ann's condition grew worse. She began to feel flushed, feverish. By the time the sky outside her lightwell was beginning to darken, she was pacing back and forth in the common room, her breathing shallow, her nerves flaring at every passing sensation, every change in the air current.

When the knock came, Ann was at the door before a second one could fall.

"Come," was all Hersa said to her.

Ann followed.

***

They carved a path through the swell of bodies in the courtyard. The space was dark, lit only by the faint glow of candlelight. Forms flitted past Ann, reddened lips, bare breasts, oiled chests. Horned masks of clay. The air seemed to vibrate against Ann's skin as they pushed their way closer to the altar. It was as if the whole city was there, drawn to its nucleus by the ring of priests who stood at its centre, bearing candles and humming.

The humming stopped. All was suddenly so still that Ann became aware of the current in the air around her – not His pulse, no, not that. It was warmer, thicker. Sweeter. Every person present moved with it, swaying together like the rippling of seaweed on the ocean floor. The current shifted, drawing Ann nearer to its epicentre.

In which stood a man.

Even masked as he was in a gold-horned bull's head, it was impossible to mistake him. And standing there, broad and commanding, he seemed to her more god than *Kyn*.

The crowd shifted and split, allowing a line of priestesses to snake through the ring of priests. There was utter silence as the *Kynra* moved to her husband's side.

Her hand flew up.

"*This man is an affront to Pritymnia!*"

Her cry had the effect of a detonating bomb. Gasps of bewilderment passed back from the core in shock waves.

"He has banished Her priestesses from Her own lands," the woman continued, "tossing them out into the streets like dogs. We shall *not* roll over. We shall *not* sanction this travesty of a holy rite! Sisters, we depart!"

And with that, she shoved through the line of priests and stormed back through the Sisterhood doorways.

The woman had planned her intrusion well: the spell of the gathering was shattered. A buzz of anger grew throughout the crowd like the drone of bees. Someone up in one of the balconies shouted out and a mask was thrown through the air, smashing against the flagstones. The crowd was moments from disbanding – or worse.

And then he began to sing.

It began softly, unheard by the outraged crowd. But slowly, it rose over the noise like a wisp of smoke from a candle, curling and floating and expanding into transparent sheets of air. Ann heard it and her heart was stilled. That voice. That deep voice, with its wordless, resonant swells. It beckoned her, reaching into the very depths of who she was and who she had been. She saw the *Kyn*'s mouth moving beneath the mask, calling them all back to him. And it was as if nothing had ever torn her away. She was there, and Nik too, she could feel him. They were all there: it was his voice that bound them together. And when it plunged back down, sinking into silence, the whole palace seemed to hold its breath.

The light from the candles flickered and went out.

There was a rumbling, a rumbling deep within her, within the ground beneath her. It grew stronger and rose higher, until Ann felt she would choke on it.

And then, like a clap of thunder, the *Kyn* cried out, releasing bedlam.

***

Ann stumbled through the dark corridors, pushed forward by the heave of bodies at her back. Hands grasped at her dress and laced through her hair, then vanished, every contact sending a shiver across her skin, disorienting her further. Hersa was gone and Ann was alone, lost in the swarm.

From the moment the priests had begun driving everyone into the passages, Ann's anticipation had quickly pitched to panic. She was trapped, trapped in a nightmare of hide-and-seek. Every refuge she sought was occupied, every corridor teeming with couples. Blood pounded in her ears as she rushed through the maze like one pursued.

Eventually, though, the herd thinned and she was able to catch her breath. She was not too far from her apartments: on the other side of what appeared to be a series of empty official chambers was a staircase that would lead directly up to the elite residences.

She was passing through the final chamber when she realized that she had company.

"Listen to me!" she heard a familiar voice hiss. "I heard her myself, this morning in the baths."

Ann stood completely still in the dark, praying that she was as invisible to Afratea as the woman was to her.

"I am no *fool*, woman," replied the High Steward. He sounded unfocused, tentative. "I know you are trying to poison me."

"No, truly. She was laughing about it. She said that she wanted you to prove yourself. She said that she wanted you to *beg*."

There was a scuffle then, and a grunt – as if someone had been shoved back against a wall – followed by a sharp intake of breath, and, a few seconds later, a groan: a low, guttural sound of both pain and gut-stirring pleasure.

Ann fled. She tore away, back in the direction she'd come from, her only thoughts of putting as much distance between her and that sound – that *sound*, that seemed to her more animal than human. That sound that hunted her through the corridors until she came to a dead end.

She was standing in a small enclave. Less than two feet away was a surge of movement, unidentifiable at first – then she realized. Two people were locked together. Rocking in that relentless, desperate way.

What little control she had left, she lost then. She ran. She flew past piles of bodies and grasping hands, she climbed stairs, almost getting caught in the tangle of limbs that stretched down its length. She bolted past open doors, with moans and cries sounding from beyond. And then, quite abruptly it seemed, she found herself in the corridor of her own apartments.

But she was not alone. As Ann neared her rooms, she could just make out two figures – one small and one large – blocking the doorway. She approached slowly. And when she was close enough to determine their features, she clamped both hands over her mouth and froze.

Hersa and Nik. Entwined. With Nik's hand groping for the door handle.

Then Hersa lurched away.

"No, Niklas, I cannot."

Nik reached out, pulling her back to him. "Yes. Yes, you can."

There was silence for a moment, and a little shiver of movement. Ann knew she should leave. But she also knew that if she was going to find shelter anywhere that night, it was beyond that door.

"Niklas, no…"

"Why not?" Nik asked softly.

"Because," came Hersa's breathless voice, "I see what happens to the women you bed."

Nik's head snapped back as if she had struck him. His hands dropped to his sides.

"I – oh, Niklas, I did not mean *that*. I meant –"

"I know what you meant."

"Niklas, *please*. I have been in this position before. It was –"

"I know what it was. Everyone does. You think the *Kyn* feels the need to keep quiet every time he fucks a servant?"

Ann realized it was really time to go. So, holding her breath, she tiptoed back down the corridor, and left the pair to their own fate.

***

Ann had taken refuge on an abandoned balcony just south of her rooms. The sky was clear and the moon was out, hovering over the mountains to the east. She leaned against the balustrade and let out a sigh. This night could only last so long.

She only realized how foolish she'd been to isolate herself when she heard the soft fall of footsteps behind her.

His mask was gone, his long hair tied back. How he'd managed to find her in a place so choked with people, she had no idea.

"There you are."

His voice was low, hoarse. Ann pressed her back against the balustrade.

He stopped within a foot of her. Eyes unfocused, mouth slightly open – Ann's brain noted these things, just as it noted the quiver that passed over her own body in response to his nearness. She stood as motionless as the stone at her back.

Then someone in a nearby room cried out and the High Steward seized her. Within an instant, his arms were around her waist, his tongue sliding into her mouth. It happened so quickly that Ann had no time to register, no time to resist. Yet it was only another second before she found that she did not want to. The fire that had been smouldering in her all day roared up to meet his, consuming her in a flash. Her hands were up, on his abdomen, across his chest, twining in his hair. From deep within him came that very same guttural groan.

"I have waited so long for this."

His breath was spicy, but also sour, like old wine. He leaned in, crushing her to him. Pressing against the very new, very tender bruises on her arms.

Ann gasped. Mistaking it for a gasp of pleasure, the man gripped her tighter. She cried out. He pulled his head away, looking dazed and unsteady.

"What is it? What is wrong?"

"You – I – I don't know what's wrong with me."

He responded by pulling her hips, hard, against his. She could feel him then, rigid against her. She flinched away. He tried to pull her closer again but she slipped out beneath his arm and backed up a few steps.

"I can't," she said holding a hand up between them. "There's something wrong –"

"It is the Tide of Darkness, Ann. Surrender to it."

He was advancing again.

"No," she said. "This doesn't change anything."

He seemed to wake up a little then. He spoke quietly but firmly.

"You are mine, Ann. I will not beg, because I have no need to. You have left your other life behind you. Who you belonged to there does not matter now. You are here –" he closed the distance between them again – "and you are mine."

He pushed his lips back down on hers painfully. This time, she shoved him away.

"Why can't you hear me? I don't belong to anyone – least of all to you!"

Standing with his back to the moon, she couldn't make out his expression. She did see his body tense, though, a split-second before he lunged at her. Then she was up against the wall, one of his hands across her chest, holding her in place, while the other groped at her skirts. She couldn't breathe, she couldn't move; the weight of his body was crushing her.

A growl from behind. The moment the man turned Ann brought her knee up into his groin. He doubled over and she staggered away. There was a loud rip as one of her sleeves tore beneath his grasp. Tugging again, she pulled free.

And then she was flying across the balcony and back into the darkness of the palace. She heard barking behind her, but she did not stop. Her heart was racing and her feet were pounding, carrying her back to the safety of her apartments.

***

After the night Nik left, Ann's stepfather seemed reformed. He drove her to school every morning. He offered her an allowance, even cleaned up after dinner. The man was terrified, Ann knew. Terrified of what would happen if she told the school counsellors what had really caused the purple blotch that still covered half her face. She knew that the moment that the bruise faded, things would return to normal. And yet that was not the reason she left, two weeks later.

He'd driven Nik away, driven him away from her, and every day that she remained in his house that loss became harder to bear.

She went to the lawyer's. And he was more than happy to have her. He welcomed her into his apartment, offering to sleep on the couch, to cook her dinner. He seemed overjoyed by her presence and Ann was overwhelmed by the sense that, for once, she was actually wanted.

And then, about a month after she'd arrived, he asked her to marry him. She'd initially thought he was joking, yet when it became clear that he wasn't, she didn't know what to say. She told him that she wasn't even of age. They'd only been seeing each other for a few months, she said. But he was insistent. He was older, he knew something special when he had it. They would wait, he assured her. It was less than a year until she turned eighteen, and then they would be married. Finally, Ann accepted.

Late that night, Ann was woken by a shaft of light falling across her face. Then the light went out and the door clicked shut again.

He had also smelled of wine, Ann remembered. The celebratory wine they'd had at dinner. He'd slipped into her bed and began by kissing her neck, and then her shoulders, and then her breasts. She'd lain still, unsure of what to do. But when his hands had wandered under the waist of her shorts, she'd laughed nervously and wriggled away. His responding laugh had been thick and slow. He'd reached out again. She'd pulled away, and he'd pulled her closer.

Afterward, Ann laid awake, pinned under his arm, not daring to risk waking him by moving. Her limbs began to grow numb and still she lay motionless. She let the cold spread, the numbness taking hold. And it was only then, in the chill of that early morning, that she let herself think of Nik.

Where was he?

Was he okay? How was he living?

Should she have gone with him?

Would he even have let her?

And as the man on top of her began to stir and tighten his grasp, she wondered if she would ever see her brother again.

*****

Ann bolted the door of her apartments, heart still pounding. She listened for a moment. There was no sound from Nik's bedroom.

"Ann?"

Her back was against the door, her hand on the latch in an instant. There was a stirring of movement in the shadows as the *Kyn* stepped into the dim glow of the lightwell.

"Forgive me for startling you, Ann. I had to speak with you."

Ann peered into his face uncertainly.

"Do you have a light in here?" he asked.

She nodded.

"Ann?"

"Yes – I think so."

"Good. Fetch it."

Ann sidled into her bedroom, unwilling to turn her back to the man. She brought out her brazier, embers still glowing. She could just make out the *Kyn*'s expression. He seemed calm.

Yet as she watched him his face began to change, his eyes widening as he took in her missing sleeve, her mussed hair and torn skirt. He moved toward her and she flinched back again, toward the door. He frowned, then slowly, brought his hands up. She let him approach. With great care, he took hold of her arm, his thumb brushing over the bruises that were clear even in the gloom.

"Who did this to you?"

Ann said nothing.

"Who did this to you?" he repeated.

"Ask your friend," she whispered.

"My –?"

"Why are you here?"

"I was told…" He shook his head as if trying to clear it. "I heard that there was a commotion at the initiation rites yesterday. Heremus came to me last night…" He paused, his eyes widening again. "*He* did not do this to you?"

Even in the orange glow she could see the man's face drain of colour. After a long moment, he whispered,

"It pains me to know this."

He turned away, pacing back to the other side of the room. When he turned back to speak to her, his voice – that voice which had enchanted her only hours before – was shaking.

"I will speak to him, Ann. I will. It will never happen again, I swear to you. He is a good man, he is, he is only… used to getting what he wants, I suppose. It will not happen again." There was a pause, and then – "Please reconsider, Ann."

She could not believe what she was hearing. "You still want me to *accept* him?"

The *Kyn*'s gaze faltered for just an instant. "Yes."

"Why? So I can be his *Kynra*? So I can be everything you've been training me to be?"

"My training, as you put it, has not been much. And you would be the making of him, Ann."

He moved forward again, reaching out to touch her face. She jerked away.

"What a *Kynra* you would make," he whispered.

Ann felt tears stinging at the corners of her eyes. But she would not cry – not in front of him. Never again.

"I will not marry him, *Kyn*."

"You do not know what you are refusing, Ann. No one would question your claim to anger, yet you must not let it cloud your judgment."

"I know exactly what I'm refusing. I've seen it in your wife –"

The man scoffed.

"I've seen it in *you* –"

"Me?"

"Yes, you. You're alone, completely alone and you're miserable." As soon as she said it, she knew it was true. "You have no true partner, no family – nothing except an obsession with your city –" she recalled Hersa with a pang – "and the occasional mistress to warm your bed for you. You chose a woman you couldn't love for the good it might do your people and now you're asking me to do the same."

The *Kyn* was quiet for a moment. "You are right, Ann. I have given all for this city – more than you could know. Yet I have never regretted it. Because it was my *duty*. And now I am asking you to take up yours."

"What duty? I don't owe you anything. You want me to lead this city so badly, then name me your heir directly!"

The words flew out as if by themselves – and the *Kyn* looked as astonished as she felt. He was silent for a long time.

"You do not know what you ask, Ann. It *must* be a man who inherits the governance of Kabyrnos."

Ann was nodding. She wasn't sure if she was more relieved or enraged. "I see. You want me to give my life for your city, but only in a way that suits you."

"You do not know what you ask," he repeated. "And I do not regret my choices."

Ann moved to the door. But before she left, she turned to take one last look at the man who seemed to take up all the space in the twins' tiny chamber.

"Then neither do I," she said.

***

She moved out into the eastern pastures, Kaenus with her again, no worse for the wear. She shivered. The wind had picked up and was tearing through her ruined dress, bending the trees around her, ripping leaves from branches. Kaenus whined.

"You can go back if you want," she snapped over her shoulder.

But he followed her through the grove of wild fig trees, past the ring of cypresses that were whipping in the wind, and to the edge of the city. Then he clamped his teeth on the hem of her dress and refused to go any further.

"Are you coming or not?" she demanded.

He looked up at her with round, pleading eyes.

"Fine then."

She ripped her skirt free and turned away from him.

She couldn't say why she needed to move forward so badly. Or what was drawing her out into the moonlit streets of the city. She had an idea though, and for once, the thought didn't frighten her.

The streets were empty. Ann headed north, pushed along by the gust of wind that blew in from the valley. She did not shiver now. She kept on moving north, past the silent workshops and into the streets of the Northern District. The alleys were barren, the wind keening over the rooftops. She continued onward. And as she turned another corner into a narrow street, she spotted a small figure huddled on the steps of a house.

Here. Now.

The woman was dressed in a plain woollen tunic, with a shock of white hair whipping around her. Her eyes were sunken, two tiny beads staring out of a ravaged face. A face that pulled at Ann's memory.

"This is no night to be outside, *Prona*," Ann said as that face turned up toward her. "Why are you not by your hearth?"

"My hearth no longer holds any warmth for me."

And then Ann knew where she'd seen her before. She recalled a flash of white lightning as she stared down into the mother's face. She kneeled.

"Your boy…"

"He is dead."

"Yes. I'm sorry."

The two remained as they were for some minutes, silent, a lonely pair amidst the storm of the night. Then the woman whispered,

"It was not always so."

"What was not, *Prona*?"

"Not long ago, he would not have had to die. Zelkanus, he – he altered it. He told us that the gods were demanding more. They would no longer be appeased by the willing life of a poppy-addled priest. They demanded a young life now, a life full of potential, full of…" The woman's voice died away.

"The *Kyn* said this?"

"Almost ten years ago. The year my boy was born. And yet our crops have not bettered, and the plague returns every year."

A *Kyn* must provide answers, he'd once told her. A *Kyn* cannot look to the interests of one over the interests of the city, he'd said.

The wind roared, whipping away her tears. Calling out her name.

She rose to her feet.

"Excuse me, *Prona*," she said. "There is something I must do."

As she turned away the woman reached out and grabbed her wrist. Her touch was frigid, but her eyes blazed brightly.

"God of Darkness give you strength, Huntress."

***

The moon was high now, the courtyard empty. Ann moved towards the western doorways, up to the door of the Chamber of the Earth Mother and pounded her fist against it.

It opened. Darkylus stood in the shadows there.

"She is not here," he said simply.

"Then take me to her."

He picked up a lamp, and led her out through the rear doorway of the Chamber without a word. They moved through the narrow passageways and out into the Courtyard of the Dying Sun. And there, facing the blackened oak, was the *Kynra*.

The woman was a wraith, her loose hair and robe lashing against the bones of her body. The lamp had blown out the moment Darkylus had stepped outdoors, yet the *Kynra* seemed to sense them, turning as they neared.

"I knew it."

The wind stole away the words, but Ann had seen them shaped on that lipless mouth.

And finally, she understood.

The *Kynra had* known it. Perhaps it had also been a gamble, but the woman must have been fairly certain that, given some time, Ann would come to her freely. She would have known that her threat was a flimsy one, that any power she held would be easily countered by the *Kyn*. But she would also have suspected that, in time, he would drive Ann back to her. And that was the point, Ann saw. The *Kynra* needed her to come willingly. The task required it.

"You will begin training tomorrow," she called over the wind. "Meet my man at dawn in the bull's pasture to the east."

Ann nodded and turned back to the palace. And as she walked away from the twisted tree, she remembered something the *Kyn* had said to her, many moons back.

You must stop holding yourself back.

"If that's what you want," she whispered into the night, "then that's exactly what you'll get."

Book V

Chapter One

Dawn was cold and crisp. Ann shivered beneath her fur mantle and watched her breath expand and dissipate into the morning light.

She had come out well before sunrise. And although it could not have been below freezing even then – it rarely even frosted here, not so close to the sea – it was cold enough to numb her booted toes before she'd made it out of the pine grove.

It had been a night of upheaval. Branches torn from trees, fences blown over, doors hanging from hinges. And it was a morning of stark realities. As the light had grown in the east to reveal the full scope of the windstorm's wreckage, Ann had settled in to wait. Alone.

Kaenus had not returned to the apartments the night before. Ann had scoured the copses, the stables, the paddocks but eventually had been forced to accept that he would find her when he wanted to.

So she waited. When she first spotted a movement in the pines, it was nothing more than a stirring of the shadows. Then, slowly, very slowly, a shape began to form. Hulking, three-legged and fur-covered, the man limped toward the boundary of the trees and out into the sun.

The *Kynra*'s trainer halted before Ann, leaning on a walking stick and heaving a sigh that momentarily clouded the air between them. Ann waited for him to say something, but the man only looked at her, raking her with keen black eyes. Somehow making it clear without speaking that he'd come expecting one thing and had found another.

Then the man whipped his stick up and she flinched.

"Expecting someone?" he asked in a gruff, sand-paper voice.

The stick was pointing over her shoulder toward the valley. Ann turned.

A lean figure was trotting out of the slanting light toward her. Forgetting the stranger, she ran to meet her dog, throwing herself down onto the dewy grass to let him cover her face in licks.

"I don't deserve you," she muttered into his mangled ear.

The stranger thumped up behind them and Kaenus squirmed out of her grasp to investigate.

"I thought he was – lost," she explained as she rose to her feet.

The stranger grunted – one blunt, monosyllabic sound – and shoved Kaenus away with his stick. The dog had been sniffing at the man's weaker leg. Before Ann could take a proper look, the man turned away and started limping north.

Ann followed, careful to keep at least two steps behind. Kaenus, however, pranced next to the man, sniffing at his bear-like cape as the three of them moved north, past the houses of the city and into the countryside beyond.

When they reached a clearing in a small wooded area, the stranger finally stopped, dropping onto a flat boulder with another sigh. He then pointed his stick into the glade.

"Show me," he grumbled.

Kaenus flopped down next to the man's rock.

"E-excuse me?" Ann asked.

"What you can do. Show me."

Ann moved out into the centre of the space and turned round to face him. She hesitated.

"You must be able to do something," the man growled. "Show me!"

Feeling like a fool, Ann removed her mantle and tried a tentative somersault. She peered back at the man. He made no protest, so she proceeded to take him through the whole routine: the somersaults, the front and back handsprings, the front flips, a rough-but-effective back flip. When she had finished, out-of-breath and sweating, she stood in front of him, waiting for further direction.

All she got was a grumbled, "That is all?"

"...Unless you want to see me run?"

Another grunt. Ann stared at him, trying to decide whether it had been a no-grunt or a yes-grunt. When the man only continued to frown at her, she backed up, kneeled and launched forward, quickly ramping up into a full sprint. She hurtled through the clearing and another forty metres or so beyond, then circled back.

Again, she stood breathless before him. The man cleared his throat, the sound like two stones grating together.

"I see."

Those black eyes combed over her body once more.

"Do you box?"

"Me?" Ann asked.

"No, the dog. Yes, you."

"Not really, no."

"Grapple?"

"No."

"Shoot?"

She blinked at him.

"Bows. Arrows. Shooting."

She shook her head.

"Hmph. Spar?"

Another shake.

"Jump?" he asked, looking as if he knew the answer to this one too.

Ann was confused. "Like…" She hopped a bit into the air, then blushed furiously, realizing just how stupid she must look.

"Hmph."

Then the stranger rested both paw-like hands on his stick and peered over them at Ann for another full minute before speaking.

"First, we will work on strength," he grumbled as he heaved himself to his feet. "You will need muscle if you are to stand even a chance."

The man fumbled beneath his cape and pulled out two objects: a Y-shaped implement, and a flat bronze disc with a hole in the centre. He wedged his stick into the crook of his arm and loaded the disc into the band of the Y. Then he leaned back on his good leg and shot the disc, with impeccable aim, into the top branches of a nearby tree. He procured five more discs and shot them into five other trees.

"Fetch those," he muttered, already limping away. "And if you are still alive tomorrow, meet me here at dawn."

***

It took Ann the better part of the day to collect the six discs. By the time she'd dragged herself back to the palace, bruised, scratched and still trembling from her many near-falls, she was half-convinced that the *Kynra* was playing an elaborate joke on her. Hobbling straight up to the dining hall, where Athyla, Tefkelerea and Trydus were already eating their dinners, she collapsed on the bench next to them. Her forehead hit the table with a *thunk*.

"You look like death come alive," Athyla commented as Tefkelerea leaned across the table to pluck a twig out of Ann's hair.

"What did you do?" Trydus asked. "Slay another monster?"

Ann thought of the stranger. "Not yet," she grumbled, reaching for a piece of salted fish on Athyla's plate.

The girl smacked her hand away. "Get your own!"

Sighing, Ann began to struggle back to her feet, when Tefkelerea – kind, giving, saintly Tefka – offered to fetch her plate.

Trydus pointed one work-hardened finger at Ann's fist, now propped beneath her chin. She was still gripping the six bronze discs like the hard-won trophies they were.

"Where did you get those?" he asked.

"They're for training," Ann mumbled. "I think."

"So you are doing it, then?" Athyla asked. "You are going out for one of the Five?"

Ann grunted – then snorted, realizing who she sounded like. But Trydus was still staring at the discs.

"Is someone – *assisting* you, Ann?"

She peered at him curiously. "Yeah. In theory."

"A man with a limp?"

"Yes. How –?"

Trydus was shaking his head. "I thought as much, yet..."

"What?" Ann asked, sitting up straight now. "What is it?"

"Your trainer is Hefanos, our Master Bronzesmith."

Ann's mouth fell open. "*Afratea's husband?*"

Both Trydus and Athyla nodded, smiling at her expression. Then Tefkelerea returned, putting Ann's plate down in front of her.

"Did I miss something?" the girl asked, looking between Trydus, Athyla and Ann – who had fallen on her small rations like a starved animal.

"She –" Trydus jabbed his finger at Ann – "is being trained by the Master Bronzesmith."

Tefkelerea was impressed. "I thought he had refused to have anything to do with the Tournament."

"Huh?" Ann looked up, mouth full. "Why?"

Her friends were silent for a moment, then Athyla leaned forward. "Hefanos was Champion of Kabyrnos three times over. The first time he won, he was the youngest Champion at eighteen years of age, the last as the oldest, at twenty-eight."

"Yet," Trydus added in a whisper, "he was gored on his final leap of the bull."

Ann choked on her bread. "His *what*?" she asked, coughing.

"At the end of the Tournament, the top ranking contestants must leap the horns of a bull, twice." Trydus went on as Tefkelerea patted Ann's back sympathetically. "He made it over, yet the bull's horn caught his leg. He was lucky not to be killed. Many are, you know."

Ann slowly pushed her plate away.

"It is *said*," Athyla added, "that there was some trickery –"

"That is just gossip," Tefkelerea reproached.

"That is what we are doing, is it not – gossiping? It is *said* that a flash of light distracted Hefanos at the crucial moment. They *say* –"

"Come now, Athyla," Trydus sighed.

Athyla glared at her friends and leaned in closer to Ann. "They say that Zelkanus was responsible for it."

"But – why would he do that?"

"They say that he desired Afratea, and that he was very upset when she chose to marry Hefanos instead of becoming his mistress. Although there is nothing to say she has not done so since."

"That really is enough now," Tefkelerea said quietly.

Athyla folded her arms and sat back, as if to say her work here was done anyway.

"I apprenticed under Hefanos as a bronzesmith for four years," Trydus added, watching Ann closely. "He would not have taken this role unless he had a very good reason."

Then the young man's gaze flicked up to something beyond Ann. Someone cleared their throat.

"Pardon me, Huntress."

Ann twisted in her seat to see the *Kyn*'s manservant, bowing low.

"The *Kyn* has requested your company, Huntress. He said that you had a matter that needed to be attended to this morning."

The *Kynra*. They were supposed to have gone to refuse her together.

Ann took a deep breath. "Tell him that I have already done so."

"Perhaps," the manservant said slowly, "you would like to tell him yourself? He is waiting, even now."

"Tell him that I cannot," she said, voice hard.

The man stared at her.

"Tell him," she went on, "that I have to wake early. For training."

The manservant's face was very still for a moment before he bowed again. "Very well, *Prona*. I will do so."

When he was gone, Ann turned back to her friends, who were looking at her as if she'd lost her mind.

"What was *that* about?" Athyla asked.

"Nothing."

"Ann," Tefkelerea began, "surely it is not wise to refuse the *Kyn* so…"

"Rudely," Athyla finished for her.

Ann said nothing. Trydus was looking at her again, eyes narrowed. She stood.

"Well, I'm tired, so…"

She turned to go, but a soft touch held her back.

"Just be careful, Ann," Tefkelerea said.

"Easy, Tefka," Trydus said, crossing his arms over his chest. "I am sure the Huntress knows exactly what she has gotten herself into."

***

The next morning, Hefanos was already settled on his rock by the time Ann and Kaenus arrived in the clearing. He glared at Ann over his walking stick as she placed the bronze discs at his feet and backed away. And then his stick flashed out, pointing east through the trees.

"You see that mountain?"

Ann nodded.

"I expect you to be here before the sun touches its peak."

Ann gulped and nodded again.

"Every time you are late, I will shoot three more discs. You waste my time, I waste yours." He fixed her with a long, keen stare. "You will train from dawn till dusk. You have work?"

"I – I weave."

"I will speak to the Mistress of the Loom. At dusk, you will eat, you will bathe, you will receive a massage – every day, mind you. If the women in the baths complain, refer them to me – and then you will sleep. This will be your life from now on. Understand?"

Ann nodded.

"You will train here. Always. You will not approach the other trainees. Excellence is attained by focusing on your own abilities, not fixating on others'."

He paused to take a long drink from the waterskin at his belt.

"Understand me, girl. You have four moons to become the best. Not good, not great – the best. And even *if* you manage that, the muttonheads who run this city may simply decide that you are too great a risk. So, for the next season, you will do exactly as I say. You will live for my command. Have I made myself clear?"

Ann swallowed. "You have."

"Good." He pointed his stick at a small boulder. "Now go fetch me that stone."

***

In the next moon cycle, Hefanos put Ann through a series of labours that left her in a perpetual state of agony. Trial by pain, he said – as if it was a joke. He had her sprinting at dawn ("if you can push *now*, imagine how fast you will be when you are fully awake.") and building balance and strength for the rest of the day. She heaved and pitched stones ("Back *straight*!"). She did pull-ups off branches ("Chest to wood, girl!"). She did lunges with bags of sand balanced on her shoulders – and if her trainer thought she was not sinking close enough to the ground with each step, he would trip her with his stick and make her rise – sandbags and all – without the aid of her hands. He drove her relentlessly. Every day she would hobble to and from the clearing, aching, throbbing and stiff. She only once made the mistake of remarking to her trainer that her body might need a break to heal itself. She spent the rest of that day fetching discs out of trees. And perched up there, thirty feet off the ground, Ann realized just how easy it would be to put herself out of her misery.

In fact, the more she trained under Hefanos the more she understood how much this truly was a game of life or death. The man was wearing her into the ground: if she survived, she'd be remade as one of the finest athletes on the island; if not, well, that was her problem. She drove her body so hard that her monthly blood simply stopped coming. She fell asleep in the baths so often that she considered it a miracle that she never drowned. But she was always woken in time for her massage – more torture – and then sent tottering back up to her rooms to continue sleeping.

Her brother was almost always in their apartments in the evenings now. At first, Ann was too exhausted to notice the change in him – she would simply stumble into her room, where she would collapse into a deep, coma-like slumber. Yet it was impossible to ignore the snubbed greetings for long – or the way he would often leave the common room when she entered it, without having said a word. Soon she began wondering if she'd done something wrong. If maybe his pride was bruised by her training for the Five, or if Hersa's continued absence was hurting him more than he wanted to let on. But after almost half a month of this silent treatment, Ann stopped wondering. Since when had her brother needed an excuse to be cruel?

"*He* left *me*," she said to herself one evening as she watched the door close – yet again – behind him.

The next day, she trained even harder.

And as the days wore on (the twins' twenty second birthday passing unnoticed) the Master

Bronzesmith continued to find creative ways to keep her pushing to the limit. She did squats on one leg while holding a large rock out in front of her. She balanced on a low branch, while raising the rest of her body parallel to the ground. Through all this, Hefanos would sit on his rock, take swigs out of his waterskin – which Ann had become fairly sure did not contain water – and feed Kaenus little scraps of salted meat that he carried in a pouch on his belt. Soon, the man had instilled in Ann such respect for proper form that he rarely felt the need to give any instruction at all – except, of course, when he felt that her breaks between drills were bordering on the profane, at which points he would simply growl at her. Growling or not, Ann found his constant, watchful presence intensely annoying. But she could not deny the effect that his tutelage was having on her body. He was reworking her into a cohesive machine.

What was becoming increasingly apparent, though, was that Ann did not have enough to eat. Three times a day she would devour her meagre rations – which seemed to be getting smaller as the weather got colder – leaving her stomach still rumbling. And the harder she tried to push, the harder it became to move through the dizzy spells. She never complained though: she'd learned her lesson. And Hefanos didn't seem to notice. Yet on one chilly, overcast afternoon, he limped into the clearing and tossed a large bag onto the ground by her feet.

"Where did this come from?" she asked in amazement as she stared into the bag. It contained a few large lumps of cheese, two hunks of bread and a waterskin full of olive oil, all sitting atop a small mountain of raisins, dried figs and pistachios.

Hefanos responded with a particularly dismissive grunt. But Ann persisted.

"I can't take your rations, Teacher."

"They are not mine."

"Then whose are they?"

Hefanos shot her a glare, but then, surprisingly, he told her.

"They are Erea's."

Ann thought of the *Kynra*, already dangerously thin as it was. "I don't think I can –"

"Do you think that your whining will make any difference?" he growled. "Repeat that exercise. Twice. Your blood has cooled."

Despite the regular gifts of extra food, Hefanos continued to be a harsh master. The rainy season began in earnest, yet it did not bring the downpours that Ann had been warned of. Instead the sky seemed to linger in a state of perpetual grey, choking the air with a cold damp that seemed to permeate Ann's bones. Hefanos pushed her harder, refusing even to let her return to the palace to change her tunic, while he himself sat beneath a waxed woollen cloth that he had tied between branches. Ann began bringing her spare tunics out into the clearing, but as nothing ever seemed to dry anymore, she resigned herself to training in wet, chafing wool. Every day, she expected to wake up with a cold or worse. And yet, whether through miracle or sheer terror of what Hefanos would do to her if she fell ill, she remained healthy. In constant pain, but otherwise strong.

Then the Plague arrived. It rolled into the city like a fog of pestilence, and the palace corridors began to ring with the coughs of those who had fallen prey to its chills and fevers. Ann thought she recognized the common flu when she saw it, but without the safety net of modern medicine, she was not even tempted to argue when Hefanos forbade her from entering the common places of the palace. He arranged with the cooks to have her food specially prepared and delivered to her room once a day. He insisted that she fetch her own water for cleaning and drinking. Sponge-bathing once again became a daily necessity. Almost overnight, Ann's world shrank to that empty, lonely clearing. She spoke to no one but Hefanos – which, of course, meant that she hardly spoke at all. She felt like a ghost, a restless spirit haunting a city that had taken on an insubstantial quality, like a photograph whose lines have been blurred. Half the population seemed to be in quarantine; the other half, in hiding. So it came as a particular shock to Ann one morning when she was met at the eastern exit by the Guard Commander.

The woman looked different – thinner, harder. More brittle. Then again, they all looked like that these days. Yet her gaze was as direct as ever.

"The *Kyn* wishes to see you," she said simply.

Ann pushed around her to continue walking. "I thought you'd given up playing messenger."

"It is not a message," the guardswoman replied, keeping pace. "It is a fact."

"Then it won't be rude for me not to respond, will it?"

The woman walked in silence for a moment, then asked, "What makes you more entitled than the rest of us?"

"I'm entitled to see or not see whoever I like – without having to explain myself."

"I was not asking for an explanation. I *was* concerned for the *Kyn* and I thought that you might be as well. Clearly, you are not." She paused. "Yet, in truth, I was speaking of the Tournament."

Ann peered at her, frowning. The woman stopped walking.

"What entitles *you*," she repeated slowly, "to compete against the men?"

A genuine question. Ann took a breath.

"Nothing," she said, exhaling. "Nothing that doesn't entitle every other person."

The Guard Commander was very still for a moment. Then she dipped her head once, in a curt bow.

Ann watched her move back through the pine grove. Then she picked up her pace in order to make it to the clearing on time. The sky behind the clouds in the east was brightening in a hazy flush that spread behind the mountains. And all Ann could think about was what the guardswoman had said.

She was concerned for the *Kyn*. But, clearly, Ann was not.

Ann pushed into a run. It was better this way.

***

Time moved at an irregular, disorienting pace. In Ann's exhaustion, every moment felt like it lasted an age, and yet the days seemed to melt in to one another. She often found that she would only have to blink for the world around her to change. Nearby meadows and hills were suddenly dotted with grazing sheep, brought down from their mountain plateaus for the season. Unusual activity sparked in the valley as those labourers with some strength left began the harvest of the black olives. Overnight it seemed that the island had transformed yet again, the colours sharpening into a palette of vivid contrasts, with the alabaster of the mountains, the emerald blush of the lowlands and the sapphire of the sea. A brilliant picture that would take Ann by surprise on those few occasions that she stopped to notice it.

The only change that she was constantly aware of was the transformation of her body. There was no escaping the firmness where there had been softness, the new ripples and bulges – the ease with which she flew through the exercises that once had knocked her out cold. After nearly a full moon cycle, she had forgotten what it was to live without physical discomfort, but she had also forgotten what it was not to feel her body respond to her slightest command. It was as if she had willed herself into being. Out of sheer resolve, she had created power. And for the first time since the *Kynra* had mentioned the idea to her, she allowed herself to feel hope.

Chapter Two

"Five competitions."

Ann halted at the edge of the clearing. It was dusk, the sky shining a ruddy brown through the trees to the west, but Hefanos was still seated, hands resting on his stick as he peered up at her.

"Wrestling. Archery. Jumping. Boxing. And the races. There will be almost fifty competitors. Roughly half from the six cities of Kapreitu, half from the six southern Gyklanean tribes. The top five contestants in each competition are ranked, first place receiving five points, second place four points, and so on. The competitor with the highest score at the end of the Tournament wins the role of Champion – provided he can clear the bull twice."

Ann was careful to keep her eyes on his shadowed face. His scarred leg, tucked behind his strong one, did not stir.

"All five top-ranked athletes will try the leap. If there is only one who completes it, he will win. Regardless of rank. Are you still breathing, girl?"

Ann nodded.

"A Champion must be skilled in every field. A competitor who does fairly well in every competition stands a higher chance of winning than one who excels in only one."

He took a deep drink from his waterskin and went on.

"Wrestling is the first competition," he muttered, coughing slightly. "One-on-one matches, first person to score three points wins. You score by forcing your opponent's back, hips or shoulders to the ground, or ejecting them from the arena – or by forcing them to submit."

Ann shifted her weight uneasily.

"Next is archery. Very simple. The targets are moved back until only one contestant can hit. Then the jumps. The athlete who leaps the furthest across the pit wins. Fourth is boxing. Have you seen a sparring match?"

Ann thought of the High Steward and the *Kyn* that day in the courtyard and nodded.

"It is very similar, yet without weapons. You strike at the ribs, chest and shoulders with your fists and feet. Again, first to reach three points is victor. And finally, there is the race. Two laps around the arena. Very straightforward. You still with me?"

Ann swallowed and tried to say "yes".

"Good," he muttered, taking a final swig from his waterskin and pulling himself to his feet. "Then I will see you at the armouries tomorrow at dawn."

***

When Ann had lugged all the necessary equipment to the clearing the next morning, Hefanos was sitting on his rock again, sharing his breakfast with Kaenus. She dropped the final load into the newly built storage box and surveyed the lot. Several spools of sinew string and a mountain of arrows (no bow yet), four wooden staffs, some leather guards for shins, forearms, hands and head, and two clay weights with handles.

Hefanos beckoned her with a grunt.

"First thing you need to know," he said, gnawing on a piece of smoked pig meat, "is that every other trainee will have been honing these skills since he was a boy. We keep our men strong and fighting ready. You will have to catch up quickly and the only advantages you will have is your height and your speed."

Ann hid a smile; his very first compliment.

"Second thing is that you need to forget all that now. You practice as if you are the only person out there and you compete that way too. Doubt will undermine you more swiftly than any injury.

"Third, I have increased your rations."

Ann opened her mouth to ask but Hefanos silenced her with a glare.

"Now go to your sprints," he grumbled. "We begin with wrestling."

***

After Hefanos had explained the rules of the competition ("No hitting, kicking, biting, eye-gouging, finger-bending, nut-grabbing, or nipple-twisting. Everything else goes."), he had proceeded to show her the many ways in which she could be grounded. This involved – among other things – arm-twisting, joint and arm locks, grapple-holds and throws, and a surprisingly diverse array of chokeholds. At first, Ann had not been able to focus on anything beyond the overwhelming nearness of the man, which had provoked in her a kind of raw animal panic. It took nine hard landings and a chokehold that had made her see spots before her mind had cleared enough to register exactly what he was doing and how he was doing it. Not that it helped much.

"Especially for you," Hefanos told her at one point when he'd forced her to her knees, her arm wrenched up behind her, "wrestling is strategy. It is about foreseeing your opponent's move and using his weight and strength against him. Never meet him head on. And always remember that even the strongest man can be made weak if you find his vulnerable points."

He then pressed his fingers into the fleshy area between her thumb and index finger. Ann gasped, he released her, and as she lay on the grass, arm cradled against her chest, he took another drink from his waterskin and grunted. Point made.

He showed her all the pressure points – in between the tendons of the wrist, at the hollows of the neck, behind the collarbone, in the crease of the elbow, at various spots around the knee, the ankles. He applied only a small amount of force, but by the time he'd gone through the rota, Ann was sweating from pain. He then ordered her to try them on him. Initially, she couldn't work up the nerve to really press into him – but when Hefanos swept her into a lock that made her want to scream, she had little difficulty finding the right spot and digging in. Grunting, he let her go.

Over the course of the next few days, Hefanos took her slowly through all of the potential grips, holds and flips, showing her different ways to free herself and how to reverse each to her own advantage. He taught her to use her attacker's momentum to unbalance and force him down, how to twist and fall on her stomach if she was driven to the ground, how to flip her aggressor if he then tried to choke her from behind. He taught her how to throw a man twice her weight over her hip and how to anchor herself against her opponent's body. He drilled her in these manoeuvres so repetitively that they began to feel choreographed – a dance that her muscles could spin through without any interference from her brain. And yet, when put to the test in a real match, it was always she who went sailing through the air, she who landed in the dirt, she whose body became dappled with bruises of every colour. Only once did she manage to throw her trainer – and the sight of him on his back, shaggy brows raised in astonishment, was enough to bring a rusty smile to her face.

But he soon got his revenge.

One unusually bright morning, Ann arrived in the clearing to find Hefanos sitting in his usual spot with an enormous pile of pebbles by his feet. He pointed to a spot in front of him with his stick. Ann moved to stand there without question. But when he took out his slingshot, loaded a pebble and aimed, she began to protest.

"Wait –"

The pebble flew and smacked her in the ribcage. She gasped.

"If you do not want the pain," Hefanos warned as he loaded another pebble, "then dodge."

The next pebble flew, striking Ann in the breast. She doubled over and another bounced against her collarbone. Another pebble was loaded and released before she had finished gasping. This time, she tried to twist out of the way. It struck her hip. The next one grazed her arm. The next one missed.

"Boxing," he said, still firing away, "is about reflexes. Agility and speed. You dodge the strike, you do not lose. You get in a few of your own, you win."

"But –" A pebble landed on her knee cap and she yelped.

"No talking." He fired another. "Just dodge."

The pebbles continued to fly for the rest of the morning – and every morning after that until she learned to evade almost every shot. Welted and aching, she was then taken on to staffs. Competitors used to spar with staffs – Hefanos told her – but men were maimed and killed too often from illegal blows to the groin, head and neck. Not ideal for foreign relations, he added with a grating chuckle. But he still regarded familiarity with this kind of fighting as excellent training. Hefanos taught her to watch his muscles closely and detect the movement before he struck. He taught her that, like wrestling, she should never try to match strength to strength, but use her opponent's force to deflect and unbalance. When they abandoned the sticks and moved to hand-to-hand combat, he forced her to practice without the protective leather guards, telling her that if she could work through the pain now, she wouldn't be handicapped by it during the competition. He taught her to evade his strikes, to feint, to kick and punch with careful accuracy. And for a heavy man with a damaged leg, Hefanos proved to be a swift boxer. But his agility was limited: he soon brought in reinforcements.

Trydus joined them in the afternoon.

"My former apprentice has agreed to practice with you. In one-on-one combat, he is –" Hefanos coughed uncomfortably – "most skilled."

"Not in wrestling, Teacher," Trydus said in his easy way. "There you will always remain Champion."

Hefanos grunted but Ann could tell he was pleased. Trydus moved to centre of the clearing and Ann followed. The young bronzesmith was a full four inches shorter, but he had at least forty pounds on her, mostly in upper body muscle.

"Shall we box first, Teacher?" the young man called over his shoulder.

Grunt.

Trydus nodded briskly and crouched down, explaining, "He wants us to wrestle."

Ann crouched down too. Clearly, it took years of exposure to decipher the intricacies of the Master Bronzesmith's grunts.

The walking stick thumped twice. Ann was in the process of setting her shoulders back when Trydus swept in. She was on the ground within a second. When she glanced at her teacher, he was watching her over his stick with a small grin playing on his face. Even Kaenus seemed to be laughing at her, his maw spread wide.

"I wasn't ready," she muttered.

"Exactly," Hefanos said.

Trydus gave her a hand up and they began again.

She lost every match that afternoon. There were a few times that she managed to stay vertical for several minutes, but she never once even knocked Trydus off-balance. It was like coming at a wall – or having a wall come at her. When their final match of the day had concluded, the young man offered her another hand up but, annoyed, she swatted it away.

"Do not upset yourself, sweetling," he teased. "You will have another chance to lose tomorrow."

"Can't wait."

The next afternoon, they boxed. Ann proved herself to be marginally more competent in this sport, yet by the end of the afternoon, not only had she failed to come close to landing a strike, but every joint in her upper body was aching fiercely.

"I told you," Hefanos grumbled as he watched her rubbing her shoulders. "The instinct is to brace, protect the body. Yet if you block stiffly, you waste your strength and the impact jars you. Sweep it away."

Their matches improved after that. It was not too long before Ann could almost hold her own. Faced with a bit of a challenge for once, Trydus was forced to start trying, and the harder he tried, the better Ann became. Hefanos pushed them both, all the while watching Ann in a piercing way that made her feel, somehow, that he was looking for something in her that he knew was there but hadn't yet found. He barked orders at her, grumbled insults, chuckled at her failures, and yet when she finally managed to land her first strike, he did not seem at all surprised.

In the meantime, she spent her mornings on running technique. As Hefanos had explained to her, she was a natural runner and already very fast, but she needed to retrain her muscles, which were conditioned to longer distances. Two laps around the track was more of a prolonged sprint. Her trainer carefully measured out the distance – about four hundred metres or so, to Ann's eye – and had her doing sprinting intervals to increase both her speed and high-intensity endurance. He also made her execute regular drills, pumping knees to chin, heels to buttock. To train her muscles in proper form, he told her.

"Remember," he said to her, "you keep your form, it keeps you. Look forward, land on the balls of your feet. Keep your stomach tight, relax your shoulders, and make sure to draw your elbows all the way back with every stride. Your knees will balance out."

Then, one morning, he revealed his final racing tip to her. Ann was returning to the clearing after her last sprint of the day, exhausted but very pleased with her pace and expecting – if not praise, then some acknowledgement of a job well done. Instead, Hefanos glared at her.

"You are too cool," he accused her.

Ann planted her hands on her hips and waited for him to elaborate.

"You want to be faster?"

She shrugged: of course.

"Then stoke the flames."

It took her a moment to grasp his meaning, but when she did, she was shocked at how easy it was – at how much fuel she found right there beneath the surface, rising to her slightest call. And how quickly her body responded to it, her limbs tensing, her chest tightening.

"Good," she heard her trainer say. "Now fly."

She flew. Drained though her muscles were, they pumped and propelled and pushed her to her peak and past. For a few glorious moments, she lost track of the land racing beneath her feet – or the finish line marker that zipped by. She could only feel her heart thundering in her ribs like a wild animal, clawing for release. She pushed harder.

Her knee gave out and she went pitching into the shrubbery. She lay there for a moment, spread-eagled, watching the clouds spin above her. Then she dragged herself to her feet and limped to the clearing.

"Hmph," was all her trainer said.

But Ann was permitted a day's break before they moved on to jumping practice.

Ann had always done very well in high school track-and-field. As Hefanos had said, her height and speed were great assets – especially in the long jumps. But she soon learned that the Kapreitan "jumps" involved entirely different mechanics and muscle development. Instead of the long run-up, the flying leap and the forward tuck of hands and feet, the Kapreitan sport hinged – quite literally – on the proper use of hand-held weights. In theory, there was a short run-up and a wide forward swing of the weights into the air, throwing the body – hands first – into a dive; near the end of the arc, the weights would be swept back through the air, allowing the legs to swing forward like a pendulum and stretch outward for maximum distance. In practice, however, (at least for Ann) it looked more like a very enthusiastic belly flop. The final swing of the legs required not only immense core and shoulder power, but a highly specific dexterity that took years to perfect. Eventually, Ann did manage to learn, but she never could tell if her distances were any good. Nor did her trainer ever tell her.

Generally, though, Ann never gave a thought to her overall progress. She ploughed forward with single-minded focus, barely taking the time to register when she first managed to ground Trydus or land the winning strike in a boxing match. There was an immediacy to her training that was all-consuming, that kept her body driving and her mind absorbed in the moment. And never was this more pronounced than when she held a bow in her hand.

From the instant she'd picked out her new weapon from the armoury, it was as if she had reclaimed a limb she hadn't known was missing. At first, just a long, straight, polished staff with a handle in the centre, the wood responded to her touch, curving for her as she pressed her thigh against it and slipped the string over its tip. Warming as she ran her fingers over its stave, assessing its balance and integrity.

"Keep it in line with your shoulders," Hefanos instructed her one evening as she held the bow before her face. "Left foot forward. Neck tall, and rotate your chin over your shoulder now – all the way, girl. You should see your target there, above your forefinger. Now draw to your ear."

Ann lowered the bow. Her gut was telling her that something was off. "But it's cold," she said. "Shouldn't I, I don't know, warm the wood first? I mean, before drawing?"

Hefanos's brows snapped together, but he did not look angry. He simply regarded her for a moment, then said, "I doubt you would have been able to pull it to a full draw first try. Yet you may warm it, if you like. Gently draw part way, then release slowly. Gradually increase. Do that until I return."

He limped off to a distant tree, carving an X into its bark with his knife. When he returned, he tossed Ann a leather glove and arm guard – "No sense in slicing yourself open." – and then retrieved three arrows from their hoard.

"Since you seem to know so much about bows, you can hit that target for me."

Hefanos stepped back to watch. Ann tentatively picked an arrow and nocked it as she had seen others do.

"Am I doing this right?" she asked him.

He didn't even grunt. Ann turned away and refocused, inhaling deeply and closing her eyes for a moment. She opened her eyes, found her target immediately, exhaled and released.

The arrow sailed through the air and thudded into the trunk in the exact centre of the X.

Ann turned back to her trainer. He continued to stare at the X, face completely blank. Eventually he cleared his throat and told her, voice gruff,

"Move back fifteen paces and try again."

Ann moved back, took aim and released. Her second arrow nestled in next to her first.

"Back again!"

Back she went, into the trees. This time, her aim was slightly off – but not by much.

"Come here, girl!" Hefanos barked.

Ann approached.

"You have never shot, you said?"

She shook her head mechanically.

"From that distance, you could hardly have seen my target. Not in this light."

She didn't have an explanation for him. She glanced down at her hand – still gripping the bone of the bow's handle – as if it belonged to someone else.

"Again!" her trainer barked.

Hefanos had her shooting until the last glow of the sun had disappeared. She only missed the target ten times in the hundred rounds she shot and by the time she'd retrieved the last arrow, Hefanos was looking thoroughly annoyed. He simply threw the bow's waxed wrappings at her and stalked away.

The next day, he made her wait until twilight again before allowing her to retrieve her bow. And then he pulled out his slingshot.

Ann winced automatically: nothing good ever came from that slingshot. Yet when he loaded it with a round wooden disc and aimed it into the air, her bow was up, her arrow aimed by the time the disc had been released. She missed by a hair's breadth. He released another and her arrow grazed it, knocking it to the ground. She took a deep breath and calmed her mind. The third disc she struck. And every one after it.

Hefanos watched the last of his discs fall to the ground with an arrow embedded in its heart.

"Hmph," he grumbled. "Well... At least we can focus on your wrestling now."

But Ann couldn't get enough. She spent every evening – which were growing longer with the passing of each day – sending her arrows flying through the sky. There was a stern beauty to it that held her captivated, like watching a falcon flash after its prey. And it felt so natural to feel her bow arc around her in its perfect half-moon – so good to feel the sinew of the string stretch out with the fibres of her muscles. So *right* to see the tension building into that focal point in her mind only to be released in one flawless trajectory. The more she practiced the more she understood that this was something that had always been within her. And she would smile to herself as she shot, realizing that as much as it had mortified her at the time, there was something fitting about the title she'd been given.

Huntress.

This ability was built into her DNA – a dormant gene, just waiting to be roused. Which she did without thought or hesitation.

Chapter Three

One morning, Ann opened her eyes and the clouds had cleared. The island was a bower of wildflowers – the sky, a limitless dome of blue. And there were only ten days left until the Selection of Five began.

The moment Ann stepped foot in the clearing, Hefanos beckoned her to his rock.

"Bull leaping," he said, voice unusually clear, "is not about showmanship. It is about making it over the horns twice. That is all. This is no ceremonial leap, girl. There will be no team of acrobats to coax the animal into position and make it look dangerous. It *is* dangerous. You will be facing a wild, violent beast. Alone."

The man then summoned Kaenus from around a tree where the dog had been relieving himself and said that he wanted to try something.

They spent the rest of the day coaxing Kaenus into charging in a straight line. By dusk, Hefanos's supply of salted meat had run dry (as had his waterskin), and Ann was covered in fresh bruises from being repeatedly bucked into the dirt by an errant, prancing bull. She left the clearing thinking that the steady rush of the real thing would be something of a blessing.

It was a comforting thought, which she tried her very best to hold on to.

***

Ann had known, of course, that the season had taken its toll on the city. But when she joined the others in the dining hall that night for the first time in over two moons, she saw the proof of it on her friends' faces – and in the emptiness of the hall itself. Afterward, she sought out Hersa and, like the others, the girl was thinner, paler, and had a quietness to her that was more concerning even than Tefkelerea's absence at the table had been. Ann had expected to suffer through at least a few snipes about her new unfeminine physique, but the girl moved directly into city news: the mass graves being dug to accommodate the hundreds of elderly and young dead; the sparseness of the rains – the closure of the baths and fountains; the few brawls that had broken out in the streets over the decreasing rations. Then there was the merchant vessel that had disappeared on its trip north. People were saying – the girl added matter-of-factly – that the Makronans were behind it.

"Sounds like fear-mongering to me," Ann snapped, surprised by her sudden irritation. "Is there any real proof?"

Hersa didn't know.

"Then it's not very smart to be spreading that kind of talk, is it?"

Hersa didn't respond. And Ann left soon after that, telling her friend that she was tired.

There was something in the girl's reserve that had put her off. Something in her way of glancing sidelong at Ann, opening her mouth as if to speak, then closing it again quickly. Something that later made Ann pause at her bedroom door to glance over at the closed curtain on the other side of the common room.

She knew what the girl had been longing to ask about. But Ann had no intention of going there. It simply wasn't worth it anymore.

***

In the days that followed, Ann was gripped by a kind of frenzy. Hefanos watched from his rock, saying nothing as she powered through her drills, shifting from one to the next without pause, muscles always moving, always pushing. Then came the morning before the Selection, and the man unceremoniously informed her that her training was complete. Until her try-out before the committee, she was permitted only the most basic exercises to keep herself limber. So, for the first day in a very long time, Ann found herself with nothing do.

She wandered north, away from the palace, carefully restricting herself to a brisk walk. She felt empty, restless. Her body ached to sprint, to fly over the hills until she had burned through the nervous energy that trilled in her bones like the vibrations of an approaching quake. But onward she walked, always north, until she had reached a small promontory overlooking the sea.

She had only seen the sea up close once, that day in Kylondo last summer. A day not too dissimilar from today, she thought. The air was already unseasonably hot, blossoms and grass already edged with brown. And the water was still, glowing in jewel-like clarity. It was not even spring yet: the Day of Life and its bloodless sacrifice lay on the other side of the nine days of Selection. It would still be the month of March, back home.

Back home.

She'd arrived here nearly a year ago. Nearly a year since she'd met the god and He had promised to return them. Almost a year exactly, she guessed, since she'd first heard Him call her name.

Ann remained on the cliff watching the sun arc down, eventually sinking behind the mountains to the west. She stayed longer still, staring out at the water, which slowly darkened to a deep, glittering black. There was a new moon tonight – the Virgin Crescent, which would soon disappear, taking its meagre light with it. Ann headed back in the near blackness. And even far as she was from the palace, His pulse was with her. As it always seemed to be now, when she listened for it. A soft, oddly reassuring presence. She walked on to its gentle beat. She drifted off to its lullaby. And, in the hour before dawn, it was its absence that woke her.

***

In the darkest hour of the morning, when the first of the spring birds had begun the first of their pre-dawn harmonies, Ann was visited by Death. He came into her bedchamber in a silence so thick that it woke her from her slumber. He came in and He simply looked at her.

He stood at the door to the chamber, barely distinguishable from the shadows. She could feel His eyes on her, but she remained as she was, waiting and silent in the darkness. The stillness stretched out, unbroken.

Until He spoke.

Antigone…

His soft, rasping voice embraced her like a fog. Ann smelled the cold damp of Him, a smell of deep places. She felt the sharp edge of His finger run down her cheek. She sighed and her eyes drifted closed.

Antigone.

***

The first day of Selection. There were about two hundred men in the courtyard when Ann arrived. She loitered near the edge of the space, watching as the other contenders milled about, talking, clasping hands, clapping each other's backs. Comrades, even in rivalry.

Ann noticed her brother arrive just as a voice began to speak near the altar. She could not see the speaker, nor could she hear what they were saying, but soon after, the small crowd shuffled apart and a group of lesser stewards began wading through, speaking to people individually. One approached her brother. Ann saw the man speak briefly; she saw her brother nod. Then he left the courtyard.

The crowd thinned, and Ann's eye was caught by a flash of silver. The Guard Commander, also waiting along the perimeter. The woman nodded at her once then looked away.

"*Prona.*"

A steward had approached her.

"You are to present yourself by the stables at midday on the ninth day of Selection."

The steward moved on to the man beside her. Midmorning of second day, the steward told the man. Ann glanced back to the Guard Commander. The woman was gone. Slowly, Ann turned and left the courtyard too.

Nine days. Nine more days to wait, with nothing to occupy her. It should have been hell, but it wasn't. Ann waited, every day wandering away from the palace with just her dog for company. Aware only of the sun glaring down on her, and of the pulse that was now with her always. Returning at night to feel the tremors that ran through the stone of the palace walls like shivers over a smooth stretch of skin. It made Ann think of a growing appetite. Of a hungry god, awaiting His sacrifice.

On the ninth day, she joined the group of men beside the stables. There were fifteen of them in total, fidgeting and shifting from foot to foot just outside a makeshift arena on the cusp of the valley. At the far end of the space sat the five judges. Ann gripped her bow hard. She'd brought it with her for luck.

The final contestant of the morning group was bowing to the judges. When he turned to make his way back toward the palace, Ann recognized him. When the High Steward noticed her, he slowed, his eyes raking her from head to foot. Lingering on her bow.

"Huntress," he greeted in his smooth, mocking way. "I wish you luck."

"How generous of you," she replied.

She stepped away before he had a chance to retort, refocusing her attention on the next man who was called into the arena.

She had been the last to arrive so she would be the last to compete. She waited, careful not to watch too closely as the others sparred, sprinted and shot. The afternoon wore on. Finally, she was called forward.

She walked across the thinning grass, her eyes fixed over the heads of the judges. A familiar, deep voice called her name.

"Huntress."

By now, Ann had grown used to seeing the evidence of the past season, its deprivations etched on faces like barely healed scars. But the change in the *Kyn*'s appearance was something else entirely: he was a shadow of his former self. He sat gazing up at her through dulled eyes, the skin surrounding them dark and sunken. His curls had greyed and deep lines now cut the once-smooth surface of his forehead. Seeing him there, shrunken and subdued, Ann was overcome by an impulse to rush to him – to beg to know what was wrong, what had happened. Instead, she met that dulled gaze head on then looked away, down the line of judges.

The *Kynra* was sitting further along, wrapped in furs, despite the heat of the day. Between her and the *Kyn* sat three men Ann did not recognize: the generals that her trainer had told her about. With the *Kyn*'s and *Kynra*'s votes likely cancelling each other's out, it was essential that she impress these three men.

"You may begin, Chosen," the *Kynra* said.

And so she began.

***

They had started off, as Hefanos had told her they would, with the combat sports. Ann had been forced to display her skills against the human version of a pile of bricks, a large man with a low centre of gravity that made him nearly impossible to ground. That she'd managed to remain upright – and even once knock him off-balance – she considered a coup. She had also landed two strikes in the boxing match before one of the generals had said they'd seen enough and instructed her to leap the pit.

She'd fumbled a bit here, skidding beyond the leaping point in her run-up and into the sand itself. She'd been permitted to try again. Shaken, she'd fallen short of her personal record. Yet she'd managed to collect herself before moving on to the sprint.

With the *Kyn* watching her in that strange, dulled way, it had been difficult to recall those thoughts that had made her blood thunder. Yet she'd done well enough without them, soaring around the paddocks at a speed that liberated her from the oppression of the long days of waiting. When she'd finished, she'd scooped up her bow, backed as far away as the weapon's range would permit, and then pinned the five, miniscule targets on the back of the stable wall. She'd then returned to the judges, given a quick, perfunctory bow, and marched away without waiting for their dismissal.

Hefanos had been right. Well rested for once, her body had performed better than she'd imagined it could. She'd done well, she knew. Very well.

Whether that would be enough, she could not say.

**

The pulse echoed into her dreams that night, like the steady dripping of water into a deep, lonely pool. It stayed with her until she woke at dawn. Dawn of the Day of Life.

She washed her face, combed her hair. Put on a dress, dark blue, the colour of the eastern sky at dusk. It felt so strange, so restricting after months spent in training gear. Ann focused on that feeling – the tightness across her chest, the compression of her shoulders. It was easier than thinking of what lay ahead. Of the many things this day could bring.

Once in the courtyard, she again remained along the periphery, watching the others gather in their finest, seeing their anticipation, listening to the susurration of their whispers. It was so like that day she'd arrived. She rested her back against the shaded wall of the eastern façade, feeling the night-cooled stone, allowing herself to be calmed by the steady beating within it. It would not be long now.

The sunlight that had been dragging down the western wall inched across the floor, lighting on the altar. Glinting off the axe that lay there still. All sound quieted. The judges had entered.

They formed a loose line in front of the altar. None of them looked as though they'd had any sleep. The *Kyn* stepped forward.

"The first of the Five of Kabyrnos," he announced without ceremony, "is Ekysus of the clan Kaftanu."

The people applauded. Ann had never heard the name before, nor did she recognize the stocky man who approached the altar. The applause died away and the *Kyn* continued.

"The second to represent Kabyrnos is our very own High Steward, Heremus of the clan Trynu."

Ann watched the man approach the altar, the *Kyn* greeting him with a clap on the shoulder.

"The third of the Five," the *Kyn* went on as the High Steward took his place beside him, "is Niklas, our esteemed Hunter."

The fiasco that had followed the stolen horses was clearly long forgotten: the crowd cheered and howled as Nik strode forward, combing his shoulder-length hair back from his face with one casual sweep of his hand. Always the rock star. Ann pressed her back harder against the wall and felt the pulse flare in response.

Then the *Kyn* drew a deep breath.

"The fourth of the Five shall be the Huntress."

Even the thrumming in the stones seemed to stop then. Ann found herself walking forward across the silent courtyard. She felt the Kyn's eyes on her face as she stopped before the altar, felt her arm clutched by a familiar vice-like grip. A muffled noise blared in the background as the *Kynra* whispered in her ear,

"Well done, Chosen. I knew it would be so."

Another drawn-out pause. Again, the crowd shuffled aside to let someone through. The fifth of the Five, Ann realized as the person halted before the altar.

It was the Guard Commander, stone-faced as always.

The *Kyn* was speaking again. "– arriving shortly and in ten days the Tournament will begin. We have the utmost faith that our Five will bestow great honour upon our city. Finally –" he took a breath – "there is an announcement regarding today's ceremony –"

But, again, the crowd was parting.

A small man rushed up to the altar. His hands were visibly shaking, his bald head sheened with sweat.

"This Tournament cannot proceed!"

A murmur passed through the courtyard as the *Kynra* hissed, fingernails digging into Ann's skin,

"What nonsense is this? What are you speaking of, you foolish man?"

"I am speaking, *Kynra*," the man replied, "of *theft*. On the largest scale."

Chapter Four

What happened next seemed, to Ann, almost rehearsed. Like perfectly ordered chaos. Confusion erupted in the crowd, voices rising like a cresting wave. At that same moment, the Guard Commander began to move forward with the platoon of guards that seemed to have materialized out of nowhere. Priestesses, too, had fanned out, Sister Aralys perched on the grand steps, trying to gain the attention of the people. The *Kyn* and *Kynra* had disappeared.

Ann looked for the man who had caused it all, and caught a glimpse of him just as the High Steward dragged him through the door of the *Kynra*'s Chamber.

Without a second thought, she followed.

"– and in such a public manner?" the *Kynra* was shouting as Ann eased the heavy door shut behind her. "*Have you completely taken leave of your senses?*"

No one seemed to question Ann's presence. The man was on his knees before the *Kyn* and *Kynra*. The High Steward was nowhere to be seen.

"I had not meant to," the man was whimpering. "I swear it. It, it was the shock."

A priestess appeared at the *Kynra*'s elbow. The *Kyn* guided the man – a clerk, Ann gathered by his appearance – to the bench by the now dry fountain. The doves' nest, Ann noticed, was also empty.

"I have only a moment before I must return," the *Kyn* said. "Think carefully. You made the inspection yourself?"

"Yes, *Kyn*," the man replied, nodding fervently. "More than half of the emergency stores. I swear it."

The *Kyn* was silent.

"The Tournament cannot go forward now, you see? How can Kabyrnos host so many, let alone…"

His question hung in the air, unfinished and unanswerable. The priestess left silently through the back door. The *Kynra* settled herself in throne as the *Kyn* turned away to stare into the empty basin.

It was not long before the priestess returned.

"The relic?" the *Kynra* asked.

"She is gone, Sacred Mother."

The door opened again, the buzz of voices momentarily blaring. Everyone in the room turned as the High Steward entered. He said nothing, only looked at the *Kyn* and nodded, once.

Without a word, Ann slipped back out through the door.

***

She moved out into the already scorching sun. Midmorning, in the Courtyard of the Dying Sun. The tree's twisted limbs rippling in the waves of heat that rose from the stones like steam. It was only a matter of hours now. And then a few hours more until Ann would meet Him again in the moonlit courtyard.

And after that, who knew.

But, for now, she was not alone.

Erysia sat on a rock not far from where Ann stood. The priestess's face was unusually thoughtful as she sat contemplating the tree. Ann watched her for a few moments, then asked,

"Why did you do it?"

The priestess was quiet for a minute. Then she rose to her feet.

"I do not know of what you speak," she said.

Before Ann could say anything else, Erysia walked away through the bordering trees.

Ann eased herself onto the abandoned rock. She sat, just as the priestess had, watching the blackened tree. The sun rose to its zenith above her, and still she did not move.

When the *Kyn* came to her, she felt – rather than heard – him approach.

"It will not happen," he said.

She remained facing the tree. "How can you cancel it now? The other cities are almost here."

"No, Ann. The sacrifice."

She blinked – then turned to face him. She was struck anew by his altered appearance. The deflated chest. Those sad, weary eyes.

"I have called it off," he explained.

"But – why?"

The man didn't answer right away. He was looking over her head at the tree.

"Something is coming to us, Ann."

She watched his face, his mouth working with emotion.

"I can feel it in my very bones. Something is coming. *At last.*"

Those two words, holding in them all the pain of a long, dark season. Of many long, dark years.

"Over *half* the stores, Ann. Years of labour, simply – vanished. And years off the life of the city. If it comes to that."

Ann glanced down at her feet, dust-covered on the cobbled ground. She knew she had to say something. But, at that very moment, he moved to her, placing his warm, heavy hands on her shoulders. She peered up.

"I owe you an apology, Ann. A few of them, in truth."

He did not go on. After a few more moments, his hands fell to his sides and he sighed,

"You should have been born a man."

Then he stepped away and, again, Ann resisted the urge to go to him. Instead, she allowed herself a moment to memorize the contours of his face, her eyes tracing every new crease of worry, every fresh line of sorrow.

He turned away. Took a few steps toward the palace, then paused. Turned back.

"I know I can trust you to say nothing, Ann. Morale is too low as it is." He smiled, more to himself than to her. "Something is coming. The gods have not forsaken us. With any luck, their gift will come soon."

And then his mouth curved down into a hard, lipless line. It was a bitter smile that Ann had seen many times – but never on him.

"And let us hope," he whispered, "that our Gyklanean friends will arrive in time to witness it."

With that, he left her, walking across the courtyard and disappearing into the vast double portal of the palace. Ann sighed and peered at the building that rose up and sprawled out before her.

In a way, she thought, the *Kyn* was like the palace itself. Standing outside, you were overwhelmed by its size, its grandeur. Once you'd wound your way within, you became captive, lost in its many corridors and halls, dazzled by its light and colour. You could never, not from any vantage, take in its full shape or complexity. And no matter how long you remained, or how well you thought you knew those well-worn tracts, there was always something else hidden further within.

She turned back to the tree. The hot air contracted around her.

Come, He called to her.

And so she went.

***

The mountainside was a refuge. Wildflowers blanketed its slopes, bees laden with their pollen; shepherds led their flocks up away from the early heat. It was cooler here, the breeze teasing Ann's hair as she stopped to drink at a brook. But she didn't dare pause for long. The urge to rise was a constant pressure, a string around her neck, dragging upward.

She was almost surprised to find it there still, that windy terrace, with its long, jagged fissure and decrepit building.

The women were waiting for her.

Ann climbed the steps and approached the eldest, who was, if anything, more bizarre-looking than she remembered.

"Did you bring them?" the old woman asked immediately.

"Bring…?"

"The lentils."

"Er – no. I forgot. Sorry."

Klochistropa's face puckered into a thousand little lines as one of the Andryleas gripped Ann by the elbow and guided her up the steps.

She was brought to the same tiny chamber. Same fire pit, same pile of filthy mattresses, same rickety stool. Ann was told to sit. She sat. A steaming mug was deposited in her hands.

"So," Klochistropa said, folding herself into a bundle on the ground. "What can I do for you this day, my dear?"

Ann sipped the warm liquid: it tasted of earth. She took another sip and only then did she realize that the pulsing had stopped. The wind whistled through the many holes in the roof, but otherwise, the sanctuary was quiet. Peaceful.

"I think," Ann began, "that I'm meant to ask some questions."

The old woman swept a bony hand out in invitation.

Ann was silent for a long time then, thinking over the events of the day. When her first question occurred to her, she took her time in formulating it. She would only have three chances.

"The Day of Life ceremony. What is gained by sacrificing those boys?"

The old woman wagged her head sadly. "Only time, my dear, only time. The young lives appease the gods – for the time being. They will still require what is due, and they will take their toll until it is given."

Ann listened, absorbing the woman's words carefully. She recalled what the *Kynra* had said, exactly a year ago, as she'd stood beneath the gathered clouds with that poor boy tied to the tree.

The sacred balance maintained, she'd said. The price of life.

Then Hersa's voice came to her, as it had been last summer.

"It has been this way since Kabyrn."

Ann took another sip of the tea and teased the memory forward. She'd been asking Hersa about the *Kyn*'s father.

"So Zelkanus killed his own father?" she had asked.

"It is rumoured," the girl had replied, "that Cryklonus was not quite dead when he was brought to the oak later that day."

Ann's heart went cold.

Time. He was *buying time*. Years of earthquakes, poor rainfall and devastating illness, to be exact. The price of life unpaid.

"Because they say when a *Kyn* hears his call," she whispered aloud, "he must offer himself to Pritymnia…"

Klochistropa's beady eyes watched her, giving nothing.

"But – how could he do such a thing?"

"That is a difficult question to answer," the old woman said, working her fingertips into the dirt on the floor. "Perhaps the best answer is simply 'fear'. Fear of failure. Fear of death – of the darkness beyond. Fear of the past coming alive again." She scooped up a handful of dirt and let it pour through her fist, like sand from an hourglass. "Fear of the prophecy."

"The prophecy?"

Ann realized her mistake the moment the question was out. Hard as she'd tried never to think of it, she *knew* the prophecy. The coming of a new age. It had been drummed into her head since the day of her arrival.

But, to her surprise, the old woman was smiling at her.

"Very good. Very good indeed, my dear. The prophecy I speak of is that which led me to banishment and the blood oath that binds me still." She paused, taking in a deep, ragged breath. "Eighteen long years ago, I foretold the coming of a boy. A boy who, like his father before him, was destined to be his father's undoing. A boy who was destined to be *Kyn*."

"But… wait," Ann whispered. "Zelkanus… He has a *son*?"

"No, no, no, my dear. You have had your three."

And with that, the mug was plucked from Ann's hands and she was hauled off her stool. Before she had a moment to steady herself, the Andryleas had ushered her out, down the stairs and onto the terrace, where she stood, swaying on her feet. She grabbed the wall for support.

The fissure was there, only metres away, like a gaping mouth ripped into the face of the mountain. Ann could feel the air within it tugging at her hairs like static electricity. Her vision swam; she felt her knees start to buckle.

Klochistropa steadied her with an unexpectedly strong grip. "No, no, no, my dear. Not yet."

Ann dragged her eyes away from the fissure as the woman guided her into the opening of the ramp.

"One final thought," the old woman whispered when they were both out of sight of the building. "You must remember: there is both light and darkness in us all. Hold on to that, my dear, and do not judge too harshly."

***

By the time Ann had returned to the palace, night had fallen. The building was silent but for the beating of His pulse. Hours had passed, and still she could not wrap her mind around what she had learned.

Nearly ten years. The boy's mother had told her on the night of Darkness that it had been nearly ten years since Zelkanus had announced to his people that the gods were demanding more. A young life, full of potential.

"What I am," the *Kyn* had once said to her, "is *desperate*."

Nine boys, then. Nine. And another one, still destined to come. The bastard son of the bastard son.

"Something is coming to us," he'd told her.

No one would believe her, Ann realized. Zelkanus was, in many ways, still their *Kounros*, their boy hero, and she was only the foreign girl who had the gall to compete against the men.

Ann made her way through the Blessed Courtyard without stopping. The moon was already out, almost directly above her. The space was empty. No one, she knew, would be coming for her tonight.

***

It was on the following morning that the first two waves of Gyklaneans arrived. The companies from Prilna and – it was whispered – Makrona. Ann was passing along one of the upper balconies just in time to catch a glimpse of them – about thirty in total, slaves included – being ushered up the grand staircase by a lesser steward and a small group of servants. No welcome wagon for them, it seemed.

Even at a distance, these men made an impression. Shorter, broader and paler than their Kapreitan counterparts, they lacked the elegance, the style that so defined the men of Kabyrnos. Yet there was one man who caught Ann's eye. A tall, barrel-chested youth whose very way of walking told her that here was someone of whom to take note. A noble of some kind – or a key competitor. It was not long before the palace gossips gleaned the facts: he was both.

He was the son of the *Makrax* – Athyla told her at dinner – and said to be the undefeated Makronan champion. Though he looked a little young for it.

And, watching from across the ambassador's hall that evening, Ann was forced to agree. Tefkelerea, who had only just grown strong enough to leave her rooms, had begged Ann to accompany her to the feast that was being thrown in the boy's honour. There was fresh wine, suckling pig, octopus, honeyed cakes – everything. But no *Kyn*.

The Gyklaneans seemed unaware of the insult. By the look of their flushed faces, it was clear that these men were already well into their host's fine beer.

Ann found the *Makrax*'s son right away, sitting next to her brother of all people. He was soliloquizing – she could hear clearly from across the room – on the virtues of Makronan ale. And Makronan horses. And Makronan women.

"Perhaps I will be able to tempt you away from this great, winding crypt," he laughed, seemingly unaware of the thirty or so Kapreitan clansfolk all within ear's reach of his booming voice. "We truly do have the *finest* –"

He stopped short, his gaze resting on Ann.

"Ah! And now we have our matching set!"

Ann braced herself as the prince lurched to his feet and weaved across the hall, swaying dangerously in the last step. She grabbed his arm to steady him. The thick cords of muscle beneath her fingers flexed for a moment before he pulled free.

"So Kabyrnos had to scrounge up two foreigners to represent them, did they?" he boomed at her in his thickly-accented Kapreitan. "No – it is *three*, is it not?"

Another Gyklanean – middle-aged and gentle-faced – had come up to lay a hand on the young man's shoulder.

"Deothesus, you have forgotten your manners."

"Very true, Selpenor, very true," said the *Makrax*'s son, never taking his eyes from Ann. "What I had meant to say, beautiful, was that you are welcome to compete for my people any time you wish."

The older man covered his face in mortification.

"Keep drinking and I'm sure you'll do just fine on your own," Ann replied.

Unexpectedly, the young man threw his head back and roared with laughter. "So the Huntress has a bit of a temper then! I like a female with bite."

"Then go find yourself a dog."

Again, he laughed. "It is chillier down south than I had expected. Where I come from, the women are not so bold."

"I wonder why."

"Meaning?"

Ann was spared having to answer by Tefkelerea's ill-timed cough, which alerted the young man to the presence of easier prey. Abandoning her friend to her fate, Ann turned from the drunken prince and made her exit.

But half-way up to her rooms, she found herself thinking about the boy's eyes. Drunk as he was, they'd been remarkably steady as they'd met hers. As had his grip. A little too steady, she thought.

***

The rest of the guests trickled in over the course of the next few days. Gyklaneans from the cities of Valpis, Arkanea, Laredea and Trynas, followed shortly by the Kapreitans from Xanu, Phernos, Gyrnos, Zaffronos, and, finally, Melkus. Hundreds in total, all of whom Kabyrnos absorbed into itself like water into a sponge. Though some were welcomed more warmly than others. While the rest of the Gyklaneans were hustled in like livestock for tallying, the Kapreitans were met at palace entrances by scores of Kabyrnossian elite, given food, drink and official blessings before being escorted to their accommodations by the High Steward and his fleet of underlings.

The baths were reopened. Feasts were held every evening in the upper western halls, with the Kapreitans in one hall, Gyklaneans in the other, and guards patrolling the corridor between. At every table, there was slaughtered cow, sheep, pig, and a never-ending supply of wine. Where Kabyrnos managed to scrounge up the resources for this charade, this outrageous spectacle of decadence and hostility, Ann could not guess. Nor did she want to.

She escaped the palace whenever she could, initially wandering out into the city. But what she found in the faces of the cityfolk soon drove her further out. That others should feast when they had only just finished burying their dead. She could not stand the way they looked at any Gyklanean foolish enough to stray from the relative shelter of the palace – the way the men would come out of their workshops to line the streets with spades and saws and hammers resting on their shoulders. She fled north. To the sea and the emptiness it offered. In the evenings, she took refuge in her rooms, grateful, at least, that her brother was kept occupied.

Soon it was the day before the Tournament and Ann found herself standing up at the altar of the Blessed Courtyard, as she had so many times before. The opening ceremony was surprisingly dull. Ann waited as a herald introduced all forty-eight contestants by name. She waited through the deafening cheers for the Kabyrnossian Five (herself and the Guard Commander included) and the still enthusiastic applause for the other Kapreitan contestants. Then she waited through the hissing as the Gyklanean names were called out. She glanced down the line of contestants, all stiff beneath the city's gaze: the High Steward, the Makronan prince Deothesus – and a short, powerfully-built Gyklanean man, with an ugly scowl and thighs like tree trunks.

"Gauging the competition?" the Guard Commander whispered from next to her.

Ann snapped round to face the front, and she heard the woman snort.

The presentation of contestants had come its end. The noise simmered and Ann held her breath as the *Kyn* stepped forward to say a few closing words.

There would be no feast that evening. It was a night of vigil. A night to come to terms with what was to come. And what lay inside.

The Tournament would try at man's strength and speed and skill. It would take him to the edge of his endurance.

Yet, more than anything, the coming trials were a test of courage and of faith.

A test of honour.

May Mavros grant victory to the most deserving.

Chapter Five

Ann halted in one of the gaps of the vast circle of stone bleachers. The ring of cypresses had been felled, canopies erected over the stands to protect spectators from the sun. In the sand stretching out before her, four rings had been marked out with wooden stakes.

She was met at the contestants' stand by her trainer.

"Get any sleep?"

She shook her head and he passed her his waterskin. She took a cautious sip. The liquor burned.

"Time to warm up," Hefanos grunted.

Ann began the process of warming and loosening her muscles, and slowly, the stands began to fill. She noticed the *Makrax*'s son and the scowling Gyklanean march in and begin their own preparations.

"As we discussed," Hefanos said. "Tunic off, oil up."

Most of the other contestants had already disrobed down to their loincloths and slathered on the olive oil that would impair their opponents' grip. But none of them had to endure the stares she did when she pulled her tunic over her head, and rubbed the oil beneath the edges of her breastband. Yet this soon passed and the whispers pitched to an expectant hum. The sun had climbed almost a quarter up the eastern sky. The matches would soon begin.

Ann moved to the contestants' stand. Across the arena, two thrones had been placed just outside the track that ran around the sand. One was still empty; in the other sat the *Kynra*. Perched on the edge of her seat, Ann found herself looking at the woman more closely than she had in months. Even at this distance, she could tell that the old woman was not well. Still wrapped in furs, still uncomfortably thin, her thinness had taken on a sharper quality. She had a brittleness to her, as if even the smallest impact would shatter her into a thousand pieces.

Then the *Kyn* took his seat and Ann looked away.

Something rapped her on the chest. She turned to find her trainer, holding his stick and giving her one of his longest, most piercing stares.

"Harness it," he said.

***

There would be five rounds in total, each round cutting the number of contestants down by a half, until the final round where there would be only six contestants remaining: the three losers and three winners from the previous round. While the losers competed for the fourth and fifth rankings, the three winners would vie for the top positions in the competition. Ann knew that how she fared would depend largely on the luck of the draw: if she was set against one of the better wrestlers in the early rounds, she wouldn't stand a chance of ranking.

Yet, by midday, she was beginning to doubt that it would even take that much to push her out of the running. She had watched three series of matches already, and every time the crowd had roared, every time a contestant had gone down or cried out, her stomach had surged up into her throat. Each time the next eight contestants were announced, she'd held her breath. Yet when the fourth round was announced, she was not called. Deothesus was. Her brother was.

Out of the contestants she knew, only the Guard Commander had competed so far. And the woman had won, handily. All the pent-up power that Ann had always sensed in her had poured out in a fluid efficiency that her opponent – a man both larger and taller than she – had been helpless against. And the way those eyes had gazed up at him, coolly appraising. Ann knew that gaze. The guardswoman had been wearing him down before the match had even begun.

Ann had also watched the Gyklanean with the enormous thighs compete in the second series. He'd obliterated his opponent, all the while scowling in a way that made Ann feel that he was relishing every moment of it. The match was short and she was glad when it was over.

The contestants for the fourth series were now in place. The Makronan prince was in the ring nearest to her, her brother two over. The starting horn was blown.

It became immediately clear that the Makronan was a natural – the perfect combination of speed, strength and pure instinct. There was nothing calculated about his movements, no apparent strategy to his attacks, he simply seemed to act and react, grinning all the while like child tussling in a sandbox.

Her brother, on the other hand, was entirely calculated. After the signal was made, he and his opponent had remained in the crouched, neutral position for a few seconds before the other man had lunged in. In a swift, but carefully measured move, Nik had twisted free and unbalanced the man – yet he had not attacked. He had waited, again, for his opponent to go on the offensive, and again, he had freed himself. He did this so many times that, eventually, the other man charged him, at which point Nik dropped to one knee, clamped his arms around his opponent's legs and swivelled to launch him sideways into the sand. The crowd cheered, but Ann was not so easily impressed. Her brother was holding back. And for some reason, it pissed her off.

But the fourth series was soon over and the fifth was being called. Her name was being called.

The noise of the crowd blurred out into a background drone. Ann rose to her feet, her legs unsteady. Somehow, she managed to cross the packed dirt of the track, through the sand and over the stakes into the third ring. She was soon joined by a man – a Kapreitan from Zaffronos with a nasty sneer. He was shorter than her, not much larger than her, but clearly, he was not concerned.

The announcer instructed them to take their positions. Ann sunk into a crouch and waited, holding her breath.

The signal was called and the man dove in. She only just managed to swing free of his grasp. When he came in again a second later, though, he found purchase, his arm snaking up around her shoulder – and before she knew what was happening, he'd wrenched up her leg, released her shoulder and she was down, back slamming into the ground.

The referee called the point. Ann dragged herself up. She felt the sand plastered to her back, a splinter of pain shooting through her neck. She rolled out her shoulders, desperately trying to smother the panic that was rising in her throat. She managed it – just barely – as they were called again to their positions.

The referee signalled and her opponent pounced forward in the very same manoeuvre – he really was that cocky. And she really was that flustered. Practically without effort, the man hooked her shoulder again and dropped, reaching for her leg. But it was at that moment that her training finally kicked in: completely through muscle memory, she swung out of his way and grabbed at him. But he was too quick. He bore down on top of her, driving her to her knees, and within three seconds, he was in total control. All she could think of was the man's weight on top of her, the sharp reek of his sweat – then his arm around her neck, dragging her – oddly – to her feet. She struggled like a wild, helpless creature, writhing and thrashing in his grasp. She felt his chest rumbling against her back. It was a moment before she realized that he was laughing – actually *laughing*.

The fucker.

Her mind cleared. She swept her leg out and hooked it in behind his, bending her knee to buckle him forward. She slipped her head free. Then, keeping a firm hold of his arm, she twisted it, wrenching it up behind his back. The man gasped and sank forward. She wrenched it higher, hearing the joints crackle as the man fell onto his other arm. Then, with one swing of her leg, she swept out the supporting arm and the man's face smashed into the sand.

The referee called the point.

The next two points were simple. The man's confidence was gone; wearing the rest of him down was only a matter of time. She evaded and unbalanced, grappled and hooked, going through every step of the routine that she'd learned by heart. And when her third point was called, she simply dusted off her shoulders and strode out of the ring without a backwards glance at the man who still lay flat on his back in the sand.

Hefanos was waiting for her in the stands. He held out a jug of water.

"Thanks," she said with a grin.

Grunt. "Do not gloat yet."

She drained half the water then poured the rest of it over her head.

***

The second round of matches started the next morning. In the first series, Ann watched her brother defeat another man in the same neat-but-cautious way, and she witnessed the second of the Guard Commander's cool, efficient triumphs. In the next series, she saw the High Steward compete for the first time, and she was forced to admit that the man knew how to handle himself. But then, she already knew that.

The Gyklanean Thighs was called in the third series. As was she. Her confidence lagged a little as she was directed to his ring.

"So this is the famed Huntress," the man said in a surprisingly high-pitched voice.

She met his eyes squarely. They were small and closely set in a red, meaty face.

"You are not much to look at, are you?" the man jeered.

"We're not here to chat."

She watched those tiny eyes narrow. The announcer called them into position. They both crouched down. The signal was called.

The Gyklanean was not particularly quick, but he was skilled, he was very strong, and he was vicious. Ann evaded his first few grabs, buying time until he presented her with an opening. She knew she needed to catch him off-balance – he was far too dense, far too powerful to take down any other way. Once, she did almost manage to trip him up, but her advantage was fleeting: the man took hold of her forearm, and, as she was pulling away, he twisted and *squeezed*. A cry tore out of her throat – she only just managed to avoid being tossed over his hip. Breaking free, she scrambled back, cradling her arm to her chest.

The Gyklanean's scowl spread into an arrogant little smirk. Slowly, she let her arms fall to her sides. She beckoned him with a tilt of her chin.

Thighs rushed her again. Ann twisted aside and reached out to grab his outstretched arm. The moment she made contact, though, the man heaved her toward him, stepping in to clamp his arms around her. Again, he squeezed, so tightly that her breath rushed from her lungs, choking out her scream. She knew the impact was coming, any moment now. Yet, instead of dropping her back over one massive leg, the man held her for a few seconds longer. She felt her ribs begin to protest, her vision blotching. She wanted to signal submission, but she was completely helpless.

Then it was over and she was lying in the sand, gasping for dear life.

She took her time in rising. Her whole body ached, her breath was coming out in painful wheezes. She'd have to make the most of her energy now – he'd taken too much out of her. And he knew it. The second the signal went, Thighs rushed forward in a reckless charge. Stepping to the side at the last second, Ann grabbed his wrist and, in a lightning quick manoeuvre, twirled round him to wrap his arm up around his throat like a noose. Then, threading her own arms through, she wedged her elbows against the side of his neck, braced herself against his back, and *pushed*. She knew full well that he'd be able to break free soon – he was too strong for her – but she only needed a few more seconds before he started blacking out.

At this point, only the side with the man's locked arm was exposed to the referee. And he making a big show of trying to struggle free. Ann was too focused to wonder. Yet the moment he arched his back out away from her, she knew. Not in time to stop his elbow from smashing into her breast.

She cried out and he threw her off him. He was smiling now – fully smiling at her.

"Halt!" a voice commanded from the stands. "Halt the match!"

The *Kynra* was out of her throne and the crowd in the eastern stands was shrieking its outrage at the illegal strike. The Gyklanean was summoned out of the ring as the referee approached, pulling a thin leather whip out of his belt.

Three lashes. Three long, angry welts across the man's shoulders, and he never stopped smiling.

Ann knew it was over then.

And when the referee called the match to a close just minutes later, she returned to the stands, head down.

***

The following morning, Ann dragged herself back to the arena. Her trainer had visited her the previous evening and sat with her in the common room, saying nothing other than to refuse a glass of water. When Nik had returned, both Hefanos and

Ann had risen to leave. But the man had paused at the door.

"It is done," he'd grumbled. "It was never your strong point. Time to move forward."

Move forward, she repeated to herself as she settled in to watch the third round. Easier said than done. She watched the High Steward subdue another opponent. She watched Thighs thrash another helpless victim, and the Guard Commander sweep another man out of her way. She witnesses yet another of the Makronan's flawless victories. And then she watched her brother move to face down his third rival.

The man was a Gyklanean from Prilna, who proved himself to be particularly skilled at sneaking in just at the moment of Nik's hesitation. In the end, Nik lost, two-to-three, and the crowd booed the Gyklanean out of the arena.

Round four was down to six contestants: the Prilnan, Thighs, Kabyrnos' Guard Commander and High Steward, the Makronan prince and a Kapreitan from Melkus. All three matches occurred at once. The High Steward was facing Thighs; the Guard Commander, Deothesus.

The latter match was mesmerizing, more dance than battle. The young Makronan moved like the wind blew, in smooth, sweeping bursts of force; the guardswoman was precise, never wasting a single opportunity, never letting down her guard. The two wove around each other with perfect grace.

Which was a glaring contrast to grunts and roars that came from the next ring over. The longer the High Steward withstood his attacks, the more aggressive Thighs became. By the time they'd reached a tie of two-to-two, the Gyklanean was practically spitting in rage, and Heremus – the elegant High Steward of Kabyrnos – was dishevelled and doubled-over in pain. Ann wasn't sure which man she wanted to lose more, but she became so engrossed in their battle that she failed to notice when Deothesus beat the Guard Commander, three-to-zero. And when Thighs managed to pin the High Steward down on his stomach, the whole stadium – Ann included – was on the edge of their seats. There was one tense moment when she was sure that the High Steward would be able to free himself, but then the big man's hands fastened around his neck and everyone knew it was over. Heremus flung his arms out, signalling defeat and the referee called the final point.

But Thighs would not let go. Ann saw the muscles in his forearms flex, she saw the High Steward's eyes bulge as the thousands of spectators jumped to their feet and roared. The referee plunged into the ring and tried to pull Thighs off, but the Gyklanean only tightened his grip.

Then the *Kyn* was there, pinching into the tender spots of Thighs's wrists. The man's fingers sprung open and the High Steward's head smacked into the sand, unconscious. As the healers rushed in and Thighs was hauled out of the ring, Ann saw the *Kyn* speaking to the man, his lips barely moving. Then the noise of the crowd pitched, people cheering as the Gyklanean was subjected to twenty strokes of the lash.

Yet Ann only sat, hands clasped in her lap, silently looking on.

***

The final matches were scheduled for the next day. Competing for the fourth and fifth ranking were the High Steward (bruised around the neck, but apparently still in fighting form), the Guard Commander, and the Prilnan. Competing for first, second and third were the Makronan, Thighs and the Kapreitan from Melkus. In the first series, both the High Steward and the Makronan prince emerged the easy victors. That afternoon, the Prilnan moved on to face the Guard Commander, and Deothesus fought Thighs.

Ann doubted that a single person saw even a point of the Guard Commander's victory. And from the reactions of the crowd, it would have been impossible to guess that the two men competing in the other ring were both Gyklanean. Deothesus was an instant hero. Every time he unbalanced the savage Thighs, every time he freed himself from a hold, or successfully tossed the larger man into the sand, the crowd erupted into cheers. And yet, the young man hardly seemed to notice. He fought on as effortlessly as he had from the first. Which, of course, only made Thighs more furious. The man was like an incensed bull, charging forward without thought, making it even easier for his opponent to slip through his defences in one sinuous manoeuvre after another. And although Thighs did manage to ground Deothesus once – the very first point scored against the young man – it was not long before the Makronan prince achieved his sixth and final victory.

Unexpectedly, Thighs then lost to the Melkian – a perceptive man who used his opponent's frustration against him. The crowd seemed to regard this as a form of divine justice, and Thighs skulked out of the arena to the sound of laughter.

Meanwhile, the Guard Commander and High Steward were still circling each other in the next ring. The man clearly had the upper hand in size and strength, but he also had the handicap of an enormous ego. Despite having seen his opponent prove her skill again and again, he continued to underestimate her. The final point of the match was scored when the guardswoman deliberately opened herself up for attack, then twirled back to intercept as the High Steward descended for what he thought was a sure kill. Ann could see on his face as he stormed out of the arena that he had never quite believed that he could be bested by a woman. A lesson she hoped he'd finally learned.

That evening, the rankings were announced. The Makronan was in first rank with five points, the Melkian in second with four, Thighs in third with three, the Guard Commander in fourth with two, and the High Steward in fifth with one. A modest triumph for Kabyrnos; just salt in the wound for Ann.

But the next competition was archery.

Rounds one and two occurred in the arena – the wrestling rings now removed. The wooden targets were set three quarters of the way back along its length, and then as far back as the stands would allow. Ann struck the black bull's eye in dead centre both times. Each time she fired was as effortless and as glorious as the very first. She simply extended herself out, found the target in her mind and released.

Round three was moved out into the open pastures outside the stadium. The spectators crowded in behind the line of shooters as they aimed at targets that appeared as small as thumbtacks. Ann was one of the last to shoot, and again, she struck centre. The top ten contestants then moved on to the next round. Nik was one of them, and Deothesus another. There were two others that seemed particularly skilled: a Kapreitan from Phernos with a nose like an eagle's beak, and a Gyklanean from Valpis, by far the smallest of the contestants.

By this round, the single target was set only metres within longbow range. Ann watched contestant after contestant miss – by feet, not inches. Nik managed to land his arrow just within the outer border of the target. Deothesus's was further in by a sliver, and the eagle-beaked Phernian's was a hand's length closer still. Only two struck bull's eye: Ann and the tiny Gyklanean.

It was then – inexplicably – that Ann's confidence began to waver.

She wanted this. She couldn't believe how badly, but she did.

She needed it.

And that thought terrified her.

***

The first phase of the fifth round was straightforward. The target was moved back to the very furthest of their range and she and the tiny Gyklanean were given two attempts to hit centre. Ann's arrows – to her shame – struck the edge of the black bull's eye. Luckily, the Gyklanean's were not perceptibly closer.

They then moved on to the second phase: airborne targets. It was Tiny's turn first. He nocked his arrow and drew his bow. The slingshot was loaded with a palm-sized, double-ringed target. Tiny nodded and the disc was fired. The little man took his time to aim and release, and half-way through its arc, the target was sent flying back. A runner went to fetch it and held it up. The arrow had struck the outer ring. A few of the spectators applauded.

Ann stepped into Tiny's position. She rolled out her neck and shoulders. She nocked her arrow. Her eyes closed, and, blocking out the voices behind her, she settled her mind on the new disc being loaded into the slingshot. She drew her bow and nodded. Her eyes opened just as the disc was fired.

But, just as she was bringing her bow up, something incomprehensible happened. There was a loud *twang* and she felt a lash of heat above her right brow. She dropped her bow, the arrow thudding into the ground metres ahead, and her hands flew to her face. The pain came a second later.

"*Move back!*" a voice thundered above the rest.

Ann pulled her hand away to see it slicked with blood. A pair of strong hands grabbed her and forced her to the ground. Her head was tilted back. She blinked through the blood and the grizzled face of her trainer swam into view. A few others had approached but he growled them away as he crashed gracelessly to his knees.

Where the bandages and sutures came from, Ann didn't know, but she easily recognized the warm liquid that poured over her face, burning.

"Did I lose?" she asked as Hefanos stowed his flask. When he didn't respond, she half-yelled, "*Did I lose?*"

"Sit *down*, girl!" he barked, pushing her back to the ground. "You did not lose."

Ann was so relieved that she sat still as the wound was stitched, the ointment applied, and the wool secured over her head. But when it was all done, she asked,

"Can I shoot now?"

"Do not be a fool," the *Kynra* snapped.

How long had the woman been there, leaning on Darkylus's arm?

"Best wait until morning, Huntress," the priest said flatly.

"There's still enough light," Ann said. "I want to shoot."

"No," the *Kynra* said.

Hefanos stirred on the ground beside her. "This has been tampered with," he murmured.

Everyone peered down at the bow in his hands. At the two pieces of string, frayed along the edges.

"I want to shoot," Ann repeated.

"Chosen –"

"I'll do it now."

And as she restrung her bow, the sun low behind her, the crowd waiting for her still, she focused her mind on the throbbing on her forehead. It hurt, yes, but it wouldn't distract. When it came down to it, it was like the ridge on her palm, or the slash beneath her collarbone: hard experience tattooed on her body like emblems of endurance. Of what the *Kyn* had once called "fight".

She would win this and she would win it now.

The disc was loaded. Again, Ann nocked her arrow, drew her bow, and closed her eyes. She inhaled deeply.

"Fire."

The disc was released. Ann's bow flew up. She unhooked her fingers from the string and released her arrow.

The disc was knocked clean out of its path. Ann didn't blink as the runner went to retrieve it; her vision blurred but on she stared, watching the man's shape trot away into the growing darkness.

She heard the screams of the crowd before she saw the man. Hands clamped her shoulders, shaking her, almost lifting her off her feet.

"Did I do it, Teacher?" she asked Hefanos beside her.

"That you did, girl," he said. "That you did."

***

Later, standing in the torchlit courtyard, Ann heard her name called out.

"First rank in archery, the Huntress of Kabyrnos, to receive five points."

She was now in second place overall, behind the Makronan Deothesus by two points. Ahead of her brother by four.

But there were three more competitions.

She didn't know who had cut her string or why – a few names came to mind – and she'd probably never know. In all honesty, she didn't particularly care.

There would be no more "accidents". No more false starts, no more hesitation.

There were three competitions left, and no one – no one – was going to get in her way.

Chapter Six

The sand in the stadium had been converted into three jumping trenches. Running alongside of each trench were five markers, evenly spaced. Each contestant would be given three attempts to leap to the furthest possible marker.

The healers had assured Ann that she'd be fine to jump – her wound wasn't a deep one. But it looked pretty bad and felt even worse under the tight wrappings of wool.

She was called in the first round of contestants. She emptied her mind and focused, putting all of her power into the run-up, into flinging the weights forward as she dove, and sweeping them back just at the last moment. In all three attempts, she landed somewhere between the second and third markers. Most of the men – she saw from the side-lines minutes later – were routinely making it past the third marker. Her brother made it halfway past the fourth. Thighs – that compact tank of muscle – landed just shy of that, with the eagle-beaked Phernian close behind. And on each of his three tries, the High Steward managed to sail cleanly through the air to touch the sand just in front of the fifth.

She didn't attend the announcement of the rankings that night. She didn't need a herald to inform her that she'd been bumped out of second and that both Thighs and the High Steward were ahead of her. She didn't need to hear it announced that she was now tied with her brother.

The stadium was already baking in the sun by the time Ann arrived the next day. Waves of heat rose from the sand where the wooden combat rings had been re-built to waist height. Servants wandered through the stands refilling jugs and waterskins, and waving fans.

"You ready?" her trainer asked when he arrived.

"Yes."

"Your head?"

"Clear."

He looked at her briefly. "Good."

The first four pairs of contestants were then announced. By the time the eight men had geared up and made their way into the rings, their leather guards were already dark with sweat. Ann took a long drink from her waterskin and settled in to watch. She watched as men jabbed and dodged, kicked and blocked, noting any irregularities, any weaknesses. She sat there for the whole morning, draining waterskin after waterskin, never taking her eyes from the rings. And when her name was called, she rose without hesitation. She strapped into her gear, taking care to ease her helmet over the bandage that would serve the double purpose of protecting her wound and keeping sweat from her eyes. Then, fully equipped, she walked out from under the canopy and felt the full force of the sun at noon bearing down on her.

She stepped into the appointed ring and waited for her opponent. A Kapreitan from Xanu – she'd seen him in the wrestling matches. Strong, not too quick. Perfect. The announcer called them to position. Ann brought her forearms up in front of her face and rolled forward onto the balls of her feet.

The signal was made and Ann swept in, driving her fist directly in toward the man's chest. He blocked, as she'd meant him to, and swung out with his own strike – which she deflected upward while snapping in again for his exposed armpit. He just barely managed to twist out of the way. She backed up, luring him to her and he advanced slowly. He now knew how fast she was. As he circled, Ann kept her eyes on his face, waiting for the smallest hint of movement. And when it came, his jab was deflected downward and her fist swung around to hammer him in the shoulder.

The referee called the point. Ann wiped the sweat off her face and resumed her stance. The signal was called again and the man flew forward, throwing a left hook in toward her shoulder. Ann ducked, leaning into it; his fist zoomed past her ear as she reached out beneath his arm, her own strike landing on his upper arm. The man jerked back, shaken by the close call.

But Ann gave him no time to recover. She flew in, assailing him with jab after jab, careful not to put too much strength into each hit – she only needed to make contact. And she was wearing him down. When she judged it time, she aimed her fist a little lower, toward his lower ribs, tempting him to overextend to block it. Which he did. Before he had time to bring his other arm forward in defence, she shot in and landed her fist, yet again, on his shoulder.

Point called. As her opponent tried to rally himself, Ann licked her lips, tasting the salt of her own sweat. The signal was called.

Without a second's delay, the man swung his fist in and around at her side. A frantic last effort – which she chose not to deflect. Keeping her arm tucked in to protect herself, Ann twisted and snapped her leg up to land her foot on his exposed ribs.

And that was it. The match was over. The sun was blazing down on her, the crowd was screaming, and Ann was stripping out of her gear. She took a waterskin from a waiting servant, and returned to the contestants' stand to continue watching.

***

Rounds two and three flashed by. The Makronan knocked the High Steward out in the second round, the Melkian was dispatched by Thighs in the third, and just like that, two of the better fighters were out of the running. Ann continued to sweep her opponents out of the way, never stopping to wonder at how very easy it was.

She did pause, however, when she was directed to the Guard Commander's ring in round four. There were only six of them left at this point, and the woman was formidable. Ann would have to keep her at a distance, neutralizing the guardswoman's much shorter reach.

But, from the very first, the Guard Commander had Ann on the defence. She followed strike with lightning strike, ducking low and leaning in, herding Ann back into the barrier, restricting her mobility. Ann did manage a few hits of her own, even landing a point by feinting a retreat then swinging back up and in. But this only seemed to add fire to the Guard Commander's assault. The two women fought on under the sun long after the other matches had finished. Yet where Ann's movements eventually grew slower, the guardswoman maintained a steady windmill of attacks. She was indefatigable, her gaze unwavering.

The moment the final hit landed, Ann sagged back against the wooden barrier, staggered by the other woman's endurance. Yet when she glanced over, she found the Guard Commander sitting in the sand, head between her knees.

"You rat," Ann gasped.

The woman looked up, wet hair plastered to her face. Her mouth curled into a tiny, exhausted grin.

"Well fought, Huntress."

The water arrived and the two women each chugged the contents of a waterskin and doused themselves with a second. And as they stumbled across the sand together, Ann felt the guardswoman's eyes on her.

"If I may say so, Huntress," she began, "you surrender too easily."

"You call that easy?"

The woman hitched a weary shoulder. "Could you not have held out longer?"

Unsure of how to respond, Ann said nothing at all.

***

While the women had been battling through the morning, the other two matches had resolved quickly and definitively. Deothesus had thrashed his opponent – a Gyklanean from Laredea – and, more surprisingly, Nik had beat Thighs, three-to-one.

This was not welcome news to Ann. It meant that where she was left to scrabble for fourth or fifth rank, her brother was assured one of the top three. It also meant that she'd have to face Thighs again.

The first series of the fifth round was announced: she was to fight the Laredean, and Nik would be facing his Guard Commander.

The Laredean was disappointingly easy, especially after the Guard Commander. His technique was good, his speed excellent, but he was so utterly predictable that Ann was able to make fast work of him. Nik, on the other hand, stood strong against the Guard Commander for some time. He was far less tentative in boxing than he had been in wrestling, but he was still strangely far from aggressive. His strikes, when he made them, were incredibly swift, but without real power. Ann took a visceral sort of pleasure in watching the guardswoman drive him down with a pure offensive force that Ann felt sure he could have held up against, had he really let himself. But, for whatever reason, he didn't, and the guardswoman dispatched her subordinate twice as quickly as she had his sister.

In the next series of fights, Thighs was matched with the Laredean, and the Guard Commander was once more set to face the Makronan prince. Ann watched the former match only long enough to see one of Thighs's powerful swings land with devastating effect on the other man's back. Grimacing, she turned her attention to the next ring.

The duel between Palthenra and Deothesus was a breath-taking thing to behold. There was barely a sound in the stadium as the two figures weaved in and out in their swift, feral dance. In wrestling, the woman had not stood a real chance against the Makronan's size; now, she used her smaller body to her advantage, plunging and twirling under and around his strikes to lash out with her own. She was at her most predatory. They were fighting for first rank – the Makronan's victory over Nik a sure thing – and it was a long, drawn-out battle. By the time they were tied two-to-two, both fighters had slowed perceptibly, sweat spraying off their bodies with every move.

But then, through what means only the gods knew, Deothesus rallied. The silence of the stadium was taut with dread as the Gyklanean man bore down on the Guard Commander of Kabyrnos, forcing her – as she had done to so many others – into the outer barrier. The thousands in the crowd groaned together as the Makronan's final strike came plummeting toward her and the woman seemed to cower away, away from the loss of her hard-earned glory.

Then there was a collective gasp as the guardswoman dropped to the ground, her legs folding beneath her – and as the Makronan's fist sailed cleanly over her head, her own came shooting up to land directly over his heart.

No one seemed to believe it at first. But the explosion eventually came, people screaming, hugging each other, crying out for the triumph of Kabyrnos. Deothesus helped the Guard Commander up off the ground and clapped her soundly on the back. The woman smiled – a weary, but brilliant smile – and left the ring for the last time to the sound of the crowd chanting her name.

***

It was later that afternoon that Ann found herself staring again into the beady eyes of the Gyklanean Thighs. The man said nothing this time, only leered silently. She looked back, unblinking, unsmiling. Then she drew in a long, deep breath and listened.

She heard the crowd cheering encouragement to her and to her brother two rings over – desperate in their knowledge of sure defeat, the thousands of voices blending into one pulsing rhythm. She felt their eyes on her, the eyes of her fellow contestants, of her trainer, the *Kynra*. The *Kyn*. She let them all go. She felt the bolstering grip of leather on her skin, and the sand beneath the toughened soles of her feet searing, hotter even than the sun on her face. She felt the steady throb of her forehead. She let out her breath, low and even.

She brought her fists up and bent into readiness.

The signal went.

Thighs charged forward with a roar, swinging the club of his arm around at Ann's ribs. She spun out of the way, hair whipping across her face as her fist lashed out at his shoulder. Blocked, but barely. Good. Outside of the close-quarters of wrestling, the man's heft was a real impediment. But those fists were lethal. They came in at her again; she ducked and twisted away, circling around him, releasing a volley of strikes to disorient. She danced out of his range, then shot in, again, again, watching his frustration climb. She swept in again, feinting left, then right, then coming at him from the centre. But there was no attempt to block this time: instead, his arm hammered down, his whole body behind the strike. He was aiming to crush.

Ann lunged back, a hair's breadth out of reach. Growling, the man snapped one massive leg out toward her ribs. She whirled to the side: his foot flew past her body as she hooked her arm around his calf and heaved. Thighs pitched forward, directly into her waiting fist.

The referee called the point. Thighs's nostrils were flaring as they were called to resume their positions. Then the signal was made and he was charging her again, his fist pulled back, then released like a spring-loaded canon ball. Ann leaned into it, rolling her shoulder out of the way.

Yet he was not aiming for her shoulder.

There was a white explosion on the right side of her head and Ann was flying, skidding in the sand, ears ringing. Pain entered her consciousness slowly, dulling her brain. She could hear the muffled sounds of people shouting and the Gyklanean's high, crazy laughter. She rested her forehead in the hot sand, clinging to consciousness by a thread.

And then the cold took hold of her.

It started in her chest and spread outwards, icy tentacles rippling into her veins, gripping her hard. She gripped back. Her mind was sharp again, crystalline – no room for thought, no room for feeling. No room for anything but that one, singular drive.

Antigone…

She stood. Removed her helmet, stripped off her arm guards. The referee was stepping into the ring, whip in hand.

"No."

The referee turned to her. "Huntress?"

"Leave it."

The din of the crowd surged as Ann turned back to Thighs. The man's smile faltered and the referee took another step forward.

"I said *leave it*."

Reluctantly, the referee backed out.

She descended, not waiting for the signal. She saw those tiny eyes widen, saw the vein on the man's neck bulge as she lashed out with strength not her own, battering pelvis, abdomen, wrist – any spot free of point or foul. She watched the shiver of pain pass over his face as her heel slammed into his kneecap. Her leg snapped up, into stomach, sending him back into the edge of the barrier. She kicked again, hearing ribs cracking, his head snapping back against the wood. There was blood on him now – its sharp, metallic tang filling the air. She reached down, grabbed his wrists and dragged his body through the sand to the centre of the ring. She could hear his ragged breathing over the roar of the stadium and felt nothing but the ice within her.

Antigone...

"Get up."

He rose, trembling.

She savoured every morsel of it. Every rush of air from his lungs, the blood smeared across his teeth. And when she sent him reeling back into the sand for the last time, she merely stood above him, looking down onto his massive, prostrate form. Daring him to rise again.

"Ann?"

Unwillingly, she turned away.

Nik's golden eyes – *her* eyes – looked warily from the opening in the ring.

"Ann, you're bleeding."

She didn't move. He gestured to his forehead.

"You need to have that looked at."

She looked into those eyes a moment longer. Those yellow eyes, staring out at her from a face that made the coldness in her throb and sizzle.

Antigone...

She passed a hand over her brow, wiping the blood away.

"Enough," she whispered. "*Enough.*"

***

Ann watched the announcement of the scores from the rooftop. Looking down on the mass of tiny figures below, she heard the Makronan's name called out. First rank with eleven points. Then her brother's was called. Eight points – one point ahead now.

Her own name was called in sequence with the Guard Commander's and Siprano of Arkanea's.

Siprano of Arkanea. She hadn't known his name. And she cared even less now. Thighs wouldn't be fit for the announcements that evening, she knew. Not that many of the other Gyklaneans attended these days.

Ann turned to descend back into the palace as the High Steward's name was called out. Sixth rank, with six points.

A tight race. With only one more left to go.

***

The air was thick with the haze of the morning, the grass dewed but already brown, hardly a month into spring. Ann walked the length of the track before any of the others arrived, her eyes combing its surface, noting its dents and hills, the way the dust kicked up behind her. She waited as the stadium filled, the air soon buzzing with voices. Nik entered, crossing over to the other side of the contestants' stand. Ann watched him as he sat, as he rubbed his face with both hands.

He was nervous – very nervous. She didn't need the twinge in her mind to tell her that. He was by far the tallest contestant, and slender, like her: a natural runner. And he was a man. He had every advantage. And yet – he was nervous.

He peered up then, meeting her gaze.

This was between him and her. Finally.

The morning passed quickly, the preliminary races concluding much as was to be expected. Ann watched, unsurprised, as the High Steward outstripped the pack in the first race, as a bruised and bandaged Thighs pumped mechanically into the lead in the second, and Deothesus secured a narrow triumph in the third. She watched as her brother came out the easy victor in the fourth. She herself barely had to try in the fifth. The only surprise came in the sixth race, in which the Gyklanean Tiny zipped ahead of the others like a mouse before cats.

The six victors stationed themselves in a staggering line along the track. Ann stood behind Tiny and in front of the Makronan, her brother four over, furthest in along the inner curve. She kept her eyes ahead, but she was aware of him. Of the thrumming in his chest, the dryness in his mouth. She blocked him out – and was left only with herself. The cold inside.

The preparation call was made. She crouched down, fingertips brushing the ground. She inhaled slowly. The smell of the dry earth beneath her. The silence in the hot, still air.

The horn blew and she was off to the cry of the crowd, launching forward on the balls of her feet – focusing on nothing but getting out and getting out fast, with knees flying up, arms pumping, head tall.

The six contestants drew level with each other, evening out around the curve of the track. Ann could sense their bodies in the shift of the air around her. She picked up the pace, knowing she'd have to establish herself at the head of the pack now. She inched out.

But he was with her, his body pumping alongside hers, leaning in even closer along the next bend. They were so close that Ann felt the wall between them momentarily crumble, and for an instant, the thumping in her ribcage was not her own.

But the first half of the track was done: time to coast a little. Ann maintained her speed, still going hard, but not killing it. With any luck, her brother would burn out trying to pass her here. Consistency was never his strong point.

Sure enough, Nik pulled ahead by a few steps. She let him have it. The second half-track was nearing its end, the starting line close at hand. She'd have to pick it up again. She hugged in close behind her brother, flecks of his sweat flying off onto her skin. The voices of the crowd crested like a wave as the twins crossed the line.

Then she leaned in and *pushed*, hammering forward in a near all-out effort – soon drawing level with Nik. For a moment, the twins seemed to hover next to each other, two streaks of gold sweeping along the track, the others left well behind. And then, slowly, Ann began to creep ahead.

Nik let out a low grunt and threw himself forward. They were nearing the last half-track mark. He pushed ahead a bit along the inner curve. Air burning her lungs, Ann bided her time, knowing that mere seconds would bring the last straight stretch of sprinting.

The curve evened out and Ann pulled in beside her brother. She could feel his body contracting and releasing, driving at its hardest. She heard the crowd shrieking, their names lost in the wordless roar. She clamped down.

Here. Now.

Gritting her teeth, she pressed forward, past, pushing, pushing, pushing as hard as she could, drawing on her last reserves, pulling it out of every fibre, every cell, muscles screaming as she tore across the last ten metres to the line. She felt Nik's rush of desperation, felt him prepare to dive.

Letting rip one cry, Ann surged forward and flew across the finish line.

The roar of the crowd was so thunderous that it shook the ground. Ann staggered sideways into the sand and crumpled to her hands and knees. She heaved. The other racers had crossed now and the crowd was out of control, pouring out of the stands, flinging food and waterskins into the arena. Ann rolled over onto her back. The cloudless sky spun above her, the blue fading and sharpening with each pound of her heart – until it simply blotted out to black.

Chapter Seven

It felt nothing like she'd thought it would. In fact, it felt like nothing at all.

The Hunter and Huntress of Kabyrnos had stolen first rank together, beating out the Makronan Deothesus by a single point. And sneaking in just behind the Gyklanean Thighs, the High Steward had secured fifth. A great day for Kabyrnos. For *her*.

And yet it felt like nothing.

The city was in celebration, plunging headfirst into bacchanal abandon. The alcohol had materialized; the Gyklaneans had, wisely, disappeared – all but Deothesus, who was at the centre of it all, mayhem's conductor, bellowing with laughter, shouting out dirty chants, one arm around Nik's shoulder and the other around a truly enormous jug of beer. Both men laughing, flushed, alight with their triumph.

Ann left. She went north, to the sea. Its stillness in the windless evening. The sun disappeared, its light sweeping after it. Soon, the sea was as dark and glittering as one of the *Kynra*'s beads and the day's heat began to dissipate. Ann sat with arms wrapped around her knees, staring always north. Skin soon chilling to match the frost within.

Nothing.

She stayed there all night. Not sleeping. Waiting. Always waiting.

In the glowing hour before dawn, she crept back to the palace, sneaking in through the silent corridors and up into her apartments. The curtains to her brother's room were closed, and she could hear his breathing from within.

First rank. The golden twins, together. And him there now, just metres away. Always just metres away. Lacing in and out of her life like a golden thread, brilliant and shining on the one side, and dulled to dark on the other. The pattern always unfinished.

She hadn't won, not really. Not while they shared the victory. And yet, strangely, it didn't seem to matter much anymore. Whatever she'd been assuming it would fix, whatever hole it should have filled, there was still only nothing. Tomorrow – *today*, she reminded herself – they would leap the bull. And that would be the end of it.

***

Ann woke at midday, muscles aching, head throbbing. Walls pulsing steadily around her.

It was time and He was here for her.

Nik's curtain was already open, the common room empty. The corridors too. The pastures were unusually hushed as she padded through. No buzz of early cicadas, no dry rustle of leaves, no bird song. No hum of voices from the stadium ahead.

Which was – she soon found – already full. And what she initially took for the silence of a massive, collective hangover, she quickly saw was something else. She peered at the faces of the crowd, rigid and pale. That hunted look in their eyes. An expression she recognized well from the past season, though she couldn't comprehend it here, in this place.

Darkylus appeared before her.

"You are to come with me."

So she'd been summoned then. Ann followed the man out of the stadium and into a nearby olive grove. But it was not the *Kynra* who stood framed in the shadows of the twisted boughs. The *Kyn* greeted her with a stiff nod as Darkylus drew back.

"Ann," he whispered. "Ann, they know. Word has spread."

His lips were white and barely moving.

"Ann, do you not hear? Can you not feel it coming? It is near – so very near. Yet perhaps not near enough."

She looked at the man, his eyes darting, never resting in one place for long. He seemed genuinely afraid. And for once, she felt no pity.

"The *emergency stores*, Ann," he was saying. "Someone – that woman, no doubt – has let word slip. I will deal with her in due course – yet we cannot wait. You must secure this now. You must *win* this for me, Ann."

For me.

She felt the ice within her crackle.

"You *must*," he went on. "If one of the others were to succeed…"

A hand at her elbow. The priest.

"It is time, Ann," she heard the *Kyn* whisper as she was drawn back. "It is here."

She was led back to her seat. She glanced at the others in the contestants' stand. Her brother, drawn and expressionless. Deothesus next to him, and Thighs.

If one of the Gyklaneans were to succeed.

She looked out into the stadium again. The tension was so thick it was almost a tangible thing, an invisible weight, pinning them to the spot.

And beneath it, the ever-present pulse.

The *Kynra* was being escorted to her throne. The skin that stretched over her bones was so pale it looked almost translucent, even from across the sand. The *Kyn* settled in his seat next to her, face averted, eyes fixed on nothing.

The twin pillars of Kabyrnos.

But there was no space for them now: He was here and it was time.

***

The five contestants stood outside the horned barrier that circled the sand while the cart was hauled in from the north. There was a stirring in the stands, a nervous shuffle of bodies. A muffled roar pierced the air of the stadium, leaving the silence deeper in its wake.

"Ann."

Nik, at her side. The boxed cart was brought to the lip of the barrier, and as the attendants wedged stones behind its wheels, it began to shake.

"Ann, I don't think I can do this."

The attendants took hold of both sides of the hatch, and swung it open.

In that instant, the spell of silence was broken. The crowd screamed with the bull as the animal galloped into the arena, a cloud of sand rising behind it. The creature's horns were long and curved, the muscles of its shoulders rippling a satin black under the sun. It bellowed again, tossing its horns into the air as the fifth ranking contestant was called forward.

Ann watched the High Steward climb stiffly over the barrier. The crowd's voices pitched, their fists pumping as the animal swung those beautiful horns towards him. The High Steward took a few steps further into the sand then halted.

The creature lowered its nose. It pawed the sand with its hoof. No one moved. Then the High Steward let out two shouts and began to sprint toward the bull – and within seconds, both animal and man were charging each other at top speed. Ann held her breath. She would not look away.

Then, in one smooth, beautiful motion, the High Steward vaulted forward to take a leaping dive straight over the bull's head. Within a heartbeat, he had landed, somersaulting across the sand and bouncing back to his feet. Making it look effortless.

The crowd erupted into near-hysterical cheers. The bull was slowing now at the contestants' end of the arena and Ann took an involuntary step back. Up close, the creature was enormous: not tall – chest height, at most – but massively, horribly powerful.

The High Steward was holding his arms up, turning slowly for his shrieking fans. But the thunder of hooves soon called him back. Ann watched as the man sank into a crouch. She watched as the bull picked up speed, its horns lowered. She watched as it drew closer. And still the man had not moved.

Then, when the creature was within mere meters, the High Steward sprang up in a low arc – aiming just barely above the animal's shoulders.

The idiot was going for a handspring.

Sure enough, instead of sailing over that lowered head, the High Steward reached down, one hand wrapping firmly around a horn – the other grasping at air.

Whether he'd simply miscalculated, or whether the creature had somehow twisted out of the way, Ann could not say. All she knew as the High Steward's shoulder hit the sand was that the people of Kabyrnos were irate. They shrieked abuse before the man even had a chance to roll out of the hooves' path. They hurled food, sandals and insults as he slunk back through the barrier. Ann scanned the crowd nervously. It was only the first contestant and they were already almost out of control.

The next ranked was called and the noise simmered. All eyes fixed on the southern point of the arena as Thighs heaved himself over the barrier with a grunt.

The Gyklanean's ribs were still bandaged, the bruises that covered his body now purple. He stopped at the edge of the arena; there would be no bravado here. The crowd began to shout again as the bull picked up into a trot, their voices rising, spurring the creature on. Thighs waited, eyes fixed on the beast. And then, when the animal was about thirty feet away, those powerful legs bunched and the man hurtled forward. He flung his arms up and out, hurling himself at the charging bull.

There was no grace to his leap, but it was effective: the man soared over the beast and landed face down in the sand. The crowd roared furiously as the Gyklanean peeled himself up, wheeling to face the circling animal.

Ann could see that he was in real pain now. His ruddy face was drained of colour, his hand at his bandaged ribs. As the creature picked up into a gallop again, Thighs crouched down with a wince.

Again, the man waited, the bull tearing toward him, the crowd shrieking bloody murder. And, just as he had before, he sprinted forward in the last few seconds, swung his arms out and launched himself at the bull.

Ann would remember what happened then for all her remaining days. It haunted her because she knew it had been her fault – her fault he hadn't been able to swing himself to the proper height. For all his bulk, the man looked like a skewered puppet as the bull thrashed, flinging him into the air.

Not a sound could be heard in the stadium except the grunts of the animal. Even as the attendants ran forward to distract the creature, the crowd remained silent. Looking back on it in the days afterward, Ann understood that it was simply that it had been too ugly, too abrupt. The violence they'd been craving from the start had come upon them too quickly, knocking the wind out of them.

Yet the event would go on. The stretcher had barely left the arena when the third ranking contestant was called. And by the time Deothesus had climbed the barrier, the only testament to the passing of the much-hated Gyklanean man was a dark stain in the sand, soon covered by the tracks of stampeding hooves.

The Makronan's first leap over the bull was clean and simple, and he was on his feet again before the creature seemed to realize that its target had vanished. The beast was enraged, its mouth foaming now as it circled round again and hurtled at the waiting man. This time, however, instead of diving, the young Makronan twisted sideways at the last second, launching himself into a mid-air roll. It was beautifully executed – almost. Coming out of his three-sixty turn, Deothesus's feet untucked and stretched downward to alight in the sand. Watching closely, Ann could have sworn he'd landed it perfectly. Yet, oddly, he then seemed to lose balance, his arms flailing as he sat down with a thump.

At first, the young man just sat in the sand, blinking his surprise. And then he threw his head back and *howled* with laughter. Soon, the crowd was tittering along with him. And as he waddled out of the arena, making a great show of dusting off his rump, their titters turned to chuckles, soon breaking out into full laughter. Ann watched Deothesus's grinning face as he made his way over to the contestants' stand. The boy really was a lot more competent than he seemed.

It was to the sound of dying laughter that the announcer came forward for the fourth time.

"Tied in first rank, the Hunter of Kabyrnos."

The laughter died away completely then, and Ann, peering up into her brother's face, felt a chill pass through her like an icy blast of wind.

She had seen that look before.

The bull turned its head the moment Nik's foot touched the sand. Its nostrils flared, its horns lowered, its breath stirred the sand at its hooves. Nik moved forward another few paces then stopped, arms hanging at his sides.

Like one touched by the god.

Ann had seen this before. On the mountain – with the boar. She reached out with her mind, urging her brother to snap out of it – to *move* – but he was utterly closed off. And the bull was closing the distance between them with alarming speed.

She flew to the barrier. "*Nik!*" she screamed.

His body tensed to alertness. The bull only metres away, Ann felt the panic, then the lightning quick thought, wondering if he could still try a leap.

No time! she called out to him.

She felt his assent, felt his muscles twist, arcing his body out, away from the bull's horns.

But it wasn't quite enough.

He went down, clutching at his leg, blood pouring out through his fingers as he dragged himself backward, away from the hooves that were dancing dangerously near. Ann launched herself over the barrier. Now close – so close – to the enormous beast, she shouted, one wordless, desperate cry, and those red-stained horns swung toward her.

And then the world around her stilled. It was an instant only, where nothing seemed to exist except her and the animal, trapped together in a storm of sand. Its black eyes regarding her with a sudden, unnatural calm. Her heart swelling with the feeling within it. The raw power. The anger. The simple, heart-rending grief.

Then the sand settled. The bull extended one foreleg out and lowered its horns in an unmistakable bow.

**

"And so it is done."

The air pulsed around her. The *Kyn* was in the arena, the *Kynra* just beyond. Nik was gone, carried out on another stretcher, and Ann was kneeling by the beast, one hand on its broad cheek. She smelled the grass on its breath. She saw the intelligence in its black, glossy eye.

But she could feel the god there with her, and He was pulling her away.

"All behold," the *Kyn*'s voice was ringing out, "the glory of Mavros and His blessing on Kabyrnos!"

"Praise be the Mother," Ann heard the *Kynra* say.

The people of the stadium were murmuring, gaping at Ann and the bull in amazement. But there was something else in their faces – something that made her lean instinctively closer to the animal.

She felt Him hiss, drawing her away again.

"And now," the *Kyn* continued, "in the company of all of Kapreitu and Gyklanea, Kabyrnos shall honour the divine powers that honour us."

Ann felt His sigh of anticipation, His hunger echoed in the eyes of the people who ringed the space like vultures.

The handlers had entered the arena and were approaching with ropes. The bull remained on its knees behind her, its head bucking nervously.

"I don't think this is a good idea," Ann said.

Antigone.

A cautionary growl, His voice in her mind like the strike of a hammer. The *Kyn* turned to her, frowning.

"What did you say?"

"I don't think this is a good idea," she repeated, pressing back into the animal's warmth. "I don't think you should sacrifice it."

Antigone.

Then the *Kyn* was there, crouching next to her. "This is the way of things, Ann."

Leave it, the voice was commanding her. You have no power here.

"Move aside, Ann," the *Kyn* uttered.

The animal stirred at her back. Its breathing shallow, its heartbeat rapid beneath her palm.

It could not die, she knew. Not by their hands. She did not know how she knew, but she was certain of it. More certain than she'd ever been of anything.

"Move aside, Ann!"

Antigone! the voice snarled.

"I can't."

She looked up at the *Kyn*, the *Kynra* only steps beyond.

"You were right," she found herself saying. "This is your gift. Accept it. Be humble before it. Then release it."

The pulse was building, bearing down.

"Or," she went on slowly, "you can reject it. And be rejected in turn."

"Ann."

The *Kyn*'s hand on her now, gripping painfully.

"We need this," he whispered. "I need this."

"That – doesn't matter."

A flicker of something passed through the man's eyes.

"That is enough, girl. You do not understand."

One wave and the handlers were there, the animal braying and backing up into the barrier as the people cheered and shouted. Two men took Ann by the arms, and hauled her back, out of the arena.

She was left beneath the pines. Air throbbing and ringing with distant screams.

"Oh gods," she whispered. "What have they done?"

***

She was running through the abandoned corridors, following the flickering trace of her brother's presence.

Ann burst through the door of the infirmary and three faces turned to her – then snapped back to the cot beneath them. Nik was unconscious, pads of red-soaked wool piled on the floor around his bed.

Ann remained by the door. She wouldn't distract them now, not for the world. Instead, she beckoned one of the nearby servants.

"Find the servant Hersephona. Bring her here immediately."

The servant left and it was then that Ann noticed the cot in the corner of the room, bearing the motionless form of the Gyklanean. She looked away quickly, peering into her brother's face. It was so still, so pale. He looked no more alive than the corpse in the corner.

Hersa arrived and the women waited together, watching as the healers worked. Nik's foot turned blue from the tourniquet tied just below his hip, his chest rose and fell almost imperceptibly.

Looking at him now, it was easy to see the boy he used to be. And so hard to recall why she'd been so angry with him.

He left me, Ann told herself. Again and again, he left me.

Yet, staring down at that pale, boyish face, she understood that in some twisted, unfathomable way, he had pushed her away to protect himself. Maybe even to protect her.

"Huntress."

One of the healers was standing before her. Her breath caught in her throat.

"He will live," the healer said. "And the wound should heal quickly, if it is kept clean."

"Oh, God," she whispered. "Oh thank God."

Hersa was already at Nik's side, wiping the dust from his face with a damp cloth. Ann lingered near the door, giving her space. The healers cleared away their implements, gave the girl a few instructions, and left the chamber. Ann settled on a nearby cot, her back to the now covered body in the corner. She watched as her brother's colour slowly returned.

"It grows dark," Hersa said eventually, rising to fetch a lamp.

For the first time in hours, Ann's mind returned to the stadium. The butchery there long over, people would soon be returning to the palace.

And, suddenly, she knew she was not safe here.

Her public act of defiance would not go unpunished. She was sure of it, just as she was sure, now, that the voice that had been with her for over a year, coaxing and coercing, was not Mavros.

It could not be. Not even in His darkest form.

"He is waking."

Ann turned as her brother's eyes fluttered open, landing on Hersa. He smiled – a weak smile, but beautiful nonetheless. Soft and tender, all defences down. Hersa leaned over him, cupping his cheek with her palm and smoothing the hair off his forehead. Ann rose to leave them.

His eyes found her then. The smile disappeared. And what was left in its place was enough to make her blood turn to ice.

Ann stumbled back, knocking a table to the ground.

She'd seen this before. Mercifully forgotten – blotted out.

Until now.

Five years, it was five years ago almost exactly, just after she'd left school, left the lawyer – for good, she'd thought – in search of Nik. She'd taken her mother's money. She had meant it for them both. To build a new life together. She returned after many years to their old family home, and there he'd been. Waiting for her. But the creature she'd found there, half-starved, driven half-crazy, barely resembling the boy she knew so well... She'd run. She'd given him the money and run, all the way back to her safe, bleak future.

He hadn't left her, not really. She had abandoned him, when he'd needed her most.

"I –" she choked out, "I can't stay here."

And, turning her back on her brother once more, Ann fled. North, always north. To the sea. And to nothing.

Book VI

Chapter One

She was gone. Again, just – gone.

Nik lay, staring at the empty doorway. Thinking of the last time.

But then, she'd found her way back to him, hadn't she? He could see her still, cowering in the airport lobby like some frightened little creature.

He'd barely been able to suppress it then. He'd panicked – frozen her out.

Better than it could have been. Better by far.

He'd given her one day. It was all he could spare from work, he'd said. But it had turned out much longer than that, hadn't it?

And since that day there'd been so many times when she'd caught him off guard, so many times he'd almost let it out...

But she'd run before. And now she'd run again.

He was glad. It was for the best. It was better with her gone.

But that look in her eyes. Those yellow eyes, so like his own.

"Niklas – Nik."

Hersa, shaking him gently – pulling him back to the moment. Bringing him back to the pain.

Nik gasped, clutching at his thigh.

"Niklas, no, it must *heal*," Hersa said, prying his hands away. "Tell me, Nik, what has happened?

Where has she gone?"

He swallowed, looking up into that soft, lovely face. This bossy little woman. He didn't deserve her.

And she'd hate him too, if she knew.

"I don't know," he whispered eventually. "But I don't think she's coming back this time."

***

Ann paused on the crest of the hill that overlooked Kylondo. Lights were winking through windows and glowing in the streets. She turned onto a footpath that wound through the rocky hills toward the foot of the cliffs. The town was soon out of sight. Humanity out of sight.

You spoil everything around you, he'd once said to her.

It was the truth. She'd torn down everything she'd painstakingly built for herself, and now she had nothing. Nothing, no one – nowhere, even, to go.

The footpath led to a strip of sand by the sea. Ann moved toward the water, feeling the lingering heat of the sun on the soles of her feet, between her toes. The air was thick and moist. A thunderstorm was brewing on the horizon, tiny splinters of lightning shooting down to meet the water's edge.

This was a raw, elemental world – so different from the one she'd just left behind. Once again, she'd crossed the borders of one life to the next. Her existence no more than one dislocation after another.

The path forward never less clear.

Ann stood at the shoreline, listening to the gentle lapping of water, watching the ripples of moonlight along the sea floor.

She began to undress, stripping off every garment until she stood bare in the humid night.

Then she stepped into the water. It was cool, but not unpleasant. She moved in slowly, feeling the ocean parting around her calves, then her thighs, then touching the warmth between her legs. She dove. The salt stung at the cuts and scrapes on her skin. She propelled herself deeper. The water grew colder, currents sweeping in from further out.

Yet the pain and cold soon ebbed away, and Ann stopped kicking. She hung in the shadows, weightless, the streaks of milky light sifting through the floating curtain of her hair. This was a place of in-between, soft and dark. Her own private purgatory.

But it was no place for mortals.

By the time she made it back to the shore, a slight breeze had picked up. Shivering, Ann waded out of the water and moved to where her clothes lay in the sand. She reached down for her tunic.

And paused.

Someone was here. She snapped up and glanced to the cliffs – to the hills. Then back to the sea.

And her heart stilled within her.

There, standing in the shallows, was an enormous white bull.

Ann didn't dare move. The beast was walking forward now, the air shimmering around it – as if the creature was pulling in the moonlight and reworking it – reworking itself – as it approached. Ann stared, disbelieving, as the bull reared upright, shrinking and growing brighter until she was forced to shade her eyes. The smell of ozone met her nostrils – the lightning storm upon them. But when she peered over her hand, the sky was still clear. And the bull had become a man.

Ann dropped to her knees in the sand.

Rise.

Slowly, she rose and looked up into the face of Mavros.

How could she ever have mistaken the horned figure in the courtyard for Him? It had been a crude caricature – nothing more. There could be no imitation of the way the moonlight caught the fine white hairs of His body, no copying the expression in His black, glossy eyes. No mimicry of His voice ringing in her mind like a bell, clear and oscillating. It was inconceivable to her now that she could ever had thought that the other voice, that rasping hiss within her mind, could be His.

"You showed great courage today, child," the god said to her.

She shook her head. "It wasn't enough."

"It is always enough when all is given. You cannot save others from their own folly."

He stepped closer.

"What–" she swallowed – "what will happen now?"

He did not answer right away. "You will have to beware."

"Of?"

She knew the answer before He spoke, yet her breath still caught at His words.

"He who lurks in the shadow of the palace. For His heart is corrupted beyond repair."

The god was reaching His hand out now, fingers rising to touch her cheek.

"If ever you had need of My aid, you have only to ask. Know first, however, that the aid of the gods is, as always, a double-edged weapon."

Then His fingertips brushed her skin and she gasped – suddenly aware of what she had somehow been blind to before.

"You need not fear Me," the god said quietly. "I have taken before what was not given. I do not often err, yet I did so then."

He paused.

"Shall I leave you, Huntress?"

A choice. But her head was already shaking.

"No," she whispered. "Stay."

He closed the gap between them, His body pressing against hers. Ann looked down, embarrassed, but His hand was on her chin, forcing her to meet His eyes as His fingers traced the bones of her face, then the curves of her breasts, lingering for a moment on scars old and new. He butted His nose against her cheek and she could smell His breath, which told of windy fields and high mountains. He pulled her closer. She felt Him hard against her then and felt a flutter deep within. Another gasp escaped. He looked up at the sound, His nostrils flaring.

All softness was abruptly gone. His hands clutched at her buttocks, lifting her onto Him. He let out a low, rumbling moan as she twined her fingers into His curls, tightening her legs around Him.

Never had she known that there could be so much ease, so much pleasure. When Mavros lay down in the sand, pulling her on top of Him, her body moved in ways she'd never imagined it knew how, following rhythms as old as the ocean tides. She felt a warmth building within her, rising in waves, her head falling back, her hands roaming across His chest, then her own, unselfconscious in her need. And when the last wave rose up to envelop her, she cried out, shuddering against Him.

She collapsed on top of Him, utterly spent. She felt the heat of His body beneath her, the rise and fall of His breath. And as she drifted away, she was vaguely aware of fingers stroking her hair and a rumbling voice telling her to sleep peacefully. For all would be well, in time.

**

Ann woke filled with a sense of urgency.

She sat up in the sand, the crust of salt cracking on her skin. She was alone. The sun was rising. And it was time to go.

When she reached the footpath that would take her out of sight of the beach, she looked back. There, in the sand, were her footsteps from the night before. First leading into the water, then heading back out again, to the place where they met a second pair.

She sighed, smiling.

But the urgency in her mind was growing. She jogged back along the path, squinting as the early morning sun peaked over the mountains. Once she reached the main road, she paused, looking north.

Half-way down to Kylondo was a company of thirty men, laden with packs. And walking at the head of the group, a barrel-chested young man, accompanied by a dog.

Two barks and Kaenus was loping back up the hill – Deothesus waving his company to a halt. Ann trotted down to meet them. Kaenus reached her first, rearing up to paw her shoulders and bathe her face in kisses.

"Huntress!"

The Makronan prince was smiling as he came back to greet her, his middle-aged companion at his shoulder.

"I should have guessed the reason that the mutt insisted on coming with us."

"You're leaving?" she asked. "So soon?"

Deothesus's smile fell away. "I am afraid we must."

The sense of urgency flared. "Tell me."

"I received a message from your *Kynra* last night, advising us to leave at first light. For our safety, her manservant said. It seems that your people are under the impression that we have stolen their goods."

Ann was speechless – but somehow not surprised. The young prince regarded her with one long, steady look.

"Come with us."

Ann blinked. "What?"

"Come to Makrona with us. You will be most welcome."

She met his gaze, then glanced at his companion behind him, who smiled at her shyly but kindly. Then she turned to look south.

"Okay," she whispered. "I'll come."

They walked back to the head of the company. As they resumed their march into the port town, she turned to her new companion.

"Deothesus?"

"Yes?"

"Thank you."

His smile was bright, as if there were not a care in the world. "It is truly my pleasure. And please. Call me Deo."

Chapter Two

A pounding on the door.

Nik bolted upright, wiping the sweat from his brow.

"What is it?" came Hersa's voice from next to him.

"I'll go see. Go back to sleep."

Sleep. He felt like he hadn't slept in days. He heard Hersa turn over as he eased his leg out of the bed and grabbed his loincloth off the floor.

The pounding got louder.

"I'm coming."

Nik groped around till his fingers found his stick, which had rolled under the bed. The pounding continued.

"*Jesus,*" he muttered. "I'm coming."

He'd been told to keep off his leg for at least ten days, which he'd done. And now that he was back up and running – figuratively speaking – he relied on this miserable little cane to get anywhere. Even to the corner of his room for a piss.

He limped into the common room, the door practically shaking off its hinges now.

He hauled it open. "*What?*"

The *Kyn* was leaning heavily against the doorframe, mouth open and emitting the unmistakable smack of half-digested wine.

"Where is she, boy?"

Nik tightened his grip on the stick. "Not here."

"Then *where*? You must know!"

The man lurched forward, hand slamming into the door that Nik had wedged between them.

"Where in the name of the wretched gods did she go?"

The light from the man's candle had flickered as he'd lurched, highlighting the ragged lines of his face. Nik supposed he should feel sorry for him, but he didn't. He'd never liked the man and he didn't think that the man much liked him either. He'd always been able to feel those steady, scrutinizing eyes following him whenever they'd crossed paths.

Which wasn't often anymore. The *Kyn* hadn't been seen in public since the Tournament's premature finale.

"Where *is* she?" the man repeated, leaning his forehead against the door.

"Your guess is as good as mine."

The *Kyn* glanced up sharply – as if Nik had somehow confirmed something for him. Then the man pushed away from the door, reeling back into the shadows of the corridor.

Nik shut the door, and slid the bolt into place. He took one quick look at the curtain on the other side of the common room, then hobbled back into his own bedchamber.

"Who was it?" Hersa asked sleepily as he sank onto the bed.

"Oh, just our old friend the *Kyn*."

The total silence next to him told him that the girl was wide awake now.

"I think he's finally lost it."

"...This is no time for jokes, Niklas."

"I'm not joking."

There was a shuffle of covers and he felt a warm cheek against his shoulder. "I am frightened."

"Don't be," he said, twisting round to tuck her under his arm. She felt so good there, her bare breasts brushing against him.

"How can I not be?" she said as he started kissing her neck. "When our leader disregards the most sacred duties of a host? The Gyklaneans will not quickly forget being thrown into the streets only a day after the Tournament, Niklas. And the crops? The – Niklas, *stop*."

"Come on." He needed this.

"No, Niklas. I cannot."

Nik paused, then lay down. Turned away.

"Go to sleep, Hersa. It'll be fine."

"No, Niklas, there is something very wrong here. The people are hungry, they are scared, and with Ann disappearing –"

Nik grunted, pulling the blanket up over his shoulder.

"– only the gods knowing what has happened to her, or where she has gone…"

"Give me some credit, Hersa. I may not be a god, but I've got a pretty good idea where she went. Even your *Kyn* must know it, or he wouldn't be bursting in here in the middle of the night."

Hersa was silent.

"She's fine, okay? She's better off than we are at the moment, so let's just go back to sleep."

After a few more seconds, Hersa lay back down. Nik lay absolutely still, waiting for her breathing to even out. He knew he would get no more sleep tonight.

***

Their company had been trundling across the plains since dawn. Ann walked between Kaenus and the middle-aged Selpenor, head bowed against the relentless glare of the sun.

The voyage had been long and uneventful. At first, Ann had been filled with the thrill of adventure: this was the passage of heroes, the epic journey, with the prow of the boat soaring and plunging into aquamarine waters and the salty air whipping against her face. Yet it had not been long before the winds had died, taking all glory with them. From sun-up to sundown, the men had been forced to their oars. At night, the tiny cabin in the centre of the vessel had overflowed with their prostrate bodies. Ann had elected to sleep on deck, opting for chill and damp over the snoring, body odour and midnight erections of thirty or so unwashed men.

For thirteen days, time had seemed to stretch on with the endless expanse of blue. Other than helping to assemble meals of salted fish and stale bread, there had been little for Ann to do, so she'd had more than enough opportunity to get to know the only two men on board who ever spoke to her. And by the time they'd berthed in the heavily defended Makronan port, Ann had felt as if she'd known the young prince and his tutor all her life.

There was something so familiar about the younger man. He'd born the hot, still days with humour, always taking on more than his share of rowing. And it was clear that his men adored him. Selpenor most of all, Ann had quickly seen.

The man had told her that he'd helped to raise Deo from the death of the boy's mother. Ann, who had been under the impression that the *Makrax*'s wife still lived, tactfully refrained from asking more, but Selpenor was a perceptive man: he had smiled and explained to her that Deo was no less dear to the *Makrax* – or his people – than if he had been a son born of legitimate lines.

"Of course, this might not have been so if Deothesus was heir to the chiefdom," he'd added. "Yet, as his mother was only a refugee from the south, there was no question of it. As it stands, it is his half-brother, Tritolanor, who will one day be *Makrax*, and Deothesus is free to seek out his own fate in the world."

Ann readjusted the pack on her back and watched the prince march on ahead of her through the long grass. Even with two packs on his shoulders and a heavy-looking broadsword at his belt, he set a brisk pace, guiding the company steadily onward – northwest toward the ring of mountains in the distance. And nestled there, on a ridge overlooking this sea of grass and scrub, was the citadel of Makrona.

By the time the land began to rise, the hottest hour of the day had passed. Clusters of houses – tiny, hut-like structures – were scattered on the hillsides here, with labourers kneeling in the dirt as the company passed, and herds of goats and cattle wandering freely throughout. The path grew steeper. There were a few brief respites as the land dipped downward, but it was not long before the houses disappeared and they were climbing again, up a steep, snaking path.

"How much longer?" Ann asked Selpenor over her shoulder.

"Soon," was all he could manage.

Ann put her head back down and kept climbing. So many days on the ship had made her weaker. And indescribably filthier. She couldn't wait to reach the citadel. Hot food, baths, proper beds, clean underwear – a modicum of privacy. The glories of civilization.

And yet, it was not – in her opinion – civilization that waited for them. At long last, the path ended in a gate set in a vast stone wall, and rising up above it was what the men had been calling 'the city' – what appeared, in fact, to be no more than a collection of wooden buildings smattered across the upper slope of a hill.

The company passed into the settlement. Slave girls hauling buckets of water hurried out of their way. Hostlers leading strings of horses waited for them to pass. And as they climbed further up the packed dirt roads, Deo pointed up ahead to a long building set on the peak of the ridge.

"The palace," he called back to her.

Most of the company had already broken off, but Ann followed the prince, grateful for Kaenus at her side – for Selpenor only a few steps behind her as she passed through the broad porch of the longhouse and into an open, pillared room.

The poorly-lit chamber was roughly the size of one of Kabyrnos's lesser reception halls. With a round fireplace in the centre, a few benches and tables scattered here and there, and weapons hanging on the walls, it reminded Ann more of a barracks than of a palace. And standing waiting for them here was an older man, backed by a line of slaves. He was dressed plainly, his hair an untidy mane of grey, but there was no question in Ann's mind that this was the *Makrax*.

"What have you brought me, Deothesus?" the *Makrax* asked as he released his son from his embrace.

"Father, may I present to you the Huntress of Kabyrnos."

The man's shaggy brows rose ever so slightly.

"My youngest son is fond of surprises, Huntress. Yet I believe this surpasses them all. You are most welcome in Makrona. You will, of course, stay with us here, in my house. My wife will be here presently to escort you to the women's quarters."

The man barely had to gesture to send a slave scurrying across the room. Then he moved forward to clasp hands with Selpenor.

"Greetings, old friend. How did our boy fare in the southerners' games? Did he prove our mettle?"

"That he did, Pakedainon. He was outdone only by the Huntress herself, and her brother."

The *Makrax* shot Ann one shrewd look. Then a small woman appeared at his elbow.

"Ah, Phitromela," he said. "Huntress, my wife."

The woman bowed, Kapreitan style.

"Huntress," she said in a quiet voice. "What an honour you bestow on our house. If you will please follow me, we can allow the men to return to their affairs."

Weakly returning Deo's smile, Ann turned to follow the woman.

"Can I ask," Ann began as they crossed to the back of the hall, "how do you all speak Kapreitan so well?"

"It is our custom."

With that edifying response, Ann was ushered through a low door and into a small, dark room. A group of women paused in their weaving and sewing to stare up at her, their eyes taking in her filthy tunic and exposed legs.

"I am sure you will wish to bathe after your journey," Phitromela said to Ann in the same hushed way. "Amphedora will make sure you have everything that you need."

Ann was then passed on to another woman – Amphedora, presumably – who said nothing at all as she shepherded her through to an even smaller, darker room, containing a single copper tub. Ann peered around at the four plain walls, at the long, heavy dress that was draped over the bench waiting for her – at the slaves creeping in and out of the room bearing their pots of water. And in that moment she found it a little difficult to recall why she'd been in such a hurry to leave Kabyrnos.

***

The monotony of the voyage was thrilling in comparison to Ann's first days in the Makronan fortress. At least while on the water there had been an openness to her life, a feeling of possibility. Cramped up in the women's quarters, the four walls around her seemed to take on the quality of a tomb.

If she had stopped to think at all, she would have realized that, on some level, she'd been assuming that Makrona would be another Kabyrnos: a different version of the same beautiful city, with different – probably better – versions of the same people. A place to relive the last year as it should have been lived.

And in some ways, life here was very similar. The imitation of Kapreitan style of clothing, weaving, speaking. The music that was played at night in the main hall, the pottery and stoneware they used, the jewellery that the women wore. But in all ways that mattered, Makrona was nothing like the city she'd grown so used to. The city she now ached for in every hour of every long, dim day.

And then, about ten days into her sojourn, she decided she'd had enough of the hush and gloom. Crossing over the porch of the *Makrax*'s house one morning, she descended into the open air and turned her face up to the sun. Light. Wind. Space. The view was spectacular, the mountains curling in around the distant plains in fading strips of blue. Men stared at her as she moved further out, trailed by her dog. No one stopped her, though. And when she found her way to the training grounds – where she'd been told that the men spent their days when not out hunting – she hitched her skirts over the wooden fence and perched there to watch.

It was not long before one of the men paused, pointing his practice sword over his partner's shoulder toward her.

His partner turned. Blinked. Threw back his head and guffawed.

"You disappoint me, Ann," Deo called to her as his partner elbowed him in the ribs, "I had told my brother here to expect you out *days* ago."

***

That evening, after one glorious afternoon spent sparring, Deo, Trito and Ann returned to the *Makrax*'s house together to find the old man waiting for them.

"The *geslas* has been assembled," he said to his sons.

Ann peered at Deo, whose face had fallen instantly solemn.

"We shall await them in the council chamber," the *Makrax* continued. "Huntress, if you will excuse us."

As Ann reluctantly turned to leave, Deo put a hand on her arm and said something to his father in their native tongue. While the two men argued, Ann peered over at the door behind them to see a lanky boy of twelve or thirteen standing in its threshold. His weathered face was strangely familiar.

"Or perhaps you would care to accompany us, Huntress?" the *Makrax* was now saying.

She snapped her gaze back from the boy to find the old man regarding her, unamused.

"My son seems to think you have a right to hear what is said."

Not overly comforted by the thought, she followed the men into the chamber. They settled around a circular table; she was directed to a stool in the corner. The boy was left standing. Soon, the room began to fill with sombre men who sat without a word. And when the seats by the table were at last full, the *Makrax* leaned forward.

"Tell them what you told me, boy."

The boy swallowed, his eyes flicking to Ann's then away. Again, Ann was struck a sense of familiarity.

"I was told to say," the boy began, "that since the Makr – um, since your people left, Kabyrnos has been… unwell. The heat has worsened. The town of Kartissus was set aflame and burnt to cinders. What crops we had are dead or dying."

The boy paused, his mouth working, his fists clenching and unclenching as he struggled to suppress his tears.

"Go on, boy."

"And I – I was told to, to tell you that some of the palaces in the east were damaged by an earth tremor."

"And?"

"Rainless storms." He was whispering now. "Many of – of our ships… My father's –"

He fell silent, his eyes dropping to the ground.

"You're from Kylondo," Ann said softly.

She felt the attention of the room shift to her corner.

"We met in the harbour, with your friends. Laerkys – right? Your father's a fisherman there."

"This is not the time, Ann," Deo muttered.

"But now you're here," she pressed on. "Why?"

"Ann."

"I was told my family would be cursed, Huntress!" Laerkys cried, tears spilling over. "I was told the Earth Mother would double her vengeance on our people if I did not do as was asked!"

"Who?" she demanded. "Who told you this?"

The *Makrax* slammed his hand on the table.

"Huntress! You will remain silent or you will leave. The boy has agreed to help our agent, who cannot be away from the southerner's palace. That is all you need know."

Biting her lip, Ann turned away to stare out the window as the man turned back to Laerkys.

"Was there anything else you were instructed to say, boy?"

"Just before the – your agent – left for Kylondo, there was an argument in the palace."

"Between whom?" asked one of the other men.

"The *Kyn* and *Kynra*."

"And what was *said*?" the *Makrax* demanded.

"The *Kyn* accused the *Kynra* of plotting against the city. Of plotting with – with *you* to… to abduct the Huntress."

Ann's gaze snapped back to the boy. He was sweating, staring determinedly away from her.

"And then the *Kynra* told him –" his words were rushing out now – "she could see he was running mad and she would not let him take their people down this path. He then replied that she would no longer have a choice in the matter."

Ann watched the boy look down again. She watched him plucking at the hem of his salt-stained, Makronan-style tunic.

"That is all I was told," he was saying. "I swear it. The prie – your agent left then, as the ship was soon to set sail."

The *Makrax* nodded at Deo, who rose to take the boy out of the room. While Deo was gone, no one moved or spoke. And Ann was finding it hard to breathe.

How could she have left? How could she have abandoned them all? When it was possible that only she knew which thieving, double-crossing priestess had stolen their best chance of survival?

"It is clear now, is it not, my brothers?" the *Makrax* was saying.

All of the men were nodding – except Deo, who had paused by the door near Ann.

"There is no longer any doubt," Tritolanor said.

"The gods have made their will known," agreed another.

"So it is settled then." The *Makrax* sat back, looking slowly around the room. His eyes finally settling on Ann's. "We shall prepare for the worst."

Chapter Three

Sleep.
Sleep.
He hadn't slept in weeks.

No. He knew that wasn't true. He'd slept. But it wasn't to any sweet repose that he surrendered himself every night.

Nik was staring into the darkness of the common room. He hadn't spent a night in his bed for... a while. Since Hersa had become aware that something was seriously wrong with her bed companion.

She'd tried to get him to talk about it, tried to comfort him. As if she could. He just couldn't stand that look on her face anymore. That look that made him feel like he'd just murdered something inexpressibly pure and innocent.

He'd seen that look before. But not in her eyes.

So he stayed out here now. Paced until he couldn't pace anymore. Then rocked against the wall until his body fell still. Then stared, unseeingly, into the dark until his eyes drifted shut.

And then the dreams would come. Come back to him.

Every goddamn night. There used to be some reprieve. Four times a year, as regular as clockwork, they'd come to him and then he'd have months to recuperate. Months to gather the scraps left of himself and stitch them back together again. Until the next dream.

But this he couldn't take, he couldn't take it – every night, every *night*, like some curse sent down on him from the gods for his sins, these dreams that gripped him the instant he drifted off, waking him what felt like lifetimes later. Leaving him empty, hollow.

Hollow. Not really. That's only what he told himself he was, every morning as he lay there exhausted, sweat-drenched and still shaking in the aftermath. There was nothing left that could be taken, he'd try to tell himself. But every night he'd have to face the truth that there was always something more. Always something more you could lose.

Truth was, he hardly felt human anymore. His emotional spectrum had been reduced to a single-minded dread. There was no compassion left in him. Not a drop left of caring.

He'd been there the day that the *Kynra* had been arrested, dragged out of the courtyard by the guards and hauled down, out of sight. He'd been there when the priestesses had rebelled. He'd seen their silent protest, been witness to the violence, the women beaten, knocked aside by the Guard Commander and her men. And then they'd disappeared, as suddenly as if they'd vanished into the very walls. He'd been there, he'd seen it all. And he couldn't have cared one motherfucking bit.

He hadn't left the rooms for days now. He'd tried to stop Hersa from leaving too – he'd had enough in him to try for that – but she'd gone anyway.

She told him that the moment people stopped living their lives for fear was the moment they were all truly lost.

Implication clear, message received. He was a coward. He'd known it for a long time, and now she knew it too.

Nik jerked his head up. His eyelids had drooped shut. He lurched to his feet, holding the wall for support. He felt his way along the room, the stone pulsing faintly beneath his fingers.

Sleep, it whispered to him. *Sleep*.

He snapped his head up again and kept on pacing.

But it wasn't long before his legs stopped moving – before he sank back down onto the floor. Before he heard His voice, calling his name.

Niklas…

He stood in a clearing within a forest of tall, ancient trees. There was no moon. It was very dark, very cold and He was near.

Niklas…

The voice rasping, sliding into his mind.

"Please, no," he pleaded.

The oak was there beside him, as it always was, its branches thin and twisted, its trunk withered and rooted into the frosted ground. Not quite dead, but not far from it.

"*Please*."

Come, He called to him.

Nik felt the voice wrap itself around him, its icy breath prickling against his skin, urging him forward. And as he stepped out into the frozen forest, he understood that something was different tonight. Tonight, He had a task for him. And Nik knew better than to disobey.

He wasn't sure how far he walked. It was much darker now. Nik could just make out the bare forms of trees gliding past him, though sometimes they would disappear altogether and Nik thought he was looking into a dark corridor. Yet the voice continued to call to him, call him by name, and he continued to follow.

And then Nik was there, in the chamber – the chamber that he went to every night. So dark, so cavernous and cold, the steady drip of water echoing into the stale, stagnant air. A prison, his very own, the taste of the place so foul. Nik wanted to be sick, to drag his nails across his face and scream. To lie down on the cold, damp rock and die.

Niklas, Death beckoned to him. *Wake up*.

And so he woke.

At first he couldn't make sense of his surroundings. The air wasn't cold now, but hot, unbearably hot, the darkness edged with a shifting orange light. Yet the moment he saw what he held in his shaking hands, he understood. And panic consumed him in an instant.

Fire. The long, unfamiliar corridor was on fire, flames licking out of the row of doors, the air full of black, billowing smoke. Nik dropped the torch and ran, ran past the burning portals, tongues of flame shooting out to lick at his heels. He burst through a door at the end of the corridor, feeling the heat behind him flare, seeing the shocked eyes of the two guards there slide past him to the inferno beyond. He shoved them aside and kept running – running, running, as far away as fast as he could go.

He couldn't stay here. He wasn't safe here anymore.

***

There had been several more meetings of the *geslas* in the weeks since Laerkys had been sent away, but Ann was no longer permitted to attend. Men would file out of the council chamber after morning-long sessions, faces grim, and no one, not even Deo, would say a word to her.

But it was clear what they were planning. Everywhere in the citadel were the signs of an army preparing for mobilization: smithies sharpened blades and mended pleated armour in their ever-roaring forges; the air rang with the voices of men at their drills; slaves gathered food, clothing and bandages. Her own days were once again spent in the women's quarters, mending packs from dawn till dusk.

It was almost impossible in that quiet room to stop her fears from preying on her. Impossible to ignore those phantom twinges at the back of her mind that told her that something was very seriously wrong. That someone needed her.

Her only moments of peace were with Selpenor. Every evening the man would take her outside the citadel walls and talk of simple things. The uses of mountain flowers. His memories raising horses in the valley below.

One evening, they were meandering down the ridge when a man appeared on the path ahead of them, leading his horse up by the reins.

"I have news for the *Makrax*," the man told Selpenor. "Concerning Kabyrnos."

Ann grabbed the man's arm. "What is it? Tell me now."

The messenger hesitated, looking to Selpenor, who, after a moment, nodded.

"A fire," the messenger said. "In their palace storerooms."

Ann stared at the man, uncomprehending. Selpenor gently removed her hand and waved the man past.

But she spun round after him.

"How many – how many people?"

The messenger looked back. "At least two hundred."

Two hundred.

"Thank you, brother," Selpenor said quietly and the man resumed his climb.

Two hundred dead. At least. And thousands more, now condemned.

"I am truly sorry, Ann."

Her head was nodding, her mind an ocean away. The twinge sharper, tugging at the boundary of her consciousness.

"Perhaps it is a curse or perhaps it is a blessing," the man was telling her as he patted her arm comfortingly, "yet Death will come for us all. From the moment we are born, we begin to die."

She could hear it now, that soft and steady pulsing. The merest shadow of a sound, like a lover whispering, calling to her in the shared darkness of the night.

"For us mortals, it is best only to know that we exist."

Antigone…

Nik. Nik needed her.

"I – I have to go back."

"Yes. It grows dark. Let us retur–"

His words were cut off by the shaft of an arrow, protruding from his throat.

Ann screamed, lurching away as the blood sprayed into her face. She heard responding shouts from the gates above, and footsteps in the distance behind her. Then she was on her knees, clutching Selpenor's shoulders, wrenching him around. There were barks from within the citadel. And men's voices, all around her.

"Take her. Go – *go!*"

She spun round. A man, smeared with dirt, moved through the lengthening shadows toward her. She thrust herself back, tripping on her skirts and falling in the rocks and dust. She heard another shout, prematurely cut off, saw the man close in on her, raising his arm above her.

And all went black.

***

How many days had he been out here, living like an animal on the mountainside with only the stolen horse for company? No food, scant water, only the few weapons he'd taken – a sword, a bow, some arrows for game. Which grew scarcer as the days crept closer and closer to summer.

His first night on the mountain he'd spent on the lower slopes, watching for the expected glow of light from the north. A palace, consumed in flames. Yet it had never come. The thick stone walls had saved them, then. For now.

He'd found this plateau days later, following the age-worn tracks of shepherds and their sheep. And here, buried within the peaks of the mountain, surrounded by the corpses of a heat-stroked, starved flock, Nik had slept, finally slept. But the days continued to stretch on, hazy and relentless. Each day taking him a little closer to the edge.

He couldn't come back from this. He couldn't come back from what he'd seen in those burning doors. The extinction of an entire city, by his own hand. They would starve. Without any stored provisions, they would all starve before the year was out.

At least she was safe.

He could think of her now, here, at the end. Nik stared down at his hands, lying across his chest. They were cracked and crusted in filth and old blood. These were not the hands of a man. They were the claws of an animal. Of a monster.

Things were as they should be now. He would stay up here in this mountaintop graveyard until Death came to claim him. Which would not be long now.

And with that knowledge came tranquillity. Relief, even.

But the instinct for survival was strong. When Nik heard a rustle in the trees below, his head shot up, his hands groping for the bow. It was a large creature approaching – possibly a feral goat. He squinted, trying to narrow his blurred vision on the shape moving in the leaves. Slowly, with hands shaking, he raised his bow.

And found that he was staring into a human face.

***

Her hands were tied, and the world around her was moving in familiar, rocking swells.

She was on a boat. Bound, gagged, blindfolded and on a boat.

"Trust me, *Psydu*, I no more than touched her," said an unknown voice. "She will be well."

"And you trust *me*, man." Ann flinched at the sound of the second voice. "If she is not, your head will be forfeit. As will mine."

"*Psydu*," the first man whispered. "Look."

A rustle of motion, then hands lifted her head with surprising gentleness – and abruptly, there was light. Ann blinked up into the smirking face of the High Steward of Kabyrnos.

"Good morning, Ann."

She struggled against her bonds, trying to kick herself up. But her vision lurched sickeningly, and she fell back against the floor.

"Be easy, Ann. You are safe now."

Her scream was stifled through the gag.

"*Temper*, Ann," he said. "If I remove that, you will behave. Agreed?"

She went still. After a moment, the High Steward knelt down over her and untied the strip of wool from around her mouth.

"You *bastard*!"

"I would think," he said calmly, "that you would be a little more grateful."

"*Grateful?* I could gut you myself, you son of a bitch!"

"Is that any way to talk to a man who saved your life?"

Too furious to speak, Ann spat, directly into his face. The man brought his palm down across her cheek and her head snapped sideways; she saw the other man shut the cabin door behind him.

"Listen to me closely, whore," the High Steward hissed, leaning down over her. She remembered the last time, the last time he'd been this close. "I was sent to fetch you back, and back you are coming. I do not care if you fled the city like the coward I know you are, or if you were taken, as Zelkanus believes. You will return with me, and you will make this better."

"And how exactly am I supposed to do that?"

The man sat back. It was only then that Ann noticed the shadows on his face, deeper than they had been the last time she'd seen him, nearly two moons ago.

"He talks only of you," he said quietly. "You, and the Makronans."

"Don't speak to me about the Makronans!" she shouted. "You killed a good, innocent person!"

The High Steward looked at her, then reached behind his back and pulled out a knife. Ann recoiled as he reached toward her.

The rope around her hands fell away. Then the man stood and walked to the cabin door.

"You will fix this, Ann."

***

The fissure called to him.

At first, he'd thought it was his delirium. He had been half-raving when the old woman had led him around the crests of the mountain to the broken-down sanctuary. The fissure had been waiting for him then, reaching out with a raw, hungry power that had almost sent him reeling. But the woman had dragged him past, depositing him into the hands of a second, younger woman.

"Take him inside, Andrylea," she'd said.

"Where – where am I?" he'd asked, voice hoarse from dehydration and disuse.

She'd ignored him.

"And the beast. Send Andrylea to take it around back."

He'd been fed, watered and cleaned. Andrylea – or was that the other one? – had tended to him patiently, saying nothing as he'd devoured the stale bread on his hands and knees. Gently holding him as he'd broken down into sobs, right there on the floor.

After that first day, he'd been put to work. Mucking out the latrine, feeding the horse, fixing loose stones and wooden support beams. There was a kind of peace to be found in these little preoccupations. Peace in the persistent silence of the three women.

And yet still the fissure called to him.

Every night, he would wake up hearing its summons like a twinge in the back of his mind.

And he would wander out onto the terrace, never daring to move past the steps that would take him to its precipice.

But tonight the pull was strong. Tonight, he tiptoed down those steps, pausing at the mouth of the chasm. Looking down into that deep, utter blackness.

"No, child."

The old woman was there, like an apparition in the night. Gently, she took hold of one of his hands.

"Not tonight, child," she crooned as she led him back to the building. "Not tonight."

***

The crew secured their vessel and moved across the empty harbour with swords unsheathed. Ann moved with them, unbound but warned: one misstep and she'd be tied up and hauled to the palace like a pig on a sling.

The market was deserted as the harbour had been, with upturned carts littering the ground, and window shutters clacking against walls.

"What happened here?" Ann asked in a whisper.

"Riots," the High Steward replied quietly. "They were threatening to pick up when we left."

The group continued southward, soon making it through the port town and out into the open country. The fields had an abandoned, lifeless look to them, with trees browned, wheat greying and brittle, not a single labourer in sight. The first view of the city was no better. There was no one and nothing. Even the pulse was absent.

But He would be there still, she knew. Waiting for her.

As they passed into the empty streets, Ann began to sense the life stirring in the houses around her. The city was not deserted: it was in lockdown. Hints of movement flashed from behind boarded windows. Chunks of brick had been hacked out of walls, large scorch marks smeared across their facades like livid bruises. The group picked up speed, continuing toward the centre of the city as quietly as possible.

The first sight of the palace gave Ann an odd thrill. And as they slipped into the northern entrance hall, she felt its walls embrace her like a long-lost friend. They moved silently up through the Bull's Corridor, turning off just before the open space of the courtyard and climbing the steps to the elite residences.

Something fluttered within her as she followed the High Steward past her old apartments. But Nik would not be in there, she knew. She'd been told of his treachery and his subsequent flight. Though she knew as well as if she'd been in the storeroom corridor with him that night that it had not been his fault. It may have been his hand that set the fire, but it was not his fault.

The High Steward halted in the corridor outside Commerce Hall. He stood with his back to the group for a moment, then turned.

"You," he whispered to his men, "wait here. Come only if I call. You –" his eyes slid to Ann and he paused. "Do not say or do anything rash. I am asking you. Please."

He waited for her reluctant nod, then drew a breath, and walked into the hall. Ann followed.

The hall was nearly empty, a gaping cavern compared to its usual bustle. But there were guards, Ann saw: a squad of them stationed at every entrance. And sitting at the far end of the chamber on his usual stool, with his Guard Commander behind him, was the *Kyn*.

Ann walked behind the High Steward as they approached, watching the way the *Kyn*'s mouth twitched as he sat hunched over, staring at the floor. Noting his hands flicking out as if gesturing to someone that no one else could see.

But then he looked up.

"Ann!" he cried, so loudly that her name echoed in the hall. "Oh merciful gods, Ann."

He flew off his stool, rushing toward her and taking her hands. The High Steward moved a few steps back.

"I thought they had taken you from me, Ann. I thought they had hurt you."

"No," she said, barely able to articulate the word. "No, they – they didn't hurt me."

"Yes, yes, I can see that." The *Kyn* put an arm around her shoulder and began drawing her to his seat. "You must come with me, Ann. You must stay with me now."

Ann peered at the Guard Commander. The woman stood staring at the opposite wall, as if she had finally been turned to stone.

"Come, Ann. You must sit here."

The *Kyn* urged her down onto his stool, then kneeled before her.

"These are hard times, Ann. Hard times. Those villains conspired with Erea, with the Hunter – they have driven us to beggardom. Yet – there is always a 'yet', is there not?" He gave a stunted little laugh. "We will soon teach them what it is to scheme against Kabyrnos."

"And how exactly," Ann began, unsure of where to start, "do you intend to do that? Your people are too afraid to leave their houses."

The smallest pinch of a frown between his brows. "We have enough."

"No. You don't. I've seen their army."

The man shook his head as if to dispel her words.

"I've lived with them," she went on. "They're not bad people. And – they did not take me."

A surge of motion behind the *Kyn*: the High Steward, stepping forward to intervene. And the *Kyn* so motionless now that she could not be sure he'd heard her.

"I went to them freely," she said. "You have to stop this. Now."

"What do *you* know?" the man cried, flying to his feet.

"I know more than you think I do."

She waited, waited for the flicker of doubt in his eyes.

"How many years will you gain?" she pressed on. "Another ten? Not at this rate."

He was looking at her now. Really looking, the way he used to.

"And at what cost?" she continued. "How many lives will it take this time?"

"You do not understand."

"You know I do."

"My actions came from the highest."

It was Ann's turn for silence.

"You *will* understand," he continued. "One day. One day, you will see."

And then, quite abruptly, she did. She saw it with perfect clarity.

"Take her away," the *Kyn* was saying to the Guard Commander. "Put her somewhere safe."

The guardswoman moved to take hold of her arm. Ann didn't fight. She let herself be led away, only turning back as the guards parted to let them pass out of the hall.

"Zelkanus," she called back to the man who still stood beside the empty stool. "He is not who you think."

Chapter Four

He could feel her now. She was close. It was growing dark – too dark to brave the journey down the mountain. Yet the chasm told him, it told him that time was running out. It told him that she was in danger.

"She was safe," he whispered into the night. "Why did she come back?"

"She came for you."

He was not surprised to find the old woman there with him, looking off at the dusk-covered hills far below.

"But why?" he asked.

"Because she loves you, of course."

He knew this. And it hurt him, because it never did any good.

"What..." he began after a few moments had passed. "What's going to happen now?"

The old woman turned to him then, her eyes like hollow pits in the darkness.

"Death."

***

Ann sat awake beneath the lightwell of her old common room. A small mercy or a parting blow, she couldn't decide, but the Guard Commander had brought her here, blockaded the door from outside, and left her. Left her to wait.

And it was not long before He found her again. His pulse was growing within the walls, slower, deeper than it had ever been. Keeping tune with every pang of her heart.

She knew that time was running out. Kabyrnos was a place of shadows, certainly, but those shadows were wrought of a light of such brilliance. A light that was now flickering out. And there was nothing Ann could do but bear witness.

So she sat, all night, listening over the beating of the walls for the cry of the owl outside. Watching the banner of stars revolve above her. Running her fingertips over the time-worn stones beneath her. And when the stars began to fade and the owls fell silent, she knew that the time had come.

The pounding had quickened – the beating of a drum now, calling men to arms. She heard the voices, the clanging of metal. The march of hundreds of footsteps – more, much more than she had thought possible. Maybe the *Kyn* had been right. Maybe the city still had more left to lose.

A pitter-patter outside her door. Ann scrambled to her feet as she heard the scraping of wood on wood – the blockade removed. The handle turned.

Kaenus was across the room within a second.

"H-how –?"

She stared past the dog and her mouth fell open.

"What in the name of the god on Crytus are *you* doing here?"

***

The sky was beginning to lighten. Nik had gathered his weapon and saddled his horse. The old woman was waiting for him with the two silent ones by the entrance to the ramp.

"Thank you," he said to them. "For everything."

"Gods all bless, Hunter."

The old woman looked sad, he thought as he turned away. So very sad.

But there was no time for her now. He led his horse swiftly down the ramp. The pebbled slope below was steep, and they went as slowly as Nik could bear. He could feel the relentless throbbing, growing, only growing now.

And they were still miles away from ground flat enough to mount – further still until they could take wing and fly the way every fibre of his body ached to fly. It took all of his willpower to keep on walking. For Nik knew that whatever was coming was almost there.

***

"It is time, Ann," Erysia said.

Ann understood. "They're here, aren't they?"

The priestess nodded. "My people tell me that they moored at midnight, off the beaches to the west of Kylondo. They will be heading south now. We must hurry."

With that, the priestess led them out through the corridors and down, stopping at the foot of a stairway to slide one of the wall's stones out of place.

Ann guided Kaenus through and swung in after him. She heard the thud of Erysia's feet landing behind her and the scraping of stone, then all went black – but only for an instant before another light flared, and she found herself staring into a familiar, lovely face.

Ann threw her arms around her friend. "*Hersa.* Oh thank god you're safe."

The girl took her by the hand and led her further down the tunnel. "Safe enough for now. There are many of us here. Tefkelerea, Athyla – the priestesses. Many of the palace women and children. Erysia came for us when the riots began."

"Is everyone ready?" Erysia asked from behind.

"Yes. We had some trouble with some of the clanswomen yet it was nothing I could not handle."

"Of course not. Get them moving, then. I will be with you as soon as I can."

With a squeeze of Ann's hand, Hersa released her and disappeared down another passage, taking the light with her. Erysia towed Ann into the blackness.

"Where are we going?" Ann asked.

"To the armoury," Erysia's voice came out of tunnel ahead. "We need to get you armed."

"What – why?"

"You have to stop them."

Ann stopped walking, Kaenus bumping her from behind.

"You want me to stop a war."

She heard the woman move back toward her, felt the furry shoulder leaning into her hip.

"Who else, Ann?" Erysia asked quietly. "We must all play our part in this."

***

The wind was tearing at Nik as he rode up the South *Kyn*'s Road at a full gallop. He was homed in on his sister's presence as she moved west across the palace. If he was not delayed, he would reach her soon – before the sun had risen over the Thyrtu mountains.

He had entered the outskirts of the city. The road leading into the Southern District was clear. He sank lower over the horse's sweaty flanks and urged the beast on faster.

But as he drew closer to the palace he reined the horse in, cursing. They skidded to a stop in a cloud of dust.

Above him, on the crest of the valley, he saw the legions of Kabyrnos stretching out from the palace walls like a sea of bronze.

He'd have to circumvent the city.

Whipping his reins around, Nik led the horse off the road, due west.

***

"This is as far as we go," Erysia said.

They had salvaged what they could from the armoury and then dashed north, racing against the sound of marching feet on the cobbles above them.

"Head straight northward," the priestess added as Ann clambered up into the light. "Stay along the fringes of the city."

"I will."

"And Ann." She passed something up through the hole. "Here."

Ann smiled to herself as her hands wrapped around the polished wood of her longbow.

"Pritymnia bless you, my friend," the woman whispered and was gone.

***

He sensed her heading north now. He wanted to reach out to her, to tell her to turn back, but he couldn't risk it. Nik needed what semblance of control he had left.

He spurred the horse onward, thundering across the last of the Kypran Hills. It was a dangerous speed on this uneven ground, but now he had no choice.

Even through the pounding of his horse's hooves, he could feel the advance of the army ahead. And he knew, he just knew, that she was running right into it.

***

The armour impeded her as she dashed from cover of building to building, but somehow, Ann and Kaenus managed to make it into the Northern District without being seen.

Erysia's people had worked quickly here: cityfolk were being evacuated from their houses, whole families of serfs streaming into the streets, heading west, out of the city and away from the approaching army.

Armies.

She could hear them now – the men coming in from the north. Ann pushed her way through the stream of people, ignoring the familiar faces. Tefkelerea, carrying two children out of a house; Afratea, greasy-haired and thin, guiding an old man through the streets while her husband limped close behind with the rest of the family. As Ann moved closer to the northern edge of the city, the streets emptied, houses already vacated. She paused at the outer border of the city.

"Mavros protect us," she whispered.

***

The horse's chest was heaving under Nik's legs as they slowed to a trot at the north-western edge of the city. Swarms of people poured out through the streets around him. She was somewhere near, he could feel her – but there were so many people and he couldn't *see*.

"Nik!"

He wheeled his horse around. Hersa was pushing through the crowd toward him. He dismounted, moving to meet her.

"Hersa, I never meant –"

"Hush, *krythea*," she said, wrapping her arms around his waist. "You are here."

For the briefest moment, he let himself be lost in the smell of her hair, the softness of her body pressed against his. And then he broke away, placing the horse's reins firmly in her hands.

"Get out of here, Hersa. No – no arguments. I won't be able to focus if I think you're in danger. Lead them up the mountain. There's a woman up there who might help."

Reluctantly, she agreed, and as he vaulted her onto the horse's back, he resumed his search.

"Have you –"

"She was here only moments ago," Hersa said as she took a child from a passing woman. "And Nik, she was armed. Running north."

Her words confirmed what he already knew, yet still he felt his heart knock against his ribcage.

"Go," he ordered her.

Shoving through the remaining lines of people, he tore past the last of the city's buildings, and broke out into the fields beyond.

Rolling in toward the city like a tidal wave was the Makronan army. And sprinting directly toward them was one small figure, with a large grey dog bounding next to her.

He launched himself after them.

***

She couldn't believe that no one had shot her yet. She was close enough to see the ivory layers of their helmets, their faces below still obscure. These were men, she tried to tell herself – with hearts and minds she could appeal to. She knew some of them. Pushing harder, she aimed for the standard bearer, his lion pennant limp in the windless morning. If Deo were here, that was where he'd be.

As she drew within range of their spears, she saw him, tall and barrel-chested, half-hidden behind his enormous shield.

"Deothesus!"

His helmeted head turned toward her but he did not stop until she staggered to a halt before him, blocking his way. His tribesmen channelled around them.

"Ann, what in the name of –"

"Deo, you have to stop this!"

"Get out of here. *Now*."

"Listen, Deo –"

"This cannot be stopped."

"*You* can stop it."

He took hold of her shoulders and removed her from his path. "They declared war the moment they raided our city. Get out of here or you will be hurt."

He marched on. She stood where he'd left her, knocked side to side by the soldiers who streamed past. He'd been her only hope.

A twitch at the back of her mind. She spun round.

The Kabyrnossian army was moving out into the fields now, stretching itself to span the width of the city. And sandwiched between the two advancing armies, a single, unprotected man.

She turned to her dog.

"Kaenus, get Nik. Bring him –" she glanced around desperately, spotting a cluster of trees and boulders to the southeast – "there. Quick. *Go!*"

***

She had been absorbed into the wall of Makronans. But he could feel her there still, feel the force of her despair. He hurried onward, both armies closing in.

A streak of grey, flying across the field toward him. The dog slid in a full circle around him, fastening his teeth on Nik's kilt and hurtling east without breaking stride.

Nik got the message.

He ran, he ran hard, the dog beside him, the two sprinting through an ever-narrowing gap toward the copse. The armies roared, the air quivering with their voices, the earth trembling under their tread. Nik was limping now, his injured leg beginning to falter as the first volley of arrows flew over his head. He was nearly there.

His leg crumpled beneath him and he went smashing into the ground. He tried to scramble to his feet, but a booted foot caught him in the ribs, sending him reeling back just as the two armies met in a booming crash of metal.

***

Ann clambered atop a boulder, her eyes already scanning the heave of bronze before her. She could feel her brother, but it was almost impossible to hold on to his presence – the battle was so close to her, the mass of it roiling and changing with each second, its terrible din threatening to shake her into mindlessness.

There. A flash of gold and grey – Kaenus was with him, fending off attackers. But there were too many, too many for him to hold on his own.

Ann whipped out her bow just as a soldier descended on her brother with spear raised. She released her arrow. It zipped through the air where the man's head had been, burying itself in another's leg. For the briefest instant, she could see the first man on the ground, mouth stretched in agony, but there was no time to wonder. She released another arrow, then another, leaving her brother free to climb to his feet, his golden head towering over the helmets around him. A perfect target.

***

It had taken him a few moments to remember he had a sword. The scream of metal, the bodies already down, the dog's lips curled back, fangs dripping crimson... But when the man had appeared, spear trained on his heart, it had all become clear. He'd slashed the man's ankles out in one sweep of his blade and clambered to his feet.

And was forced backward as another sword came slicing in. His own sword was up in a flash, knocking the second strike out of the way as an arrow flew past his face – another man dropping beside him. In the moment of distraction, Nik brought his fist in and hammered at the man's exposed throat. But as the man keeled back, Nik felt a sear of pain across his unprotected shoulder blades.

He spun round, intercepting the next blow.

This was no contest, he realized as he whipped his blade round again. This was no arena in which to weigh an opponent's strengths and weaknesses. This was about covering your fucking back. About being stronger, quicker and more brutal than the swarm that every second threatened to pull you under.

As much as it sickened him, he could do this. In his heart, he knew that he'd been born for it.

***

Her arrows flew with deadly precision, her arms working without pause while Nik and Kaenus sheared a space for themselves amidst the carnage. It was all so simple, so straightforward now, that she barely noticed Him, His pulse oozing out into the battlefield, the very air thick with its throbs. His appetite hot, like the rising sun at her back – yet cold, cold as the ice she now felt spreading within her.

Antigone…

The northernmost buildings of the city were on fire. Most civilians were out by now – but not all. She saw people running, screaming as the battle was pushed back into the streets.

Her arrows continued to fly.

Antigone…

Bodies were piling up in the field, the air reeking of a butcher's shop – His pulse quickening, almost suffocating now.

The cold within her crackled.

Antigone…

The *Kyn* – surrounded by a ring of guards, hurling spears over their shoulders like bolts of lightning as his Guard Commander pushed on ahead, cleaving through the Makronan mass with single-minded purpose.

Ann's arrows flew on.

***

Nik heard his name in the beating air, saturating the world around him like the smell of battle, thick and sour. He was drunk with it. He sliced his way forward, pushing further into the fray as if drawn by a guiding hand. The dog now left behind – while before him, a sort of clearing, a break in the turmoil.

In which two duellists, old rivals, faced each other once more. Their blades so swift they were lost to sight. The woman angling to the west, opposite the rising sun; the man already wounded, but holding his position. Nik pushed on, cutting down any in his way.

Then, a flash of light – the sun, reflected off the Guard Commander's silver diadem. And in the split second of the Makronan prince's blindness, she moved in, sword scything in toward his neck.

Niklas…

Nik's blade was there to meet it.

***

There was no choice now. Her quiver empty, her brother locked in a battle that he could not win, Ann launched herself off her perch, sword unsheathed, and threw herself into the swarm.

It was slow going, even once Kaenus appeared at her side. Clambering over the sodden ground, surging back and forth with the tide of bodies – and the pulse stronger here in the thick of it, swelling and contracting against her body, making it harder to breathe, harder to keep hold, to pull herself toward the faint sense of her brother in that cleared space – maybe only fifteen, twenty metres ahead.

She screamed her frustration and shouldered the man ahead out of her way.

A mistake, she realized too late.

The man spun on her, driving down with his spear. Lunging back out of the way, Ann's heel caught and she crashed into the mud, her helmet knocked clean off. She heard Kaenus's ripping snarl, saw the man go down – but not before his cry brought four others round. She was surrounded in an instant.

She was pulled to her knees, her hair wrenched back and held in place as the shield came down. One moment of blinding agony, her face on fire – then the shape of a man cleared in front of her, sword raised.

Not now, she thought as the blade came down. Not this way.

A howl of pain.

Kaenus.

On the ground at her knees. Sword buried in his grey, scruffy chest.

Antigone.

***

He felt her enter his mind like a current of ice, freezing him over in an instant. His mind now sharp, crystalline – but also dark, impossibly dark, as if they had both plunged down into the shadow that had always existed at their very core.

They were as one. He felt her bring her blade back, slicing through her hair, freeing herself to tear into the men around her. She felt him turn away from his duel, abandoning the wounded prince to cut through the wall of bodies that kept him from her.

Then they two were together. Rejoined and whole. They breathed in the dense, palpitating air, and tasted the reek of it. They heard Him call their names.

The twins ripped into the horde in perfect unison, blades carving into flesh, feeling it yield and split at their touch, no one free from their retribution. They were as two furies, weapons unstoppable, hunger unquenchable. Every life taken bringing them further under the shroud of darkness.

***

Then, from deep within, in a space almost entirely consumed by shadow, a gentle stirring. A breath of life.

Ann gasped, coming back to herself. She stared, uncomprehending, at the hands in front of her – cracked and crusted in filth and fresh blood. She let her weapon fall.

And she looked down upon the death that they had wrought.

Faces. Mountains of empty, almost unrecognizably human faces. And one she did know. Her wrestling partner, her friend, Trydus, lying not far from where she stood.

She heaved, acid from her empty stomach searing her throat.

So many fallen.

Yet still – so much more to lose.

This had to end.

***

Nik was brought back by a cry, strained and cracking.

"Mavros! End this now – *please*!"

He whipped round to find his sister kneeling in the muck, shorn hair haloing eyes that blazed in a bloodied face. And her body trembling, trembling violently. He reached down to steady her.

And was thrown off his feet by a sudden jolt from below. He glanced around, bewildered. The battlefield suddenly still – swords and spears frozen. Waiting.

Then, swelling up from the earth beneath him, a rumbling, a shaking that rose in bone-grinding convulsions. Nik was knocked back again, unable to rise, as the earth shifted and heaved, ripping apart with a crack so loud that his ears rang with it.

Hardly able to believe his eyes, he watched as a rift began racing along the battlefield – and men began pouring in, their mouths open, screams drowned out in the roar of the land. Then Nik was on his hands and knees, scrambling, fighting with all he had to get away from the ever-nearing chasm.

Yet his sister – he recalled too late – was on the other bank of the crevice. Unconscious and sliding dangerously close to the edge.

There was a flash of motion to his left – a long-haired figure leaping, swinging through the air over the widening gorge. The man fell to his knees on the other side, brought down by the quaking, yet still he managed to push against the flow of bodies, and crawl to where Ann lay – her feet now dangling over empty space. Hooking one arm under her shoulder, he heaved her back, away from the crevice.

Nik went weak with relief. The shaking was easing, rolling out now. He glanced toward the city, dust and smoke obscuring its rooftops. Debris still falling, wood still burning. The world as he knew it, torn apart.

And then all was still.

Slowly, Nik propped himself up. The battleground was silent but for the moans of the wounded and the distant booms of a great building, crumbling to pieces.

A twitch at the back of his mind. A tug, like a string that drew his eyes up, to where a man was climbing to his feet.

It was too far to make out the man's face, but Nik knew him nonetheless. And the man knew him.

The *Kyn* was looking right back, watching, as he always was. And lying motionless on the ground at his feet, barrel chest pinned beneath a broken branch, was his Makronan captive.

Chapter Five

She was staring into open space. A cloudless sky, just darkening – the serrated profile of the mountain in the distance. The ground over a hundred feet below.

They were imprisoned in what was left of the aviary. Half the room had been ripped away. Ann and Nik huddled along the inner wall, mere feet away from the drop, while Deo lay unconscious in the corner. Only a single bird remained, watching them from its perch.

Ann fingered the bridge of her nose. Broken, she recalled – though the memory of it was hazy. As if it had happened in another age, to another person.

"Nik," she began. Her voice, thick and hoarse, barely sounded like her own. "Nik, what happened?"

"You don't remember."

He was staring off into the approaching dusk, arms wrapped around his knees. He hadn't looked her way.

"There was an earthquake. The battle ended."

She was silent.

"Then we were rounded up and brought here."

Ann drew her knees to her chest, and instinctively reached out beside her, searching for the furry reassurance she was so used to finding there. After a moment, she let her hand fall again.

Deo moaned and stirred in his corner.

"Only one way out, I see," Deo muttered as he blinked, looking around. He dragged himself up against the wall. "What shall we do now?"

"Wait," Nik replied.

They did not have to wait long. The sun was only just disappearing over the hills to the west when they heard a scraping of metal beyond the door.

The *Kyn* stood framed in the doorway, the Guard Commander on the roof behind. He had bathed and was dressed in fresh clothing, though his hands and nails were still creased with dried blood. And they were both still armed. The man faced Deo and Nik, his back turned to Ann.

"I will not waste words. Hunter, I am prepared to show you leniency. For your treachery, you may choose exile. You, Deothesus, son of Pakedainon – you must die. Tomorrow. You will be taken to the oak and offered to the Earth Mother to pay for the sins of your people."

And with that, the door was shut, the bolt scraped back into place.

In the silence that followed, the wind began to blow, whistling past the broken walls of the aviary. The bird rustled overhead. The sun, Ann saw, was now gone.

***

She was in the forest again. It was dark and cold – very cold now. Ice fringed the branches of the trees and the dirt beneath her feet was frozen solid.

She could sense Him here, His pulse echoing in the woods around her. But something told her that He had not yet noticed her. She took a tentative step forward.

Nothing. No voice, no call. She looked up.

The moon was out, a mere sliver glowing is the sky above her. Offering no warmth, but reassuring nonetheless. Without the voice, there was no horror here. Not in this place.

But as she stepped out into the clearing she beheld the young oak, bent and withered. The thing was dying. It was nearly dead. Reluctantly, Ann moved past. There was nothing to be done for it now.

She continued further into the clearing, something drawing her forward. When she reached its centre, she knelt onto the frozen dirt and began brushing the leaves away.

And there, beneath the frosted refuse of the forest, was a pair of green saplings. Ann bent down to cup her hands around them, breathing gently into the circle of her palms. It was too cold for these little things to survive. She would have to stay with them, at least until spring came and they could grow on their own.

But He was nearer now. She felt Him approach in the gust of wintry air that swept in from further out. She shivered, drawing closer to the saplings. He still hadn't noticed her. For now, she could stay here. For now, they were safe.

***

Nik stood in the shadows of the aviary, looking down at the twist of river far below. The world had fallen quiet, the only sounds to be heard the breathing of the two sleeping behind him. And the occasional rustle of feathers.

So he was to be exiled. Again.

Where would he go? Where could be far enough away? No matter where he'd ever fled to, the voice had always followed.

Nik glanced down at his sister.

Shorn hair and broken face could not tarnish the beauty he had always seen in her. And now, now as she slept, she looked more like the girl she used to be. For the moment, she was soft and sweet in the way she'd been then, when she would reach out to him in their special way and ask for him to come. And he'd always gone to her, as she'd never doubted he would. They'd been everything to each other. They'd had to be.

But then the voice had come to him.

He'd been too vulnerable, he now knew – and the voice had been too strong. And as his needs had grown into the needs of a man, the voice had born down harder. She is your other half, He had told him again and again in the darkest hours of the night. Your better half, torn from you at birth. She is the only thing that can complete you. The only thing that can make you whole.

It was true. Even as a girl she'd been so brave, so strong in her quiet, enduring way. She was everything he wasn't. Without her – the voice whispered to him still – you are only half a man. You are nothing.

Niklas…

It had been torture this past year. Torture being so close to her, torture sleeping in the room next to hers. So he'd found other beds to occupy, other girls to take his mind off the one he could not – *would* not – have. And finally, he'd found the perfect one – or she'd found him. But it could never have been with Hersa, not in this life. Only in a life without this vile, bottomless longing. This curse.

Niklas…

She was stirring. He took a step backward, closer to the edge. Any minute now she would open those eyes – *his* eyes, and yet, not his. Never his. She would look up at him and she would see.

Niklas.

***

He was here now.

A dark shape on the dying oak – on that branch. There.

A bird, she thought. Point of a beak, sharp as a knife. Yes, a bird.

He had seen her now.

Antigone, Death beckoned to her. *Wake up.*

And so she woke.

***

Her eyes flew open. Silhouetted against the darkness of the sky, a tall figure. At first, she thought it was Him, *here*, but then she knew.

"Nik."

She couldn't make out his face, but she saw, she saw what he held in his mind.

And it all came back, the inexorable flood of all that shouldn't be. All that she'd spent years running from. Her body could barely contain the pain of it – she was only mortal. And there was no earthly solution, not to this.

His voice came out of the dark, quiet and empty.

"There's nothing left, Ann."

"... I know."

"I'm..."

"Hollow."

"Yes."

The silence stretched on as the twins looked at each other through the shadows. And then, inevitably, came the rustle of feathers.

"It's okay, my Anna," he said, backing up now. "It's all going to be okay."

Understanding came to her too late.

"... No, Nik, no, it won't be okay – no – *Nik, don't* –"

I'm so sorry, he told her.

"NO!"

And spreading his arms out like two painfully inadequate wings, he tipped backward into the night.

***

Her screams echoed through the palace. Standing only a storey below, he saw the boy plummet past, he heard her shrieking his name, heard the other one shouting to know what had happened. He wished with all his heart that he could be up there with her now to ensure she would not follow. Yet He had told him to wait. So he waited.

And He always knew, He was always right. He had said they would come to Kabyrnos and they had. And Zelkanus had known them instantly. How could he not?

Yet they were so much less than he had expected, divided in a way he could not understand. It had been plain to him that the boy had already been conquered by it, whatever it was that burdened them. He was clearly no threat. Yet still, Zelkanus had kept watch. He had asked his Guard Commander to keep the boy close. Who knew what he could have been concealing beneath that weak, charming exterior?

Evidently, he was as feeble as he had seemed.

She, she had been different. Zelkanus had seen right away that she had potential. And how she had grown into it. She was the answer to all of his prayers. The Great One had told him to keep her near. And he had almost failed – he *had* failed – yet, by the grace of Mavros, she had been returned to him.

Zelkanus sat in his empty hall within the ring of torchlight. Many of the outer walls and columns had fallen, much of the ceiling and floor caved in. He supposed it was not quite safe to be here, but He had told him to stay. So he stayed.

Yet in his deepest of hearts, Zelkanus was growing mistrustful. Mavros had also promised him that the bull – his long-awaited sign of the gods' favour – would bring in an era of bounty for his people. And now his city, the city he had given everything for, was in ruins. Yet He had told him to be patient, so he was. For now.

The Great One had not led him astray thus far. When the oak had called to Zelkanus, so many years ago, He had come, He had told him there was another way, a way to save his people from disaster. For Zelkanus had seen what had happened in his father's time, he had known that without a strong leader to take his place only ruin would lie in wait for Kabyrnos. So he had chosen to stay on. It had been necessary, he told himself. For his people. All it would take, Mavros had said then, was the life of one boy. A common serf would do. No great loss there.

Except that it had not only been one. Every year, despite the offering, the pull had gained in strength, and the cost of his delay had grown dearer. This year, the call of the oak had been so strong that he had feared it was his last, until Mavros had told him of way to rid himself of it forever. A greater sacrifice. Yet you will have to wait, He had said. So Zelkanus had waited.

Yet no longer. For the boy had finally come.

Zelkanus glanced past the broken wall into the night beyond. All was silent now. He shifted on his stool and listened, listened for any sound from above – any voices, any weeping. Yet there was nothing.

Tomorrow would be the end of it, he told himself. No more lives lost. And whether the girl liked it or not, she would have to take up her proper place now. He had no doubt in his mind that Heremus would still gladly have her as wife – although if she would not have him, another would have to be found. This was essential. To give her stewardship directly would be a death sentence. A curse. And that he could not do, not to her.

He would hold nothing back from her now.

This was the right path to take. Mavros had told him so.

And yet, as Zelkanus sat in his crumbling, torchlit hall, he remembered that it was only yesterday that she had stood in this very room and looked at him that quiet, piercing way she had.

"He is not who you think," she had said.

Zelkanus... the voice called to him out of the flickering shadows. *It is time.*

Ah, he thought. She is coming.

***

Ann rose to her feet.

"What are you doing?" Deo asked, alarmed.

She couldn't answer him. She tried to move past him toward the door, but he gripped her shoulders again, as he'd done when she'd flown after her brother.

"Where are you going, Ann?"

She could not explain. To explain would be to show him the gaping hole that was left of her heart, and that she could not do without falling to pieces. There was only one thread holding her together now, one single, tenuous strand that kept her connected to this life. And it was leading her out.

"Let me go."

He stared into her face for a moment longer and then released her.

She moved to the door, feeling no surprise to find it unlocked – no surprise to see the Guard Commander's dark shape beyond, pointing past Ann's shoulder with a sword.

"Only her," the woman said. "You stay."

When Ann was out, the guardswoman barred the door and began walking across the roof. Ann followed, barely noticing the chunks of stone gone, the missing steps. She saw only that thread in her mind, leading her down.

Yet when the glow of torchlight reached her, she found herself beginning to rouse. She knew where the woman was leading her. And as they stepped around a mountain of rubble and into the remains of Commerce Hall, Ann felt a blast of cold fury sweep through her.

"You," she uttered. "You drove him to this."

The *Kyn* rose from his stool. "Palthenra, you may go."

"You *drove* him to it."

The man said nothing as the guardswoman crossed back through the hall. And when she had disappeared into the corridors beyond, he remained silent still.

"Say something!" Ann yelled.

He sighed. "I was thinking…"

Then he paused, seeming to weigh something in his mind. And then, very slowly, he began to speak. He began to speak in perfect – if halting – English.

"I was thinking that, with your hair like that, you look so much more like your mother."

She blinked and her anger was gone.

"Not the eyes, though. Hers were blue, weren't they?"

She nodded dumbly. Zelkanus moved forward, cupping her cheek in one large palm.

"Antigone. My own Antigone. I have waited a lifetime for you."

Ann stared at him. At that strong-featured, aging face. At those brown eyes, that once again crinkled warmly at her in the torchlight.

"Your own son…" she finally managed to whisper.

She squeezed her eyes shut. She could see it – she could see it all over again, the dark silhouette, spread-armed and falling.

But she was being called away; He was calling her away again.

"Antigone!" Zelkanus cried, rushing after her. "Ann – Ann!"

She paused, letting him catch up – allowing him to pull her into an embrace. And for one moment, she let herself imagine that she was a child again and safe, safe within the stronghold of her father's arms. She looked up into his face and saw that it was there – and had been there for her to see all along. The love that came too late.

"I'm going after him," she said quietly.

The *Kyn*'s eyes widened, his arms dropped away. "He – he is gone, Antigone."

If he had been incredulous or dismissive, she might have been dissuaded. It was his fear that resolved her.

"He chose his fate," the man went on, pleading now. "He never had the strength to survive in this world. Not like you or I."

"He was never given a real chance."

She began walking away again through the hall. The thread was still there, but redirected now, leading her out and down. Deep down.

But the *Kyn* stayed with her. "You cannot go, Antigone – I am begging you. Asking a boon of the gods *always* requires a heavy sacrifice. It is in many ways a curse – a great curse. I have learned this." He grabbed her arm, spinning her around. "You cannot go to Him!"

"A curse?" she said quietly. "You are the one that did this to us. You chose your own life over those boys. *You* cursed us. The moment you left, you cursed us."

She watched the man flinch away from her words. The only words she could think of to make him let her go.

"I will not give up on him, *Kyn*."

***

He watched her go. His Antigone.

She had shaken him, shaken him deeply – capturing him, as she always did, the moment she had looked at him with those strange, sad eyes of hers. Those eyes, which belonged neither to him, nor to her mother.

He was cursed, indeed. Zelkanus knew full well the price of fulfilling his duty. He had known it when he was barely more than a child himself – just about her age now – and he had been called to leave them, his two beautiful, golden children.

Yet who else was there to sweep up the wreckage of Cryklonus's reign?

Cryklonus. That savage.

Through all this, Zelkanus had always thought of his twins as safe – safe with their mother in that soft, privileged world of theirs. It had never occurred to him, when he had first seen that wary, hunted look in his son's eyes, that he himself could have brought it upon him. Yet she had as much as told him so.

Zelkanus was cursed, as was his own father before him. And so he had cursed them.

"Kyn?"

Zelkanus looked up hopefully.

But it was only his Guard Commander who stood in the doorway.

"Yes. Palthenra. Good. You had better transfer the boy to a proper hold now. Better to keep him safe until tomorrow."

The woman departed without a word and Zelkanus buried his face in his hands.

For just a moment, he had allowed himself to think that she had returned. His Antigone. But she was gone now, and only the gods – those cruel, heartless creatures – could say if she would ever come back to him.

***

There was nothing now. No thread, no pulse. She moved through the well-known maze unguided, blind but certain in her understanding that she had to take these steps alone. She had to go freely, willingly. The task required it.

And so she pushed on until she came upon the heart of the broken palace. A desolate courtyard, whose balustrades and pillars had fallen away into rubble and dust.

Yet she was no longer alone. There, in the remains of the northern passage, a powerful figure, with two horns upon its head – moving toward her, and shifting as it came in a kind of disjointed shrinkage of its limbs, a shedding of its bulk. A costume being discarded, piece by piece. And by the time the figure was close enough to make out the general cast of its features, its shape was only that of a regular man, small and thin.

"I know you."

The priest nodded. His face had lost that queer, deadened look. There was so much purpose in it now.

"You were – the man. On the plane."

"Yes."

"You steered me here."

"Not alone."

"No, but it was you – the Makronan spy. Leaking the information about the emergency stores, then telling the Makronans to flee. You steered us – all of us – to this."

A pause.

"I had no choice, Huntress."

"No choice."

"You will understand." Darkylus turned away from her to face the crumbled remains of the western palace. "Come. I will take you to Him."

Chapter Six

The light from Darkylus's torch threw moving shadows against the walls as they descended further into the bowels of the palace. It was colder here beneath the ground, and damp, with beads of moisture clinging to the rough surface of the stone. Ann wrapped her arms around herself and walked on in silence. Only one way forward now.

Her guide paused outside the thick wooden door. Waiting – she realized – for her. She put her hand on the handle, twisted and pushed.

It opened onto a small chamber, almost entirely taken up by a massive column that stood in its centre. Little hieroglyphs had been scratched onto the column, like the absentminded doodles of a child. They were horns, or double-edged axes – Ann couldn't quite make them out. The priest had taken his torch around the pillar, leaving her in the gloom by the door.

Cautiously, she stepped further into the chamber. As she did so, she became aware of a soft, rasping breath. She saw Darkylus kneeling at the far side of the room. And beyond him, slumped against the wall, she saw was what was left of the *Kynra*.

Ann stared in horror. The torchlight showed the infinitesimal rise and fall of protruding ribs, the slackness of that lipless mouth in its skeletal face.

The woman was nothing more than a spectre, shrunken and fading away into the darkness around her.

Darkylus smoothed away the wisps of hair, now a pure white.

"All will be well, my love. You will see. It is almost over now."

Ann doubted that the woman had heard him. She may still have been breathing, her heart may still have been beating, but she was already gone. And the quiet desperation in the man's voice told Ann that he knew this as well as she did.

"Darkylus," she said quietly, calling him away.

He lingered a moment longer, then stood, moving past Ann to crouch at the base of the column, where, with a loud grating noise, one of the stones shifted aside. A wave of stench rolled out of the hole, thick and foul.

"Follow this down," the man told her. "Do not tarry and do not look back." He turned away, kneeling back down by the dying woman. "He will be waiting for you."

***

Zelkanus could feel it clearly now. The pulse beating in the very stones beneath his feet.

On some level, he had always been aware of it. On some level, he had always thought of this place as kin. A living part of him. Or he a living part of it.

Yet this pounding was different. Sharper, more erratic. These stones were angry.

Mavros had never led him astray. Mavros was always right, He always knew. Mavros had told him to be patient – and Zelkanus was trying his utmost.

For his golden age was finally coming to him. And it was she, Mavros had said, who would bring them into it.

He is not who you think.

The pulse flared in the wall beneath Zelkanus's palm. He snatched his hand away, yet it stayed with him, pounding in his ears, shaking in his bones.

"Oh gods," he whispered. "What have I done?"

***

She climbed backwards through the hole, fighting the urge to scream, her foot groping in the dark for the ground she was sure was not there. Yet within a second she was through and standing on solid stone. Steadying herself, she drew in her last lungful of clean air, turned away from the torchlight and began her descent into the blackness.

The steps were steep and slick with moisture. She proceeded slowly, gripping the cold walls, the chattering of her teeth filling the narrow space, almost drowning out the return of the pulse – which was no longer in the air around her, but at a point in the distance. A point growing slowly, very slowly, closer.

The stink became worse the further she descended. In a way, she was grateful for it: revolting though it was, it was a real, animal odour. A rotten musk – the reek of a decaying carcass. A smell that sharpened her mind as it churned her stomach, allowing her to keep hold of her reason as she moved down, one crumbling step at a time.

Eventually, her feet met level ground. It was only a few more shuffling steps before they met water, thigh-deep and so cold that it burned. Ann waded through, careful to avoid the rocks that hung from the ceiling like melting wax. The air here was frigid yet so thick that she was finding it hard to breathe now. She could feel her body failing – hands trembling uncontrollably, legs numb below the hips. Yet somehow, she continued to wade forward. Forward, always forward, never looking back.

Then, after what felt like a lifetime or more, the path rose out of the water and came to an abrupt end. A wall – another door, which smelled of rust. Very slowly, Ann placed her hand on it. It was ice against her palm. She could feel the pulse there, just on the other side. She had only to open this door.

But she could not. Ann stood frozen, listening to the beating heart of the creature she had come to meet. The creature that had been drawing her toward it for so long.

What she would have done in that moment to have Kaenus at her side. How much, in that moment, she needed Hefanos's reassuring silence, or Deo's booming laughter, or even Erysia's impish grin. Or Hersa's scolding. Or the *Kyn*'s deep voice, humming softly. What she would have given then to have Nik beside her.

Yet here, in this deepest and darkest of places, there was only her. As it always had to be. As it always was, at the end.

She opened the door.

A cave. A great, gaping mouth with fangs of rock. Dim shafts of light filtered through the stalactites above, illuminating the emptiness below. Leaving the corners to shadow. The air heavy, dank, unclean, but so cold that the reek was muted. Everything was muted.

And then, like the harbinger of Death, came the rustle of feathers.

***

Zelkanus paced the ruins of his terrace, looking south, toward the mountain. The torches were still burning brightly in the hall behind him, and the sliver of the Dying Moon had risen in the east. Midnight. She was well out of his reach now.

Yet the pulse had fallen silent and worry was eating away at him from within. This waiting would be the end of him. Zelkanus was a man of action: he needed a foe that he could face.

There were footsteps in the hall behind him – his Guard Commander. Zelkanus sighed and returned to the torchlight.

Yet as he laid eyes on the woman, he realized that something was wrong. There, in her face: a crack in the stone.

"Is it true?" she asked him.

"Is what true? Of what are you speaking, Palthenra?"

"The boys."

Zelkanus felt as though the floor had finally given beneath him.

"I would have followed you to the end, my *Kyn*."

Sadness, so much sadness in her voice. Yet firmness too – as always. That unyielding sense of justice that he had depended on for years. That he would need in the time to come.

"Child, I –"

Her hand flashed out, silencing him. "You chose your fate."

His own words, like a whip across his back. There were more footsteps now. And as his Guard Commander turned away from him, another stepped into view.

Zelkanus felt a chill pass through his heart as the boy strode into the hall, the firelight glinting off his borrowed sword.

Cursed.

***

Ann stood transfixed as He moved into the light.

Here was a thing of horror: tall, emaciated, with limbs crooked and muscles twisted, like the knotty branches of the burnt tree. And unfurling from His back to blot out the light above were two enormous wings.

The creature cocked His head to the side, bird-like.

"Antigone," He said. "Welcome."

His voice rasped and grated – but did not overwhelm her as it had in her mind. This was a human voice. More or less.

"Come," He said, beckoning her with a misshapen finger.

Ann took a step forward, then another, almost involuntarily. And as she approached, the wings stretched back and the creature stood tall in the dim light.

She gasped.

That face. Horribly handsome and sickeningly familiar. And those eyes.

Those eyes.

"Who –?" She swallowed, trying to coax up the words that had dried away.

"I am Death," the creature rasped. "I am Mavros. Or, at least, of His darkest nature."

For a moment, all she could think of was His nearness – all she could see, His eyes.

Those eyes.

"Should you like to hear a tale, Antigone?"

She did not, could not, respond. But the creature's wings were settling. He began.

"There is a young woman, only a girl still, yet she has the makings of a true leader. Brave, just and strong. She wants to rule her father's city when she is grown, yet she is told that women do not rule. Angry, she runs north, to the sea."

Ann saw it again, the white stretch of sand, the lapping of the water, the moon high above. And a girl standing at the brink of the sea, loose hair blowing around her.

"She meets a god there, who desires her. She is young, she is ambitious. She refuses Him. To no avail."

I have taken before what was not given.

"Soon after, she learns she is with child and before long her father informs her that she is to marry a *Kyn* of another city – the island's greatest. Again, she refuses, and again, she is forced."

The creature's wings moved as He spoke, beating softly, stirring the stagnant air around them.

"As soon as she is wed, the girl buries herself away from the world in a deep, dark room, with only her love-smitten kinsman to tend her. For many moons she burns with anger and hatred toward the world of men and the child within her. The child is born with much pain. The girl Erea refuses even to touch the thing. She abandons it in the dungeon to die of neglect. Yet, as she departs to take up her rightful place as *Kynra*, she leaves the creature with a parting gift: a name. *Ikades*, which means 'of the Darkness'. And so she seals His fate."

Those eyes. Like molten pools, any sorrow, any pity now long burnt away.

"Yet the creature is half-god and does not die. It grows in the darkness, twisted by its mother's hatred and its Father's indifference – watching, always watching the world above, its only company the anger in its heart – and the visits of its kinsman, who is consumed with guilt."

I had no choice, Darkylus had said.

"Once, only once does the mother visit her spawn. Years later, she comes bearing a sleeping boy – nine years of age, the same as the creature is then. 'I have need of your help, Ikades,' she says to the creature. 'I must send this child away to a place where his father cannot reach. Will you do this for me, in exchange for the gift I gave you?' The creature agrees.

"So the creature sends this boy – a child it had watched since the cursed day of its own birth – to a place not far in distance but in time. And it bestows upon him its own gift: one piece of its own black soul.

"It is an escape and a triumph. The boy will one day return, the creature knows, and on that day, the boy will be made *Kyn*. And then, the creature thinks, the world that blocked Him out will be at His mercy.

"Yet the creature did not foresee what would happen then. That the boy himself would breed and that little piece of soul, so painfully parted with, would pass to his two unborn children."

Those eyes. Those unnatural, yellow eyes.

"Antigone," Ikades said. "You belong to Me."

***

Zelkanus parried another lightning strike. That the Makronan was adept, there was no question. He moved as though he had been born to wield a sword. Which, in a way – Zelkanus thought – he had been.

There had been no accusations levied nor excuses offered. Zelkanus had looked into the boy's unwavering eyes – so like his own – and known that it was time. It was as it was always meant to be, from the moment of the child's conception. It could never have been Niklas: that one would never have had the nerve. This one, this was a true son of his.

And there was pleasure in duelling him. Wounded and worn though the boy was, he was a challenge – just what Zelkanus most needed now. In the ordinary way of things, he knew that the boy would have conquered. He had seen him in the arena. He had admired – envied, even – his prowess. And Zelkanus was not as young as he once was. Yet the boy had been through much that day. Zelkanus could see it in every laboured breath. Victory would be a simple matter of patience.

Though, great gods, the boy was dogged, pressing forward without pause, his sword slicing in again, again, his arm flying in smooth, undulating movements. Zelkanus kept pace, deflecting each strike and biding his time. There would be an instant, he knew, when the boy would falter. So he remained as he was, unyielding, letting the boy dance around him – the storm raging against the mountain.

And then Zelkanus saw his opportunity. Breathing hard, he pushed in, attacking in a flurry of strikes until he had driven the boy off-balance. Then his leg snapped out, landing on bruised ribs, and the boy went reeling into the wall, little chunks of stone and plaster raining down.

"Give in, boy," Zelkanus panted. He rolled out his sword arm in an unhurried gesture. "We both know that this is only a matter of time."

The Makronan shook his head, scattering the fallen debris. "You speak truth, old man. You have been living on stolen years for far too long."

Zelkanus laughed, the sound loud and unnatural in the hollowness of the hall.

"Twist words all you like," he said. "As long as I hold breath, *I* am *Kyn* here."

The boy sighed and wheeled his sword back up through the air. Their blades met again in a clap of thunder.

***

"Yes," Ikades rasped. "You belong here, in the darkness."

Ann's breath rushed out of her lungs in an opaque cloud. She peered up into the handsome face that had just confirmed for her what she had known all along. Her uncanny ability to always find her target. The bond she shared with her brother. The horrible things that seemed to befall anyone who got close to her. She was tainted, tainted from birth. She and Nik.

Cursed, those yellow eyes said to her.

"Fate has an unexpected way of unwinding itself," Ikades went on. "In time, I discovered that I had received far more than I had bargained for."

His hand came up, claw tracing the line of her jaw. A lover's touch.

"You, Antigone, you were the central thread in My tapestry. You drew them all together for Me to unravel."

Cursed.

"You hate the world that much?"

It was a simple question, uttered in a small, unsteady voice. But it seemed to incense the creature, who swept in toward her.

"How could I *not* hate the world that did this to Me?"

His face was now inches from hers, His rancid breath seeping out in stomach-rolling waves, scattering her thoughts.

Cursed. All of them – cursed before they were born.
But something in her rebelled.

No, it said. Not a curse.

"A choice," she whispered.

The creature was silent, His head cocked to the side once more. He stepped back. Inviting her – she realized – to go on.

"The world didn't do this to You," she said quietly. "I know what it is to be… hurt. To block out the world because you think it will protect you. Maybe you even want to hurt them too. But festering alone in that pain… that's what twists you. That's what hardens you up and hollows you out inside."

She took a steadying breath. The creature still hadn't moved.

"And then one day you realize that the darkness can't last forever. If you open yourself up to what's – what's *good*, then eventually… there's light."

Then the creature smiled. It was a ragged, twisted thing that spread across His face like a growing tumour, sending a tremor down Ann's spine.

"But there is no light, Antigone," Ikades rasped. "I have taken it all."

He stepped aside. And lying sprawled in a puddle beyond was the broken form that the creature had shaped in His own image. Her brother. Her Nik.

One wordless cry, like the keening of an injured animal, and Ann was on her knees, curling around her twin's cold body.

"His life was never worth much to me," Ikades hissed in her ear. "It never satisfied. Yet with you, I had to be defter than ever before – and even then there were times when you resisted. When you disobeyed."

His black wings surrounded her. The light now truly gone.

"I have taken them all, Antigone. Only one remains. Only one."

***

They fought on as two immortals trapped in an eternal battle. The boy was bleeding now from a wound on his abdomen, and Zelkanus could see pain and exhaustion dragging at every line of his strong face. He too was tired, with muscles burning and joints aching, but he would keep on fighting. He had no other choice.

With a grunt of effort, the boy threw himself back at Zelkanus. Zelkanus dove in and grabbed the raised forearm, stabbing in beneath. Dodged – narrowly. The Makronan twisted free and swung his weapon in from the other side, yet, as always, Zelkanus's was there to meet it. Their blades slipped along the length of the other's, locking hilts. Bringing their sweating, shaking faces within inches of each other.

Zelkanus roared and shoved the boy back.

So cursedly *stubborn*! Who did the damned boy think he was – a *god*? Did he think he could escape his death here?

"Had enough yet?" the boy panted as he wiped his brow.

Zelkanus brought his sword back up.

He had fought so hard. To do better – to *be* better – than his father before him. He had given everything for his people, to bring them back into glory. And still they suffered. Still he had suffered, only the gods knew how much. And here stood this young man – as arrogant as his grandfather before him – all but telling him it had been for naught? This bastard whelp, who had snuck in from the heart of his enemy, despoiling his beautiful, shining city.

Yet there was still hope for it. Hope that it could be remade as it once was, as it was meant to be – not in this foreigner's crude vision. Zelkanus could not let this be the end.

All he had ever wanted was to build a golden haven in the darkness of the world. A place where people could live bound together by shared duty and fairness and love. Where no one would ever be unprotected – or alone.

Was that not worth one more life?

Only one.

***

"I have waited so long for this," Ikades hissed, fastening His claws around her head and wrenching it up.

Her eyes were open now and forced to every shattered bone, every twisted limb of her brother's corpse. She moaned.

"I will break you, girl."

His hands tightening, His claws digging in, piercing her skin.

"W–wait."

Ikades paused. Her breath was coming in shallow sobs. She'd known, hadn't she, that it would come to this?

"A bargain," she gasped. "My life – for his."

For a moment there was only the sound of the dripping of water into the pool around her brother's body. And then she heard Ikades's crow-like laughter, loud and mocking.

"Why would I barter for something I already possess? *I could take your life this very moment*."

Ann fought to keep hold of her senses. This barely thought-out plan was a long shot, and this would be the trickiest part.

"Yes," she panted. "You can kill me. But You can't – break me."

The seconds passed and Ikades said nothing. His wings stirred around her. She didn't dare move, didn't dare breathe. It was a battle of wills she had presented to Him and she could feel His interest piqued.

"If what you say is true," He began, "and I cannot break you..."

"My brother will go free."

"Free..."

"Alive," she said. "And untainted."

A long pause. Then Ikades nodded.

"We have a wager, then?" he hissed.

Ann felt her heart hammering in her chest, protesting. She'd barely had a chance to live. But what did that matter now? What was before her was a choice. And here, at the end of it all, it was a remarkably simple one.

"Yes."

The word left her mouth and she felt it wrap itself around her, choking. Binding them both.

"You are Mine, Antigone," Ikades rasped. "And you will suffer."

She heard His crow's laughter, felt His wings once again enfolding her, pulling in the putrid air. The stench of a ravenous appetite. An unquenchable need that devoured any who opened themselves to it. And she had opened herself now. Completely.

The pain of it was – impossible. The weight of a mountain settling on her, burying her alive. She could feel Him in every fiber of her being, like an acid eating away, corroding her organs, her bones, her very marrow.

There was screaming, a shrieking in her ears – her own voice, unrecognizable now.

Then, just as she was flickering out, it stopped, and she was left limp against the wet stone, gasping for breath. But the claws were on her still, dragging her up like a rag doll.

"Look at Me."

There was no more choice here. She looked.

And His handsome face – Nik's face – smiled that ghastly smile, yellow eyes voracious, feeding on her every whimper.

"Antigone," Death beckoned her. "You are Mine."

***

Zelkanus broke off in his attack and staggered back. The pulse was flaring again, pressing into his mind.

She was in peril. He could see her now – her body collapsed in the deep, her golden hair soaked through, her breath rising in a feeble mist. And a figure kneeling over her, so bent, so hideous, blocking out the streaks of sallow light. The only light left.

"No," he whispered. "*No*…"

The boy's hacking brought him back. The Makronan had retreated to a corner and his body shook from his coughs, blood spattering the broken tiles of the floor. Yet in his hand he gripped his sword as firmly as ever.

Sensing Zelkanus's gaze, the boy straightened and began to limp forward again. His body almost broken, yet still he came.

Antigone.

Zelkanus's heart stilled as the voice reverberated in the hall. The boy continued forward as if he had not heard. As if he was not walking to certain death.

Antigone.

The boy heaved his sword up and brought it down in a scything cut. Zelkanus barely managed to bring his own weapon up in time and was forced to use his other hand to brace against the boy's unexpected strength. The blade bit deep into his palm.

Antigone.

Putting all of his weight behind it, he thrust the boy off and slashed out desperately, warding him away. Yet the boy simply would not stay back.

Antigone. She had been his light and his joy since the moment of her birth. And as he battled for his city, for his very life, he realized that above all else he should have protected her. He should have protected them both. Instead, he had sent them directly into His hands.

He had sent her to her death.

***

At some point the pain had changed, mutating into something far more terrible. He was in her mind now, prying open every door, taking what was there in the darkest recesses of her soul and twisting it, shaping it as He Himself was shaped.

Before her, she saw a boy strapped to the limbs of a tree. Ann cringed away from the memory but another was ready to take its place. A girl now, black eyes staring, an axe buried in her neck – and then the girl was a man, large and muscular but no longer strong as he lay broken in the sand. And as that image dissolved, another came, and another, raining down on her like cast stones. An older man, shot down merely for being her friend; a younger man, another friend, butchered like a bull in a pen. All of their faces, the faces of the men she'd slaughtered, of the countless others whose homes and lives she had stolen by calling down a disaster more devastating than the battle it was meant to end. And finally, it was Nik's face she saw. Cheeks hollow, eyes pleading with her not to leave – not to leave him alone again. Because, really, that's all he had ever asked of her.

You spoil everything, He hissed in her mind.

It was true.

You tore them all down, Antigone.

She had.

Monster.

Yes.

And yet.

There was always a 'yet', wasn't there?

Ikades held her still, hands pressing into her flesh. Those twisted, bloodstained claws.

You poison, she told Him. *You prey on weaknesses and watch as the venom spreads.*

"I am not the monster here," she whispered.

But His laughter swatted her words away.

"You think you are a hero then? The golden Huntress of Kabyrnos – saviour of a broken city? You are *nothing*."

He was inside her again, pulling up memories like fibres from a cloth. The High Steward's hands on her, pushing her against the wall. Her stepfather's bloodshot eyes, his palm across her face. Then, a darkened bedroom, and the lawyer slipping between her sheets, between her legs, grunting over top of her. Yet soon it was not his face, but Nik's, his yellow eyes harder, crueller than they could ever have been in life.

The shame rose up to choke her like a mouthful of bleach, scouring out everything, everything but that voice that told her that she was nothing more than a pretty face – and not even that anymore. You are only wanted, it said, for the pleasure you give. It is the only worth you ever had.

Ikades was stripping her down, picking away like the scavenger He was until there was nothing left but bones. Ann hung within the cage of His wings, and wished, hoped, *prayed* for the strength to endure it.

Then she could smell it – a wisp of air piercing the foulness of the dungeon, fresh and lively, whispering faintly of trees. And she could see it too, just for a moment, that clearing deep within a moonlit forest. A space to breathe.

And then it was gone. But it had been there. In the deepest, most sickening pit of her soul, it had been there.

It is best only to know that we exist.

And as long as she existed, she was never truly alone.

Ah, He sighed in her mind, as if He had been waiting for this moment. *But you* are *alone.*

Ann whimpered as the last images came falling down on her like the sweep of an axe. Her mother's blond hair, disappearing behind the door; the deep crags of Zelkanus's face as he left them to the night only hours before. Then Ikades's wings opened and there was Nik, as he was now. Grey, broken and still.

"Alone," Ikades hissed.

As it always had to be. As it always was, at the end.

"There is nothing left for you here."

No light. He had taken it all.

"Why hold on?"

Why?

She lifted her eyes one last time to the broken form of her brother. And there, beneath the wreckage of his face, a look of peace. More like the child he had once been.

She knew she could not hold on any longer. Ikades knew it too – she could feel the triumph rolling off Him like a fog, engulfing her. She was now forfeit.

Ann just hoped it would be enough.

It is always enough when all is given.

The claws fastened around her neck. "*You are Mine.*"

"But," she gasped, "it is – a gift."

She saw the tremor of hesitation. Then she saw the colourless flesh of His face tighten as He realized what had been done.

He had torn her down, stolen everything she had. But He had lost. He had lost the moment the deal was made. As long as the life was given, and given freely, He could never truly break her.

Yet the life was still His.

There was fury in His eyes now, no longer yellow, but black – so dark she was lost in them, drowning, choked out. Ikades shrieked, a high, grating scream that shook the cave as His claws tightened on her throat, and the shadows consumed her.

***

He felt her let go. Antigone. His little girl.

Both gone now, with the third only moments away from his own end – yet still staggering forward, sword tip dragging on the tiles. This one most foreign, most hated, yet, out of the three of them, the most like him.

Why would he not give up?

What was he still holding on to?

The boy Deothesus shouted with the pain it took to sweep his final blow at Zelkanus's face.

Zelkanus knew he could block it. He could keep on fighting until there was nothing left.

But he chose not to.

Book VII

Chapter One

After the darkest hour had passed, when the first of the summer birds were trilling their sunrise harmony, Nik opened his eyes.

Wisps of cloud floated in the dark sky above, edged with the hints of a golden dawn. And someone was calling his name.

He struggled to prop himself up on his elbows. His body ached, but – incredibly – it was whole.

Soft arms enfolded him. He smelled the scent of Hersa's hair as her face pressed into his chest and she began to weep.

"Nik – oh, merciful Mother, *Nik*."

"I – I fell…"

She held him tighter. He peered over her head. An altar – and a fissure, now quiet. Nothing more than a crack in the rock of Mount Crytus.

"How – what am I doing here?"

She pulled away only far enough to peer into his face, her lovely eyes brimming over. Looking into them, Nik felt a warmth spread within his chest. It was as if the barriers of his heart were melting and reaching outward to draw her in.

"I do not know, *krythea*," she said, laughing through her tears. "And I do not care."

"Where –" he coughed, bracing himself for what he knew would follow the mention of her name – "where's Ann?"

But, to his immense surprise, nothing came. No surge of guilt or self-loathing – no loneliness so acute that it caused him physical pain. He felt just as he did before: hazy, sore – and the slightest bit uneasy.

"I do not know," Hersa said, glancing around. "Was she supposed to be –"

Nik felt her stiffen.

"Stay here," she whispered.

Slowly, the girl rose to her feet. And slowly, Nik's eyes inched ahead of her toward the edge of the terrace.

A body. On its side, facing away from him. It was too dark still to make out much but the shape, but he knew her. How could he not?

Nik watched as Hersa knelt down by his sister's body. There was no grief, not yet. There was only a vague picture unfolding in his mind. A dark cave, two immense wings. And his own face – but older, sharper, and twisted with bitterness. His face as it might have been. As it still could be, if he did not choose otherwise.

But how had they both come to be here?

There was someone else with him now. A bony hand on his shoulder.

She came for you, the old woman had told him.

Nik looked up into the woman's ancient face. There was so much sadness there.

"All will be well," the old woman crooned.

"How?" he managed to whisper.

"In time."

The woman bent down to him then and smiled. It was a kind, sad smile – with just a hint of something else.

"Nik!" Hersa screamed from the brink of the terrace. "Nik – she breathes – she *breathes*!"

He was on his hands and knees, scrambling around the fissure – pulling his sister into his arms.

"Ann," he whispered, shaking her gently. "Wake up, Ann."

Hersa was shouting something over his shoulder, but he couldn't hear her. He was desperately trying to reach out – to rouse his sister with his mind. But that place within was gone. Not closed up, not scarred over – just gone.

Yet she was stirring. A long draw of breath, eyelashes fluttering. She blinked up at him. At first, just looking, just seeing. Then, the softening of her bruised face – the peace there.

Followed by a crease of confusion. And then, most horribly, a convulsion of pain.

Hersa was prying his fingers away, easing Ann out of his arms. Nik looked up at her, bewildered.

"Move aside," Hersa ordered, her eyes still on Ann. "We must hurry."

Nik followed her gaze down Ann's body. The sky was brighter now and he could see that what he had mistaken for the old stains of battle was really fresh blood. And it was spreading quickly.

"What – what's wrong with her?" he asked as the two silent ones pushed past him, blocking him out.

The old one had come up behind him again.

"She is losing her child."

He stared up at her, mouth open. "Her – child?"

"Yes. The child of Mavros."

***

The passing of day and night. The earth moving in its full circle, first warmed in the sun, then cooled in the dark of a moonless sky. Only to begin again. The fall of rain outside. The smell of hay beneath her, with the faintest tang of salt, carried in on the wet breeze. The sound of hushed voices. Her brother's hands, smoothing her hair. Hersa's voice, singing her to sleep.

Sleep, child. For all will be well.

***

Nik peered at Hersa over his sister's sleeping form. "Will she be okay, you think?"

Hersa took his hand in hers and nodded.

"But how can you know that?"

His voice small, pleading, a child begging for guarantee.

Hersa guided him out of the room, pausing at the door that led out onto the terrace. The rain was still coming down in sheets. Nik thought of all the others below, taking shelter in their makeshift tents. And they, the lucky ones.

"Her alloy is a strong one," Hersa said, leaning her head against his arm. "Do not worry, *krythea*. All will be well."

Nik sighed and kissed her hair.

"All will be well," he whispered. "In time."

Chapter Two

It was a wound still too tender to touch. What had been done to her in that cave – what had happened afterward. His last attempt to shatter her, she now knew. And it had been shockingly painful – shocking, because she had not known that there was anything left to lose. But there always was, wasn't there?

Ann sat in a wagon, trundling along the uneven surface of what used to be the South *Kyn*'s Road. The rain had finally stopped and they were returning to the city, all of them – Ann, Nik, Hersa, the hundreds of others that had fled to the mountain. One long procession, working its way around the rubble. Returning home.

But the land had changed. The quarries had been replenished with fallen stone, the river redirected and refilled. Green sprouted at the base of fallen trees. And already, there were people in the fields, trying to salvage what they could of their crops.

The land would heal. In a different shape, perhaps, and bearing many scars, but it would heal. They all would. It had already begun.

***

As they came in along the western road, their wagon drew to a halt. The road was blocked by a crowd of priests and priestesses, all rolling large ceramic *pethys* up the hill toward the palace. Ann scanned the area and found Erysia, as expected, at the head of the crowd, shouting directions.

The emergency supplies, it turned out, had been locked in the storeroom at the back of the Royal Armoury for months. When asked how she'd obtained the *Kyn*'s personal seal to open and re-seal the chamber, the priestess only smiled. When asked how she'd known to protect the supplies in the first place, she said simply,

"I had a feeling."

Erysia was now – Ann learned as the wagon made its way through the commotion – one of the forerunning candidates for the position of Sacred Mother. She was young for the position, and there were certain Sisters who were dead against it, but Erysia didn't seem concerned.

"Gods protect us," Hersa muttered, shaking her head at the sky.

The *Kynra*, unsurprisingly, was no more. She had been found the morning after the quake, hanging by the neck in a lower dungeon. Her kinsman was still missing. Erysia didn't seem to think that he would be seen again. Ann was inclined to agree.

More surprising was the news about Deo.

"He is being hailed as the Foreign *Kyn* come again," the priestess told them. "He is to be enthroned the day after tomorrow."

The day after tomorrow.

When the wagon rolled to a stop again, Ann let her brother help her out. She still tired easily. Erysia came to her side and offered her arm.

"So, tomorrow then," Ann said quietly.

The priestess nodded. "Tomorrow at midday."

***

The Courtyard of the Dying Sun was a wasteland of rubble. Sitting on a rock by the black tree, Ann eyed the remnants of the great building and waited. She was early.

When they had arrived the day before, Ann had immediately felt that the hum was gone. The palace was no more than a building now, broken and empty. But, sitting there under the clouded sky, Ann realized that this was the kind of emptiness found in open fields, and in meadows and clear skies. An emptiness filled with the small whispers of life.

But with life, there must always be death. The sacred balance, the Kapreitans called it.

Ann sat unmoving as the courtyard filled with people. No one approached her.

The skies were now dark. Not a word was uttered. It would not be long.

When he came out, he came out unfettered. Bandages covered the upper half of his face, and his Guard Commander walked at his side – not to guard, but to guide.

The crowd parted as Zelkanus walked toward the tree, shoulders squared and chin high. Ann felt heat stinging at her eyes, but she did not cry. She did not cry as he was stopped before the tree. Nor as he was hoisted up. Nor did she cry when the guards backed away, leaving his powerful body limp against the charred bark. But when his face turned unseeingly to where she sat, the tears finally spilled over, pouring down her face in a silent river.

She moved to his side. The clouds overhead began to rumble and the crowd shuffled back.

"Ann," he said quietly. His deep voice clear and steady.

"I am here."

"I knew you would be, my girl."

She placed her palm against his cheek.

"Ann, I never meant for any of this to happen."

"I know."

The rumbling grew louder.

"You had better leave me," he whispered.

"Yes."

She did not move.

"Ann. Please. Do not watch."

There was a flash of light, which left the world dark in its wake. The skies snarled in response.

"Remember me as I once was."

She turned then and walked away. She moved through the crowd that stood transfixed, staring at the man that she'd left behind. That the world had left behind. She never once looked back. Not even when the heavens roared and there was a brilliant flash of white, reflected against the broken walls of Kabyrnos.

***

She stood in the clearing, lit only by the sliver of a new moon. The forest was silent. It was a thick, fulsome silence. The silence of many little growing things. Green buds dusted the branches of the trees, small shoots pushed up through the dirt.

Ann walked toward the young oak. It was no longer dying, but somehow, it was no longer young either. In so short a time, it had grown taller, fuller, shooting up to meet its kin. She ran her hand over its bark, and smiling, she turned away.

Something was drawing her to the centre of the clearing. Ann crouched, pushing away the dead leaves.

The smallest green sprout. Weak, but growing.

It is spring now. All is well.

***

Ann woke in the blackness of her old bedroom. The south-eastern part of the palace had escaped the worst of the damage, so she and Nik – and Hersa – had been able to move back in directly. It had only been a few months since Ann had occupied the narrow bed, but it felt like so much longer. She had woken many times the previous night wondering where she was. The silence was alien to her.

But tonight the shadows were not silent. Tonight, she was being called out.

Ann tiptoed out of the common room and into the corridors, and soon she was padding out on the grass of the eastern pastures. Branches bent back as the wind picked up, but she continued onward, following the thread in her mind.

She moved into the fields north of the city. The ground here was still trodden, the vegetation trampled, but the blood had been washed away and the bodies had been buried. Kapreitan and Makronan alike, sent on with the proper blessings and ceremony.

The old woman was standing at the edge of the new chasm, hair blowing around her. For a moment, Ann was reminded of another old woman, on another night, similar to this.

"You're back."

"Indeed," Klochistropa cackled. "My exile is over."

"I'm glad."

"Kind of you to say so, dear, very kind."

They were silent for several minutes. Then Ann released a long breath into the wind.

"What will happen to Ikades?"

"I cannot say for certain," Klochistropa said. "He shut out the world, and now, I believe it will do the same to Him. No god lasts long without believers."

Ann nodded, feeling moisture pricking at the corners of her eyes. She went to wipe the tears away, but the wind had already taken them.

"Was it all my fault?" she whispered.

Klochistropa made a soft cooing sound and moved toward her, taking hold of both her hands. Her skin was dry and cool, and felt of paper.

"No, no, no, my dear, do not think it for a moment. Nothing is meant to last forever."

The old woman dropped her hands, stepping away, back toward the rift. "It is a sad thing, though, is it not? This grief we inherit? For all its faults, Kabyrnos was a bright spot – a beacon of grace and beauty. A new, hard age lies ahead. For centuries to come, the world will be plunged back into shadows."

Her eyes drifted upward. Beyond the raging winds, the sky was black, dusted over with stars. And in that moment, the old woman seemed to fade, blending in with the torrent of the night.

"And yet we must remember," she breathed, "that it is only from darkness that we know light."

When the woman's eyes returned to earth once more, Ann was ready with her final question. So much depended on the answer.

"Am I... am I my *own* now?"

Klochistropa stared at her for so long that Ann felt her heart sink. The woman was going to tell her no, that Ikades's soul still lived within her.

"No," the woman said slowly. "No, I think not."

No. Of course not.

"Yet it is not as you fear."

The old woman was walking toward her again, her hand outstretched once more. She paused before Ann and very slowly, very gently placed it on her stomach.

"No mother is ever wholly her own again."

For a moment, Ann thought that she had imagined it. That the wind had whispered it, this newest, most tender desire of hers.

"He could not take it," Klochistropa said. "He tried, yet its sibling drew it into itself. To keep it safe."

Ann blinked. "Twins?"

The woman smiled her hole-punched smile and Ann felt that she had never seen anything so beautiful.

"Two spirits, now joined in one. A gifted child."

This was more than Ann could take in at once. More than she could have ever dreamed to hope for. But even now, she knew it was right. After all that had happened, it was right.

"Now," Klochistropa said, burying her hands in her bony armpits. "I must return. Andrylea's home is not much – more of a hovel than a house – yet one cannot be too particular when one returns to civilization after nearly twenty years. These old bones need a fire, and a blanket, perhaps a bowl of soup…"

Ann watched the woman scurry back toward the city, still muttering to herself. She knew she should follow – it was cold out and she would have to take care of herself now. But the thread was pulling her onward. So onward she went.

***

When she came to the beach, He was already waiting for her.

"Antigone."

He made no move to draw closer. And she was glad of it, because looking up into His calm, inhuman face, Ann found that she was furious.

"How?" she demanded. "How could You have let it happen?"

"It is the way of things, Antigone," Mavros offered simply.

"But – Ikades… He poisoned, He corrupted Your people. He made them believe that *You* –" Ann paused, struck by a thought. "He was trying to blot You out of existence – and You just don't care?"

Mavros said nothing.

"Why, *why* didn't You *stop* Him?"

"These struggles are not for Me to decide," He said. "People must always be given a choice. Antigone, He could not have done what He did alone."

"But He was part *god*," she shouted. "*How could we even stand a chance?*"

"Yet you did."

Mavros stood utterly still, a glowing statue in the moonlight. And when He spoke again, it was with a sorrow so deep, so ancient that Ann's anger was simply gone, blown away on the breeze.

"He is My Son, Antigone. What would you have had Me do?"

Ann could not reply. Her hands drifted to her stomach.

"Our child," He said after a moment. "It cannot stay here."

"Why?" she asked quietly. "Why not?"

The god did not respond. Ann looked into His black eyes and remembered something that the old woman had once said to her.

Perhaps the best answer is simply 'fear'. Fear of death – of the darkness beyond. Fear of the past coming alive again.

"But – this is my home now," she said, pleading.

"I am sorry. Yet the child will be safe with you."

The moon had set and without its glow Mavros looked flatter somehow. Almost like a mortal creature.

"If you choose not to keep it, you may stay," He said. "Otherwise, go to the Blessed Courtyard at midday tomorrow. She will guide you from there."

He turned away, toward the darkened hills.

"The choice is yours, Antigone."

After he had gone, Ann knelt down in the sand and took a pile of it in her hands. Slowly, she let the grains spill through her fingers and return to the earth.

Her choice, she thought.

And here, at the beginning of it all, it was a remarkably simple one.

Chapter Three

It was just before midday on the longest day of the year. There was to be no celebration; the Day of Light was a day of mourning this year. Ann walked into the sunlight of the Blessed Courtyard with her brother at her side.

Not many had been told of the departure, so Ann was surprised to find that a small crowd had gathered.

She said her goodbyes. The Mistress of the Loom, Athyla and the others. She clasped hands with the Guard Commander. She nodded at Afratea and hugged the Master Bronzesmith, eliciting a grunt of surprise and reluctant embrace. Then she saw the High Steward leaning in the shadows of the columns beyond.

"My brother told me what you did for me," she said to him. "During the earthquake. Thank you."

The man did not reply. Yet when she turned to leave, he stopped her.

"I – I did love you. In my way."

She nodded. "Good luck to you, Heremus."

She walked on. Most had left the courtyard; only a handful remained. Ann approached Deo, who leaned against Tefkelerea, his bandaged arm around her shoulders. They embraced.

"Farewell, brother," she said, smiling. "I'm sorry that there wasn't more time."

The young *Kyn* kissed her cheek. "You have taught me much already, sister."

Ann turned to her friend. "Don't let him get away with anything, Tefka."

"If such a thing is possible," Tefkelerea sighed.

With a laugh, Ann moved away.

The priestess was waiting for her by the altar, eyes twinkling. The axe – Ann now noticed – was gone, and in its place stood a small, yellow-haired statue.

"Those blessed by the Earth Mother are always together in spirit," Erysia said as she approached.

"Playing the part already," Ann teased.

The woman shot the sky a tragic look. "No one understands me."

"Or we understand you too well. Stay out of trouble, Erysia."

"Perhaps I should say that same to you?" The woman's eyes flitted down to Ann's belly and she winked. "I was given to understand that your world has not seen divine blood so pure for millennia."

For a moment, Ann could only stare. "You never cease to amaze."

"And I never shall. Now get moving. It is almost time."

There were only two left.

Hersa was already crying. And as Ann came up and wrapped her arms around her, the tiny woman tried several times to speak, but eventually gave up, weeping softly into her shoulder. When she was done, she looked up at Ann, sniffling.

"Not so perfect now."

"What?"

The girl gently tapped the scar over Ann's eye, then her nose, which was mostly healed in its new, crooked form.

"Not so perfect. Though anyone will think twice before picking a fight with you."

"Exactly what I was going for."

The girl smiled, but her eyes was solemn.

"Do not worry, Ann," she said quietly. "I will take care of him."

Ann's lip began to quiver then. "I know you will."

"Goodbye, dear friend."

And, after one last embrace, the girl left the courtyard. One left. Only one.

He was waiting for her, hands hanging at his sides. "What will you do now?"

"Don't know yet. Find a job, I guess... I'll be fine."

"Of course you will."

Ann looked at her brother. He was so changed. Not just with long hair and brown skin – a total native now – but he seemed taller, somehow. Fuller. As if he was finally filling in his proper outlines.

Then the thread was in her mind.

"Nik."

He closed the distance between them, taking her hands and resting his forehead against hers. For a moment, Ann was unable to move or speak. For just a moment, she stood with her twin, and for that moment, it was as it always should have been.

Then that moment was over. Too soon, the thread was pulling, leading her west.

"Nik," she choked, "I –"

He squeezed her hands. "I know, my Anna. I know."

Ann took in one deep, shaking breath and let go. And with one last look at him, standing tall in the empty, sunlit courtyard, she turned away to follow the thread down through the darkness and back up into the light.

ACKNOWLEDGEMENTS

For allowing me to study the ancient world from afar, I am grateful to Rodney Castleden (author of *Minoans: Life in Bronze Age Crete*, *The Knossos Labyrinth: A view of the 'Palace of Minos" at Knossos* and *Myceneans*), to John C. McEnroe (author of *Architecture of Minoan Crete: Constructing Identity in the Aegean Bronze Age*) to Ian Morris and Barry B. Powell (authors of *The Greeks: History, Culture and Society*) and to D. Brendan Nagle (author of *The Ancient World: A Social and Cultural History*). Barry B. Powell's *Classical Myth*, and Robert Graves's *The Greek Myths* were treasured resources.

I am so grateful to my publisher Harry Markos, and everyone at Markosia who allowed my dream to become a reality.

My thanks to my dear friend Mike Ellis for helping me put together a beautiful and personal – and properly formatted – cover.

I shall always be thankful to my husband, Bryce Hill, for the many forms of his assistance in piecing this book together over the years. He deserves as much credit for this book as I do.

Credit also goes to my brother, Paul Karvanis, for his enthusiasm and general awesomeness – his *kefi*. He is, and ever shall be, a mighty influence for me. He inspired all that was good in Nik. For the character's flaws, I had to invent. As Paul would say, he has so few to choose from.

To my parents, Athanassios Tom Karvanis and Andromache Karakatsanis, thank you, thank you, thank you. For everything. For connecting me to my Greek roots. For bringing me to Crete so many years ago to fall in love with the stones of Knossos. For their help in the different stages of this book's creation. My father's interest and enthusiasm for the creation of an entire world was indefatigable. My mother's editing skills and time, invaluable. Thank you, again.

My deepest love and gratitude to my grandparents, Despina and Apostolos Karvanis, and Xanthippe and Emmanuel Karakatsanis, for the gift of a Greek heritage. Words cannot express my respect for the courage and fortitude it must have taken to leave their beautiful country and seek a brighter future for their children. My dream began with them.

And, finally, to my grandmother Xanthippe Antigone, my enormous appreciation for sharing her own breath-taking tales of courage, love and heartbreak. Her stories were my inspiration.

Manufactured by Amazon.ca
Bolton, ON

33775372R00278